The Feed

A Novel

Nick Clark Windo

HARPER LUXE

An Imprint of HarperCollins*Publishers*

THE FEED. Copyright © 2018 by Windlark Ltd. All rights reserved. Printed in the United States of America. No part of this book may be used or reproduced in any manner whatsoever without written permission except in the case of brief quotations embodied in critical articles and reviews. For information address HarperCollins Publishers, 195 Broadway, New York, NY 10007.

HarperCollins books may be purchased for educational, business, or sales promotional use. For information please e-mail the Special Markets Department at SPsales@harpercollins.com.

FIRST HARPERLUXE EDITION

ISBN: 978-0-06-279172-6

HarperLuxe™ is a trademark of HarperCollins Publishers.

Library of Congress Cataloging-in-Publication Data is available upon request.

18 19 20 21 22 ID/LSC 10 9 8 7 6 5 4 3 2 1

For Eleanor

Psychoanalysts are fond of pointing out that the past is alive in the present. But the future is alive in the present too. The future is not some place we're going to, but an idea in our mind now. It is something we're creating, that in turn creates us. The future is a fantasy that shapes our present.

—STEPHEN GROSZ,
The Examined Life (2013)

The Feed

KATE
What Would You Sacrifice?

Is this what you realize when you turn off the Feed? The restaurant's other diners hustle around me, yet I am absolutely alone. I should be nestling in amid the raucous chatter of this busy place, but instead I'm embalmed in real silence, and it's as that weird ringing thing happens in my ears that it hits me: Tom is right. I must really remember this. Even though this unconnected stillness feels deeply unnatural, it *is* good to be slow—if I can just ignore the itch in my brain.

I was spraying nonstop between classes earlier and I'm still buzzed from it now, even though I took Rafa for a big walk in the park after school. Marooning myself on a bench with my Feed off and my Do Not Disturb on, I threw his ball and watched the children play. That was it. That was all I did. No chats, no news streams. I had homework to mark (Class 9K filleting *The Tempest* with trowels in a filtered-thinking test I'd set them) and I should have messaged JasonStark27 to release him from detention, but I didn't. I didn't even check my pool. I simply sat and winced at the repetitive torture of the rusty swings and forced my thoughts to slow. And slowly the buzz subsided. My heart calmed and I felt the baby inside me relax: her agitations eased as my mind unknotted. Action: reaction—nice and clear. Tom would have been proud; I slip my Feed on now, here in the restaurant, just our PrivateStream, and nudge him to tell him he's right. The connection makes my heart race, and without thinking I dip into the chatter of the restaurant's hectic PublicStream, I plunge with ease into the—

"No!" Tom's thick eyebrows go up and his eyes widen, in surprise or irritation I can't tell, as his Feed stays off and his emotis are therefore unknown to me.

I turn my Feed off again like one of my troublesome pupils and we sit in silence some more. He smiles at me but I don't return it. I can't, for a while, while I concentrate. *I can do this, I can go slow.* Why does Tom have to make it look so damn easy, though? My eyes rove, hungry for information. The cutlery of the thirty-three other diners scrapes. The occasional, unintended real laugh rasps around the room. Someone

THE FEED · 3

coughs. No words, though, no talking in the real, and I hear birdsong over the super-road's growl. I realize I haven't heard a bird consciously for so long, and it's a really lovely thing. But the problem with being off is— it's—so—slow!

"How long will this take?"

"Could take forever," Tom agrees, nodding his broad forehead patiently before swivelling toward the kitchen. "How long have we been waiting?"

"I'll check."

"*Kate*," Tom warns gently. "We are being *slow* tonight."

And there it is: the psychotherapist's tone. It implies far more authority than the length of Tom's experience deserves; in fact I think I first noticed it right when he started practicing last year, but I can't check my mundles to see without going on. If it riles *me*, though, why wouldn't it rile his clients? And that wouldn't be good; he has to make this work. It's taken him a while to find himself, and he loves the work. He's really good at it. It's *his*.

So I disengage my eyes again and look around the real, past the diners and outside. It's not yet dark, though the super-road brings an early murk to these older parts of the city. We moved in around the corner two years ago, just before we got married. A beautiful old house (new-builds lack soul—I like a home to have a past) and way more expensive than we could dream of affording, but Tom's parents helped us out. I'm still mixed about that. So's Tom. But we're on the hilltop up here. The super-road arches close above us and the city is an urban growth, laid out below. So many people down there before me, the millions of lights sparking like so many vibrant lives, and I could be chatting with any of them, my thoughts prismed out from the lit-up tower over toward the river, the main Hub of the Feed. Tom's father's place. Watching over us all: the eye of a needle through which everyone threads.

Just seeing it, I'm tempted to dive into my pool; I'm itching to check the new poll I set. Two hundred million followers I have now! (If I accepted endorsements, and I wanted to, I'd be able to give up teaching—but *no*.) I'm tempted to do a GPS trawl to see how near I am to any of my followers, but I smother it back and try to ignore the itching in my brain. I gulped in some pool the other day that it's not actually the implant itself that itches. The Feed doesn't create any physical sensation at all. It's just an *urge* that, to make sense of, we attribute to something physical, so our brain tells us that it's itching. I resprayed that fact. One hundred and thirty-seven million people "liked" it, though I doubt they actually did.

I close my eyes, and my memories of the Feed's phantom images score the darkness like neon and starlight, an internal global cityscape where everyone lives close by. So beautiful. So inevitable. So comfortable.

I can't believe I've become hooked.

Tom's right about that too, damn it and love him at once. Eyes back open and, off as I am, the billboards across the street display nothing but giant square quickcodes on their pristine expanses. The world is quiet. The social hubbub of the restaurant's PublicStream is silenced. I have no idea what the menu is and we can't get the waiter's attention. It's like we don't exist. We're here, cocooned in slow-moving silence as everyone around us communicates, eats, and laughs, and it's like—

The waiter's boots echo off the wooden floor as he leaves the kitchen, tattoos strangling his arms. He dumps plates before two young women whose lips twitch, swollen into semi-smiles, while their eyes roll and judder. He grinds pepper on the blond girl's food but not on her friend's; the communication was silent but clear. Though the waiter stares up into a cobwebbed corner, I know that's not what he's seeing. "*This is a strange repose, to be asleep / With eyes wide open,*" as Class 9K would effortlessly reference, fresh from their filtered-thinking test (they wouldn't). Rather, he's accessing an infinite multitude, streaming with his friends, internalizing a sound track, messaging his girlfriend . . . or not, I guess, as the trio's mouths twitch into synchronized smiles, because it looks like he's flirting with them and I'm left itching to go on even more than I had been before, a dry urge, the interface of the Feed teasing my brain like a catch in the back of my throat.

Tom strides over and grabs the waiter, who jerks at the contact and gapes when he realizes Tom is talking to him—actually speaking words. He disengages his eyes as Tom forces him to really *look* at the world and see the real. Tom drags him back to our table and the young waiter rocks nervously. He has a tiny quickcode tattooed above his eyebrow, shaped like an eagle, instantly scannable and ready to enhance my world, and I wonder: What would I see if I turned on my Feed? What skin does he have set? He's pale, so maybe those girls just saw him with a tan. His teeth aren't even, but maybe to them he has a perfect smile. Or maybe he's set himself to look like someone famous. Turning off the Feed is like drawing back a veil. It might not be as pretty, but it's real, and Tom is right, I know he is, of course I do; it's not just because he hates his father: it *is* a healthy thing to do.

"No, no, *no*." Tom snaps his fingers and the startled

waiter's gaze jerks back to him. "We aren't on," he articulates exaggeratedly, and mimes a mouth with his hands. "It's just *talk-ing.*"

"You're . . . *off?*" the waiter asks, his voice croaky through disuse. His eyes glaze for a moment. Who did he just message? His manager, for help? Those girls? Probably not; they don't turn to look. Has he sprayed a grab of us? Doubtful—Tom's security settings are so high he's virtually impossible to grab; his father has seen to that.

"Do—you—have—a—menu?" Tom asks, glancing at me. He's having fun with this.

"Not real." The waiter points at his temple like we're the idiots. "Just Feed."

Tom smiles up at him in a way I know means trouble, and it's been a long day, so . . .

"Pasta?" I interrupt, and the waiter nods. Real words feel strange in my mouth, but I speak quickly. "Bolognese for me, then, and carbonara for him. And a side salad, please. Just green."

Once the waiter flees, Tom's expression makes me laugh despite my mood. This in turn makes him smile, which is nice, his grin still soft, still young around his cheeks, beneath his drooping hair. It's a touch longer than it had been when we got married. I lean back and clasp my hands over my baby-filling tummy. Mummy and Daddy happy again, little girl, just like we used to be. Enjoying being off together. We can still do it, you know. We're good together; it's just the other things that get in the way. The distractions. This life.

Tom leans toward me and marks each word on the tabletop: "Kate, it's so fucked up!"

He means it, very genuinely, but as it's our routine to come to public places and bemoan the state of the world, his angst is rounded and warm. I take his finger before he breaks it, though.

"It is. We're the only ones who're sane."

"Seriously, *look* at these people. No one's living in the real world anymore!"

Something turns fierce despite his speaking in a whisper. And of course, as we're off, I have no idea what he's thinking as his face folds into a scowl and something dies in his eyes. He pulls his hand away and there he goes, his thoughts most likely rolling down that rut that has to do with his father, his family, the Feed, but I have no way of knowing for sure. His isolating his thoughts like this is almost rude. What is he thinking about? His alternative life, maybe, the one he chose never to live, where he stayed involved with the Feed rather than running away. We discussed that one loads while he was training to be a psychotherapist. Chasing *that* career—the talking cure—when his father had set up the Feed. Well, you don't have to be Freud, do you? I remember Tom's glee before he told him, and I remember his father's reported silent rage. We talk, Tom and I. We talk a lot. It's one of our strengths, when we find the time. Like tonight, when we're going slow. But I wish he'd give himself some peace. He chews his lower lip and stares out the window, his eyes darting around for all the world as if he were on and spraying away, but I check and he isn't; his Feed is still off.

As is mine.

The blonde and the brunette work through their food silently, mechanically, lost in conversation with each other, or others, or many people at once. From the outside, who knows? Their eyes are moving even quicker than Tom's, but what they're seeing is not the tables and old prints on the walls but the pulsing, strobing colors of their Feeds. My brain itch, I'm suddenly aware, is now unbearable. It's making my fingers flex and clench. My mouth is super-dry. I could be checking my poll. I could be surfing newspools for developments about Energen. Everyone was surprised by the company's announcement, but no one seems to be asking *why* it's made the Arctic drilling stop, why it's made this decision *now*, Anthony Levin, its CEO, smiling sincerely at the world. I don't trust him. Something is building. The world is disturbed and people are doing strange things: businesses unpredictable, politicians perverse.

It's all very odd, and my brain (my actual brain, working really hard here without my Feed) is starting to hurt now. I could, if I were on, be relaxing it, catching up on some ents. Mum and Martha wanted to message tonight because Martha has mundles of her new house to share; I could leave my own world and experience her memory bundles of a place so many miles away in a time now past as if I were actually *there*. I could be checking my pool: "What Would You Sacrifice?" has been getting tens of millions of resprays a day. Everyone loves a poll. But I need to keep it fresh. People's attention needs constant feeding, and if I want to influence them to *think* about the world, I need to be smart. I need to be heard above the chatter. That's what Tom doesn't get: I'm using the Feed as a tool for good. I'm not *addicted*!

One of the first polls on "What Would You Sacrifice?" had been ". . . for the Arctic?" Fitting, given Energen's news today, but barely anyone had taken part back then, and I learned from that that it's not stupidity or carelessness; it's just distraction. It's the enticing noise that surrounds us. So now I slip the political ones between things like ". . . to look good?" and ". . . to get the man of your dreams?" I got more than sixty million sprays with that particular poll and then hit them with ". . . to be kinder to the planet?" Eighty million sprays for that one. Smashed it. Newspools scraped my stats. (Politicians "won," naturally—who wouldn't sacrifice them?) What matters is making people focus for a moment on what we're doing to our world. If we can get a toehold, just crack open people's brains a bit, then greater changes might follow. I don't know yet what the next poll will be, but from where I'm sitting I'm thinking something like "What would you sacrifice . . . for the good of your brain?" because—and there is no way I could tell Tom this, though I'd like to scream it in his face—I don't think I'd sacrifice the Feed! I don't think I could! I can't! I want to go on right now, I'm screaming for it inside! But . . . I breathe . . . *Come on now, Kate, come on* . . . I breathe and soften my voice, because this was supposed to be a nice evening and I'm just being distracted. Like everyone else. I need to focus here.

"Why don't we do some anagrams, hey, Tom? Get the old brains working . . ."

He grimaces and shifts in his chair. "So what have you done today, Kate?"

And then—I can't help it; it's because I was thinking about it and I've been spraying about it all day, so all those links are fresh and I'm so desperate to check my pool—it's like a slip of the tongue, a habit that lives by itself—I go on, and—

—where the hell have you been? Martha messages, & Mum's rightbehind her, her emotis making it veryclear that she's about to unleash at me, but I blockher and interrupt. We're being off tonight, I chat, Tom reckons it's good for the brain to be slow, to keep it workingproperly. Don't be ridiculous, Mum chat-snaps, have a look at yoursister's mundle, & before I can blockher again she sends me one that bursts like a newlyformedbraincell in my-mind, the senses & emotis of Martha's bun-dledmemory expanding into existence like a polyp in mybrain, so I'm her not me for a while:

—I'm on the lawn looking up at the new house, white frontage (the new [*cloudbreath*] shade from [*Perfect-Paint*], an ident links me), peaked-windows, cloudysky above. I step onto the path (that lawn looks weedy, use new [*Weedaway*], an ident links me) & myheartrate increases as I reach out toward the door; myheart is thumping 42% faster & a 2.3% endorphin rush flows in. It's soexciting! The BioLock—*mine*—recognizes me, because it's mylock in *myhouse*! and the door opens automatically & I hear the kids 6.72m behind me running up the path, but I'm in the hallway now, the coolshadows and the freshsmell of polish & it's—

—I freeze the mundle & explain I'll message them later because I've been on for 4millisecs already & Tom'll notice if I'm on much longer & I still haven't surfed any pools for Energen news or looked at the [*WhatWould-YouSacrifice?*] pool & I can see my boards are flashing with 57,603 messages, so the poll must be doingwell. A message from someone called ChloeKarlson437 comes in as I watch—*Keep up the good work, Kate!*—but there's no time to reply because—Oh, come *on*, Kate, Martha messages me, & I flash her an adrenalspike and at the same time quickly search for [*Energen*] & news streams out of all the pools, but there's nothing new so I spray at my friendgroup to see if they know anything new & send a quick-

apology to Martha & a wobblyface to Mum &
tell them I'll message later & I go off & it's only
been 11millisecs—

—but Tom noticed.

"You're *addicted*, Kate," he hisses.

"Come on," I scoff, and gesture at everyone around us, though I know he's right.

"You're just like the rest of them!"

"You're such a snob! No, I know," I say, snapping my fingers, thinking as fast as I can without the Feed. "You have a transgendered intrasexual abandonment-induced Oedipus complex."

We played this game just before he completed his psychotherapy training: How overly complicated can you make simple psychological syndromes sound? This one actually makes him laugh.

"It's a daddy complex," I explain, pleased with myself, proud of my brain, riding his good humor, "but more deeply complex."

But his laughter stops. He glances at me and shakes his head. No emotis needed.

"You Feed too much, Kate. Come on. You're . . . you didn't do this before. I'm sorry I annoy you, but it's because I care. You'll be freaking out the baby . . ."

We fall into silence again, but the silence isn't like it was. There's more to it now. We both agree the Feed is out of control. It's what we bonded over when we first met at his brother's wedding. We're both worried about the state of the world too, and Tom agrees it's gotten so much worse in the five years since then. My parents don't believe that Tom is a good person, because of his family—he's a Hatfield—but he is; I know he is with all my heart. He's not like his brother or his father. But it feels like he has their absolutist streak, like he's making me choose here. Between him and the Feed. Like I can't have both. I turn away from him and pat my bump again, one of the many kids that I regularly tell my two hundred million followers we're consigning to death because of the way we live. She's a Hatfield too.

"Do you want to go on again then, Kate? We can be slow tomorrow night instead."

But before I can reply, it happens like a wave. Clatters of cutlery and chairs thrown back. Gasps and a gabble of confused words actually vocalized out in the real, and then silence again, like everyone has taken a breath but what has happened is everyone's eyes have started to flicker even more rapidly. Someone sobs; the blond girl's hands are clasped over her mouth. The waiter runs for the door.

"Tom?"

"Get back on!" he says, and he's on a snap second before I am and—

—I'm deluged with mysister. Martha is hystericallyshouting so I blockher & gland testosterone to counter the adrenalspike I feel, her panic contagious, & Mum is desperatelymessaging, Where are you, where are you? I've been messaging you for *seconds*, Kate, what's the *matter* with you? I blockher too & notice myboards have thousands of newmesssages & I've never felt anything like it: theFeed warps with a coalescingweight that nearly makes me fall off my chair in the real. I try to slow myendocrinesystem down because Mum's now chat-screeching at me that Martha's shouting at *her whydidIblockmysister?* Then a silence falls on theFeed as billions of FeedIDs pause, like a wave drawing out, before breakingnews gushes like a tsunami. Memes flood & rumors ripple like a swellingcontagion. Newspools burst into form in a swollentide. Clusters grow around them as people swarm to look, & Mum's panic-bursting me, *What's happening?* My adrenal medulla pumps mysystem with epinephrine as I rush to look at one of the pools, but something slams down in front of it. *But nothing's dammed:* theFeed is free & people swarmflow to other pools, which are dammed & dammed again, blocked by . . . the company?

The government? Within 3nanosecs 127,734pools are created & dammed & I tell Mum I don't know what's happening & I panic-nudge Tom, but he flash-messages me he's trying to message his-brother, Ben, & then something filters out from the seething Feedchatter & there is a vid, a vid is going viral, it's spreading faster than anything before & they're trying to stop it & [*dariancharles*] the news is that PresidentTaylor1 has been killed. Everything goes quiet. All FeedIDs are stilled. *PresidentTaylor1 has been killed.* It fractals across theFeed, then mutates to say *assassinated.* Already there's chaos in the U.S., contagious panic, the economy has flatlined & weapons have been mobilized toward the east. My cortisol levels are up 18.2%, my heartrate beating 2.93times too fast, & there are now 100,000s of thisvid & as fast as 1pool is dammed, 2,000others appear, & I'm looking up what's the difference between *murder* & *assassination* & Mum is still shouting but she's drowned out by the roar & it's something to do with the word *hash,* which is an archaic term for $C_{21}H_{30}O_2$, & I access one of the newspools & what's there, the thing that everyone's absorbing, that's at the center of all these newspools coming repeatedly and unstoppably into existence, is a vid tagged [*RichardDrake62SeniorSecurityAnalystWH. USA.StaffFID#22886284912*] and time-stamped 7.23secs ago. I go into his memory bundle. I have no idea where this room is because the GPSloc is blocked, but it looks like every special-ops room from any ent I've ever gulped. A lacquered table reflects cold-buzzing neons. Thinscreens & decks adorn the soundproofed walls. Then PresidentTaylor1 walks in with a creamsweater (the new line from [*Muitton*], an ident links me) slung across his shoulders, a big mug of dark and fragrant coffee (the [*arabeanica*] blend from [*Nesspro*], an ident links me) in one hand, & this is the WhiteHouseUSA, this *was* the WhiteHouseUSA 7.34secs ago, & this mundle getting out is an insane security breach, no wonder pools are being dammed, &—

—Good morning all, PresidentTaylor1 says in thereal with that warm-gruff tone, & sits. I understand, he says, given Energen's surprising news, that the race is now on for the ArcticSouth. We will not let it fall into the wrong hands. Folks, we have war in a cold climate. But before the president's smile can fully form, Richard-Drake62's view is obscured as a silhouetted figure—PatrickVaughn59, it's tagged—stands & raises a gun. The president's head becomes a cloud of red. The room upturns as Richard-Drake62 dives for cover & RichardDrake62's mundle crashes to black & there's the sounds of upheaval & someone screams something that sounds like "Dariancharles!" & right away [*dariancharles*] is spurting off into thousands of pools saying [*whoisdariancharles?*] & then the vid repeats—repeats—repeats. Whoever's sprayed it zooms in each time on the president's face as his head bursts apart and the mundle slows to split-frame grabs—the president's head splits open in slo-mo & this vid is streaming into 47,196,255FeedIDs *from this pool alone* & in a stomachdropping cascade all pools are suddenly dammed. Everything stops—

It's like going over the edge of the world. There is nothing; just the samemessage appearing everywhere on theFeed, wherever I look. It's from the government, telling me to *go home quietly,* to *go home now.* All other content is dammed, & in thereal, in the restaurant, we all stand like a herd & flood into the street. Everywhere people stumble, stunned in the hilltop dusk by the absence of anything on theFeed. All communications are culled. The tower, the Hub of theFeed, is still lit in the distance, but it's broadcasting nothing now but the government. On as I am, the quickcodes now make the billboards alive with the samemessage endlessly reproducing itself in spooling neonbrights, expanding off the boards, filling the air, choking the eveningsky with gaudycolors telling us to gohome, there is a curfew, gohome, there is a curfew, gohome, there is a curfew, gohome.

Six Years Later

TOM
The Memory Facility

He leaves through the double doors at the side of the facility and loops the chain back around the handles as he'd found it. Chains are good weapons now. He considers taking it with him—it's not too rusty—but no: better to secure the place and protect what he's found.

The forecourt is empty, the windows in the high walls dust-stained in the still, early light. In places pipes have cracked and the concrete has exploded outward in gaping rocky wounds. Tom thumps the yellow fuel tanks again, dirt-streaked and resonant, and nods in satisfaction. He has weathered skin now and wind-tousled hair. His smile is a crevice in a hardened face. This unlikely discovery could save their lives.

Across the deserted parking area, he climbs a verge

and walks along the perimeter fence, still keeping an eye on the storage facility to see if there's anybody there. Finding where he cut the wire, he stoops through. A road leads off north. There's a car and a trailer farther up, jackknifed. The tarmac is crumbling, in some places chasm-deep, and in the distance he can see the facility's main entrance: a thick, dirty gateway that, like the entrances to all his father's places, used to be translucent, fluid, and clean.

He drops off the other side of the road and goes into the wood. From the inside, its run of beeches strikes silhouettes against the clouded sky. Dark and light, it's like trudging through an old-fashioned bar code. It's cool for summer as another cold dip rips unpredictably across the land, the stormy weather, still turbulent, scudding in from the east. Will it ever settle now? They used to smell bad things carried on the wind, but that was a long time ago.

As Tom's boots crush the long grass, a cackling brings him up short and two magpies beat away into the woods, swerving around the trees. "Bring on the joy," he says, and scans the surroundings for any other movement. He pats the bulges in his pockets to check his bounties are still there, then opens his arms to the canopy above. Through the trees, the hulk of the storage facility sits silently behind him, slowly decaying

into the hills, as he forgets his way and has to back-
track to find the glade where the breeze wrestles the
branches and the long grasses writhe.

"Guy?" he whisper-calls, and a horde of squirrels
chatter amid the conspiring leaves.

Something smacks the earth by his feet. Something
else speeds past his face, and then a hard object hits him
on the shoulder. Another cracks the side of his head.
Semi-stunned, he turns around to finally see Guy pos-
ing on a branch tossing unsplit, unripened chestnuts
between his hands, an expectant smile filling his face
beneath his frenetic ash-blond hair.

"What's the password, then?"

"Well done, you got me." Tom rubs his head and
raises his hands in surrender.

"Incorrect."

Another chestnut scuds past Tom's cheek. "Careful,
Guy!"

"Still not right!"

Guy throws the final chestnut in the air, a high lob,
and dangles himself from the branch, his sweater riding
up around his skinny stomach before he tumbles to the
ground. He smooths his hair back, grinning with his
mouth though his eyes, as always, are worried. "So?"

"Empty. The place was deserted."

"Already ripped out?"

"No. There are tanks of fuel. And the seals looked good."

Guy rubs his powder-white, thin-fingered hands together, clearly nearly daring to hope. "And were there cables?"

Tom nods slowly.

"And transistors?"

Tom pulls from one pocket in slo-mo victory an angular lump of metal with many pins for legs and a trailing wire for a tail. Guy beams. He actually claps. "This is going to change *everything,* Tom! With the turbines working we can use the fuel for the plow. We can dig *deep,* we can plant things better. We can relax, Tom, we can *relax.*"

They pat each other's shoulders, sharing the triumph. How life has changed. They hug.

"You haven't been asleep?" Tom asks Guy, breaking the embrace at last.

"No, Tom, I have not. You?"

"Guy," he says pointedly, "what do *you* think?"

Walking fast, and halfway home, they camp in a gentle fold in the hill. Rocks penetrate the earth above them and long fronds of grass give the place a fringe. The sides of the dip have been rubbed at until the earth is smoothed.

"The dogs have been here," Guy muses as he spreads the dry soil with a foot, peering at the horizon around them.

"Then it's good enough for us."

They build a fire, a small one. They haven't seen anyone else for a long time, but it's not worth the risk: when things go wrong now, they do it more absolutely than before. So: just five sticks to heat their tins as the sun sets and the clouds pull apart. A skyful of stars is scattered overhead. The fire *tinks* and snaps, its core a fluttering orange, as Guy lies back, arms behind his head, the transistor bulging his backpack pillow. The silence of the world.

"Pretty perfect, hey, Tom?"

Tom nods, holding his knees for balance as he looks up, lines etched around his eyes as he squints. Night skies. So clear. They've become the norm. He can barely remember the scuzzed-out faded grays of yesteryear, those skies bleached by city lights. A poorly recalled dream.

Guy watches Tom first as he sleeps, as he must, then they swap. Tom stretches his legs in the cooling air, yawning, running in place to wake up as Guy clambers under the rugs. He watches the young man's face relax. Guy is soon asleep. His mind blank, Tom stares up at the stars again, at the moon, whose light catches the grasses above them like large silver lashes, until, just before dawn, the colors in the sky meld through black to blue to the beginnings of green as the stars slowly fade to nothing. Guy jerks abruptly beside him. Then, still asleep, he seems to stop breathing. His fists curl and his face twitches, then his eyes screw tight.

"Guy?" Tom whispers, his heart suddenly painful, all his senses alert. The morning is at that moment brighter than he'd realized.

Guy continues to twist and chew on nothing, even as Tom hauls him up and shakes him. But he will not wake—it's like he's tethered too hard to sleep. His eyelids flutter and his mouth stretches into a tighter and tighter grimace until suddenly the spasms stop. Then a breath escapes his lips, his face eases to peace, and he starts to breathe normally again.

Tom's eyes fill. His own breath is now ragged. The lonely silence of this place is so dense. He wants to run, but instead he strokes Guy's cheek; he touches where the skin looks sore around the young man's mouth and traces the soft part of Guy's neck with his fingers. Then he wraps his hands around Guy's throat and chokes him. He digs between the tendons with his thumbs and feels the cartilage warp. Guy's eyes burst open. His mouth gapes, his tongue gags out, and his hands swipe ineffectually through the air.

It takes a long time. The noise is animal, until something snaps. Tom keeps on squeezing, keeps shouting, keeps clutching the bones as Guy's body gradually stops jerking.

Keeping constant lookout, his brain scoured with sleeplessness, Tom hurries through the next day homeward, dozing briefly at intervals, never letting sleep take him deeply away. He avoids the roads and villages, preferring to work his way across the fields, which have mostly merged into one. Panicked and exhaustion-fuzzed, he sees a tree stump as a person, but no, of course, it's not. His mind is deeply agitated. His thoughts have, over time, generally relaxed. Raw with panic like everyone else's during the years following the Collapse, they now tend toward peace. They have all learned methods to calm the disconnected fear, and the regrowth of hope has gradually soothed Tom's mind; he can feel it even now embalming the panic as he forces himself to breathe. He sits in the deep grass and *breathes*. Explores the earth with his fingertips. Smells the sap of nearby trees. The sun suddenly smacks his skin as it breaks a cloud. He concentrates on the air in his throat.

He hasn't killed anybody since he killed his brother.

It comes from nowhere, this memory, this sickening revelation, long buried. It's as if the muscles in his hands have remembered it: the softness of Guy's throat snapping under his palms, but instead of Guy's face it's suddenly Ben's, as twisted with surprise in his bedroom as Guy's had been there on that hill. Ben's face. Tom hasn't seen it for years, but there it is. Twisted. How had he forgotten this? It should have haunted him daily. Shards of broken memories cascade, and amid them some tiny voice tells him he has to calm down. He vaguely senses tears on his face and that his body is jerking in the grass, but he's trapped here in an ancient maze, smothered and surrounded by these images from before.

He had to do it. He'd had no choice. Their mother. He almost feels memories of snatches of her Feed, the scorched silhouette of how she used to chat—but no, they're gone. Other scraps of memory are dislodged by the strength of his thumping heart: the smoke-filled sky; jagged piles of vehicles crushed up around the tower; staring down at them from the apartment. And then a big one, detaching like an iceberg: child-height in a darkened room, hiding from his brother when they were boys. Tom had buzzed him, turning his Feed on and off. It had driven Ben to a frenzy. *What y . . . doing? . . . upid! . . . Tom! . . . Dad'll kill you . . . stop turni . . . om! . . .* Off and on and off and on. And then

THE FEED • 31

stunning pain as he was cuffed about the head. His father towered over him. He simply forced Tom's Feed on. *I don't have time for this, Tom. I'm working.* Ben's face, his smile, as he reached up to take their father's hand. Tom had watched them leave the room, and now he forces himself up out of the grass, shaking, gasping, blinking, barely seeing the world around him, picking up rocks and throwing them at trees to *focus on the now.* Some memories are better left lost.

He rubs his fingers into his straining eyes. He runs for a while and slowly the memories subside, and with them his body calms. He walks. He breathes. The heat comes off the day and the animals emerge. At dusk he startles an army of rabbits. A pack of dogs has taken a horse down and is halfway through it. A kestrel follows him for hours, riding the thermals, carving through the sky.

He marches through the second day, calm again. Then, that night, dogs prowl. Hearing their breathing, a guttural pack of sniffing and growling sounds not far enough away, Tom finds a nook up an oak to hide in. He thinks, tentatively, about the first time he had tried to remember things after the Collapse, after they had lost the Feed. Even the rough, warped memory of it is sickening as he'd tried to access things that were no longer there and his body had stalled in panic. The stunning rawness of a hacked-away limb. Exhausted, aware of the tumult of his thoughts below, his eyes droop and he pinches his face to stay awake. Birds pace. He mustn't sleep. The stars are brushed by the shadows of the tree's hushing leaves, and by the time they have faded and the sky has turned opal, he is finally stumbling down the hill toward home.

With the dew undisturbed and the sun topping the hill, the camp is peaceful before the others awake. Corridors of trellises branch out from the farmhouse toward the shower stall and huts. The house itself has patched-up walls and scavenged, rusted turbines hammered to the roof by Guy. As an Electrician, they had coaxed that valuable knowledge out, so he had partially remembered what to do. The turbines spin gratingly in the morning breeze, so close to giving them power, so close to saving their lives, but so far, useless.

Tom heaves himself up onto the porch of the children's hut and glances through the window, breathless. There she is: Bea, in bed, a frown of dreaming concentration crumpling her face. Jack, too large for his cot, is squeezed in nonetheless. Danny is the adult watching them this morning. A slice of sunlight catches the young man's rusty hair while he points an earth-caked finger at a book's scuffed page. Unaware he is being observed, his mouth curls around the shape of each slow word.

At the farmhouse's sun-peeled door, Tom toes off his boots by the shells of upturned monitor cases filled with herbs, where insects buzz. He pats the remaining lump in his pocket to check it's there again, fixes a smile in place, and flips the latch, and there she is too. Kate, skinning something he can't see, turns from the kitchen counter. The light from the window halos her head, her blond hair glowing while shadows hide her face.

"Well, there's a lot of fuel," he starts off positively. "It'll see us through the winter. And cables to—"

"But was there any food?" Kate's fists, smeared with the blood of the tiny animal she has been preparing, are clenched before he has finished inhaling. "We have to get *out* of here, Tom. We're not going to survive!"

"Of course we are—"

"No, Tom. We can't *grow* anything. Open your eyes!"

"Kate," Tom says, trying to hush her voice. He feels his thoughts troubling his mind again, uncontrolled as his pulse rises. His mouth is unwieldy as he hears himself gabble. "With the fuel we can run the plow. With the cables we can—"

"I don't care. I want to go."

"We can't abandon everyone."

"Yes, we can."

"Kate—"

"We have to fight for our family, Tom. We agreed! You, me, and Bea, *we're* the number ones."

Kate stops her words with puckered lips. Her fingers flare in frustration as, again, Tom goes silent, but his mind is overwhelmed. There is too much to process here: his love for Kate, his relief at being home, his anger, his fear, his *massive* love for Bea, the animal drive to protect her, them, to look after Guy and Ben. All these emotions cannot coexist with the absolute necessity of what he did on that hill, the renewed frazzling fear unleashed by what he had to do to Guy, and his thoughts collapse under the weight of it all.

"Look . . ." he starts, closing the distance between them. He takes a deep breath and tries to reset this. He's pleased with the surprise he had found her; that had been how he'd wanted this to start. "Kate. Listen. Please slow down. I know it's not much, but . . ." He extracts the apple from his pocket. Without the Feed, he doesn't know her thoughts, however hard he scrutinizes her face. Does she remember? Of course she does—it's one of their secret questions. "Katherine Hatfield," he murmurs.

"Shh," she concedes. She wipes her hands before clasping his and the apple they hold. She looks into his eyes. "Someone might hear."

"Katherine *Brown,* then." He kisses the top of her head. The smell of her hair is a comfort. "I can't find you diamonds, but I can still get you apples. Right?"

Kate thumbs her engagement ring and rubs the apple's surface, indents it with her thumbnail. Many things move in her eyes. "I still want to go, Tom."

"I promise you I'll protect us."

She shakes her head. "We're going to starve. I'm sorry."

"Give it another six months. It's so dangerous to move." His mouth goes dry. "What would happen to Bea if one of us was taken?"

Kate bites her lip. There is heat in her eyes. "Things aren't fine just because you *think* they are, blindly hoping away!" She pulls away in exasperation. "Where's Guy? Have you both eaten?"

Guy's choking face flickers through Tom's mind. It's etched there now, with Ben's, it seems, undeletable. He blinks them both away. He sees the dark room, this small kitchen, but can still feel them, rotting inside his brain. "He was taken, Kate." He hadn't wanted to do it. He hadn't even wanted to say it. He doesn't want to scare her. *He* doesn't want to be scared anymore. He shrugs slowly and looks away. He won't cry. He buries it all within. "There was nothing I could do."

Kate takes his hands, her voice tight. He can hear the fear there—he's not stupid. They're still trapped, like fish in a pond. "We . . . need to get out of here, Tom."

"But that didn't stop *him* from being taken. That wouldn't protect us, would it? There *is* no protection!" His voice is quivering. "Kate, all we have is the hope it won't happen to us."

Left alone in the dusty silence of the kitchen, Tom drops the transistor on the tabletop. He slumps against a chair. Closes his eyes. Then, after a few moments' rest, he heaves water from the rain tanks across the lawn and up an unsteady ladder to fill the shower. Bottles nestled in the curves of corrugated sheets hold mildly warmed water, which he pours in too. From up high, looking over the moldy plywood wall of the shower stall, he surveys their patchy vegetable plots and disintegrating barn. Everything was so much easier when it was full of supplies. But food aside, they had thought they were safe.

He sees Graham stoop out of a hut, the one he shares with Jane. Wearing his habitual loose trousers and sole-flapping sandals, the old man eases himself into the chair on his porch, draws his hair into a soft gray wave, and folds open a dog-eared book, pen in hand. Tom climbs back down into the cubicle before he is seen and undresses. He'll have to tell the camp about Guy. Shatter their fragile peace. Slapping his feet on the soggy ground, he unleashes a cascade of near-freezing water. He rubs it into his eyes, rubs his scalp through his gritty hair, the water blocking and unblocking his ears. He washes his hands and arms. Washes them and washes them, flexing his fingers and getting into the flesh between the thumb and the palm.

While he's dressing, dried off and nearly done, he hears breathing—slivers of sound on the other side of the shower-stall wall. Whispers scuffing the breezy air. He buttons his trousers and grips the latch slowly. As he sweeps open the door, the freckle-spattered children freeze in their sewn-up clothes, eyes widened with their discovery.

"Bea . . . What are you up to, Jack?"

"Nothing!" the boy blurts out too quickly, a bundle of wires gripped in his hands and pressed into his stomach to hide it. Bea doesn't say anything, but shrugs and won't meet his eye.

"Come *on,* you two. Old tech is dangerous." Tom flicks the towel over his shoulder and holds out a hand. "Give it over, Jack. Where's your dad?"

Jack's voice is a birdlike trill as his grip tightens on the wires. "But what's it for, Tom?"

So much has gone from the world, Tom thinks, yet a child's stubbornness remains. Bea, beside the boy, peers up through her matted hair with inquisitive eyes—another instinctive trait, it seems, that somehow survived the Collapse.

"I thought you were supposed to know everything, Tom," Jack whispers. He sidles closer to grasp Tom's hand. "Daddy says you can read people's minds."

"Go on, get away," Tom snaps, shaking the boy off. He glowers as Jack runs to the farmhouse and takes Bea's hand. Who tells the children these things? Who even talks about reading people's minds—where has Jack gotten the *words* for this, let alone the concept?

"Where have you been, Daddy?"

His eyes still on Jack's retreating form, his thoughts locked, he mutters, "I was at work." It sounds strange even as it leaves his mouth, some old phrase rising from the unknown, dredged up on the tide of his returning memories of Ben.

Bea scrunches her nose at the unfamiliar word. "At . . . *work,*" she pronounces, and grips his forearms in such a way that he's lifted her up before he's even thought about it. "Will you take me too next time, Daddy?"

"Probably not, no."

"Why?" She's fiddling with his hair, trying to look inside his ear.

"Why do you think?" he asks, shaking her fingers away, glancing toward the farmhouse again. Kate is in the doorway, arms folded, watching them across the lawn, Jack crying behind her legs.

"Hmm. Because the fairies might catch me?"

"Exactly."

"Oh! Let's plant something, Daddy!" Bea cries, and wriggles to be let out of his arms.

He chases her across the grass and uses his towel to capture her, wrap her up, and lift her again, kidnapped, kicking and shrieking, into the air.

"But what's the point in going back if Guy's gone?"

They are squeezed around the heavy kitchen table, their plates licked clean after breakfast. It's not the biggest table, but they're not the biggest group anymore. The insipid smell of rotten vegetables lingers, and another scent too: the acrid tang of argument.

"Hey?" Sean grunts when no one answers him. His skin is pocked and patchy, the shadows beneath his eyes very deep. His hands and forearms are laced with strands of scars, the story behind them still raw in his exhausted eyes but imprisoned there, untold. A policeman before the Collapse, Sean had brought his son, Jack, and little else to the camp, other than a determined instinct to protect. It had calmed Tom at first, being swept along in the wake of Sean's fervent plans to secure the camp, but over time they had all realized the eviscerating truth: that the threat was not solely from outside; it was lurking inside them all. And what could they do to defend against *that*?

"Without Guy's knowledge," Sean continues, "we can't connect the windmills, so what's the point? We can't risk people finding us. We'll be attacked!"

"More importantly," Graham states, "Guy was *taken*."

Everyone eyes the transistor, the inert electrical insect squatting on the table. Kate has taken the children foraging to give the rest this space to talk. Old Graham and his wife, Jane; Sean hunched opposite them; Danny leaning by the sink, his face screwed up in thought. Tom knows they must be thinking about their survival right now—but are they contemplating the day-to-day mechanics of the challenge or the bigger thing: What happened to Guy, and its implications for themselves?

"The point is, Sean," Tom says in the end, trying to sound patient, "that if we can't get the windmills to work, we'll need fuel more than ever. We need to power the plow if we want to grow food. It doesn't matter if people find us when we've died of starvation!"

"So you're happy to lead more people to their deaths," Sean declares.

Tom thumps the table. "Guy was—"

"Tom, Sean—*please!*" Jane's skin is paper-wrinkled, her voice softened by age. She lowers her shaking hands as if to part the waters of this argument. "Tom has told us all there is to tell. Guy was taken." She shakes her head. "Who knows what that will mean for us? But there is fuel that we now *desperately* need. Any food?" Tom shakes his head. "Well. It sounds like an opportunity too good to miss, and a miracle if others have. If we don't get fuel, we'll die. We need light, we need heat. We need to be able to cook. So I vote yes. Going back is worth the risk."

Graham doesn't need to say he seconds his wife; he nods his slim forehead at the table, his gray fringe falling in front of his eyes. He swipes it back and gently takes Jane's hand. Tom stares at them. The ease of their age. Their silent understanding of each other. It's beautiful.

"Still, we can't rely on fuel forever." Danny pushes

himself away from the sink, his scowl, now that he's worked out what he thinks, determined. His skin, which flushes at the least provocation, is dappled. He has a quickcode, almost unnoticeable, tattooed into his hairline, round like some Celtic symbol, and the frays of his sweater wave as he gesticulates. "Now I can't mem everything—"

"*Remember,*" Graham quietly corrects.

"Yeah, I can't re*member* Guy's skills about wiring, I'm no Electrician, but what good are those windmills on the roof if we don't try to hook them up? They could save us. We need cables so that transmuter can work—"

"Transistor," Jane amends.

"Whatever. I'll give it a go. But we *need* those cables from the facility. Guy's put the windmills in the right loc, at least."

"*Location,*" Graham corrects. "Or *place.*"

"Exactly." Danny nods. "Yes vote from me."

"Maybe you led people back here, Tom," Sean states, his thoughts clearly still stuck elsewhere. His bloodshot eyes flicker and catch. His hands drum the tabletop, his feet, the floor. The energy is of exhaustion: a chronic lack of sleep. "If you've exposed the camp, we're *dead*—"

"There's no one else," Tom replies sharply. "Danny, you up for the journey?"

"You *betcha!*"

"Good." Tom nods and taps the table. "We'll go the day after tomorrow. We'll get the fuel. We'll get the cables. We'll get those windmills working. We'll be safe."

"Tom . . ." Jane's slow voice rises through the silence. She crumples a smile at the transistor. "We should talk about Guy. This hasn't happened for years. We're all in considerable danger . . ."

Tom breathes. Sean drums the table. Graham and Jane clasp hands. Danny wraps his arms around himself and looks physically sick with fear. They must talk about this thing that no one wants to admit. Danny is staring at Tom, his wide green eyes pleading for some comfort.

"So tell us, Tom," Jane says, her voice hardening. "How was he taken?"

Tom flexes his thumbs, clasping his hands in his lap. Won't meet their eyes. Some memory in his head is bursting to be let out. "The usual signs. You know. I did what we were told to do."

He had once told Bea that pumpkins creak as they grow, and that if you listen hard at night, you can hear them groaning in their sleep. This information has been reshaped in her mind, and before any work can be started on the vegetables, a systematic procedure must take place.

"Miriam's okay too," she calls, kneeling by the penultimate pumpkin in the patch, which is deflated like the rest of them. "It's cold at night and she nearly got eaten by a bird, but she likes it here and she's friends with the carrots."

Tom nods solemnly, shading his eyes. "Thank you, Bea, you're doing a very good job."

"Daddy, Miriam also wants to know, did you leave Guy at *work*?"

Tom purses his lips. A dry breeze lifts the leaves of the browning rhubarb and shivers them. It's a good memory that this girl has.

"Will he come home later?" Bea persists. "He said he'd show me fish!"

When Tom still doesn't answer, confusion darkens her face. He'll have to tell her something, he sees, but the truth? No way. Not yet. Please. "Bea, you know those fairies?" he asks, and the girl nods sternly. She knows them well. "Well, they took him. So . . ." He shrugs and retreats over the corduroy earth. He doesn't know what else to say, or how to put it into words, but he knows she mustn't see his face. Bea and Jack, born after the Collapse, who never knew of the Feed, are the most instinctive people-readers of them all. Not only is her memory good; Bea knows when she's being lied to.

"Hello!"

Jane is trudging up the hill with an easel in one hand and a canvas in the other, and Tom turns gratefully from his daughter. He jogs over to take the canvas. "Another painting?"

"Why not? Except we're running out of space." Out of breath and hot, she sets up the easel and waves cheerily at Bea, who turns abruptly back to the pumpkins. "But Graham lost that battle long ago. He knows it makes me happy."

"You're good at it."

"Well." Jane's eyes often gleam at a joke that no one else has heard. "You are kind, Tom, but my days of painting for others are over. One good thing about this almighty mess is who has time for critics anymore?" She wipes her brushes on a rag. "Which is lucky, because I'm low on russet, I've already lost my favorite yellow, and I'll soon be painting endless studies in brown."

"Can we make you up some more?"

"I don't know. Can you? All this *stuff* we took for granted . . ." Jane sighs and stares away. "So, I had a funny dream while you were gone," she says evenly after a while.

"A comedy dream?"

"Oh, you." She elbows him, staring at the sunbaked hills with unerring intent. "No, it was scary . . ." She trails off while opening a tube of white, and when she turns back to her painting, a smile is veneered across her eyes. "Time was this would have been worth a lot of money. I enjoy it much more again now." Her smile softens.

"Tell me about that dream."

She pauses. "Is there any knowledge Graham or I can help you with for the facility?"

"There were instructions written on the fuel tanks. They looked complicated. What about—"

"Did you copy them down?"

Tom shakes his head and frowns. "Look, Jane. Thanks for your support earlier."

"Sean's threatened by you, that's all. Before you came along, he was the alpha."

"The . . . ?"

Jane paints a curve on her canvas, a stylized fish. "The main man," she explains. "You're not complicated, you men. You were the psychotherapist. Tell me I'm wrong."

"That was years ago. He'll tear the camp apart!"

"Oh, a fight needs two, Tom. He's just scared. We all deal with it in different ways."

"Well, we need to get him to sleep properly. Enough already. He's paranoid!"

"If only he were . . ." She turns from him and starts on the sky, patches of blue spreading into form. She works the canvas with seemingly unplanned swipes, but the chunks of color take surprising shape. A cloud covers the sun and its rough edges gleam. A flock of birds circles afar, above the dark forest. Bea's head bobs, disappears, and occasionally reemerges amid the straggly browning plants.

That afternoon, he sits in the consulting hut. Sean won't come to talk, despite it being their rules, one of the ways they have learned and agreed to process the fear, taking advantage of Tom's knowledge, his talking cure, and there are so many better things he could be doing with his time. Checking the filtration tanks down by the stream that they've just about worked out how to use. Preparing provisions for the journey to the facility. Talking the route through with Danny, discussing the dangers, the details, so he is prepared enough that Feed reflexes won't kick in. Of them all, Danny is still the most prone to them. He had been young when it happened, a student. Enabled in the womb, he had spent his entire life in the infinite web of the Feed's connections, from before he was even born. His natural brain had been barely wired when everything had collapsed, and Tom's proud of the work they've done since.

The distance from the storage facility sits tight in Tom's thighs, and the night's scant rest in the tree aches his back. Bea's insistent probing about Guy plays on his mind. Her inquisitiveness endangers her. How long until she'll have to be told the truth? He closes his eyes and falls toward sleep, though he knows he shouldn't; no one's watching him, but he does it anyway. A fragmented dream of heat and darkness and a child that's his but not. Animals prowling through ruins. Guy too, grinning, and he realizes Guy's face somehow survives; he can remember him clearly, and he grasps this dreamily, with pleasant surprise. Ben's face too. It's there, in his head. Watching him sleep that fateful night. The memories flood unstoppable. It had happened before Tom's eyes. Ben had convulsed and grimaced as something found its way in. Tom had seen that. He was sure of it. He'd shouted for their parents, he'd shouted for Kate, but he had known Ben was dead already. He'd seen the vid on loop, showing them the signs. So he'd choked his brother to death—

He jerks awake, a hand over his drum-thumping heart. "It's me!" Jane sing-speaks, opening the door. She assesses him. "Were you just asleep?"

"How's the painting?"

She makes a noise of mock disgust and waves her hands away.

"Go on then," he says, and nods. Contrails of the past stream before his eyes. It's all he can do to focus on the present. He had killed only Ben's body. His mind had already been taken. "Sit down, Jane. What do you want to talk about?"

"The children, Jack and Bea . . . It feels like we've made it because of them. They're first generation. Never knew the way things were. Never had old-style jobs. And now Bea's going to be *six* next week. I remember when I turned six. It was a very big thing, you know."

There's something in her eyes that she's not saying; Tom thinks he can see that at least. Something strained, something tearful. He's learning these people signs.

"Your memory, Jane," he says quietly, shaking his head. "Since Guy, mine's been all . . ." His fingers swirl around his head.

"We'll get you all there," she says smartly. "We're getting your brains working again."

"You and Graham were lucky, not having the Feed."

"It gave us a head start," she concedes. She taps her temple and winks. "I can't remember my brief fling with the thing, can't even remember what it felt like, it was that long ago." She makes a face like she's eaten something bad. "If I could go back in time and change one thing in my life, that's what it would be. The only way I've ever been untrue to that man is by not telling him about it, but it would make him so unhappy. It's still in there somewhere . . ."

"And that's where it'll stay. Graham need never know. Your secret's safe with me. So tell me about that dream. The funny dream. You said you had one earlier."

Jane blinks, caught off guard. A scowl shadows her face but then she fixes him with her eyes. "Well, it wasn't funny *ha-ha*—"

"But that's why you're here, isn't it? To talk it out?"

She makes a noise in the back of her throat. "*Fine.* I've had it before. I was inside a stinking, hot metal place. Outside was . . . awful. Like a desert. I knew it was here, but it was like Mars. Do you remember the pictures? Dunes of earth, all scorched. I had a desperate hope that things might change . . . And that was it. That was the dream. It was really horrible. Happy, Mr. Freud?"

"It's strange," Tom muses. "You just made me mem the vids—"

"Remember."

"*Remember* the vids Fed back from the expedition

to Mars. I was fascinated by those underground cities they said they'd make. I remember—you just reminded me—realizing Mars had been there for thousands of years and that it would always outlive us. And it has. It's up there now, undisturbed by what we've done." He shakes his head. "I wonder what happened to those colonists, abandoned up there . . ."

"Doesn't bear thinking about," Jane says, and shivers. "And you and Danny better look after yourselves too, going back to the facility again. Here's no more forgiving than Mars."

After dinner, Graham runs a knowledge session on the lawn. As the colors drain from the sky, they discuss famous paintings and what they imagine they looked like. Jane sketches them out to order and Bea and Jack watch, rapt, as the images unfurl. Still in dirty shorts and T-shirts near translucent with wear, they chatter in the warm evening. They try to remember the names of the planets, but apart from Mars and the Moon, they can't, not even Graham and Jane, who, as Resisters who'd never had the Feed, can usually bring more to mind than the others.

Graham reminds them of the use of some words. He quivers between seriousness and glee as he describes how *mem* is *to remember* and how *mundles* are *memo-*

ries. *Emotis* are *emotions.* How to talk is *to talk* and not *stream,* which is a small river, like a *brook.* He spreads his fingers in delight. He makes them do grammar drills and write. That's the journalist coming through. They do memory exercises, remembering what plants they can eat, what happened that day, the day before, the previous weeks and months, stretching the muscles of their brains.

As the last rays of sun pick out the treetops on the hills, Graham reminds them how important a thing it is to remember, and at his cue, Danny lays three lanterns on the lawn. He has constructed them from thin willow ribs and what scraps of paper he could find. He is trying to hide his tears, Tom notices, but only when Bea wraps her arms around the young man's leg and Danny squats down to be hugged by her. She plants a little kiss on his forehead, on the old circular quickcode there; she thinks it's something special.

"So . . ." Graham says. He stands to look at them all. Sean lays a hand on Jack's shoulder. Tom glances at Kate. Jane toes a shape into the dirt. Deep breaths all around. "We must remember Guy, folks. Remembrance lets us learn. It reminds us. Re-minds us. Right? What are we if not what we remember?" He presents the children with pencils and taps the side of his head.

"Jack, Bea. This is your chance to say to Guy whatever you would like to say and to remember it forever."

"Can I ask if he'll still show me the fish?" Bea asks.

"What if I don't have anything to say?" Jack warbles, and Sean's scarred fingers tighten.

"Then you have nothing to say. That's all right," Graham reassures the boy and his father. "But if you do, write it here. Nice and gently. It might just be *goodbye*. And don't forget your *d*s and *b*s, Jack; make sure they go the right way around."

Tom watches first Danny, then Kate and Sean, write on another of the lanterns. Graham and Jane take the third. What the hell can he say? What does he actually want to remember here? Not the way it ended. The good work Guy did, positioning the turbines; the . . . how he . . . Tom shakes his head. No more memories will come, and in the end he simply writes, *Sorry*.

When all three lanterns are patterned with words, Danny holds out an oil-soaked rag. Sean takes up a rusted, gummy battery and rubs steel wool over the terminals, after a while spitting sparks, igniting it. It's a trick Guy showed them, some knowledge that he had brought as an Electrician that they will now practice to remember, for however long it works. The flaming light flickers Sean's face, licking into the hollows of his eyes. He sets fire to the wicks and passes the lanterns to Bea and Jack, who in silence let them go. They rise, glowing from within. They are taken by a breeze and spread apart, drawn separately away toward the south, small points above the dark canopy of leaves. Tom glances at Kate, at Bea; through the thickening blue of night he scrutinizes their faces, tries to imagine what they're thinking and fails. But he feels the imprint of them on himself, the weight of their meaning on his life. He looks up again. The three lanterns have risen. He wonders, fleetingly, if anyone else, elsewhere, has seen them too. And then, in silence, they disperse.

They lie in bed as the curtains flutter in a balmy breeze and it's still just light outside. The leaves patterned on the wallpaper are faded. Late-night flies still drone around as he rubs the back of Kate's neck.

"What kind of a world is this to grow up in?" she whispers. "Weren't we better off with Energen and all that lot? Remember them? That company? All that time I spent trying to stop it. And look at the world now."

"Oh, Kate. She doesn't know any other. She's happy. I look at Bea and I think there's hope, you know? Her brain works better than ours. Her memory's amazing. She reads all the people signs—it's like she sometimes reads my mind. We're achieving something here. How shall we celebrate her birthday?"

"*What* are we achieving?"

The tone of her voice makes Tom's thoughts lock defensively. "Knowledge. Food. Science: the filtration tanks."

"But why, Tom?" Something eases in her voice. Something becomes softer, eroded. Maybe she's not angry with him, he thinks; maybe she's angry with the world. "What are we doing this for?" she continues. "Let's imagine they don't get taken, it's just Bea and Jack. What, are we going to *mate* them? And then . . . ?"

This stuns him. He's not really thought about the future in any real way; it's enough to concentrate on the present. Kate shrugs his hands off and turns to him.

"I really think we should leave, Tom. Something bad is going to happen, I can feel it. Please don't go back to the facility."

She rolls toward him and wraps his heavy arms around herself. Tom listens to the sound her eyelids make as she blinks beside his ear, as she settles onto his chest. He doesn't want to believe her, but he's worried too, of course. The world has stopped being predictable. The structures they had put on it have been destroyed. The stats and metrics to bring understanding to chaos have been dissolved, burned away like paper. He feels her breathing, high and fast, with no idea what she's thinking, or who she is anymore. With the Feed he would have felt her emotions directly, like they were his own. He would have called up a mundle to remind himself of their catalog of happy times. Not even to remember them: to put himself right back in his mind exactly as it had been then, like a wormhole through time. But curled together in the future on this bed, they've become different people, their memories of the past fractured at best, painful at worst. Good things in there somewhere, he hopes.

"If we don't get that fuel, we'll die, Kate." He tries to sound patient. "It's not like I *want* to go, you know."

"Let's not fight, Tom. We're both tired." She rolls away. "Can I sleep first?"

He nods, watches her as she falls asleep, and then, when she's deeply gone, eases out of bed. Looking down at her, he flexes his fingers in the gloom. He tests himself: tries to remember the bedroom in their old house. Nothing comes. He touches her throat. Then, though he knows he shouldn't, he goes out walking. Not far. Just around the grass, keeping to the shadows so he isn't seen. Sean is watching the children tonight, upright, his hands spread flat on their little table. He has the stillness of a waxwork, and who knows what deeply entrenched thoughts ooze through his sleep-deprived brain. Danny dozes on a thin mattress in Graham and Jane's hut, with Graham asleep in bed and Jane watching. They changed the sleeping rota to give Tom and Kate some time alone tonight. The rotas will have to be changed again now Guy's gone, and Tom will be away again so soon with Danny. Back inside, he winds the old grandfather clock in the corridor. The rotas are pinned to a noticeboard here: for cooking, for foraging; who's on washing; the vegetables; checking the dam, the generator; the sleeping schedule, who's in with whom. Questions they have, about knowledge. Their lives are contained on this board. The world they have forged.

As he eases open the bedroom door to slip back inside, he sees that Kate is sitting up in bed. His heart jolts as she turns to stare at him, turns to look at the empty chair, sleepily confused. Back at him. "What are you *doing?*"

"Come on." He reaches for her shoulders.

"No, Tom!" She shakes him off, her eyes wild. "What are you—"

"Kate—"

"Don't you dare leave me asleep alone!"

"Kate," Tom groans. "You're overreacting. I was gone for a moment and nothing happened. Come *on.*"

"You have to watch—"

"You think I don't *know* that? I just killed Guy! It was . . . I couldn't . . . I . . ."

"And you'd have to kill me too if—"

"Kate!"

"I don't want someone joyriding my corpse, Tom!"

She flinches as he shoves past her, his hands to his face, a meaningless noise roaring from his throat. He opens the curtains. Forces the window closed. Thumps the frame. Throws the curtains shut again. The candle's greasy light flickers bronze shadows as he stands, fists clenched, shoulders heaving. The shadows stop moving. The darkened mirror, florid with age, reflects only darkness. The room so cold, so quiet. The flies have all disappeared. Tom undresses silently, but his heart's thumps are still escalating. He suspects she's expecting him to talk, but he won't. And he won't think about this, he won't think about her being taken, or any of them, or the consequences. He will sleep, and he knows that she'll watch him while he does so; she'll be watching him for signs.

The next morning, leaving the house by the back door, he climbs the slope to the barn. The plow squats inside, its missing blades replaced with ancient phone cases and spoons. Its fuel tank is open, hungry, dry. He fumbles in the darkness under the hayloft, where a stinking pile of barley they don't know how to process lurks. It doesn't smell healthy anymore. A diminishing row of tins with square-blotched quickcodes grins at him from the shadows. Impossible to know what's in them now; they're keeping what they think is dog food for a special occasion. He slips into the harness and heaves the cart outside. It's made of slight planks of dry and whitened wood with a metal rim and rusted wheels that resist the slope down the hill to Danny, in the vegetable patch. Together they coax the cart to the mildew smell of the generator shed, where they load on four empty fuel kegs. Then, back in the farmhouse, in the study, Tom takes maps from a dusty shelf and lays them out on the table.

"Here's where we're aiming for, then."

"And where are we starting from?"

A blank patch sits between the contours at the end of Tom's earthy finger. On the page it looks unassuming. Unimportant. But it is everything to them.

"That's quite a way." Danny blows out his cheeks.

"Yes, it is."

"I didn't realize."

Tom kneels, reaches deep into a cupboard, and brings out a metal box. Flips the catches. Opens the lid and gives Danny the gun. "Have you ever used one?"

Danny shakes his head. His eyes are bright, but

something nervous flickers inside them. The useless quickcode on his forehead crumples as he frowns, trying to scoop out a memory. "My uncle always used to say, 'It's better to have a gun and not need it than to need a gun and not have it.' He was a right Prepper," Danny adds, and judges the weapon's weight. "No preparation would have saved Guy, though, would it? I mean, is what w-we—" Danny's eyes twitch. Again. Again. Again. His mouth contorts as his breathing sticks. "I f-feel—I—I—look, I—"

"Danny!" Tom grabs Danny's shoulders. "Tell me what you're looking for." He talks fast, seeing that Danny has lost the outside world to the Feed reflexes within. Like someone still reaching for a branch that snapped long ago, he will fall unless Tom catches him.

"I—look, I—I'm—I'm looking for my uncle—*have a gun need a gun*—I'm in his house but—but—but—" Danny's eyes lock, flicker, fix, and skew about in his head as he tries to access a memory that's no longer there. Cleaved off but twitching. Tom takes Danny's face and pinches the skin, trying to lead him back to reality. "A map, Tom, a *map*!"

"That's great, Danny. Why do you need a map?"

"To, to, to—look, I—a map, Tom, to, to, to work out our route. Route. Rou—I'm, I'm—" A smile breaks through the pain. "I'm trying to get the G, the GP, GPSloc. *Location.* The *place.* Like he said. To work out where we are. Plot the route to the facility. I'm—"

"Okay, Danny. Just breathe. Come on now. What do you know about where we are?"

"I know we're at the camp, Tom. I know we're here. *Now.*" Danny stops. He flaps his lips and shakes his hands. His eyes focus back on Tom. "Fuck me, that hasn't happened in a while."

"What were you trying to access?"

Danny shrugs, quiet. "Something about my uncle. Some memory when I was a kid. Those maps were his, you know. After the Collapse, I got to his place but he wasn't there. I grabbed some tools, the maps . . . I think I was locked on the smell of his place, a memory that . . ." He twirls a spindly finger at his own head and vaporizes his fist. Then he grins, but Tom can tell his voice is falsely keen. "I'm damaged goods, mate! Still want to take me?"

Tom's expression doesn't change. He doesn't want anything bad to befall this man. He's always been so good with Bea. But can he trust him? Probably. Can he assure his safety? No way. But he has no choice if they want to get the turbines working.

"Sure." He smiles and takes the weapon back.

———————

"It's incredibly annoying," Graham says. "I can remember it clearly in a book, an actual *book* about Aztecs. One of the characters is shortsighted and learns to polish a clear stone so finely that, when placed over his eyes, he can see again. The memory of this scene comes into my mind daily. *Hourly.* Tom, it's driving me frantic! Every time I can't see something properly, there it is."

"It sounds frustrating."

"I can't remember the name of the book. That's the torment."

"Can Danny and me try and find you some glasses at the facility?"

"I. Danny and *I.* I had my eyes lasered, with a lifetime guarantee." Graham eases himself back into his chair and raises an admonishing finger. "They called it a miracle cure."

Tom stretches his feet out. "Do you believe in miracles?"

"No." Graham pats his palms flat on the arms of his chair. "No God; no miracles."

Tom rubs his fingertips into the fuzz of his own armchair. "And how's the writing?"

"The Feed going down is the best thing to happen

for books for years, Tom. My Chronicle shall be a best-seller."

"Still the Resister."

"Listen, young man, we need to remember basic knowledge. Metalwork. How to make clothes rather than patch and repair." The old man points to their few ancient books. "*Quantum Mechanics Made Simple.* What use is that? Think of all the knowledge that was lost because it was never printed. Stored on the Feed, or some computer *thing*." He splays his hands. "We're doing our best with you all, Jane and I, trying to remember everything before we croak. And I record it in my Chronicle. That's why one of you simply must learn to read. I honestly don't know why it's proving so difficult!" He looks sideways, lost in thought, then changes his tone. "You should get some pictures on the walls in here. Brighten the place up. We've got some spare. Or make a commission, Tom. A family portrait. I always told Jane she should try portraits. Good money in portraits."

"Not anymore. No money."

"Find her some more orange paint and she'd do anything for you."

"And what's your . . . what was it called? Cut?"

"Commission?"

"Right. Your commission."

A crease pulls at Graham's eyebrows. "That she be happy," he says eventually, and then, after a while, "What do I do if she's taken?"

"You'd get through it. We've all coped with loss."

"No," Graham says steadily. He raises his hands. Flexes his fingers. "How do I *do* it? Show me what you did to Guy."

Guy's face, then Ben's. Tom's heart swells, his chest contracts. He nearly chokes, but hides it. "Don't you remember the vid?" he coughs out, and he has barely said the word before something clicks in. Sudden swathes of his memories of the vid, as Ben had first shown it to him in the family's apartment at the top of the tower, and the ensuing argument, one of so many, as they'd been caught in the sunset's amber glow while the first black tendrils of terror tightened the streets below them.

A man had slept, camera close, his face filling the screen. REAL-TIME SIGNS, it had flashed. The man breathed deeply, then his eyebrows rose. He winced. The movement took his mouth. More contortions. A grimacing of his jaw . . . and then he had relaxed. A timer in the bottom of the screen had glowed red: barely five seconds was all the time it took. The man breathed out again, in again, and opened his eyes. His fiery bloodred eyes. Their color leaked away to the densest black, like orbs of glass were staring out of his face, and WATCH OUT had faded in across the screen.

"Tom?"

Tom jerks at Graham's touch. He can feel him, hear him somewhere . . .

"You're fitting, Tom. Listen to me!"

. . . but this is what's real: the man, the signs, the eyes, the argument with Ben, telling him to take those eyes out, those ridiculous, untrue eyes. Ben's vid would breed paranoia and intense fear, he knew. It would tip people somewhere dark. But Ben had sprayed it. That instant, the vid had gone live onto the Feed, sprayed out from the Hub in the tower. The signs to watch out for. The twitches. The fear. As you suspected your loved one's mind was being carved away—

"Tom!" And the sound and the slap on his cheek thrum away between the past and the present like reflections between two mirrors, and Graham is there, lit by the sun through the open windows, holding his shoulders firmly, sweating, his gray hair falling over his eyes, worried. "You were fitting, Tom!"

Tom squeezes his eyes shut. Opens them, blinking the images away, concentrating on the interior of the hut. The smell of the warm wood. The countryside silence from outside. The world's reality around him. His hands are frantically trembling.

"It's . . ." he says. "I c-can't explain it." He points at an invisible thread from his mind to the sky, and rests it in the end on his head. "More must have been saved than we thought."

"Remembered, Tom," Graham scowls. "We're not computers."

"Whatever," Tom says with a sigh, because other memories have come, and he sinks—

"Tom!" Graham's grip on Tom's shoulders, despite his age, is strong. "Tom, *look* at me."

Tom brushes the man away and wipes a hand across his face. "I'm here. It's fine. I'm here. And in terms of what you *do*, Graham . . ." He slumps into his chair. He raises his hands and weakly squeezes the air. "You just do what you have to."

He wakes from troubled sleep to the sound of stifled tears. They are in the children's hut tonight, watching the kids. Kate is in the armchair, feet tucked under, the cold moonlight catching her skin, trying to keep her sobbing silent, trying not to disturb the children.

"Kate . . ."

"Go back to sleep, Tom," she whispers. "You've got a big journey tomorrow."

"Hey . . ." he murmurs, stretching his fingers to caress the curves of her ribs, leaning up. Jack is buried in a rug. Bea's face is scrunched up, like she's working things out in her sleep.

"I don't want to worry every day that you're never coming back—"

"I'll be fine. Danny's coming too."

Kate rubs her nose. Checks the children. Lowers her voice. "Can you trust him?"

Tom squints, trying to see her better through the darkness. "It's Danny."

"Can you, though? Even if it *is* him?" She pulls back as he tries to take her in his arms. "I feel like it's all falling apart again. Why's it so difficult, Tom? Why do we argue all the time?"

"We're fine, Kate. It's just that we're scared, and we show it in different ways. Guy being taken has—"

"But if you get a cut, you might die. You eat the wrong food, you die. You sleep unwatched and . . . It's a time bomb, Tom, any time it could . . . one of us could . . ." She turns her face away. She shudders and moves back as he touches her arm again. "Why weren't you watching me last night, Tom?"

"Kate. Listen. Sometimes I—"

"Is that you in there?"

He closes his eyes and exhales. "We met at Ben's

wedding. Our dog was called Rafa. If she'd been a boy"—he nods at Bea—"we'd have called her Daniel. I proposed to you with a ring pushed into an apple because they're your favorite fruit. We—"

"I'm just scared," Kate says, but a smile quivers her lips. "So please . . ."

"Kate," Tom whispers, wrapping his arms around her, "listen. Guy was taken. It hadn't happened for *so long* before that. It's unlikely it'll happen again. Can we be sure of that? No. Okay, it's a time bomb, but it's one that might not go off. It will happen or it won't. So we have to *live*. What other choice do we have? And you're the most important thing in the world to me. I'll protect us all, I promise. Come on now, you know *that*."

He reaches up to lean into the chair and wraps his arms around her. She runs her fingers through his hair. They both smile and close their eyes. In the darkness, Bea opens hers.

A gentle breeze ripples across the lawn and the ground is hard and dry: perfect for their journey. Even this early in the day, the sun has started to bake the air, and the trees' susurrus fills the camp. Tom watches the woods. He scans the track running up the hill and away, over the top to the road and the storage facility, miles and miles away. A clatter knocks across the lawn as Graham stumbles out of his hut and loses his footing on the steps.

"She was taken," Graham moans, his voice cracked.

Tom's thoughts reduce. They contract to deal with the enormity of this, and he feels Feed reflexes judder in. Forces them back as he unsteadily climbs the stairs. As he takes the old man's arms, he realizes how terribly thin he is. This can't be, can't be happening. Another? His skin contracts. Their hut is bare inside: some books, Jane's pictures on the walls, including the half-completed painting from before. And Jane in bed. Her hands are clawed. Her eyes glassy. Her hair spills like a silver floe, while earth-red finger marks grip her crushed throat and thumb-shaped welts push up under her chin.

All other plans are discarded as they prepare to bury Jane that afternoon. They've learned it's unsafe to delay with a corpse. They climb the hill from the farmhouse to a plot above the vegetable patches. Tom and Danny carry the body and the others trail up behind them. With a clear view of the hills where the sun rises, Sean stands back from the hole he has barely finished digging.

There is little formality; few rituals have a point anymore, and they have not had time to create new ones of meaning. "She loved the sunrise," Graham tells them when they have lowered her into the ground, wrapped in a tarpaulin and covered with planks to stop the dogs. His voice is empty, barely more than air weakly shaped by his shaking lips; his cheeks, daily shaved, are rough with points of silver. He can't stop kneading his hands, his squeezing fingers marking his skin with white like Jane's neck was seared with red. "The orange of the clouds at sunrise was her favorite color. You know? She was simple like that, content with the beauty of the world. I think that was why her pictures sold so well. Windows of peace in a frenzied world. She was . . . my peace . . . She was . . . everything that . . ." His jaw trembles so much that he cannot speak. He gulps—air, words, who knows. Tom can barely watch. Only when Graham pulls his swollen eyes from the grave and turns them on the others can he continue with what sounds almost like a plea. "I know you call us old Resisters, but she never needed the Feed. We didn't want it. The real world was enough."

Everyone surrounds the hole, the shallow valley around them vast in the summer's heat. Tom and Kate hold Bea's hands; Jack is cocooned in Sean's stiff arms, crying. Sean stares fixedly ahead, the tendons in his neck tense, his face juddering as his eyes tether him to the world, fixating on Jane's grave. For a long time everyone is still. Who should move first? They don't have rules for this. When Danny eventually pushes the soil back into the hole, it somehow ends up level with the sides. Still, no one else moves. As Danny plants the spade deep into the earth, Graham unleashes a wail, and Kate takes his arm and leads him toward his hut. Sean lifts Jack onto his shoulders and marches stiffly toward the woods. For all their differences, Tom considers following him—first Guy, now Jane; it will be reminding Sean of his past, surely, and what he did to Jack's mother, so soon after the boy's birth, and he probably needs to talk—but Bea tugs his finger.

"What is soil made of, Daddy?"

"Um . . ." He watches Sean disappear into the woods with Jack slumped on his shoulders. "It's a good question, Bea. I'll put it on the knowledge board."

He starts down the hill, with Bea at his legs. Danny sidles over, looking at the ground, his pale hands shaking. Suddenly his green eyes snap up to Tom's. *Who's next?* he mouths, his eyes ghost-wide. Tom blinks, stops, thinks—

"Why did Jane die, Daddy?"

He looks down at Bea. "In her sleep, darling."

"But what *of*?"

Tom realizes with a lurch how destructive knowledge can be. He sees his daughter, days off being six, and feels with unachievable urgency the need to stop her aging, to protect her innocence from the world, to shield her from all of this. But how is that possible? They had thought it was over, but Guy, now Jane. Any of them could be taken as they sleep. *Who's next?* He glances at Danny, who, hands in pockets, avoids his gaze now, staring, staring at the ground.

"She just died," Tom tells Bea. "In her sleep."

He feels the utter weight of the look she gives him then and knows it will lodge in his mind forever. Something in the upward tilt of her eyes, while the sides of her mouth droop down. She plainly knows he's lying, even if she cannot work out why. She doesn't need the Feed to see this, and Tom is left with the echoing realization that his daughter doesn't trust him; there is a distance in her withdrawing gaze that he's never seen before. Danny catches his eye and nods Tom's attention across the lawn. Kate is coming back. She is pale. Hollows are carved into her cheeks.

"Graham's not good. He's just . . . making this . . . *noise.* I don't know what to do."

All Tom can do, while she looks to him expectantly, is work his mouth while no ideas come. Are they under threat? Are they in danger? No one taken for years, and now this? Two of them? Over days? Five seconds. That's all it takes. His jaw opens and closes but no sounds come out.

"I'll just take her in," Kate says stiffly, and Bea silently takes her mother's hand.

Danny, chewing on his lip, looks fleetingly at Tom before examining the ground until they're gone. "She asked me why we watch her and Jack while they sleep, Tom. She's not stupid."

"What did you say?"

Danny shrugs. "For safety. Are we going to tell them?"

Tom sees Bea in his mind's eye, her dubious face as he dodged her questions. She will grow old. The age is waiting within her. How long can he hope to protect her?

"I can't believe Jane's gone, Tom," Danny says quietly. "What's happening? Are we being . . . targeted here?"

"Don't be stupid," Tom mutters. "And she's not really gone. We can still remember her."

Danny snorts. "How?"

Tom touches his temple. "And we must."

Danny shakes his head disgustedly. "Then your brain's working better than mine. Nothing goes in without downloads." He nods down the hill after Kate.

"Listen, should we take Graham with us to the facility? You know, to distract him?"

"That's a good idea. We'll leave . . . tomorrow if we can."

"Sure. But, Tom . . . the kids will need to know. What happens. Sometime they will. I know you say we shouldn't talk about the past," Danny says uncertainly, "but we have to. We can't ignore the pain. We have to talk about it. I'm scared that if I stop talking about my uncle, he'll . . ." He raises a hand to his head and blows his fingers out. His eyes are achingly sincere. "When Mum was killed . . ." His head goes down and his shoulders shudder. "I want the Feed back, Tom. I want to talk to them, even if it's just their BackUps. Do you think I can find them at the facility? Do you think they were saved? And what can we do? What can we do to save ourselves from . . ." He turns, pointing around, at himself, pointing at *all of this.*

Tom's mind stalls. His thoughts shift. "There is nothing," he says, "that we *can* do."

That night, with Danny watching the children and Graham in with Sean, Tom sits up against the headboard, watching Kate sleep. Somewhere in the darkness things merge and his mind goes back before the Collapse, while he was training, reading Freud and

Lacan late into the night. He had found expensive paper editions of the books because he had wanted to understand them slowly, thoughtfully, rather than gulping them down with the Feed. (He'd told Ben he was doing this, of course, just to piss him off.) He had watched Kate, his fiancée then, sleep in their new house, this person who had come from nowhere and with kindness had changed his world. The world had then changed around them, unstoppably: a fragility they must have been living over for years without knowing it, their lives paper-thin. Bea's distrusting expression resounds in his memory, and Danny's question—"Do you think they were saved?"—and Tom nearly sees his parents again. His father's face doesn't quite emerge from the shadows of his mind. The tower. His mother blocking his Feed after Ben had died. *Were* they saved? His father must have had plans.

A wind heaves and brings him back to the world where Kate frowns beside him. She clenches her jaw. She gurgles and rolls her head. Tom watches her move, aghast, and gets up and stares out the window. He pulls the curtains tightly shut behind him to block out her sounds, forehead pressed against the cool, cracked glass, eyes closed. Could he kill her? Even the thought of it, of Guy, of Ben, of that vid, makes his hands shake, his breath tighten, his face go numb, panic rising as he tries to hide from what might be happening to Kate *right now*. The huts are dark, the night sky deeply black, as she coughs behind him, smothered by the curtain, coughs—and then goes silent. Two ghostly clouds are sped across the sky by a wind that ripples through the forest and rattles the window.

When he ducks back out, she is awake.

"I'm here," he says.

"I can see that." She smiles and pats the bed. When he doesn't move, she observes him across the room. "Leave the facility to rot, Tom. Let's go. Let's go now. Let's take Bea and find somewhere new. Don't leave me, Tom. Please. Let's be just us again."

"There's safety in numbers."

"Guy and Jane are dead. Danny thinks we're being targeted."

"I won't be long, Kate. You're going to be fine."

"But what if—"

"Listen," he says impatiently. "I *promise* you'll be fine. You and Sean, you can both sleep in with the children. I know it's not ideal, but . . . I'll be back in a few days. And listen, Kate. Listen." He takes her chin, which only then he realizes is wet with tears, and raises her face to his. Her lips are salty and slick. "If we can't find food and the plow doesn't work, we'll leave after

Bea's birthday. If Danny can't get the turbines to work, we'll just go. Like that. Okay?"

"It's just the fear's bigger than everything else sometimes."

"I know. Come on." He holds her for a while and then encourages her out of bed, past Sean's room where Graham's sandals wait outside, down the stairs, and outdoors. He pulls the kitchen door shut behind them, his thumb fitting snugly in the latch as they pause in the doorway.

"It's so quiet," she murmurs, spreading her arms out into the night. The sky's eastern edge is already starting to melt. The blades of grass tickle Tom's feet and he loops an arm around Kate's waist as they walk. A lick of candle comes from the children's hut, where Danny watches them. They walk until the house is murky-dark and then he kisses her. She holds his head. His hands move to her back, her neck, her waist, and undo the little buttons between her shoulders. She lifts his shirt. The grass is long and cool beneath them.

In the morning, they use the cart to haul large bottles of water up from the filtration tanks by the stream. They wedge bags of supplies between the empty fuel kegs. Danny climbs into the harness, and when Jack laughs, a golden chortle that brightens the mood for a moment, he shakes his rear and starts the thing rolling over the grass with a bray. Sean mechanically pats Jack's head. Kate leans back to hold Bea uncomfortably in her arms as Tom gives them both another final kiss. The girl is barely awake, squinting through her sleep-swollen face. Kate clasps Tom's arm. Her eyes are red-rimmed but her smile is warm, before she nods him sternly up the track.

As Danny heaves the cart up the long incline through the woods behind Graham, the camp is lost below them. The track is shaded and cool. Dense undergrowth crowds them, edging into their path. The busy sounds of animals, insects, birds, mostly hidden. When they reach the road they glance at one another nervously before leaving the cover of the trees. Stepping onto the tarmac feels very wrong. They have learned to avoid roads. For reasons of safety, but also for this: the aged asphalt, slowly tending to powder; the cracks, in places gulfs, where the earth bulges and plants have ripped through in a freeze-thaw cycle of decay; the growths of grass on the verges where hedgerows roll into the road. There's a van on its side and carpeted with moss, and a motorbike grown over with plants. Simply, the differences between then and now still do not elide.

Tom's brow furrows and his eyes lock and flicker as the fear rises, as splinters of half-complete memories slide through his mind: shards of super-roads clogged with crushed cars, people moaning on the tarmac, half dead but desperate in their animal way to escape; the repetitive vertiginous plummeting in his mind as he tried to find help, as he tried to access knowledge from the lopped-off Feed, as he's nearly trying to do again now.

That first night they stop in a copse at the bottom of a hill. They pull the cart off the road and wait until dark to light their fire so the smoke will not be seen. There are so few people left now that the ones there are must be dangerous. They heat a few of their dwindling supply of tins until they are blackened by the flames and they have to take them off with rags.

"Beans," Danny utters through a full mouth, and shudders with glee. He glances briefly up at the heavens and winks. "You know this is why I came."

"Well, don't choke yourself," Graham advises. "That would be a damn fool thing to do."

Danny raises his eyebrows. It's the only thing Graham has said all day. Then he lies back on the earth to stare at the stars while Graham writes his Chronicle in the firelight and Tom lashes a tarpaulin between trees and lays down rugs beneath.

"I'll watch," Tom says.

Graham wafts his offer away with his pen. "No, you two sleep first."

Tom goes under the shelter and Danny crawls over, pretending to be fat, not bothering to stand. "Don't touch me," he whispers as he nestles himself comfy and drapes an arm over Tom.

"In your dreams."

"That's what I'm worried about, pal."

Something wakes him, something more than Danny snuffling against his neck. He peers into the gloom as things ebb away: dreams, touches of things in his mind. The trees are a dark cushion under the starlit sky and the silence here is thick. What woke him? He interprets a shadow as Graham, then the spread-out darkness of the extinguished fire as the old man lying prone. But it's not.

"Graham, are you there?"

It takes time for Tom's eyes to adjust, to see the figure lying unmoving by a tree. No sound but his own hoarse breathing. He crawls past the embers to where Graham is bundled, hands in his jacket, head bent forward, his book and pen on the ground. He grabs the old man's shoulder.

"I'm watching the fire." Graham jerks and tries to fight him off. "Leave me alone!"

"The fire's gone out. You're supposed to be watching!"

"I'm fine!"

"Graham, would you like to talk about it?"

But Graham, grumbling darkly, simply turns away.

Tom fetches a blanket from the shelter and wraps it around the old man. Then he sits under the tarpaulin and watches Danny. Listens to him breathe. Watches the two sleeping men intently until powder blue starts to edge the sky.

For some reason Danny looks the tiredest of them all as they near the top of the hill, although he had slept the most. "Rabbits," he explains as he pushes the cart up the final stretch of slope with Tom. "I kept dreaming there were rabbits under the camp, burrowing around until there wasn't anything left for them to burrow *through;* it was all just hole, right? And as soon as I realized *that,* everything started to crumble, everything caved in."

"What happened to the rabbits?"

"I stopped worrying about them then, to be honest."

They survey the gentle folds of the hills, low light

lying over the rolls of earth. Everything is subtle move-ment: the expanse of the trees' sun-clipped leaves; the grasses and crops, untamed for years, with the wind playing patterns in their waves. Birds swerve and duck in flocks out in the air. In the distance something—an airplane—had scooped out a long furl of earth as it crashed. Now, covered in foliage, it is another mini-hill.

"When are we going to have breakfast?"

Tom scores a mark on the map with a dirty thumb-nail. "How about here?"

Danny cranes to look. "And where's the facility?"

Tom points somewhere off the top of the map: about eight inches more. "Today and tomorrow at least. Around that village and on the other side."

"We'll add weeks to the journey if we go around every village. It's not that dangerous, is it? I mean, who's here anymore?" Danny opens his arms expan-sively, lord of all he can see.

They pluck wild radishes and charlock and stuff them in the cart as they descend the hill, avoiding a motorbike and warily eyeing a dirt-mottled van as they pass. Hand-swirls have cleaned the windscreen at some point. A drawn-out curl of color on the back doors could be rust or blood. Climbing the next hill, stomp-ing up the dried-up tarmac, Danny leaps on a small plum tree, and when they reach the bottom again, Tom pulls the pods from a slender plant with triangular leaves. "Pignuts." He shows them. "We can eat them while we walk."

They are passing a bus, rusted, smashed.

"What about breakfast?"

"This is breakfast."

"You're kidding!"

"No."

"Oh," Danny says, looking glum. Then he brightens. "Are we nearly there yet?"

A narrow stalk of smoke rises in front of them, splitting the evening sky like a crack through glass.

"How far away is that?" Graham asks. "My eyes . . ."

"A few miles?" Tom murmurs as he brings the cart to a stop.

"It's thick, isn't it?" Graham says. "Not wood?"

Tom glances back along the distant length of the darkening road behind them. He peers into the nearer, hidden depth of the crowded flanking trees.

"Is it people?" Danny whispers at his side.

Tom scowls. "Let's stop somewhere soon."

They light a fire, off the road and behind a hillock. Tom watches the woods, strains to see along the road. It looks empty. The clouds obscure the moon and, as if the trail of smoke itself has spread above them, a darker mood descends. Then Danny discovers that tonight's beans have bits of sausage in them and can't stop himself from dancing in delight. He unleashes a yodel into the night.

After dinner, Tom lays out the tarpaulin and blankets. Again, as he and Danny go to bed, Graham says he'll tend the fire; he'll take first watch while they sleep. But again Tom wakes to see him shivering in the dark and not watching them at all. He is asleep instead. Danny is too. Both men look relaxed, their faces at peace. So vulnerable. So open to attack while they sleep, from outside and from within. They are so reliant on one another in this world. And then Danny grimaces. Chokes in a tight breath of air. Tom kneels and reaches toward his neck. Danny's eyes squeeze, his mouth chews and then spreads into a smile. He chuckles. Then he relaxes, shifts, and rolls onto his side, and Tom lowers his shaking hands and turns back to watch the shadows in the trees, clustering all around them.

There are five columns of smoke stretching into the powder-blue sky when they wake. One is a sparse scuff rubbed sideways by the wind. The others are thicker, and one is a roiling stream of live and looping blackness.

"You didn't show me how to use the gun." Danny's voice is subdued.

They walk to the cart, where Graham sits perched on a keg, frowning as he firmly writes his Chronicle. Inside Tom's rucksack is a pair of bolt cutters and a hard shape in rags that he hands to Danny.

"No firing. Whoever they are, there's no need to let them know we're here."

Danny squints down the barrel at the trees.

"There's bullets already in there. We don't have many. You let the bullet holder out by—"

"The cartridge."

"Isn't *cartridge* another word for a bullet? Graham?"

Graham doesn't know or doesn't care; either way, he ignores them.

"Doesn't matter," Danny mutters, and then, talking like he's a crook, "*I know whatcha mean.* You let it out by . . . ?"

"Thumb that switch there. That's the one. So push it back in. Good. And take the safety off. That's right. And now shoot. Except don't. Just pretend."

"*Pow,*" Danny says.

"Nice shot."

Graham looks up from his book, squints and shakes his head.

———

Soon they pass a car. It's not the first—they've passed so many they've stopped checking for fuel that's never there—but it is the first that's freshly burned. The metal clicks as it cools.

"Why did they do that?" Danny whispers, backing away from the thing.

"I don't know," Tom mutters. He eyes the tree line and glances, again, back up the road. Searches the surface of the earth-scattered tarmac for tracks. Right now—are they being watched? Is this it? He looks rapidly around them. "A signal? Fun?"

"That sort of shit stopped being fun years ago," Danny remarks as he too scans around with widened eyes.

There's no way of knowing how many others are left, but it's surely not a lot; it can't be. It took them many months to die, in differing states of lobotomy, lying in the roads, but die they mostly did. The shock. Knowledge ripped violently out. Animals again. Stunned like cows in an abattoir, bolts through their brains. And all the systems gone, all the help, the infrastructures, all dissolved in seconds: there was nothing left and no one able to help them. They were surrounded but alone. Their systems stalled and shorted out because of the fused elements of their brains. They could barely function. For years the stench had been unbearable as slowly the corpses had withered, collapsed, and . . . ultimately disappeared. This car is blistered inside, its innards like charred bones, sterilized, like their firestorm-stripped brains had been. The seats have melted like their lives, like their dreams, like their dangerously malleable world. The dash is viscously dripping and the tires have spread onto the tarmac. They have to turn the cart around and use it like a ram to move the wreck, still too hot to touch, away.

Wind in their hair, touched by the faint smell of smoke. The village looks deserted. An ivy-choked sign asks them to drive carefully. A digital display telling them their speed stays blank. Advertising billboards line the road, naked now that there's nothing to make the quickcodes anything but the reality of what they are: ink on weather-streaked paper, the augmented veil pulled away. The first house has been smashed. A curtain is sucked between window shards, in and out, like that for years. Dirt smears. There are haphazard cars in the streets. Tires flat. Windows crazed. Doors pulled from their hinges. There are old bones beside the hedgerows.

They creep onward, Tom in the harness, up the center of the plant-cracked road. He tries to keep the cart's roll constant, to keep it quiet, but all the debris makes it hard. There's an unspoken agreement that they're not talking. They pass a shop from whose open door a paste-like mulch spreads, and Tom brings the cart to a stop. Silence suddenly. Sun-scorched quietness. Graham crouches, keeping watch, his hair and jacket ruffled by a warm breeze, and Danny goes in first, his feet skidding on the muck as Tom follows. The shop's shadows hide the mess across the floor. Shelves have sagged. It's a shock to see faces on the older printed posters. Smiling children holding piggy banks. Families in cars. ARE YOU INSURED? they ask, smiling. Tom remembers being in the back of a car with Ben, streaming vids and messaging each other on their Private-Stream. Their parents were in the front with their own Feeds muted to their children's . . .

Whether it's the memories or the putrid stench clogging his nostrils like oil, something makes Tom's eyes sting and run. He backs out blinking into the sunlight and Danny bursts out moments later, gasping for air with streaming eyes, a security-locked pack of pens and a notebook held aloft.

"For your Chronicle, Graham," he chokes out. "And teaching the kids."

There is a movement down the street, crossing the road.

Tom freezes. Looks from the corner of his eye.

A fox stops, steady on its legs and large. Another

jumps down to the pavement from a wall. And another. Then three more. All of them watching, circling, waiting. These things are huge and well fed.

"Let's . . . go now," Tom murmurs. Keeping his eyes on the first fox, he kneels for a lump of tarmac and hurls it at the pack, which scatters, circles, and reforms. Teeth bared. Tails straight. They bark. Danny slides into the harness, shaking, and sets it moving, Tom and Graham edging beside it, watched by the foxes and the dusty broken windows, the breeze gently teasing the refuse and the dust as the foxes finally rest in the road, gnawing again at the splintered, meat-free bones.

With the village down behind them, the facility emerges at last in the near distance: a squat concrete fortress, gray amid the healthy green, the multitudes of leaves flickering in the wind, just as Tom had left it days before.

"Well done, boys," Tom says, and nods. "We're nearly there. Let's do this. Let's get this fuel."

Danny, grunting, a hunted look in his eyes, hauls the cart to a stop and palms the dirty sweat from his brow. Then, making a noise like a strangled groan, he grabs Tom's arm and points. On the winding road below them, through the foliage, a dark shape moves.

"What is it?" Graham whispers, his hands to his eyes. "I can't see."

The shape is revealed for an instant in a break between the leaves: a vehicle, low-slung, ovoid, and gray-swirled with dust. Long metal spikes have been fixed to its curved roof and sides. It looks like a rusted, flattened old-fashioned mine, hauled ashore by the filthy and laboring horses that drag it along the road, smacked by swaggering men. At this distance its progress is silent.

"It's not good," Tom answers tightly. "But it's going the other way."

Danny's voice is tremulous. "Do you think they set fire to those cars?"

Tom has no idea. He had thought this area empty. He watches the group diminish with distance. Snatches of song sneak around on the breeze. As they top a hill, the men look like they are herding a strange and massive animal—and then they disappear over the other side.

Although they could reach the facility by nightfall, they decide to get close, camp, and approach it at dawn. There are other people. They weren't expecting this. Should they hide? They don't know. They haven't encountered others for a long, long time.

They stare at the fire in silence.

"We're doing the right thing, boys," Graham announces finally. "We need those turbines working. We *must* bring home fuel if Jack and Bea are to survive. I mean . . ." He catches Tom's eye before pouring them nettle beer, and they sit with their boots off, drinking.

"My mum used to give me beans when I was a kid," Danny says thoughtfully, after a while, staring at the unopened tins.

Tom shakes his head. "Danny, you know what happens when you try to remember the—"

"Mine did too," Graham interjects. "On toast, after cricket at school. I used to love that. Playing into the evening. Walking home while it was still light, and I'd sit at the table, all dirty, with grass stains on my whites, and I'd have baked beans on toast with cheese grated on it, and squash. Lemon-barley water. Usually we all ate together and we had to be clean for tea, but those nights it was just me and my mum and I didn't even have to wash my hands."

Tom takes a deep breath while Graham pauses. This is a mistake. Then: "I can't remember my mother ever cooking for me. Not once," he tells them, and Danny and Graham listen with interest as he breaks his own rules. He never talks about his past. And he doesn't talk truthfully now; or rather, he doesn't reveal it all. Who his father was. Where they lived. His connection with the Feed. But as he talks, from his words unspool new memories. "We had cooks. Walk-in fridges with food covered in . . . *plastic wrap.* Is that what it was called? My brother, he used to bully me. With the Feed, it never stopped. Wherever he was, wherever I hid, he could get me. He was relentless. I'd turn it off while I ate so I could have some peace, but that made my father furious. But then, his anger was the most attention I got. I remember sitting up on a high stool in the kitchen so I could reach the surface and eat eggs. I remember sitting there reading out loud to the cooks from books. Real books. That made him angry too."

"Were you *in ute?*" Danny asks.

"Oh yes." The truth was he had been the very first to be enabled before birth. A father's demonstration to the world: Look how safe this is, why *wouldn't* you have your own kids done? By the time Ben had been born, the need for proof had seemingly gone; *he* hadn't been enabled until he was four, and how Tom had forgotten this until now he can't understand, as unpleasant emotions suddenly make him feel very sick. Why had Ben not been enabled *in ute?* Things from the past reorder themselves in his head, as if a riverbed seen only through moving water is now revealing itself, stilled and dry. The arguments in restaurants. The malleability of promises. The hatred he had felt for Ben hadn't been hatred, he realizes; it had been . . . envy? And the hatred he had felt for his parents had been obscuring something else for years. Actually, Tom thinks, looking through a heat haze at his past, maybe he had been well prepared for the Collapse because he'd felt so paralyzingly alone before it.

"Me too. I never learned to read. Never had to until . . ." Danny rolls his eyes around them, at the world. The firelight collects in his irises and catches on his rusty stubble. "How come you did?"

"Oh, I was a bit perverse." Tom sighs. "I wanted to rebel. The Feed was too easy—"

"That was the beauty of it, mate."

"Of course. No need to think, no need to leave the house. But is that what life's about?"

"I always pitied your generation," Graham says forlornly. "Being a child. For me, before all that stuff was invented, that's when I felt most alive. So many joys you never had. You were never actually *present*. You lacked the opportunity for anything worked at. Your knowledge was transitory, not deep. You didn't invest in it and most of the time you didn't understand it. You certainly can't remember it. *Mem* it," he says, doing a strange little imitation of a jig. "The Feed implanted forgetfulness in your souls. You're living the most natural life you've ever lived right now."

"You're such a typical Resister, Graham," Danny snorts. He sounds bored but for a tightness in his voice: a keenness bordering on need. "It was everything. My mum, my dad, my uncle, they were miles away but with me all the time. And they were so *proud* when I went to college. Know how I know that? Because I *felt* it, raw pride, directly from them. First in my family, I was, and that would have been impossible without the Feed. It cost them a fortune to have me enabled, to give me all that knowledge at the flash of thought. Why take time to read when I knew it in a gulp? I didn't have money to travel but I saw the world. Vegas. Bangkok. Dubai. I was smart back then, cultured. The Feed made me more than I am. I was never alone. Total knowledge—"

"Blissful ignorance," Graham interrupts.

"There was everything you could wish for!" Danny exclaims.

"But you were just a *conduit*." Graham's lips barely move. "Nothing stuck, did it, Danny?"

"But I'd do *anything*," Danny croaks, "to have it back. For an *instant*, to—I'd, I'd—"

"My mother had dementia but she had a *dignified* death; none of this being saved on a machine like all of you!"

Danny's hands are shaking, his eyes twitching as he

pounces on a point, the workings of his brain nearly visible: "But if your m-mum had been saved, she'd be with us n-now, right, Graham? They could have r-restored her."

Graham smiles. "Would she, Danny? Are *your* parents saved?"

Tom's pulse pumps his neck. His mind is fizzed without his noticing it, knee-jerk instincts that make adrenaline flow. His eyes flick and try to lock on to something no longer there: a dizzying fall that repeats, repeats as he misses the connection as he tries to message Kate, as he tries to message Ben, as panic rises, his breath high, his vision swimming . . .

"I don't, I—" Danny drops to the ground, gagging. "Mum—Da-Da-Da—"

Tom, blinking furiously, fumbles Danny onto his back. Tries to ignore the man's panic, to stop it from infecting him too. "D-Danny! What are you l-l-looking for?"

"My m-mum," Danny chokes out. "Where's my mum? It's bla-black, *there's nothing here*—"

Graham strains to lift him. He sounds almost tired. So weary of it all. On the one hand there's the terror in Danny's eyes as he glitches and gasps in the old man's arms; on the other hand it's familiar. It's a tedious way to live.

"Danny," Graham says quietly, his voice hoarse. "Open your eyes: see what's *here*. See what's real!"

A tired smile melts Danny's contorted features, and a quick nod. His tongue flicks from his mouth, his breathing slows, and his muscles relax as he leans back into Graham's embrace. He sighs in the end: "Fuuuuuuck."

Up early, as the first touch of blue lines the horizon, and Tom's mind is running straightaway. It's been running all night without him, processing things, and the tempo of his dreams continues in his heart, uninterrupted by his waking. He's not here; he's *there* again, back before the Collapse. His hands shake as he wets his face with a little water and dresses. He dreamed of Ben again, he knows it; it's more a lurking sensation than a memory. He eats little and they move out as the facility's blocky shadow becomes distinct from the gloom. Then, as they reach its perimeter fence just after dawn, Tom's mind dislocates again. It plummets. With the wire in his fingers, the backpack straps biting his arms, on the crest of a heartbeat he travels back through time as another memory comes loose: breaking into the building site of the tower with Ben and imagining themselves to be a pair of survivors in a postapocalyptic scene. Kids, neither even ten, they had playacted parts of whatever ent they'd been streaming.

A Mirror for Monsters, was it called? And here he is, breaking into his father's property again, decades later. Now. Without Ben.

He blinks in the cool air, stomach lurching. His aching eye muscles spasm hopefully, an addiction re-ignited, looking for his brother. And he finds him, a refound memory suddenly icy clear in his mind's eye: Ben waiting for them in the expanse of the apartment, topping the sky at the tip of the tower. President Taylor had been killed weeks before, and many more had been murdered since then. Destruction surrounded them. Ben had airily offered them coffee as plumes of smoke grew from all over the city below them, like black daisies on a dead gray lawn, but Kate had ignored him and asked immediately about her parents. In the split second that Ben had checked himself, it was evident he'd forgotten to search for them. His eyes glazed as he went on.

"They're in . . . ?"

"Southampton," Tom had said, exhaling in disgust.

But they hadn't heard a thing from Southampton since the power station had blown. Two million people offline, off-grid. Most likely dead. Ben had asked Kate, "Do they have SaveYou?" and of *course* they did—she had set it up for them—but after accessing more information, he put a hand on her shoulder and told her they'd never used it; no BackUps had been transmitted from their Feeds. They hadn't been saved, he told her. Then: "You're pregnant?" he asked. "Does Dad know?" he inquired, turning to Tom.

Tom had deflected the question—"So where *is* Dad?"—and that had been enough. He'd never seen his brother like this as Ben's voice was suddenly ready to break and he raised a finger and thumb and held them a shaking centimeter apart. "We're this close, Tom. To coming down. Dad's . . . we're fighting to keep the world going . . ." He focused on the gap between his fingers. Squeezed it and squeezed it, that centimeter of air, until he collapsed and cried. "We believe that something is . . . invading people while they sleep. That Sergeant Vaughn, when he killed President Taylor, wasn't Sergeant Vaughn . . ." He chewed his lip again, purple bags sloughing down his face as he told them people were going to sleep as themselves but waking up someone else. They looked the same, they sounded the same, but inside . . . something lurked. Waiting. To kill. "We have one held captive but he's resisting interrogation. His Feed's locked off. All of these murderers—their Feeds are locked off from the moment they wake—"

Tom had consciously used the tone he employed with his clients; this situation had needed taking under control. "Personality is just a bias of reaction, Ben. The way we behave once encourages a likelihood of how we'll behave again. Our brains aren't like hard drives; they can't be *wiped*. People can't be *taken over*."

Ben had merely sighed as he stood. "I didn't bring you here to argue." As he padded away, his words had been carried up into the glassy vaults toward the bedrooms and, above them, the pinnacle of the tower, the family's homeHub. "We're being invaded, Tom. Something, or someone, is hacking us while we sleep. Then they kill. We don't know what they want or why they're doing it, but we believe that things will get worse. Billions may die. I'm giving you a heads-up. That's what family does. Dad thought you'd be difficult, so we have people clearing your house already. They'll bring your dog too. So would you like that coffee?"

Tom shoulders through the gap in the dew-dripped fence, takes the bolt cutters and cracks through the chain around the gate. As it cascades to the ground, the padlock thwacks the broken tarmac like a python's head from a children's ent. He can suddenly smell— can he?—burned coffee on the breeze; can feel the joyful rush of Kate being pregnant and the overwhelming grief of loss, the vertigo of it, of being in his father's lofty apartment while the world is in free fall around him. He tries to stop thinking about the past but something has been unleashed by the night before, by Guy's death, by Jane's, by them being taken and that familiar panic again. It grates his insides. He is energized, on high alert, and utterly, utterly exhausted. Even the act of walking suddenly feels too much—as if reaching out, stepping forward, whispering a plea for help to Graham and Danny beside him could disturb the world and bring everything down around him.

Graham pushes the squealing gate open as Tom just stands there, stunned, and Danny yanks the cart through.

He hadn't noticed the smell when he'd scouted the place before, but he can feel it now in his teeth: rust. The oxidized fire escapes, a deep burnt red, overgrow the buildings like roots. They walk under them, through the narrow crevices between blocks, like excavation pits in tombs, and when they finally reach the forecourt, the bulbous yellow tanks are there waiting as before, emblazoned with the triangular logo of Energen.

"Here we *go!*" Danny claps his hands and does a little dance. "We're gonna live, we're gonna li-iii-ive! Oooooh, baby, *yeah!*"

Birds flurry away as the echo of the song rolls around the forecourt's walls. Tom grabs Danny's shoulder and peers up at the formidable storage towers. There are many darkened windows, many escarpments and places to hide. People could be anywhere, and the building is deep inside. "You're not going to do that again, are you?" he murmurs, giving Danny a dirty look before scanning the shadows and reflections in the glass once more for movement.

"Of course not," Danny mutters back. "But no one's here. Calm down."

Slowly they move again. Graham quietly reads out the instructions on the pumps, and once the fuel has slugged into the kegs, they enter the facility to find cables for the wind turbines and anything else worth taking. Murky growth over the skylights makes the corridor feel underground. Stale and dusty air. The shadows echo and the doors squeal. Beneath flappy holes in the ceiling, puddles and tidemarks spread across the vinyl floor. At school, Tom suddenly remembers, he dripped ink onto paper and watched it spread. A *chromatogram:* the ink dividing into its constituent colors, each running at a different speed. It's like what the Collapse did to them all: those who ran faster had the better chance of survival; the old, the infirm, the slow, all those who couldn't get away from the cities before the Feed collapsed, became . . . what? Prey? And his parents? If they had survived the brain trauma when the Feed went down, had they tried to run too, finally brought down from the tower to everyone else's level?

Tom sees Danny peer through milky fire glass ahead and kick the door open. Banked with memory towers, this vast room would have been automatically cooled before, people's mundles, vids, and grabs in frozen storage in energy-hungry machines. But now it's just cold. The skylight has collapsed and, weakened by rain, ceiling tiles have sloughed off to reveal a skeleton of struts around which hundreds of wires run like veins.

"Bingo," Danny says.

"Jane used to—" Graham laughs and then stops.

Skidding across the room, Danny rips open a tower. The hinges cry out. The displays are dead. By the time Tom reaches him, the circuit board that Danny has yanked out has crumbled away. He pulls out another, which flakes similarly, until he is cradling so much rust in his palms.

"These are people," Danny whispers. "All that's left of people."

Graham's face, shifting through different gradations of horror, is unable to settle.

"Are my parents here, do you think?" Danny asks Tom.

"There were storage units like this all over the country. Maybe this isn't even one of the SaveYou facilities.

Maybe where your parents' BackUps are saved, it's better preserved."

"Let's be honest, though, that's pretty damn unlikely." Danny lets the fragments of rust trickle between his fingers, then turns to hide his tears. He pushes his forehead against a grille. After some time he sniffs and mutters, "Come *on*, Danny. We're here for Jack and Bea," and Tom watches as, galvanized, Danny uses the sheets of circuits like splintering ladder rungs to scrabble up the tower. At the top, it's still a leap to snare some cables, but he brings a clutch down and crashes to the floor, tiles cascading, as billows of dust mushroom like downward clouds.

"Will these work?" Tom splutters through the murk. "For the turbines?"

Danny examines them. In the end, he shrugs. "Guy would have known. I think so."

And all their hopes for survival, for the culmination of Guy's plan for a self-sufficient future, resting on that, they set to work. They climb, pull, and coil in the dust-hazy room. They reap the cables, slicing them off, and soon multicolored bales lie by the door. Graham sits on one, head in hands. "Haven't we found enough?" he murmurs behind Tom as Danny reaches the end of the room. "Can we go now? Let's get back to the camp, Tom."

Tom hesitates, looking around. "Well, let's see what else is here. More bulbs would be good. I want to give Bea a party for her birthday. Light up the place like magic." He chuckles. "Maybe some acetate to color them?"

The word, that word, *acetate,* sits surprisingly on Tom's teeth. With the Feed, with some spasms in his eyes, he would already have had information on its chemical structure, the etymology of the word, and the last time he had used it. He would have asked his mother about his childhood parties and filtered through her mundles and grabs, not so much remembering as reexperiencing them. She had always enjoyed those parties more than he had. She had always loved a crowd. All this information assimilated without thinking, his mind and muscles working in synchrony, seeing things without them being there, knowing things without words. A deeper, connected, malleable world, and all his thoughts, his memories, stored on a private Hub back home, in machines like these but just for his family, and seamlessly integrated and activated by instinct, by the tiniest muscle movements sending messages to and from the implant in his brain.

Tom's heart lurches with panic as he looks for the Feed and it isn't there. Instead of connectivity, there is a void, horrifically huge. Silence and slowness. Blackness, thick and deep. Tired muscles twitch painfully in his eyes, locking like a faulty mechanism. He looks for the link to his father, his mother, to find out where they are. He tries to link to Kate. There is nothing. Breath without air. Nothing in his gaze except the room, this depressed and disintegrating room in the tomb of an obsolete storage facility in the ruin of a world. And Danny, he sees, has slipped away through doors still swinging, loops turning in the dusty air.

"Danny!" Tom hisses down another stairwell. Nothing. His voice is swallowed by the rough twilight darkness, then something rustles in response. A rat, not a man, and barely a rat at that.

Tom runs up dingy corridors, searching for footprints in the dust. Nothing. He retraces his steps, running. He turns a corner and pulls up short to avoid colliding with Graham, whose eyes are unfocused, his mind still stuck somewhere else, somewhere sad. Rust-mottled memory banks loom in the murk as they walk slowly, silently, listening. The dead silence in those cavernous rooms, swollen with time, makes Tom's ears ring. Then he hears the distant screeching swing of doors. He passes Graham the rucksack, creeps down the corridor to a stairwell that stretches vertical darkness above. Nothing. Then a movement catches in the corner of his eye and he leaps, turning, going down, his hands over his head as glass detonates around him.

"Shit! Sorry, Tom! I'll get you next time, yeah?"

He takes the stairs two at a time and finds Danny on the next floor up, a machine held unsteadily between his thigh and elbow, and another in his arms.

"What the *hell* is that?"

"Microwave. And that"—Danny nods over the banister—"was a fucking TV!"

"What do we want a TV for?"

"I don't know, I thought you'd want to see it. This is a mini-oven. I've already put a music machine in the cart—"

"We don't need this stuff, Danny," Tom snaps.

"Radios. Maybe we can contact people!" Danny's keen green eyes catch the little light in the darkness. Fragile hope pools in them. "If there's anyone out there. To help. Listen, we've come all this way, Tom, you may as well take a look."

Tom, after a moment, grunts and leans over into the stairwell. "Graham?"

In the silence of the shadows below someone moves but no one speaks.

"Graham, are you with us or waiting?"

Danny nudges Tom's arm. "Leave him be. We'll be quicker without him," he whispers.

Upstairs, the windows are smeared with tar. The flooring is crumpled, the walls rotten, but there's less dust than in the corridors below. It's clean. Danny kicks open the door to a large room and reveals thin-screens and radio kits spread across desks. It's quite a find, Tom sees as he riffles through the machinery, twists dials, and lifts speakers to his ears. Nothing—of course nothing. He isn't expecting anything, but reality and hope live parallel lives. He moves between the desks, thinking through what they can use back in the camp, and it's as he rests his thumb on the screen of an ancient monitor and draws his skin juddering across the glass—a feeling unfelt for a long time—that three things happen at once. What he has been looking at makes sense: a dark and bundled mess on the other side of the table is a heap of blankets on the floor, and there are others, he sees, beyond. The kettle he just rested his palm on, wondering how they'd been able to live without one that worked—and his heart suddenly pounds in an animal way—is warm. A man ducks into the room, toweling his hair.

Tom freezes. Danny freezes.

"Nigel, I—"

They all freeze. Then the bare-chested man hurls his towel at Danny's face with a cry and barges a table over. They haven't seen outsiders this near, up close, for so many years, and Tom at first can't move. This can't be real. Computers avalanche to the floor as the man careens toward a jacket on a chair, making a jabbering noise as he runs. Tom still stands while Danny leaps, but the man is too fast: he knocks Danny back with an elbow to his face and stamps on his knee. Then he grapples a gun from the jacket and thrusts it at Danny, at Tom, at Danny again. His hands are shaking and the safety is off. His mouth chews at the air before choking out malformed words.

"Who you? What you done with Margaret?"

"I—I don't know," Danny stammers. "Listen, friend, we're not a threat."

"*Back!*" The man jabs the gun's snout at them. The sinews in his neck strain and his bloodshot eyes are bulbous. "No you move or I fucking *shoot* you. Nigel?" he calls back into the corridor. His speech is slow, words still clearly hard to find even after all these years. "Margaret? The fuck you *done* to them?" His eyes are wild as he whips the gun back and forth, the ugly, stubby thing. A shot from this distance will be brutal.

Danny, his voice a calming murmur, raises himself on his elbows. "Hey, pal, why don't you just—"

"Said don't *move!*" the man screeches, then corrects himself. "You," he commands Danny, "there." He flicks the muzzle between them, drawing Danny across the room like an angler until he is next to Tom, a gun's narrow arc between them. "You got *food?*"

It's dark, near impossible to see, but Tom catches a very animal expression in his eyes. How pale the man is. How the filthy skin sucks his ribs. The sores coloring his skin. "Yes, we have food," Tom whispers, and nods. "Outside." The gun steadies on his chest. "It's hidden," he adds, but the sound of the explosion is too loud for the size of the room, and muzzle flash eradicates the shadows for a blinding instant. The man's bare chest erupts in a tangle of gristle and bone as he is flipped around, his gun spasm-firing, the room flaring bright again. Chips fleck up from the floor. Something sears across Tom's thigh as the man collapses against a table, unleashing an animal sound. Danny jumps on him, smothering him, while Tom limps across the room and, coming at him from the side, pushes Graham's arm down and rolls the gun out of the old man's grasp.

They skid through puddles, shoulder their way through doors and back out onto the forecourt, where Tom snatches up the chain. Take it as a weapon? His hands are uncontrollable. He tries to tie it, misses, misses again. Anything to slow these people down. Which people? Who? A shot smacks out. Fragments of tarmac burst. Danny and Graham flinch wildly as they push the cart to speed, while Tom scans the blank windows above them. Another shot and a feeling like a massive beetle flying unimaginably quickly past his ear. A long muzzle emerges. Tom raises his own gun and shoots. Turns. Runs. No more shots have been fired by the time he catches them, their eyes wild, their feet flying, the cart's wheels thrumming the tarmac, jarring on the cracks.

"Are they after us?" Danny gasps. "Are they coming?"

They force the cart around corners, heaving it and ramming it through the guardhouse gates. The empty road is different now. It stretches before them. Wrecked cars are places of ambush; leafy trees where people can hide. Behind them, from the facility, the buzz of motorbikes fires up.

"We need to put roads between us," Tom shouts as he runs. "Crossroads!"

As they career down a slope, the cart picks up speed. They let it.

"We need to hide," Danny yells back.

"We have to hide the cables and fuel!"

Graham's breath heaves, his gray-blue eyes petrified. With small, rapid strides, his gait is neither fast nor sustainable. He clearly doesn't have the strength for this. As the cart hits a crevice, the wheels crunch and jump. It goes faster.

"We need to ditch this!" Danny shouts, yanked forward even as he's trying to control it.

"It's what we came for!"

"Tom, we have to *hide*!"

A motorbike buzzes over the crossroads behind them, doesn't take their turn. Tom spins to look, trips, rips his knuckles to the bone, and Danny and Graham are twenty feet away, thirty, more. He gets up. Hand to face. Feet pounding. The motorbikes' roar drowns all else under the low-clouded sky.

"Flip the cart," he shouts after them, his stomach clenching with pain.

"Fuck the cart!" Danny cries back.

"No!" He sprints to catch up with them, grasps the metal lip, heaves and digs his feet in to stop it. His thigh explodes with pain as more blood bursts into his jeans. "Get these off," he pants, hauling off a keg, which nearly smashes his foot. He uncaps it and rolls it away, gushing fuel, as Danny wrestles the others. "Tip the cart! Roll the kegs off the road!"

Tom pushes, and runs, and looks back, and runs, the keg ringing like a bell, its rolling dents scuffing his palms, ENERGEN-GEN-GEN whizzing around. Fuel on his feet, the ends of his trousers slapping. Danny and Graham race for the trees. Tom abandons his keg to gulp out fuel and jumps off the road. Winded, he stands and runs again, lifting his legs like a hurdler over the grass. Two motorbikes crest the hill as he reaches the trees. Will he vomit? His throat is too dry; it won't be possible. He does and tries to keep it quiet as the bikes stop by the cart. People shout and point. The bikes race off: one away, while the other stops by his keg in the road. The man dismounts. Woman. It's a woman. Would he kill her if he had to? Crush her throat like Guy's, like Ben's— She looks at the keg and then up off the road directly at him.

He pulls back.

Is she now approaching, gun out, gun up, halfway here? Should he glance out again?

He does. The road is empty. The motorbike's still running; could he make it there in time? Then he sees her some trees away. Searching. She takes tall steps over the undergrowth, her pointed features framed by a dark bob. A breeze blows up. The branches shake and the leaves hiss. Tom creeps backward, keeping the thick trunk between them. She's so close he dare not breathe. And one of the sticks under his feet will snap, surely? Now that he has circled around the tree he is in plain view of the road, and he sees a motorbike in the

distance, tearing back toward them, its growl irritating
the air. Still the woman peers into the wood, her back
to him, and he rests his hands on the bark. Blood on his
hands. Graham shot someone. Why shouldn't he? All
in self-defense.

Tom pulls out the gun and thumbs off the safety.
The motorbike has disappeared in a dip, but when it
reappears, he will be caught. The woman moves to the
next tree, her eyes on the deeper wood. They both hear
the motorbike. She turns to look; he doesn't; he pushes
in against the trunk, pulling the gun to his chest. The
motorbike comes in loud and the woman is back on the
verge beside it, shouting, pointing. They both rev up
and spin around and speed back up the road until he
can't hear the engines anymore, only the bashing of the
trees and the crackle of the leaves. There's the sodden
smell of moss. A massive pain crushes his lower back.
His legs are jellied, his skin cold with sweat. And he
has to put his hands to his face to prize open his jaw to
breathe.

When he calls for them, they take a while to emerge.
They see their own fear reflected in one another's eyes.
They see the dirt on one another's faces and where the
tears have run rivulets through it. They right the cart
in silence, raise the kegs, the colorful bundles of cables,

and all their other stuff, and lash it down with shaking hands.

They find a turnoff as soon as they can, and then they take a smaller track. Old-style warning signs tell them to keep out, that they will be prosecuted, that there is danger of death. Tom cuts the chain on the gates, and past a tangled thicket of bushes they find a sheltered overhang.

"Let's sleep," he says. "And then we'll travel by night. No fires. No sound. Let's go home."

When it is dark, they reluctantly rejoin the road—they can't move the cart over the earth. The world is spectral, the clouds silvered scuffs. Tom's injured fingers throb. His thigh stings, and through the rip across his trousers he sees a puckered-open slash, stanching and welling as he limps, dark shadows glinting on its crusting edge in the grayed-out light. They talk rarely but listen a lot. They hear engines gunning on nearby roads and their eyes widen in the night.

A bird starts to warble, a specter dipping along the hedgerows beside them. Later, another trills in. Within minutes the dawn chorus cascades through the air, the sky rounded by the heart-pumping escalation of scales. They are back on the outskirts of the village and pass one of the burning cars, now cold and rough to the touch. There are no foxes, and only a few scattered bones in the gutter.

"That's a chaffinch," Danny says after a while, pointing somewhere up ahead, the first speech among them for hours. "You can tell by the upward cadence of its call."

The bird screeches again and Tom squints as it launches from a twisted pylon: a Feed mast for a rural zone. Others follow it, arcing to branches, each and every bird as green as the translucent ash leaves catching the dawn. Their wings are like darts and their tails carry something of the Jurassic. "They're parakeets, you fool!" he says, chuckling, and Danny breaks out laughing, discovered, before they press on in silence.

Tom soon notices Danny avoiding all the manhole covers in threes.

"Every little helps," Danny quips. And then, approaching a crossroads, the three of them see it at once. The silence expands around them until: "Holy fuck," Danny whispers.

There is a man ahead. He has been stripped, flipped, and tied to a pole. His feet have been nailed to the wood. His knees have been smashed, his throat sliced, and his nose and genitals removed. Birds are on him. Dogs are beneath him, licking his blood from the pole. No sudden movements, but still the animals turn. Their blood-lipped mouths quiver. The threat of stones barely keeps them back, pawing the earth and muscular. But eventually the birds peck and tear the corpse's skin again and the dogs turn back to wait for bits to fall.

They spend the day inside a house from whose bookshelves flow gummy waterfalls of rotting mulch. The quilts are thick with floral patterns of overgrown mold that has expanded up the walls. Midday sun bakes the day outside and time pulls on like the tide. Dogs and foxes pad in clans separately through the debris. Birds land and scrabble on the roof. Sometime in the broken afternoon Tom hears the sound of engines, gunshots . . . a mass of dogs barks. Two motorbikes roll up the road, circling the debris, the helmeted riders looking. And then deep silence fills the world once more.

Dusk comes. It's the time of skylarks and house martins for a while. Then, with nothing but the creaking of wheels, they roll out into the night. Tom limps as efficiently as he can. Nothing else until a quick-moving figure slips out from another house. He leaves the door gaping wide and follows them, confidently, at a distance.

Away from the village and into the deep countryside they go, followed all the way. At its darkest, when the world is most quiet, Danny starts to sing softly, and Tom and Graham join in. Songs whose words Tom had forgotten he knows, tunes he has not heard for years, whose words rise unbidden in his mind with emotions too snagged not far behind. They stop long before dawn for food and sit on the cart, leaning against the kegs and bales. Danny passes pignuts around, throws some into his mouth. The sky is clear above them, the stars like pinpricks through space and time, and Tom shakes the nuts and selects one, pebble-sized, to hold in the air.

"I'm not sure I remember this right—I heard it as a child—but if you hold up a grain of sand, it will obscure ten thousand galaxies. Ten thousand galaxies, of billions of stars each, covered by one single grain."

Graham and Danny both tilt their heads up.

"Do you reckon there are aliens?" Danny asks after a while.

Graham chuckles. "I remember a comic strip from when *I* was a child. That one with the boy and the tiger. They said the surest sign of intelligent life in space is that it has never come to see us. They were very wise, those two."

"Do you think if we asked them nicely they'd help?" Danny says. "There must be someone up there who can save us." He arcs his arm expansively across the sky, then his face falls. "Fuck, do you think it's *aliens*?" he whispers, aghast, and points at his head. His eyes are suddenly very wide. "Y'know, who got into Guy's and Jane's minds? Aliens!"

"Oh . . . don't be *ridiculous*," Graham mutters after a shocked pause.

"More likely to be the Chinese or something, right? Those China lads," Tom adds, surprised by Danny's thoughtlessness, trying to make whatever happened to Jane better somehow, somehow more palatable than . . . *aliens*. Maybe it *had* been the Chinese; they had been an immense technological power, developing similar things. But China had collapsed with every other country. The truth was no one had known who was responsible. Not Ben, not his father—whoever these people were who had brought about the Collapse had remained anonymous to the end.

"Jane reminded me the other day of those colonists up on Mars," Graham states quietly, his voice dark. He glances briefly up at them. "Do you think—"

"No, listen," Danny interrupts, his eyes glinting; he's warming to his theme. "I'm sure I saw a whole load of ents about aliens doing this sort of thing—"

"Exactly, Danny, *ents*," Tom stresses. "They weren't real! It was *people*, but why . . . ?"

"Ooh!" Danny exclaims. "I just remembered a fact too!" He pops in another nut. "Do you know how many cells there are in the human body?"

Tom and Graham shake their heads.

"No, I mean that's a genuine question. How many cells *are* there in the human body?"

"I thought you were telling us the fact?" Tom points out.

"A million?" Graham muses. "We'll raise it in the next knowledge session. Maybe Kate or Sean knows." He shakes his head. "But our pool is getting smaller."

"Anyway, anyway," Danny races on, "the point is that all these cells are dying all the time, right? And they're being replaced. So," he says, cocking an eyebrow, "how long do you think it takes for *all* the cells in our body to change?"

Graham glances at Tom. They both shrug.

"Seven years. That's what I just remembered. Seven years ago you were actually, physically, a different man from now. Isn't that cool?" Danny nods contentedly and lobs another nut into his mouth. "I learned that at college, when I was doing law."

Tom looks at him. "You were never going to be a lawyer."

Danny shrugs. Jumps off the cart and gets into the harness. "I'd've been a millionaire by now."

And as they travel through the cool night air, talking more freely about the past than they ever have before, confident now that they've lost their pursuers, a figure follows them in the darkness, just close enough to be able to listen and quietly enough not to be heard.

During the next day, they sleep outdoors under the bramble bushes at the edge of a beech thicket, taking turns to watch each other as the crickets bask and the sun cooks the earth. They walk through the following night in silence, hearing voices on the wind and, as dawn spreads, seeing people who are not there; maybe they used to be, or will be in the future, but Tom, Danny, and Graham don't care anymore because they are ravenous and they stink. They are beat. And as the sunlight melts the sky, it feels like reality is washed away. They become effervescent with the nearness of home.

They hit the downward track, the grasses of the valley, and when they finally reach the lawn, Danny lays himself flat and, crumpled over, kisses the earth. Shouts go up, and Bea and Jack run at them. They leap on Danny, who keeps his face to the earth, hiding his tears, Tom sees, while Graham stands still, leaning back, hands in his pockets, observing their camp with a small smile on his exhausted face. And Tom feels something melt inside himself too: relief, safety, hope, all the good things in the world about being home, though when he is in the shower later, he examines the raw mouths of the blisters on his hands, the scratches etching his body, and the swollen bloody fissure on his thigh, and he notices, as if examining someone else, that he has lost weight in those few days. And Kate, later still, after dressing his wounds, watches him sleep throughout the night and into the following day.

The unfamiliar feeling of a T-shirt—threadbare— pulled over washed skin brings back memories of his childhood, of going to bed on summer nights while it was light, of the world being topsy-turvy as he was supposed to sleep while it was blatantly still day. And here washes up the dreamlike memory of an evening when he went downstairs to find his parents, his bones hurting deeply, and one of his father's friends had called him—had he?—"the Experiment." He had heard that, he was sure, holding the handle. The familiar *click* of the kitchen latch as the farmhouse door closes reminds him that he's home now. With Kate. Sean has demanded a camp meeting before lunch, but now they climb the hill together, the tree canopy cocooning them. He has left his boots unlaced, his feet unbound in their cracked leather shells. Bea collects leaves as the shadows of the branches of oaks and plane trees grab her. Kate holds the silence. Then she stops.

"I'm glad you're back, Tom."

"Me too."

"I was worried."

"Me too."

"Tell me what happened."

He tries to hide his limp as he starts to climb the dark-earthed hill again, but Kate grips his fingers and grabs his elbow while Bea is too far away to hear.

"What happened to your leg, Tom?"

He folds his arms to loosen her hold. Light sparks through the canopy, but before he can answer or avoid the question, Bea is beside them, her arms full.

"Bank, please!"

Kate holds a basket out, barely looking at her daughter, her eyes fixed on Tom. The basket is already half full with leaves and dandelions, and the new batch tumbles on top. They look in and make appreciative noises for the little girl, who shouts, "Thanks!" before she points up at them sternly. "And don't you eat any until we're home. I know what *you two* are like."

"Bossy," Kate remarks, watching Bea dash back to the undergrowth.

"I wonder where she gets that from."

"So?" Kate prompts, glaring at his leg. "I've seen gunshot wounds before."

"It was shrapnel."

Kate purses her mouth.

"There were people there, Kate."

"Shit, Tom. Why didn't you see them before?"

"Maybe they were hiding. Maybe they'd just arrived! There was one group in a spiky van like a hedgehog with horses, and another group on motorbikes."

"It's not worth it, Tom—"

"We got fuel for the plow and cabling for the turbines. It was worth it all right!"

"Not worth losing you."

"You didn't, Kate. Come on, why are you—"

"There are always other options, *but there is only one us*! And . . ." Kate glances at him. "Bea keeps asking why they're watched while they sleep. She's become obsessed. She said you told her Jane died because she was asleep. She's upsetting Jack. Sean says we have to tell her; he says if we don't, he will. He's not slept at all since you left."

Tom scowls. When they had first arrived, he had found it hard to understand Sean through his mutilated language and the sleep-deprived hallucinations of his addled brain. It had been painful to watch the man, eyes determinedly open, trying to hold his terrors at bay, the things he was keeping silent. Sleep. Sean's obsession and theirs.

They have reached the peak of the hill and left the forest now, walking along an old field on a rich seam of chalk. A fur of trees nestles in the pit between the distant hills, and low clouds hint at the only straight line. Bea is behind them with another armful.

"What are we going to do with these?" Tom's voice is raw.

"It's for a stew," Bea informs him, and rushes off again. There is a worm in this deposit.

"Tom, listen," Kate continues. "We promised each other. It's us, that's all there is. We take priority. We agreed. It's not like SaveYou is working anymore—there are no second chances. We can't be saved. So *please*. No risks. You've been so lucky with that leg. I washed it. I don't think there's anything in there."

"We could always find a Pharmacist."

Kate rolls her eyes. "Don't *joke*, Tom. Still the same: blind, blind hope! Even if there *are* any Pharmacists, why would they help *us*? Come live with me in the real world. Just—don't—get—shot. How does that sound?"

Finally he intertwines his fingers with hers and pats her stiff hand. He hugs her, and her hair, taken by the wind this high up on the hill, whips his eyes. "Okay," he concedes, "I promise not to get shot if you promise too. Deal?"

She pulls back to look at him guardedly, not sure he's being serious, then pledges: "Yes. But remember what else you promised: if those turbines don't work, we leave."

They meet on the lawn, and Danny and Graham answer Sean's and Kate's questions while Bea and Jack play by the shower stall. Without Guy, without Jane, their numbers are diminished. Their absence brings Tom up short. Soon, he notices the children edging nearer, can clearly see the hunger for knowledge in Bea's determined eyes. He shoos them away while the others continue to talk. He sits there, and it's like a dream. *Was the man shot dead? Dead dead? Were they travelers or were they settled? They had horses? Bikes?* He feels enervated. The wound on his thigh throbs, and pain, for a while, is all that tethers him to the world. Why *should* they stay here anymore? Why shouldn't he take his family away? They have to look out for themselves.

"Did they follow you here?" Sean demands. His eyes are dull, his voice lethargically slurred but driven, his deeply scarred hands wringing constantly. "Because if you've exposed the camp," he intones, "we're dead!"

And with that echoing in their thoughts, with nothing more to be said, Danny goes back to the house to lay the wires to the turbines while the others disperse and Tom remains alone. Will the cabling work? Until now it's been a dream, a hope to aim for. But it'll become real now, one way or the other. It will work or it won't. They'll survive, for a while, or not. He surveys the woods, the distant mouth of the track. He remembers the hazy curves of that van through the trees like an armored creature, moving strangely, silently, for its size, pulled steadily on by the horses. Its spikes. Is Sean right? Are they in danger from the group on motorbikes? Can they protect themselves from harm? There are people at the facility who are looking for them. Have they led them here? And there's the permanent threat from within. He has to tell Bea about sleep.

With timber they were saving for another hut, Tom and Sean build a rough gazebo on the lawn. Sean won't be drawn into talking. "Tell her," he grunts at Tom, and scowls over at Bea. She suspects they're building this thing for her birthday, and she watches them askance from around the corner of the farmhouse for a while before openly parading around. By the time Graham is teaching her and Jack to write that afternoon, she's asking for words like *presents* and *cake.*

As the afternoon turns gray, Tom and Sean erect a pole, and Danny leaves his work with the turbines on the farmhouse roof to rig some cables to the moldy car battery by the generator for the lights. They string them up, fanning them from the pole to the gazebo to the house. Turned on in the daylight, they look like dew on a huge spiderweb.

That night, Tom and Kate are in Danny's hut with Graham. Danny watches them first, surrounded by the dusty mess in which he lives: stick-bound contraptions litter the place, drawings that could have been better done by a child. Tom lies there, listening to the hut as it creaks in the night, the hushed sounds as Danny turns the pages of his book. Then he gets up and creeps past Danny, tweaking his ear as he goes. Danny flips a finger at him, barely distracted, flops out his tongue, and returns to the book he's examining.

Sean is on duty in the children's hut in the slight candlelight there. Tom observes him through the window for a while. Sean's scarred hands are flat on the tabletop, but as Tom watches, they twitch and curl into strangling shapes. Then it's as if he notices what they're doing. Dazed, he spreads them flat once more. His lips move, murmuring some unheard word again and again and again, his face creasing up in confusion. One word.

Sorry? It's difficult to tell, but with a jolt, Tom sees that Bea is watching Sean too, peering out from under her tatty comforter. Her expression is blank, but what on earth will she be making of this? Tomorrow Tom will tell her; what choice does he have? Tomorrow she'll know why they're watched, what Sean is doing now. He'll tell her the signs to look out for—the signs from the vid, Ben's vid—and she'll never sleep well again.

Dying inside, he runs across the lawn and up past the vegetable patches to the barn, where he uncovers the music machine from the facility. His thoughts about Bea agitate his mind, but he buries them, embalms them with hope and distraction by carrying the machine carefully down the dark hill, the house looming out of the night, and setting it up in the gazebo. In the generator shed he flips on the battery and outside, with a faint hum, the lights come on, crazed above him in the night sky. The nature of their light is foreign—it pulses and its color is too consistent—but instantly familiar too: a second after the surprise of seeing the bulbs incandescent, they have become normalized again already. Back in the gazebo, the small fan in the music machine starts to whir. It's been a decade since he used a machine like this, and he scrolls through menus clumsily. With a quickening heart he finds the song he wants before returning to Danny's hut. He winks at him, puts a finger to his lips, and gently brushes Kate's hair.

"What?" she says, jerking up. "What is it?"

"Come with me."

"Is everything all right?"

"Just come. Quiet. Graham's sleeping."

Danny smiles at them tightly and looks away. Does his duty like they've been trained, watching Graham for signs while, outside the hut, Tom puts his hands over Kate's eyes. Her body relaxes into his as he guides her over the night-shadowed grass and under the strings of fairy lights that hover like laced-up fireflies, converging on the makeshift gazebo.

"What is it?" she whispers, and as he murmurs in her ear, "You'll find out," he feels the heat of her earlobe on his lips and the curve of her cheeks as she smiles. Is Danny watching them? He doesn't care. It reminds him of the moment they first entered their house, their lovely house on that hill, the city's lights spread out beneath them, and he is relieved that such memories survive. It seems that as more time passes more come back to light. "Don't you dare peek," he says, then positions her in the doorway. "Okay."

Kate takes a deep breath. Goes up on her toes. Opens her eyes and gasps.

Tom presses a button and a display cascades to life.

HELLO, it says. The machine engages with a soft sound as he pushes another button, and then, after a pause, the music starts to play. Kate's hands go to her face, her mouth, her eyes, which fill with tears. She hasn't heard music in years—none of them has—and she hasn't heard this song for longer. She smiles. She laughs. She sways away from him but doesn't move her feet.

"Would you like to dance?" he asks.

"You couldn't remember the steps on the day!"

"I bet you forget them first."

"You're on," she says, and gives him her hand. "And be careful of your leg."

Tom leads her outside and holds her close, his heart beating against her chest as they clasp hands beneath the lights. Neither of them can remember the steps but neither of them stops dancing.

On the day before Bea's birthday, Tom and Kate forage with the children until Danny declares that the turbines are finally wired and ready. This moment has been years in the making. If they work, it will change everything: heat, light, and cooking powered eternally by the wind. Guy's legacy, they'll call it, to remember him by. They'll be safe. There will be progress and Kate has said they can stay—if it works. All depending on Danny as he climbs out of a window and, once atop the roof, raises his hands in unstable victory, the transistor clasped between them. He teeters toward the turbines trailing a cable tied to his belt. The other end reenters the house like an umbilical cord.

On Tom's shoulders, Bea clutches his hair and whispers, "Daddy, he's going to fall!" but Danny reaches the first rusty turbine, its blades spinning quickly, and grabs its column for support. He gropes toward the next one and fumbles the transistor into place. Jack, on Sean's shoulders, puts his hands over his ears. Sean stares, stares, stares.

"Okay!" Danny calls. He has to duck to be seen under the air-slicing blades. "Are we ready?"

All lights in the house are on but the fuel generator has been disconnected. If the turbines work, the house will light up—"In a blaze of glory," Graham had muttered wryly as Danny had explained this glorious plan before starting his ascent. But Graham is rapt now, his lips white as he whispers to himself with his fingers, Tom notices, crossed.

"I said, *are we ready?*" Danny does a little rolling of his hips to excite the crowd and grabs frantically at the turbine again when he slips. "Then let there be light!" he cries as he flips a switch and raises his arms dramatically.

———

By evening the clouds have condensed. They haven't reconnected the generator now that they have to save the fuel. Whether they will do so for Bea's party is moot; the celebration feels like a thin veneer, the hope it should represent harshly defined by the darkness this afternoon's failure has left them in. Tom places a candle on the kitchen table—it seems to be burning faster than before—and puts crockery away while Danny sits there, waiting.

"What are you going to tell her?"

"The truth. I have to."

Danny nods. He has been very quiet since the afternoon, the quietest Tom has ever seen.

"Why d'you want me here?"

"Because it's not an easy truth to tell."

Danny nods again, tightly. "But does she have to know, Tom? It seems such a shame . . ."

Tom doesn't say anything, stands by the table with a hand on the back of a chair. The candle hisses. The shadows in the room seem darker tonight, the ceiling lower.

"I remember," Danny continues quietly, "when she was being born. I went into the fields and the fuckers were still furrowed under this crust of ice. I could smell vegetables there, I swear it, I was that hungry, and I thought how this planet doesn't give a damn. It barely notices us. But I got back and there you were, you three, and Bea was this tiny scrawling little thing, and she made it worth it. The hope, you know? It'd be miserable to starve for no reason. But starving for the good of a child meant something. We meant something. Bad times are when goodness can really show. And I'm sorry about the turbines, Tom, I'm so, so *sorry*. I just don't have the knowledge Guy did. I don't know about electrics; I was learning to be a lawyer! But I promise I'll do everything I can to protect Bea. I'll defend her with my life!"

Tom has no words for this or to respond to Danny's sincere eyes filling with tears. There is joy in this world; the camp, the trust and friendship they are building here, is support enough, isn't it? It is structure. It is protection. And surely they can save it. Surely there's no need to leave like Kate wants. She's just scared. They need people around them, they need safety in numbers. Don't they?

The latch rises and Kate ushers Bea in. Kate is pale. The little girl is clearly suspicious.

"Hey, come on, Beaty-Bea," Danny says, and laughs. He jumps up from the table, chirpy again, does a little wiggly dance and gives her a smothering hug. "We just want to have a chat. It's nothing to worry about. Why don't you sit on down?"

Bea does, and her head droops toward the table. "Am I in trouble again, Daddy?" she mumbles, and glances dolefully at Kate, who sits beside her, unsmiling.

"Noo-oooo-oo," Danny reassures her.

Tom swallows. "Of course not. But . . . Bea, darling. We have to talk—"

The door opens again and Sean prowls in, bending under the lintel. He scrapes a chair back and sits. Clasps his scarred hands. Nods at Tom and Kate, commanding them to continue. He won't look at Danny, won't even spare him a glance, and, Tom notices, Danny's tears well again.

"Listen, Bea," Tom says, knitting his hands. "You asked me why Jane died. Remember? Well, the truth is . . . You're six tomorrow, that means you're a big girl and you're old enough to know about a . . . *responsibility* we have to each other. And to everyone else in the world." He takes in Sean's steely expression. "Jack's not ready to understand this yet, but you are, Bea. So can you keep a secret?"

Bea glances uneasily among the adults, her small mouth slightly open. When Kate had taken her from the hut, Graham had been telling Jack a story. The sense that maybe being six won't be quite all she thought it would be furrows her brow, but she nods nonetheless.

"When we sleep, we are vulnerable," Tom continues. "Our minds can be invaded. Do you understand? You know the world Graham has told you about? That Mummy and Daddy lived in before? There were assassinations and accidents. People started behaving in strange ways . . . There were too many incidents that became too . . . targeted, too common to be coincidence . . ."

Bea frowns at Kate in confusion.

"You know that old tech you and Jack found a few days ago, darling?" Kate takes over, but her voice is wavering so much that her words clog her throat. "You asked what it did? Well . . ."

"It's hard to explain, Bea," Danny continues when Kate falters too. His voice is gentle. He leans forward and uses his hands to portray things as he speaks. "But the world used to be different from what you're used to, right? There were big buildings, and cars, and airplanes, and we could all talk to each other in our heads . . . There were loads and *loads* of people then. But someone invaded us in our sleep—"

"Invades us," Sean interjects.

"—and for a long time we didn't realize it was happening. So many people were taken, and there was no way of knowing. Because everyone looked the same, right? But these normal-looking people suddenly started doing bad things. Very bad things. Killing other people. Destroying buildings, power stations; trying to disrupt the airports. They killed the president. We didn't know who was themselves and who was someone else. It was . . . terrible. It was the not knowing that was the killer. People were terrified. They did awful things they'd never otherwise have done. But we realized people were being taken over in their sleep. So it became law: never to sleep alone, never to sleep unwatched. And . . . there were signs we had to look for. It stopped being a law that you couldn't . . . Basically, Bea, if you saw someone being taken, it wasn't against the law to . . ."

Now Danny stops too, and the small girl, sitting alone before them, nods as if she has to tell them it's all right to continue. Kate reaches out to her. "Maybe we should—"

"Watching doesn't save them. Nothing saves them. You have to kill them when it happens," Sean states. "Miss that moment, when you see the signs, and you'll never know. Your mum and dad will look like themselves, sound like themselves; you'll think they're themselves. But they won't be. You'll think Danny's himself, but he's not. There's something else in their brains. They'll kill *you.* That's why everyone is watched. That's why everyone *wants* to be watched. Because you wouldn't want something in your brain, in your body, would you, Bea? Killing your parents? Killing all of us? You wouldn't want that, would you?"

"It's a lot for a little girl to take in, sweetie," Kate whispers softly. Her hands are shaking; she turns the little girl's pale face to hers, her hands nearly covering her ears. Her words are stranded together, a murmur, a plea. "And don't worry, Bea, don't worry. It happens so rarely, it won't happen to us, there's nothing to be afraid of. But this is why someone is always awake—"

"To kill the others," Sean restates, "if they're taken. Do you get it, Bea?"

There is a silence in which Bea starts to cry, her face, still held tightly in Kate's hands, crumpling as fat tear globes grow from her squeezed-closed eyes. Kate turns beseechingly to Tom. "That's enough!" she says, but, "This is nonnegotiable," Sean continues impassively, rapping his knuckles on the tabletop. "Lack of adherence to the rules will be met with disciplinary action. They're not rules. They're facts. Facts of survival."

"Okay," Tom says, "I think that's—"

"I had to kill my wife." Sean's voice is shaking, his hands are shaking, held out before him as if something is going to erupt. "I had to kill my *wife.* Do you think the *fuck* I wanted to do *that*? It's the way the world *is.* Get *used* to it. Strengthen *up.*"

"A-and that is what happened to Jane?" Bea stutters before Tom can even interject.

"Yes, Bea," Danny says softly, glancing from Sean to Tom to Kate, and reaching over to take Bea's little hands. "She was taken and Graham had to stop it."

Bea turns her teary gaze from Danny to look directly at Tom. Her pupils are vast as the candlelight catches the blue around them, this girl who is not even yet six. "And Guy?" she asks, her voice quivering. "You made him dead too, Daddy?"

Tom stares at her, at her round cheeks framed by her irregularly chopped hair, at her eyes, almost tired with shock. Kate's watching him too. Exhausted. Petrified. They look so similar, these two. He nods, his jaw tensing. He knows he is breaking her world. "You just have to do it, darling. You see their pain."

And now, instead of Bea's shocked face, he sees Guy's. The pain. The feeling of Guy's throat collapsing in his grasp. And then it's Ben's, and the grass beneath Guy's head is the woolen carpet under Ben's at the top of the tower, when each second flooded Tom forward from the moment he made the decision, when he saw the pained twitching on his brother's face as something broke into his brain, and he was shaking his life away. The horror of what he had to do, of what he was already doing. That horror had been flooding everyone's lives, everyone in the world. Their only choice: killing the people they loved and enduring the filthy guilt, or drowning in the lurking terror that their loved ones weren't themselves. It was turning them into monsters. The horror and the paranoia, competing with each other, tightening the city, choking the world until it broke. It broke. It collapsed and brought them here.

"And . . . that's why you watch us? Because you would do this to me?" Bea asks.

The next morning, the morning of Bea's birthday, there are no shadows. All normal tasks on the rotas are ignored. Bunting goes up beneath the clouds; tables are brought outside and decorated with leaves and flowers. All this change confuses Bea, just six, only six, and still with him, for a while.

"It's like a holiday," Tom tells her. "To celebrate your birthday."

"Lift me higher, please."

He does; he puts his hands under her feet so she can stand on his shoulders and reach higher into the tree.

"A holiday," he continues, "is a day when everyone can forget their troubles and not worry about the future for once, to be with the ones they love."

"Got it!"

When he lowers her, she is holding a large oak leaf,

very similar to every other leaf up there, including the more easily reachable ones. "Why that one, Beaty-Bea?"

"Just *look* at it, Daddy, it's a special one."

Bea stretches to get the leaf as close to his face as possible, then takes his hand. He lets himself be led by her, likes feeling the tug of her, loves feeling her fingers wrapping around his.

"Oh, I do love holidays," she says, and sighs as they stroll back down the hill.

"Do you know about the seasons?"

"Of course! It's spring."

"No . . ."

"Summer!"

"That's right. And what are the other seasons?"

"Spring, summer, autumn, winter." Bea's voice takes on the rhythm of an incanted chore.

"And what sort of weather is it in summer?"

"Hot and sunny."

"And what sort of weather is it in winter?"

"Daddy, please, can we stop talking about the weather now?"

He rolls up his lips and nods: fair enough.

"Did you find out what soil's made of?" she asks, skipping beside him.

He scowls. He'd forgotten this.

"Don't you know, Daddy?"

"There's a lot that we don't know anymore."

"Where did Guy go when you made him dead?"

She is looking up at him, snatching glances as she trots to keep up, waiting for his answer. But he just smiles and tells her he doesn't know. He doesn't. Not anymore. For a while, the world *had* known: you died, and you'd been BackedUp. People were saved, their memory states preserved in cold storage. Just before it had all collapsed, he had done something he hadn't told anyone about. Not Kate, not anyone. He had killed Ben the day before. It was night and he came quietly upstairs, into his father's empty office. The night flattened the city but the fires threw up shadows. The end was so close, but he hadn't known that then. Barely thinking, because he had already decided what to do: he accessed the homeHub and Ben's SaveYou files. His BackUps. And there he was, his brother, the stored memories of his life, rapidly moving layered skeins. All saved. Digital replications of his brain. What Tom was doing was so deeply taboo, scouring the thoughts of a dead man. But he had to *know.* That moment, when Ben had been taken, he had wanted to see it. So he had riffled right to the end of Ben's final day and gone *in.*

Ben's thoughts, Ben's emotions, Tom immersed himself in them. Ben finished working, ate dinner, bade

Tom good night. Closed his eyes. A fragmented jumble of dreams suddenly warped. Everything squeezed. Even for Tom, who had only been watching this, something behind his face had felt squashed, crushed, compressed, and then . . . there was nothing. Nothing at all. Absolute freezing. Hellish void.

Tom had withdrawn from Ben's SaveYou states and stood staring at the blackened city below, his own ghost face reflected in the glass. Who were they? That was what he had wanted to see. But no. There had been nothing after Ben had died.

Feeling sick, he looks down at his daughter. She glances up one last time and plainly fakes a smile. He asks if she's okay about their conversation, what they'd talked about the night before, and she shrugs heavily. They walk the slope in silence until she dashes to Graham on his porch. Tom watches her go. Purses his lips in response to Graham's wave and goes briefly into the kitchen. Kate is at the table, sewing together a little dress. Her movements are ragged, her face flushed.

"It's from one of Jane's," she says between her teeth. "Do you think she'll notice?" Suddenly she winces and sucks a finger. "Dammit, I can't see anything in this light!"

Silence stretches between them until Tom nods grimly, turns and goes to the generator shed. It's only as he leans to turn the power on that he notices Kate has followed him. She stands by the door, folding her arms against the dampness of the room. Her face is stiller now.

"So when are we leaving, Tom?" Her arms go out to him when he doesn't reply and then her fists clench back. "Tom, you *promised*."

"We shouldn't just leave everyone, Kate. They're good people."

"Yes, we should! Because if we stay here, we *die*. Stay and die or leave and *maybe* survive. This place is being *targeted*, Tom!"

"What are you talking about?"

"Guy, Jane, we're all being—"

"Guy was taken miles from here! There is *nothing* to suggest it's targeted. Stop stoking up the fear! It's *random*, bad luck—"

"Stop pretending, Tom, stop living in a dream! We have to make difficult decisions! And if *you* can't . . ."

"What?" He reaches for her hand.

Tears quiver in Kate's eyes. "Then I have to think about Bea."

She lets his hand drop and moves toward the door. She waits there, under the lintel again, waiting for him to speak. She clearly *wants* him to speak, desperately wants him to say something, *anything*, to have a solution for it all; wants to share some of his hope. But when he comes up with nothing, she leaves.

Bea and Jack are intoxicated—they've never had a party before—while the adults approach the celebration stoically. They decide to turn on the fairy lights, using up the meager supply of energy from the car battery. What does it matter anymore?

The clouds relax and split. There are unexpected colors before sunset. Kate's face is infused with the light; it collects, rosy, in her eyes, but she will not look at Tom. He watches her watching the woods, her gaze forever drifting toward the track, as, with an accompanying warble from Jack, Bea emerges from the farmhouse in her new dress. Leaves have been stitched onto it; as she points out to Tom, her oak leaf forms a pivotal part of the arrangement. They talk, they eat, they admire the sky's colors and wispy clouds. And then, with no warning, a noise rips the world apart. Tom drops to the ground. Bea clings to him. He lurches for Kate as a static rattle scores the air and its ringing after-noise shudders the silence. Birds burst up, away, and circle far above.

"Sorry!" Danny calls from the gazebo, and then music starts quietly.

Bea's face becomes simultaneously scared and full of awe. "What is that noise, Daddy?"

Tom breathes back his pounding heart and nods at the gazebo. "Go look."

Soon they are all dancing around the fire, dancing to songs from the past under strings of lights as forgotten voices live again. The corner of their field is lit, the grass glowing green in the night, amid the unlit trees, between the dark bodies of the hills, the deep silence of the country laid out around them, the sky above them, the stars, the world that they are on.

The music proves addictive as the fire rips into the night. Even Graham dances with Bea, a slow, flexing jive. Kate dances with Sean. Tom watches them from where he sits with Danny, who jigs Jack on his lap. He watches as Bea detaches herself from Graham and prances up to Kate, who gives her hands to Sean, who lets the little girl stand on his feet and sways her around the fire. Sean smiles, Tom is surprised to see; he actually *smiles*.

The night air is cooler now, and Tom watches the fairy lights dip as the battery loses power. He watches as, at the outer edge of firelight, the smoky swirls coalesce into a darker shape: a moving shadow that sharpens into the silhouette of a man. But all the men are here. This shape is a new one, an intrusion, a cancerous presence amid them, and something flows through Tom like the power buzzing in the lights: he shouts and grabs Bea, and with tumbling strides they group together by the table. The shadow throws dark trails into the smoke as it raises its arms. The wind turns and rolls the smoke away, revealing, for an instant, this man. He is middle-aged. He has chopped curly hair, dirty clothes, and a very level gaze. He steps forward. He holds the silence as his nostrils flare, perhaps for the smoke, perhaps for some other reason; his eyes do not flicker.

"Hello. My name is Mark."

Sean strides forward, drunken-bold. His sleeves are already rolled. "What do you want?"

"I offer you no threat," Mark soothes, his face creased, his hands held out. "And I will take nothing from you. I will give you, however, stories. This is what I do. I am a storyteller, traveling, remembering, and telling what I know. To preserve tales and let them live. If you find my stories acceptable, if you enjoy them, I would be happy to eat your food. This is what I do."

And Sean, right close to Mark now, without changing his stride, punches him in the face.

Graham ushers Jack and Bea firmly away, and with Mark tied up in the darkness against the wall of the shower stall, the others group up on the far side of the fire.

"I don't care who he *may be*," Kate shouts, shaking Tom's hand off her arm. "We don't welcome people here by hurting them, Sean!"

"He's from the storage facility!" Sean hisses, and jabs his finger. "Tom led him here!"

"We have no way of knowing—" Tom protests, and Mark watches all this from a distance as:

"This is the *attack!*" Sean snaps, pushing Tom back. His voice gets higher and higher, his spine more and more stiff. "This is it! *Someone get the gun!*"

Kate groans and strides away. She snatches a jug and a cloth from the table and, kneeling in front of the trussed-up man, wipes the dried blood from his face.

"Who are you?"

Mark stretches his lips, savoring his answer like a wine. "I'm . . . whoever you want me to be so I don't get punched again, please. I'm not taken, if that's what you're worrying about."

"Well, that's us reassured," scoffs Danny, standing close behind Kate. He has a hammer in his hands.

Tom steps forward. "Where are you from, then?"

Mark shrugs. "Where is anyone from anymore?"

"You can make this easy," Sean growls, putting a fist in his palm.

Laughing lightly, barely acknowledging the threat, Mark observes them from beneath cushioned brows. "Originally, from Loxburgh. Would the taken know of that?"

"The new suburb?" Sean asks, standing his ground.

"Well," Mark says, jutting his lower lip out, "it was looking pretty ratty when I left it."

"When was this?"

"Soon after the Collapse. So . . . what's that?" Mark shrugs again. "Years ago. I've come down from the north just now. There's not many camps, not many people, and some very dangerous ones at that. I've found enough friendlies to survive."

"And the cities?" Danny says. "Are there people left alive?"

Mark moves his eyes around them, as though looking for the hopes they hold, before he shakes his head. "Fuel stations going up, scrapers coming down. Animals have taken them now. The dogs are huge, mutated, muscular things with massive teeth. Cerberus hounds from hell. And what few people there are are savages, little better than animals."

"Have you seen this?" Sean demands, but his voice is weaker than before. Mark shakes his head. "Well, if you haven't seen it, you can't say it. Unfounded conjecture is dangerous."

Mark tilts his face. "That's going to limit my repertoire."

"So what stories can you tell?" Danny interrupts before Sean can speak again.

"I can do poems, I know a bit of Shakespeare. I can tell old news or just make something up. What would you like? Something for the birthday?"

"How do you know it's a birthday?" Sean growls.

"I've been watching you." Mark laughs, then faux scowls. "I thought you all looked friendly."

"How did you find us?"

Mark glances at Tom and Danny for a second before clearly rethinking what he was about to say. "I found your filtration tanks days ago, down by the stream. Tonight I heard your music. You should be careful. I saw men prowling. A van like a metal porcupine, pulled by horses. They're hunting for children for mating, I think."

The embers of the fire rustle behind them in a breeze that, moments later, touches the unseen trees across the grass at the entrance to the track, hidden in the darkness of the night.

"There are so few people out there," Mark continues, "so it's a solution of sorts. But you don't want to attract them here, believe me."

"So how *do* we know you're not taken?" Danny asks, agitated again all of a sudden.

"Send me away; I'll find somewhere else to settle." Mark shrugs at them from the ground. "Or we'll have to learn to trust each other. Because I don't know about you either. Are any of *you* taken? You might be, any single one of you."

Summer draws on and then one night, while it is still dark outside, there is a stretched moment when Tom is aware of his dreams. In the gulp of a heartbeat they are swallowed. By the time he sits up they are gone and all he is aware of is Kate's hands on his shoulders, shaking him, and her voice echoing in his ears.

"What's happening?"

"A noise: I heard a shout. There was glass breaking."

Tom hurls the bedclothes off. He shoulders into Kate, reaches back to grab her arm, turns to the window and pushes his face to the pane. Orange light licks the night, and there's a sound: a roar of hungry moving air racing hot into the sky.

He pulls on trousers as he charges onto the landing, shouts as he runs down the stairs: *"There's a fire in Graham's hut!"* He hears movement in Sean's room, sees the door open and Sean stumble out. Tom barrels through the kitchen and grabs the handle of the garden door. Pain sears his hand and flames burst into the room, folding up and along the ceiling. His face wet, his eyeballs dried out, the flames race, lick the wood, stretch to get inside, howling.

"Tom, here, the table!"

Sean is behind him and they turn the table and heave it at the fiery doorway. Then Graham is with them, with Sean, pulling the table back, having another go, while Tom uses a saucepan to punch out the window. He goes through, feet first, and tumbles to the ground.

In the still-dark air, the camp comprises juddering shadows and sparks and smoke. Shifting golden light carpets the lawn. *A fire?* Fire is on every hut. It licks the front of the farmhouse. Shouts and smashing glass ricochet in the night with the thump and crash of things breaking. The smell of burning everywhere. Tom dashes through the choking smoke toward the children's hut. The only one without fire, its windows are broken and the door hangs wide. Inside, the beds are overturned, sheets slack on the floor. Beside the upturned table, Danny drowns in a pool of blood. His book has been ripped in half and they have cut his throat, but not well: bubbles grow and burst from the laceration. A whistling sound. Blood congeals in his hair. His terrified eyes gulp up and rove. He can't move his head.

Tom races from the hut, frantic, looking—*for what?*

Sean clambering through the kitchen window, Kate hurling water on the flames. Graham stumbles on the grass, spinning, arms like a scarecrow. The sparks from the fires, the heaving columns of smoke, the whirling stars in the sky, as Tom sprints toward the track, stops, stares into the darkness, runs, stops again, tries to make sense of the world, tries to hear anything above the thunder of blood in his ears while the shafts of trunks knock around him as he stumbles up the empty track until he hits the road, gasping. Nothing. No one. They couldn't have come this far this fast, not with the children, and he would have seen a car, a truck, even motorbikes; he would have *heard* them. He cries out as he runs back down—for Bea, for Jack, but mostly he shouts for Bea until his throat tastes like blood and his voice is cracking as orange touches the clouds and he can see the camp in the dawn-green light back through the billows of churning smoke.

He stops, chest heaving, and watches the forest. Stares at the trees. Their lines. Their branches. Are there people there? In the undergrowth? Behind those bushes? He prowls, arms out, wild, waiting for movement. Did he hear a muffled cry?

The bushes taunt him.

Nothing.

There is nothing.

His face is numb, his heart swollen. He races back into the camp, shouting for Sean, his voice hoarse to hardly anything at all, and Sean comes tearing across the lawn. Around them, charcoal clinks and *tings*. Some of it drips, crumbling.

"The children," Tom gasps. "They've taken the children."

"We'll find them," Sean barks, and pulls him by the arm to the farmhouse.

Danny is on the kitchen table, Graham restraining him as he jerks, forcing a towel to his throat. And Kate bends, blood on her hands, to pull a needle, gore on the thread, through the lacerated skin of his throat. Tom is through the door and up the stairs. He tugs a drawer out. Grabs his rucksack and some clothes. He's back downstairs and barges into the study, flings the cupboard open and pours the gun, the bullets, into his bag before he's back through the kitchen, past the gory chaos, and out into the smoke-filled morning.

Sean shouts at him: "That's the camp's gun, Tom! Stop!"

Tom does. He stops. He looks past Sean into the kitchen, where Kate has moved away from Danny. They see each other, Kate and Tom, and she frowns. She brushes a chair aside, moving toward him. Then Mark emerges from around the house, his face black with soot, a gash on his head, and Sean roars. He lowers his shoulders and hurtles him into the wall. Hitting him, pummeling, punching madly, like a mechanism unleashed. Tom looks back to the farmhouse. Kate is now at the door, her lips trembling, her face smeared with blood. She reaches out toward him.

He turns and runs for the track. Runs. Runs under the trees, up the day-lit path, pulling his rucksack on as the sound of people shouting after him is drummed out by the blood in his ears. All he can think about is *running*.

KATE
Burning Up

The GPS says Tom is 12.45m away & about to turn into view. I'm regaining my balance after falling on the rubble. So much of OldTown is rubble now. But we couldn't stay in the tower anymore, not after what Tom's father did. I work out that the interlaceofgrazes on mypalm will take an average 206secs to cease to bleed, 3days20hours17mins12secs to heal deeply & a further 1,885mins42secs to disappear. The looter who smacked me down releases a rock toward the rowofshops. It spins through the air, 1revolution, 2, & I tell Tom we're taking Rafa with us, & he says we can't. The rock has turned 4revolutions & covered 3.24m of air. An armyhelicopter banks in the distance, tipping 27° off vertical. It's cold.

Kate? Are you there? Kate? Kate? It's Martha. She's at home, a warm WestCoast breeze rolling into the kitchen, & she wants to know when we're leaving. Come on, Kate, come now, she tells me, the kids want their auntie! & she waits for my reply. The airports are still open, the fares increasing exponentially in relation to the growingdelay between each flight out of here. I grab the looter'sface & GPSloc & Feed it to the police. An automatic log is taken & someone will reply within 17secs, I'm told—an eternity, because most of the police are at the Saltworth site, which is stillblazing, its orange heart at an estimated 1,729°C, just 3.7% under critical, the reporter says, surrounded by chokingsmoke & hordes in hazchemsuits. We're trying to get out, I assure Martha. Like a needle in my veins I feel her panic. It started simmering when PresidentTaylor1 was shot. Boiled over when the Chinesepremier was killed. Exploded in the powerless terror of losing Mum&Dad. An ad comes up. It tells me my body's showing signs of stress and dehydration and maybe it's time for a break; there's a shop that sells [*Cham O'Mile*] just 30.7m away, do I want my GPS to direct me to it? The tip of the looter'srock touches the shopwindow. Veinsofbreakage freeze out across it as the looter takes a heavystep into the road. MyFeed links me to where I can [*buyhistrainers*]. He's blocked hisFeedID, of course, but whoever he is we must share some demographics. I tell Martha to calm down, but already she's telling me she can't bear to lose me, that Mum&Dad being gone is more than she can bear, and she bombards me with mundles of when we were kids. My cortisolevels lurch up 23.68%, my heartrate jumps even though I've finally found my footing and Tom's arm has come into view around the corner. Long before I feel it, I know that dopamine is flooding mybody & the reuptake is blocked. I'm going to go into panic. My norepinephrinelevel spikes. I can see my bloodpressure rising & my adrenalglands go crazy—because of the looter? because of the fall? the uncontrollable loss&despair brought on by the memories of our dead parents Martha is pumping at me? because I can see Rafa in my mind's eye lost amid the monumental wreckage

the city will surely become? because I want to
stop being pregnant? stop this baby coming into
this horrific world? & there's a—

—She had gulped air like she was contracting in a vac-
uum. The looter had convulsed too, halfway through the
shattered window. Smoke had rolled in the sky, reflected
in the murky walls of the bulkier domiciles. Somewhere
distant an explosion rumbled toward them. Kate's eyes
jerked, unseeing, the pupils wide as though they were
gasping in light like her lungs were choking for air. Her
eyes spasmed and she couldn't breathe, couldn't cope,
and her fingers clawed at her head as she—

—flow of information is smotheringly, com-
fortingly absolute again. Fuck. My GABAlevels
dropped massively & all the stats point to the
echoingretreat of a seizure, I nearly had a seizure, & what the hell just happened? Tom? *Are
you there?* I don't know, he chat-gasps. Hisfear
floods me so I filter him, tone his levels down,
send a panic-burst back at him, pureinstinct
that I apologize for as soon as I can stop it. It
felt like theFeed went, he says. Didn't it? Kate,
are you okay? Yes, I chat-gasp too. Ask your
father what the hell just happened, but Tom's
already saying, He's not online; he's just . . .
looking at the carnage, he's on the homeHub

but he won't reply & Mum's still blocking me, & Tom says, Kate, I'm with you, I'm nearly there, & there he is, his face all compacted and serious as he turns the corner, as the glittering-fragments of the shopwindow cascade across the road, nearly all fallen now, the looter spar-kling amid them, & I tell Tom I love him, & he says, I'm here, I'm with you, we're going to be okay. I drop into my deserted pool [*What-WouldYouSacrifice?*] & spray quickly ". . . to save the world?" I don't expect anyone to vote (there are only 2people here; 3months & where are the 200million?) & I don't have time to think of pollquestions so I leave a commentsec-tion blank & I tell Tom we have to escape the city *now,* for the baby & for us, that if his par-ents aren't replying we have to save ourselves, & he knows I'm right. It'll break his heart, I know it will. My aunt's place, maybe, if we can't get a flight out, &— Martha screams at me to get out, get out, get out of there, Kate, her howling knocking out the bandwidth in my brain, that powerstation has— But it's not her—it— What was— Panic in Tom's eyes, his slate gray— No, theFeed can't— Because Mar-tha, Tom, I—

—Her muscles had stopped. She had dropped. Everyone had, that moment. Smoke rose, rolled and folded into the sky. Impacts, distant detonations, reverberated off the buildings through the stilled and wind-blown streets. Birds had sprayed upward. Dogs froze and then fled. Machines hurtled from the sky, tearing the air, brick- and glasswork spraying. A massive explosion sent tremors through the ground, sucked the windows out of walls; even the strengthened glass from domiciles disintegrated. A midnight flash ripped across the sky. And under the booms a deeper noise: as more things stopped, as more things crashed, the approaching sound of silence.

Night had come early as clouds of noxious smoke flooded from the east. Birds landed. Dogs nosed the fallen, still-lying bodies. Minutes, hours later, Kate had stirred in the cooling, unforgiving air. The silence was more immense than any noise, deeper than her own groans. Similar bestial sounds came from near her. Tom, facedown, bled from a cut on his brow. Something white and sticky congealed around his mouth. She crawled toward him. Life cauterized around her. How long it took. How achingly slow. That was all. Scratchy filth scraped inside her brain. Inside her head she was alone. The Feed was gone. Tom was beneath her. She could see his face, shadowed in the light of the moon. But she couldn't know his thoughts. She had fancied she felt her baby's thoughts, fluttering amid her own, but no: there was nothing in her mind but herself.

Rain drills onto the roof, the windscreen smothered by a moving sheet of water through which only darkness lies. First one clouded breath then others burst from her mouth. Kate shivers and cannot sleep. She hasn't felt the wrench of panic like this, this poisonous plunging grief, since the Feed went down: the panic of loss, of unsolvable loss and separation, the raw, incurable desperation to be reunited. Images flash in impulsive bursts. That looter. Rivers of wrecked cars. Crushed corpses by the road. Digital scuzzing fuzz as things interfered with the Feed. Smoke and wind. Danny's ripped throat. The warmth of blood on her hands. Bea, Bea, when she had seen her last, as they had hugged and the girl had dashed away across the lawn to the children's hut, the imprint of her short-armed cuddle across Kate's shoulders, that moment pulling away, adrift and lost forever.

The cold is getting to her bones.

She hasn't been in a car for years, can't remember the last time she drove one, or when she'd last moved quicker than her own legs can go. How her legs hurt now, from running. She'd made Tom get rid of their car, back in the days when it mattered, when the world had needed them to make some sacrifice. *When the world had needed them.* She laughs. *As if it ever had.*

She can't make out any movement outside. The dogs had stopped prowling when the rain became too heavy, their pelts too saturated to take on more. She touches her leg and pulls back instantly, tacky blood inside her damp jeans. The barking, the snapping jaws, the heavy furry mass pummeling her, sideswipes through her thoughts. Her hands shake unstoppably. The dogs? They're gone now. She crumples forward. Tom's gone too. He has left her. His face, looking back through the smoke, had been expressionless before he ran. She smothers the T-shirt to her face and cries. It had been one of the unthinkingly few things she had grabbed two panic-fragmented days before. She can smell Bea on the weave. She slumps. She sleeps. She mustn't. She jerks awake at every sound, at no sound at all, at her ceaseless thoughts, her pulse racing, her bitten leg throbbing all the time.

Early dawn comes with the jolt of waking from a threadbare sleep, her heart pounding like it hasn't since she lost the Feed. Shards of images cascade once more. Memories spurt as her brain knows she's panicking and throws up reasons why. Peace destroyed as she re-members again— *No.* She pushes her thumbs into her eyes, forcing the instinctive muscles still. There they go, there they flex, as she looks for Tom to panic-nudge him on the Feed, to find his GPSloc, to zoom on where he is. She can't. Looks. Fixes. Looks for Martha. She tries to connect with Bea even though Bea was never enabled, they've never been entwined like that.

Having lost sense of time, she becomes aware of the real: the seat's old springs push into her back, and there are straw-colored eyes close to the window beneath pointed ears. Steam spreads around her fingertip and the dog licks the glass. She removes some old bread from her bag and forces herself to chew it. Then she winds the window down and the dog gulps a chunk, then pants for more, dancing on its feet in the drizzle.

"You're out of luck," she murmurs, and its ears go flat.

The dog is still outside. It watches her, blinking in the light rain. Is it one of the pack that attacked her, or a lone one? It's impossible to tell. The lesion on her leg is tender, the skin stretching around the tooth marks, bruising red and green. So stupid! She hadn't left the camp in so long, she'd forgotten the ways: to freeze, to throw stones, to make herself look big. She washes the wound with water from the roof. With luck it wasn't rabid, whichever dog it had been. They all look the same. From nowhere, she misses Rafa.

Metal protesting, the door hinges grate her exhausted ears. The dog stays where it is, sprawled beneath a bush, its jowls spilling over the tarmac. Flickers of memory, after-images, ghost her sight—filthy canines, fire, the woods as she ran up the track—but here, two days' panicked run from the camp, it is absolutely silent. Hills line the distance. Early mist rises to meet the clouds. Dark trees, beyond it, covering the land. By the time she looks back, the dog is approaching.

"Stay back!" she shouts, and it stops. Nostrils warp and suck the air. It comes forward again. "Stay *back!*" Kate brings the rock from her jacket, puffs up her chest, and stretches her arm to throw. The dog's ears droop, its tail drops, it growls but back-walks away. She pushes herself off the car and starts up the road, leaving a bit more bread behind. The dog watches, sits up, and then trots to follow, pausing very briefly to swallow it.

That night she hides in another car. She sleeps. Barely. Tries to stop herself. Exhaustion crowds her sight. She mustn't sleep unwatched. If she's taken now, what will happen to Bea? The intruder wouldn't care. Would it even know? She wakes with the eviscerating realization of where she is, of what's happened to Bea, and what Tom did, and her head lurches, an absence, a vomitous instinct that fuzzes her sight and has her stumbling from the rust-coated car, barely seeing the things she passes as she struggles toward the only place she can think to go. She skids on something bloody. A carcass. That dog, she sees through her startled, staring eyes, lies nonchalantly back up the hill. Although its ears prick up, it steadfastly doesn't quite look at her.

"Thanks," she calls, and stumbles away with the dangling thing.

When the road bends and she's hidden by a hedge, she hurls the dead animal away. She wants to run. She has to find Bea. She needs to rest. She mustn't sleep. She runs.

She reaches a village as the first distant thunder rolls. A pack of dogs clusters in the road, nosing large dry bones. She pushes the map back into her rucksack and climbs the fences between overgrown gardens until she finds another way in, passing houses whose walls have tumbled, whose roofs have collapsed. There is a park and a playground and a church. The dusty silence in the dirt-covered streets. The broken windows and fire-blackened roads. She sees a stroller, ripped and decayed, and little bones beside it, one round like a doll's head. Fizzing and sparking, memories and Feed reflexes swarming in, this is all too much for her brain.

Clouds choke the sky like smoke by the time she finds a safe-looking barn with empty pens inside. As she hears the first heavy raindrops fall, she lobs her rucksack into a hay stall and climbs up after it. Soon rain thrashes the roof in a darkness that swims through her poisonous irresistible dreams, and slowly she realizes she isn't alone. There is breathing in the darkness, and when she opens her eyes a face is next to hers. Even though she screams, the dog doesn't move; it keeps its paws on the shelf and pants smelly hotness at her. As another roll of thunder bears down on the barn, it barks and whines and then, as more thunder roars, scrabbles to get up. She lowers herself onto her injured shin and helps it scramble onto the shelf. By the time she has climbed back up, the dog is a big ball of fur and ears and takes up most of the space with its shivering, quaking pelt.

"You better not snore," Kate whispers, and lies down beside it. She wonders whether she could train it to watch her while she sleeps. She's sure it could kill her if it chose to. But she likes the sound the dog makes as it dreams, its hushing snorts, and the weight of it lying beside her. She used to let Rafa sleep on their bed. It had driven Tom totally mad.

There had been someone lurking in her head once. She had woken one day from a sweaty, fevered dream and been absolutely sure: an unshakable sense that, for a time while she had slept, she hadn't been alone. Someone had been amid her dreams. Tom had been sitting beside the bed—they'd been ordered to watch each other sleep. Ben's vid had gone into every Feed. Everyone had been forced to watch it. The Collapse had been building. Everyone could feel it, like birds sensing a storm. Paranoia lived in people's eyes. No one could be trusted. Everyone looked exhausted, most trying not to sleep. Everything wound tightly. Something would have to snap. Southampton had gone down, her parents lost in oblivion, and that was one lost city among many. Martha had been trying to make her leave. But they had stayed. There in the tower, in the bedroom they'd made their home, they'd felt safe, hermetically sealed from the world. She had been shocked by how hard self-preservation had gripped her. She would caress the baby through her own skin and press her forehead to the thick windows and look down. The traffic had not moved for days. Occasionally someone tried to mount other vehicles or smash things out of the way. Fighting was constant. *Kill first* was the thinking, because at least you'd still be alive.

Who was doing this to them? And *why?* Their lives had been paper-thin. Smoke leaked up from the estuary like ink in water. Drifts, not of smoke but obscurity, were also swallowing the Feed: pools blocked by the company or the government (it was now difficult to tell them apart), information closed off and all privacy settings rescinded as they trawled desperately to locate the intruders. At night the clouds reflected fire from all around, the colors of blood and ink. Sucking up the smoke, they had congealed and densified above like the crushing panic in her brain, her brain that, one morning, had been touched.

"It's me," she had said from the bed when she woke that time, when there had been someone in her head.

Tom had nearly laughed—he didn't know what had happened yet—and he'd rubbed her hair as she'd frowned. Held her stomach, increasingly baby full. They had gone through their questions, as the new protocols demanded: What's your name? *Kate.* Mine? *Tom.* How did I propose to you? *With a ring, in an apple, on a hill.* Yes, it's you . . .

It had taken time to persuade Tom, but she'd been adamant. They had waited until his parents were out, at a meeting with the government. Entire cities had gone offline that morning. She had persuaded Tom up to his father's study, to access their homeHub. As she had watched, he'd gone through her BackUps. He'd been lost in her mind, looking for those moments in her dreams when she'd been sure that someone had invaded her.

Empty windows stare at her. The wind stirs up phantom movements. Her shallowest breath is deafening in this silence. The soles of her boots have aged since she wore them last, when they had escaped the city and she had been pregnant with Bea. Although cracks run through the rubber now like the cracks running through the roads, somehow everything feels the same: her pounding heart; her thoughts shorting out; seismic terror tearing up through the veneer her safe-feeling life has been; the poisoning doubt that Tom is really Tom. What's missing now is his capacity for hope. It had gotten them through before; it had raised her spirits higher than she could have achieved alone. But his hope had more stamina than hers. They saw the world so differently. And now here she is, alone.

The dog's paws pad beside her, light and ready. It seems they're now a team.

Bea's abduction hits her in the stomach harder than anything physical ever could. She would sacrifice anything for her daughter in that moment: her own life, Tom's, the entire planet; she'd give them away to get Bea.

She runs, on and on, the dog at her feet, checking the map at junctions. That afternoon she sees it in the near distance: the storage facility, squat amid the hills. Where else could Bea be? Who else could have known about the camp? They spend the night in a truck that has lain on its side so long its metal has rusted to the road. Its thin walls are being eaten away by time, but its stronger framework stands for now. She builds a small fire, taking her time with a lighter running low, while the dog disappears. It brings back an animal, still twitching in its jaws. Kate flays and then partly burns it, feeding the dog scraps of cindered flesh and throwing most of hers away when it isn't looking.

A truck blocks the gate, a dark lump of metal beneath the dust-dirtied transparent curl. It has been driven hard up against the gateposts. Its cabin has been torched and the fabric of the seats burned. The mirrors are melted, elongated and frozen. The glass is cracked and smoked from the inside, and bales of barbed wire have been rammed in. She shucks off her rucksack and goes under. The dog, sphinxlike, shifts after her. The sun is hot and the day peaceful: the type of day that waits for a noise, but no noises come. They circle the facility, keeping behind the tree line. Where the undergrowth thins out, they wait. She sees no people, no movement, nothing. She is dizzy with hunger, with the constant contraction in her stomach, but she won't ever stop. She walks. She climbs. She stumbles through the heat. She tries to imagine what Bea is feeling, to picture where she's being kept, but that way hideous images lie and they suffocate her mind. She tries to understand why Tom ran, what possessed him to leave her; she tries to structure her memories to work out how she's now alone. She tries to clear her mind of thoughts that will not be escaped.

The sun-smacked tarmac of the forecourt expands before her, a heat haze shimmering. Rusted fire escapes entwine the building. Dark watermarks color the walls. Kate holds Bea's T-shirt tightly in her hand; she has made the dog smell it, as if that will help. She smells it again herself and there Bea is, realer than real: frizzed hair, flushing cheeks, a glinting concentration in her eyes. Kate's stomach lurches and chips of tarmac fly, peppering her legs, before she even hears the shot. The dog barks up at the windows. Another bullet impacts at its paws and Kate runs without thinking in front of it with her arms wide as a third shot rings out and they dash behind a cabin together, the dog's eyes as huge as hers. It nestles closely between her legs, whimpering, as they inch along the wall.

A hand grips Kate's face. Someone flips her to the ground. Her head resounding with the dog's barks, her vision warps and a man shouts and scuffles fly around her head and there's a smack and a howl and the thump of a gun and the weight of a pelt as it lands beside her. Kate is hauled up and pushed at gunpoint through a shuttered door. Someone wrestles her rucksack off, and as her head snaps back, she glimpses the dog's corpse behind them. After rattling along a network of barely lit corridors, they emerge into an atrium, a pyramid of dirt-streaked glass with a cracked green marble floor. The doors have been smashed and metal grilles forced in their place. The original fake plants are still in their beds, and here she sees her captors. Hunger-carved faces. Skin tight to the bone.

"The fuck do you want?" one of them rasps. He has a V cut from his lip. His cheeks sag to the sides and, even with his mouth closed, Kate can see his browning teeth.

"Nothing."

"Then why you here?"

"I'm passing through."

"Where you from?"

"Why?"

"Because I'll fucking kill you if you don't tell!"

Kate chews her lips and looks into the surprisingly

hazel eyes straining beneath his bald head. "I'm going north."

He stands in front of her, hands on his hips, the butt of a blade protruding from his belt. He glances at a woman with a still, pinched face and sharply bobbed dark hair before turning back to Kate. "Where you *from*, tricksy? You taken?"

"My camp was destroyed. I'm going north. No."

As the man circles her, she sees the woman thrust her hands into her rucksack. A sweater. Her hat. Bea's T-shirt is thrown to the floor. Her food. The map. She is shoved and her head jerked back.

The man's loose lip flaps as he wheezes out on a breath of decay: "*Why?*"

"Because my family's dead, so what else can I do?" she spits with more venom than she has.

The man stays close, his breath whistling, his eyes searching hers. Arched back like this, her heart cracking her ribs, all she can see is the upward space of the atrium, the massive cobwebs across the moss-covered glass. Still holding her twisted backward, the man turns to the woman with her hands in her bag. "Anything?"

"No."

"Lock her in the storage room," he wheezes, and throws her sprawling to the floor.

She has been in the dark for a long time now, in a place of self-denied sleep. She mustn't sleep; she mustn't. She scratches the wound on her leg to stay awake with pain. Is it exhaustion, hunger, or fear that makes her imagine things? As a child, make-believe ghosted her life. She had written her parents stories and sketched out accompanying art. She never drew well, but words she could wield, and she lived for her parents' praise; they soon learned not to comment on the pictures. Martha had been the one encouraged to draw, and together they had made little books. Their parents had been teachers of art, made redundant by the Feed in a changing world, yet determined not to be changed by it.

Kate crawls to the moldy pipes now, her boundaries lost in the darkness of the room, and puts her ear to the ducts. She can hear the children in her head but not through her ears. She imagines ghost sounds like the ghost images of what might be happening to them that she tries to banish from her brain. Pain and panic engulf her. On the pulse of a heartbeat she is jerked back to another dark night, six long years ago. Everyone else had been cleared from the farmhouse apart from Graham and Jane. They were the only ones with a chance of having any idea what to do. She and Tom had reached the house a week before, trudging the last of the road-frosted miles, their heads cavernous with silence. The world had quieted. Who knew how many had died in those months? Who had known how *long* it takes people to starve? Weeks of lying gasping on the ground. The horror of the world. People stunned, most to death straightaway, others enough to be easy prey. And no help coming—no people, no apps, no systems. Time to face facts: the world wasn't rooting for them either.

She had found Tom. She had gotten them from the city, driven by the life within her: their baby growing inside. Their speech was malformed, their instincts animalized, because being attacked was now the norm. Tom's hope had gotten them through—her drive and Tom's hope. The farmhouse had been her aunt's, but they had found others there. Social obligations had died with the world, but the people there were kind. They made Kate comfortable as the contractions started and she was engulfed in panic. Gone was the data, the previously detailed experience of her life: the metrics that told her precisely what was happening to her body and kept her updated on the baby's progress and her own. The structure of information that had withheld fear and raised her above animals shattered as roaring pain burned through her body and opened her up in a damp room in the darkness of the countryside with two old people valiantly doing their terrified best while Tom backed away, horrified at the sounds and the incredible smell that saturated the room. No vids. No info to gulp on. No mundles to stream her to relaxing times. Only fear and pain and panic, and then exhilaration that pounded her heart as it pounds her heart again in imprinted memory of that time as she feels once more the weight of her baby as Bea was passed up, slick and screaming, into her arms. She remembers the tug and stretch before the cord was torn and they were parted. Parted but never closer. Never stronger. Never more bonded by anything so pure, by love burning through fear, the strongest substance in the world.

Then.

Not now.

Now Kate's limbs shake with too much emotion for her body to process, and she retches at the floor. Bea is gone. What might be happening to her daughter courses through her mind. She stays on the ground, trying to stifle the thoughts until the lock snaps, the door opens, and candlelight comes cupped in a hand. The woman's up-lit hair makes dagger-sharp shadows on the walls. Her voice is surprisingly warm, but tired, the edges worn away. "Why did you come here?"

"I told you," Kate gasps. "I'm traveling north."

The woman puts a bowl of chunks of things in a congealed stew on the floor.

"Wait!" Kate heaves in a desperate breath. "I'm so tired!"

"So sleep."

"Don't you still watch each other?"

The woman glances into the large room outside before, sighing, she pulls down a rug. She folds the musty thing over Kate, then squats on a box, drawing a hammer from her waistband and laying it on her thigh. "Sleep then, tricksy. I'll take care of you."

Kate wakes with a gasp from a dream that was sucking her down from the top of the tower through a burned-out world into a chasm that was opening in her brain. The woman is no longer there. The faint glow of candlelight touches the half-open door and she hears retching in the distance. A tired sound. But, rested at last, she feels alert and awake. Does she have time to run? To search the place, to find the children and escape? She crawls to the doorway. There are tables covered in tech. Then candlelight licks her face and she hurriedly lies back down. Exhaling, the woman sits on the box and wipes her mouth. She puts hands to her stomach and manipulates it, then squeezes her eyes tight shut and, unknowingly watched, shakes silently with tears.

"Get up, tricksy!" the man with the cloven face croaks. "Get the *fuck* up."

Kate stumbles as they ricochet through the maze of corridors. The sun has risen, the tar-smeared glass coloring the day like smudges of a desert dream. They squeeze into a breeze-blocked room with smashed windows and a sharp wind, where the split-lipped man drags her to one side. High above the forecourt, he thrusts a rifle's snout into a crook and forces her head down to the scope.

"Can you see them?"

The circular sight blurs over the ground as she scans and catches a man in the crosshairs. He has gray skin and short curly hair. He wears a frayed sweater and his bruised face is up, briefly, toward the sky. He is talking. It is Mark.

"I see one."

"Do you know him?"

"No."

She moves, blurring the ground again, and catches a leg, an elbow, then locks on someone else. Hands in his pockets, his head bent, listening to Mark. It's Tom. He looks up at the facility, unknowingly at her, with her finger on the trigger as he looms large in the scope.

"Can you see the other one?"

"Yes."

"Do you know him?"

"No!"

But she knows he abandoned her. She knows he separated them. She knows that's not how he should behave. Is it really him? Her finger tightens around the trigger, but the man wrenches the rifle away and brings it up to bear, elbowing her aside. The gun recoils and he squints back through the scope and fires three more rounds, each shot impacting Kate's ears.

"Are we done here, Nigel?" The woman has to shout to be heard.

"Yeah," Nigel spits back. "Get rid of her."

Kate's vision still has the silhouette of the scope, the center of her sight a circle scored by crosshairs, as the woman drags her from the room.

"What's happening?" she yells as the gunfire echoes after them.

"We were raided," the woman pants as they run. "They got inside and killed someone." She heaves doors open and trips down some stairs. "Then there was another group. Two days ago. Ram raid. Then you. Now this. What the hell . . . You were lucky *you* weren't shot," she adds as they reach the big room. "But we have rules. We still vote. Though now there's just us two."

Kate breathes heavily by the door to her prison.

"Then thank you. It sounds like I'm alive because of you." She puts her hand out. "Kate."

The woman grasps it. "Margaret."

"And those two men? Did he shoot them?"

Margaret's voice lowers. "I don't know. Nigel is . . . stressed." She forces Kate back into the shadows of the storage room and locks the door behind her.

After an unmeasurable time in darkness, the door is wrenched open and Mark and Tom are pushed in. "We're not here to hurt you!" Mark exclaims, bouncing back toward Nigel's silhouette, while Tom stiffly rights himself.

"Shut the *fuck up*, the lot of you!" Nigel spits.

"Wait," Mark appeals. "Let me tell you a story—"

The door is shut in his face.

"Ow!" Mark kicks something in the darkness. "Shit. Hold on, Tom."

A glow fills the room as Mark shakes a lamp, solar-powered and compact. He looks up at the shelves, at the boxes. He slowly moves the light around and then cries out.

"Welcome to the cupboard," Kate says, and sees Tom's hand lower, revealing a thin leak of blood from his nose. So he recognizes her. She's conflicted. Relief.

Anger. Fear. Is it him? Surely. Either way, the others mustn't know they're acquainted. "I'm Kate," she continues quickly, extending her hand toward Mark. "*They're probably listening, aren't they,* but what's the harm in introductions? My name is Kate. Who are you? Where are you from?"

"Oh. *Mark,*" he says, and winks exaggeratedly at her. "Nice to meet you, Kate. I'm from Loxburgh. You?"

Tom's hand falls heavily on her shoulder. His eyes are hollow, like he hasn't slept for days. She has never seen him so dimmed. "Kate," he whispers. So, there . . . it *is* him . . . surely? "How long have you been here?"

"A night. Did they hurt you?"

"They were a tough crowd," Mark concedes, interrupting them, and she turns reluctantly back his way.

"Do people always try to kill you on sight, Mark?"

"I am, I admit, having a bad streak. But I think this lot are more scared than vicious. I don't think the children are here, Tom. I think it's the others. The spiky van gang. We're kindred spirits," Mark explains to her loudly for anyone listening in. "Sworn to wander the world together in search of stolen children."

Tom's voice is hushed and urgent as he takes her to one side. "Mark managed to escape from the farmhouse. Sean tied him up."

"That's a very unromantic way of describing it."

"Just talk *quieter,* Mark," Tom snaps. "Like Kate told you to."

"I escaped against all odds so I could help you in your plight!" Mark faux whispers.

"Sean beat him to a pulp but he managed to sneak away."

Beneath his bruises and the shadows of the storeroom, Mark pulls a hurt expression. "Tom, you have to set these stories up better if we're going to work as a double act."

"There's a difference between telling tales and lying!" Tom hisses.

"Oh, come on, a little embellishment never hurt anyone! A sympathetic exaggeration of some facts, the considered exclusion of others. It's entertainment!"

"I told him I wanted to travel alone," Tom whispers fiercely to Kate.

"No one wants to travel alone," Mark counters quietly, and turns back to Kate, talking exaggeratedly loudly again for the benefit of any eavesdroppers. "And you? How did you get here? Was it *Kate,* you said? Have you been traveling alone? Who's been watching you sleep?"

Deeper exhaustion than she has ever known overwhelms her. Feeling so alone. Even a sudden flash of pain as she stumbles on her bad leg fails to energize her. It's all too much and she lowers herself to her rug.

"You know what, Mark?" she says. "Not all stories are for sharing."

Mark snores gently, bathed in the sterile glow of the solar lamp. Tom points, his eyes catching the light in the darkness, and she nods. Lifts the blanket and rolls out as he tiptoes toward the door. She has barely stopped beside him before he tries to kiss her. When he tries again, she slaps his hands away and they freeze at the sound, glancing at Mark lying unconscious on the floor.

"No. Tom, don't . . ."

"What's the—"

"What do you *think* the matter is?" Kate's voice is quiet but her consonants are hard. Her eyes are hardening too, despite the tiredness that loosens her cheeks. "You separated us, Tom. We agreed and agreed and *agreed.* I had *no* idea where you were going, *no* way of finding you."

"I thought you'd stay at the camp. I'd have come back for you—"

"With Bea missing? You thought I'd *stay*?" Her

whispers slice through the darkness, and when his hands come toward her she hits them away again. "You live in a fantasy world, Tom! We *never* split up!" she hisses. "There is no way of finding people. There is only getting lost. You do *not* do that to us. Why—did—you—do it?"

In the end, after searching for words, "To get Bea" is all he has.

Her face folds into her hands. She heaves sobs, trying to keep them silent while tears flood from her eyes. When Tom's arms enclose her, she doesn't resist: she feels him judder as he weeps.

"Is she here, Tom? Are these the people you saw?"

"I saw that woman," he whispers between tears, "but I don't know if they took Bea. It might be them. Revenge for the man Graham killed? It might be those others just as well."

She grips his jacket until her knuckles shake. "Do you trust Mark? Is he with them?"

"They hit him hard."

"They hit everyone hard. But maybe he's taken."

"Kate," he says, brushing her hair back. "Are you okay?"

Her expression locks. "What the *fuck* do you think?"

"We'll find her, Kate," he mumbles, after flinching. "If she's not here, we'll escape and keep looking. We need to befriend these people. Let's keep pretending we don't know each other. They'll get spooked otherwise. Just don't lose hope, Kate. We'll find her."

In the darkness, time loses sense, but at some point they are ordered, blinking, into the room outside. Kate notices Tom look around it as they emerge, particularly at a rectangle of floor where the stained carpet has been removed. She watches him blanch before seeing that three chairs have been arranged, in front of which Nigel and Margaret sit, armed.

"Sit," Nigel rasps, pointing his gun at the chairs, and they do.

"Why did you come here?" Margaret demands.

When none of them speaks, Nigel leans forward. "You know, your lives are paused. Since you were in my sights—you on borrowed time."

Mark laughs. "And I just thought that you were a terrible shot."

Kate turns to him. Tom stares at him. Everyone looks at Mark until he rubs his hair and examines the cuffs on his sweater, intent suddenly on their frays.

"Why you here?" Nigel wheezes after a while, like he's pleading for an answer, and Kate watches him and Margaret as Tom speaks, gauging them, intent on his every twitch, on every flicker around her eyes. Here they are if she can interpret them: the clues she has been waiting for.

"I'm looking for children," Tom says. "They were stolen. I was told to come here to find them."

"Here?"

Tom nods meaningfully and Nigel glances at Margaret, who frowns. "Who told you to come here?" Margaret asks. "For *children*?"

"A man I met said you lot would know what's happened to them."

Margaret's face is pained. "Your children?"

Kate carefully observes it all as Tom shakes his head, lying. "A friend's."

"Well, I'm sorry," Margaret says. "We keep ourselves to ourselves. It's a—"

"You?" Nigel demands of Mark.

"I'm keeping this guy company."

"And you never met *her*?" Nigel spits as he leans back into his chair and jabs his finger.

Mark looks back and forth between Kate and Nigel. "God's truth," he says. "We've never met her before. I thought she was a ghost. I saw one once, this would have been back in, oh—"

"Get out, then," Nigel interrupts. He glances at Margaret and then continues, his face seething while something softens hers with relief. "Go, get out. I don't give a shit. But if you turn, if you stop for a second, I'll shoot you." He points at Mark. "You most."

"Well, hold on!" Mark replies. "Maybe I don't want to leave!" He puts a hand to his chest. "My name is Mark, and I offer you no threat. I will take nothing from you. I will give you, however, stories. I travel from place to place, listening, remembering, and telling what I know. To keep the tales true, to preserve them, and let them live. If you find my stories acceptable, if you find them enjoyable, and you are so inclined, I would be happy to eat your food. I shall leave when finished, or before if you ask. This is what I do."

Nigel's face folds in on itself as he breathes laboriously. "A fucking storyteller," he gasps. "You can shut up. But you two? What're your skills? What knowledge you have?"

Mark claps Tom on the shoulder. "This man has one of the greatest skills of all. This man is a *fantastic* listener."

Nigel sighs. "Listen. You don't shut up, I'm going to fucking hurt you."

"But," Mark declares, "he also cooks up a storm! Just last night we were sitting in a field and I said I'd kill for a steak. Off he went, and not for very long, and when he got back, he told me not to look. I sat there while he did his stuff, and when he'd finished, there it was. Get it out," he tells Tom, and then turns back to the others. "There were leftovers."

Tom reaches into his rucksack and unfurls a package, revealing meat and potatoes.

"What is it?" Nigel whispers.

"I'd taste it first." Mark squats down and takes a piece. "It's good," he adds, and eats.

They are in the refectory, a long room with a chess-tiled floor, metal tables, and a kitchen partly obscured by a burnished old canteen. Kate sits with Margaret while things clatter in the kitchen.

"So how long have you two been here?"

Margaret looks down into her cup. "Years now."

"And where did you live before?"

"A village down the road." Margaret glances over Kate's shoulder before seeming to make a decision. "My boyfriend used to work here. That's why we originally came."

"Nigel's your boyfriend?" Kate tries to keep the surprise out of her voice. A sudden sizzling bursts from the kitchen and she looks back as Tom stirs something heavy. Cooking. One of his skills, apparently. When she turns back, Margaret is looking out the window and her mouth is tightly shut.

"Not Nigel?" Kate murmurs.

"He was shot in the raid. Killed for fuel." Margaret laughs bitterly.

"I'm . . . sorry." Kate sees Graham in her mind's eye, blood on his arms as he handed her baby to her. Face ashen as they sat on the grass and he told them about the man he shot. The way his hands had trembled.

"They both worked here. At the start, this place drew a lot of attention. A storage facility for the Feed? Come on. Not that anyone could make it work. It broke. They were desperate. But we got good at protecting it. Then . . ." A hand goes to Margaret's stomach and another to her throat. Her body buckles as she retches. "I don't know why I'm staying here anymore," she whispers after a while, glancing over Kate's shoulder. Although she smiles, the sadness stays in her eyes. "Maybe I should leave with you."

"I feel sorry for Tom's friend," Kate whispers, leaning forward. "Losing a child must be crushing. They're so innocent. The fear they feel must be so much more . . ." And then it hits her. Who needs the Feed to feel her daughter's fear? Who needs tech to empathize? She puts her finger and thumb to her eyes, but tears still leak out.

"Did you lose someone too?" Margaret reaches across the table. "A child?"

"Have you seen any?" Kate asks, her lips wet as she speaks.

"Children?"

Kate nods and wipes her nose.

"No. I haven't for years. Of everyone when the Feed went down, they were least able to cope. My daughter was . . . I wouldn't know . . ." Margaret glances at the kitchen, at Tom as he cooks, and her hands go again to her stomach. "Maybe his friend's children were in the van that tried to break in here. It was spiky and pulled by horses. The men were armed. They're sending a message like that, aren't they?"

Kate unclasps her fingers, waiting for Margaret to speak some more, feeling the sickest she has ever felt but close to something now, surely? This spiked van. Hope kindles in her stomach.

"We saw them coming up the road to the main gates, the ones you came through. They tried to move the truck first. If they'd opened it, they'd have seen it's full of concrete. Stupid fools. We took up positions. We'd already agreed to kill. That was not a difficult vote." She shivers. "And when the van stopped where the fence gets low, one of the men went to jump over and . . . we shot him." Margaret looks up at her. "I shot him . . ." She points between Kate's eyes. "They all started shooting. No thought. Like animals. But they went north after that."

"North where?"

Margaret shrugs, assessing her.

Kate puts on a smile. She really tries to make it look genuine, but she can feel it quivering. "And where the hell did you learn to shoot like that, Margaret?"

"Gaming."

Margaret's eyes are so sincere that Kate actually laughs for real, and the laugh is contagious. Soon they are both crying, mouths stretching, heaving for breath.

"Right, what's the joke?" Nigel yells, and Margaret quiets immediately.

Kate leans across the table again. "What did you do, Margaret? Before all this."

"I was a teacher."

"Me too."

"Augmented maths and VRT."

"English. For the little ones."

"It's a long time ago."

"A different world."

A hooting erupts from the kitchen, where Nigel, having tried whatever Tom is cooking, burns his mouth on a piece but swallows it nonetheless, and dances with joy at the flavor.

———————

They eat Tom's stew later. He won't tell her what the meat is, but she finds blond fur. She doesn't want to be near him. She wants to find Bea. Silence lies heavily on them as their cutlery clinks against the plates, the sound of slurping, chewing, and nothing else. The smoky candles reflect in the walls' white tiles, like the fire of some distant sun has been caught deep in the ceramic itself.

Once everyone is stuck in a satisfied stupor, Mark raises a finger. "The ancient Greeks had people like me. People who knew every story. They were like walking libraries. Remember libraries? We used to talk about primitive people, didn't we, but think what they had to do to survive. Catching things, cooking things, doing things that we in our technological excellence outsourced to machines and now have no knowledge how to do anymore. How many of you can even remember any stories? That's where I come in. So, who wants one?"

"Excuse me," Margaret says, and leaves the canteen.

"We don't need your stories here, I already told you that," Nigel says tiredly. He yawns and jabs a finger at Tom. "We want his cooking."

"In the camp I've come from," Tom tells them, "we

didn't let people tell stories about the past. The memories brought back too much pain."

"And that, my friend, is exactly what stories are for!" Mark proclaims. "The Greeks called it *catharsis*. The past is the past, but it's here to stay, that's kind of what they believed. All the emotions it caused have to be got rid of, so what we need to do is *talk*—"

"I'll make sure Margaret is okay," Kate says, and they shift to let her past. The unstoppable tune of Mark's voice follows her into the unlit corridor. She listens for other sounds. For children. The smell of damp has become an essence of this place. She feels the mold slide off the walls as she runs her fingers along them. In cavelike cold like this, the children would not survive for long. But what about that spiked van? Are they looking in the wrong place?

"Kate?" Margaret is silhouetted back by the canteen door. "Are you all right?"

"Sure." Kate can smell an acrid tang on Margaret's breath. "But I've had enough of stories."

"Come on, then."

She follows Margaret onto the tarmac at the front of the station, where the murky glass of the atrium dully reflects the stars. Like the fire in the canteen's tiles, it's like the glass holds the sky somehow, containing the galaxies above them. She hadn't been expecting it to be night.

"It's so quiet, isn't it?" Margaret remarks, hands on hips as she looks to the horizon.

"What happened to the man you shot?"

Margaret keeps breathing in the peaceful air. In the moonlight, the tarmac looks like a stretch of silvered sand. She tilts her head and takes her time to evaluate Kate. Then she grunts, a small noise, as if she has made up her mind about something.

The following morning, with a uniform cloud across the sky, Kate walks beside Margaret toward the perimeter fence. Tom and Mark erect a ladder, and some dogs sprawling in the grass on the other side prick their ears. A lump of something sodden lies amid them, and when Nigel shoots at them, they bark. He shoots closer and they curve away, sandy streaks against the green.

Parts of the man are less than a smear. Elsewhere, bones stick through the flesh. A hand with a cuff of skin lies to one side. The chest has been stripped, the stomach excavated. The blast had removed the top of his head and the soft innards are gone, tongue marks inside the skull, yet his lower face, although grayskinned, looks strangely serene. His chin is stubbledark.

"We think they're from the north," Nigel grunts. "They always use the same road."

"And did you actually see children?" Tom's voice is steady.

"No," Nigel concedes.

"But maybe there were?"

Nigel doesn't move. His mouth contorts, his split lip sagging to the sides. "They weren't good people," he grunts. "So I hope there weren't."

They don't stay out there for long. The dogs become too bold too quickly, edging back toward them and starting to snarl. Pausing to catch her breath, her head swimming, Kate lets the others go ahead, but Tom falls back.

"Kate, we have to talk."

"No, we don't."

"Are you avoiding me?"

"Just carrying on what you started."

"I wanted to find Bea!"

Mark and Nigel climb the fence ahead, but Margaret waits for Kate, watching.

"We need to get after this van," Tom mutters. "It's the same one I saw, the one with all the spikes. We'll leave tomorrow." At her continued silence, his voice rises in pitch. "Kate, can you at least tell me what happened to the others? Is Danny okay?"

She shakes her hands out and, when they reach the ladder, stops beside Margaret. Gestures Tom up first. Then she follows Margaret, feeling suddenly nauseated. As she climbs over the top, she catches her leg on the fence. Only Margaret hears her gasp, and she doesn't mention it until they are back inside the building, in the atrium, alone, where she demands to see. The puncture wounds are now vividly colored. Lightning streaks of red craze outward and are surrounded by concentric bruising. Even Kate is shocked by the sight.

"Shit," Margaret assesses. "Is that painful?"

"Yes."

"Wait here."

Margaret works quickly when she returns, pulling a tube from her pocket and applying a cream that cools Kate's skin immediately.

"Ted told me about the medical stash. Nigel doesn't know I know. But this looks nasty, Kate."

"What's the cream?"

Margaret shows her the tube. It's crinkled and white with nothing but a quickcode. "Not much use without the Feed. It smells right, though. But you need to find a Pharmacist."

"They don't exist."

"Of course they do. But that type of knowledge is rare, not to mention the drugs, so it'll cost you," Margaret says. "What's a leg worth, though? You need to find a Pharmacist."

With that word, and the dusty dryness of the place, Kate is in the pharmacy of her youth, there with Martha while their mother talked to a man in a white lab coat. It was the earlier days of the Feed, and while some packaging was quickcoded, others still had colorful designs. The pharmacist stared through his spectacles at her and her memory warps to the last medic she had seen: in the tower, a physician peering at her, one of a horde of lab-coated drones who worked for Tom's father. The Collapse was imminent, she and Tom had been moved into the tower, and she was undergoing many tests. Checkups, Tom's father had said, and he'd apologized: he would have helped them before, if only they'd told him she was pregnant. If only he'd known. Why hadn't they said? And again, that feeling of nausea, the morning sickness; she feels sick like that at the more recent memory of the acrid tang on Margaret's breath as the real world and the dusty atrium swim back around her.

"Ted was your boyfriend?"

Margaret's application of the cream slows slightly.

"Margaret, are you pregnant?"

Kneeling amid the dust and crystals of shattered glass, Margaret glances up. "I don't know."

"You have morning sickness, don't you?"

"What am I going to do?"

"Have you told Nigel?"

"What if he throws me out?"

"Why would he do that?"

Margaret pauses. "It's not part of his plan."

Kate looks away from Margaret at the smashed tiles across the floor, at the fake plant she is leaning against, its leaves smothered in dust. The fragments of glass in the children's hut flash into her mind, the grass covered in ash from the fires. The blood. The van, how she imagines it: hard and heavy with rusted spikes. The inside oven dry. Bea and Jack bound together, parched and bruised . . .

"Margaret. Children *have* to be part of the plan."

They stand in the still and empty atrium until Margaret rolls Kate's trouser leg back down and pushes the tube into her palm. "Take it with you tomorrow."

"What's happening tomorrow?"

"Tom said you'd go with them."

Kate looks at the tube in her hand, at her infected leg, at her worn-out boots and the trails she has made in the dust. If she doesn't go with Tom and Mark, where will she go?

"Kate . . . are they actually your kids? In the van. Yours and Tom's?"

Kate bites her lips, which are suddenly trembling as everything wells. Those tests, in the lab in the tower, with Tom always at her side. The scans of their healthy, moving baby were Fed straight into their brains. Hers and Tom's. Tom's father absorbed them too, and even he had smiled: the full and growing form of their daughter, sleeping in her stomach, filling their brains as the world outside collapsed to utter hell. Her daughter was safe then. When she'd had her inside her, she could keep her safe.

"There's enough room for you here," Margaret tells her, putting a hand on Kate's arm to try to stop her crying. "If you want to stay with us."

They stand on the forecourt as the sun clears the tree line and birds turn in the early-morning air. Kate and Mark wait with their rucksacks on, watching Tom search through his. "My gun," he says, and turns to Nigel, who shrugs. His mouth folds in on itself.

"Not yours."

Kate watches Tom eye Nigel up and down. The gun is there in his waistband. Tom lifts his rucksack on. He stands aside, his face flushing. Then Margaret, in front of everyone, hugs Kate. She whispers, "Find a Pharmacist, Kate. Please." Kate nods at her and looks at Margaret's stomach. The others are watching them.

Kate doesn't say anything, but Margaret nods too, though her expression does not change.

They walk for a long time in silence around the vehicles, across the fissures in the road. They cross a stream over a collapsing bridge and follow the road through a wood until the facility is the size of a fist behind them. They wait until Mark stops behind a bush, and as they continue, the sound of the man-high barley mutation swaying in the field is all there is to hear.

"You left us."

Tom thinks for a long time while the barley waves.

"You left *me,*" she states.

"But I was going to come back. I didn't *abandon* you."

"We promised."

"I'll never do it again. But, Kate, you've got to—"

"Don't . . ." She turns her head. "You have no right to tell me what to do."

"Kate, calm down. I thought I—"

"No you *didn't,*" she snaps. "You didn't think at all. Not about anyone but yourself." She scowls at him and then looks down at her feet. "What was our dog called, Tom?"

"Are you serious?" he tuts. "It's me, Kate. It's me."

Kate's expression darkens. "What was our dog called, then?"

"Rafa," he says, scowling too. "Thanks so much, that's really nice, Kate—"

"No, it's not, Tom! None of this is nice! From the fucking start! The way the world collapsed, what your father did to me, the way we've had to live. Living in fear every time I go to sleep. Every time *you* go to sleep, I'm terrified you won't wake up as yourself. The way you fucking ran away, *none* of this is fucking *nice!*"

Tom barely blinks. His voice sounds weary in its intonation: "Your sister was called Martha. Your parents were teachers and they hated me too."

"Oh, grow up."

When she turns away from him, the barley, the sunlight catching its tops, is tear-blurred. She feels so many things: relief and fear, desolation and hope. Tiredness too. Exhaustion. Something in her has leveled out. She had hoped with burning fervor that Bea was in the facility, because where else would she be? Now something is numbed because she wasn't there, but it's focused. On this van. They must find this van with spikes. The road stretches on ahead. This is the road that Nigel set them on, that he said those people used. She sees that the few vehicles on it have been barged to the side. She stares at the horizon, looking for the silhouette that she can clearly see in her imagination: a low-slung oval, metallic and hard, led by horses, covered in spikes, and black with the sun behind it.

There is nowhere for her to wash her wound that day or the next. They hurry on. Her skin chafes her as she marches, and Mark's constant talking chafes her too, texturing the air like pollen: a stream that smothers yet continues to evade, because no matter what he's asked, he is impervious to revealing himself. He hides behind his stories like smoke. He knew a man who changed his name. He knew a hairdresser who was bald. He misses the Feed, he loved the Feed; he segues and twists and hides.

They crest a hill and examine the road below them, heading always north. Nothing. Maybe—is that something? Kate grabs Tom's arm and points. A movement? Or just the reflection of the sun, sparking on something distant? Or nothing, nothing at all.

By the time they find a stream late the following day, salt stains Kate's top. She leaves Tom and Mark to set up camp by the road and carefully descends to the water. In squatting to dunk her clothes, the wound on her leg tears. The ragged slit leaks pus and a pinkish flow dribbles out. She washes it and squeezes cream into it and waits for the water on her skin and the ointment on her leg to dry before she pulls her clothes back on and climbs exhaustedly up to camp, trying to hide her limp.

Whether it is a noise or a dream that wakes her, it's gone the moment she stirs. Mark is lying on his side as he sleeps and Tom is . . . not there. Not watching them. She reaches over to wake Mark, but stops. How long can she leave him unwatched? How long would it take? In those vids it was only seconds. Mark breathes noisily, stuffed up, then gulps in some air and subsides again to peace. She crawls away before getting to her feet, reaching out into the darkness. With no light to see, her ears become sensitive: every clicking blade of grass; the branches of the trees getting nearer, knocking. Somewhere close by an animal skits away through the grass, gulping to itself. She waits for her pulse to calm and continues, wheezing Tom's name into the night, and as she nears the shadowy, hustling trees, she collides with a form on the ground.

Tom, lying in the grass, blinks back his dazed look.

"What the hell are you *doing*?"

"I came to look at the stars. Just for a moment. I must have fallen asleep."

She kicks him, actually kicks him, in the ribs.

"It was an accident!" he cries, pulling himself up. Something in his voice undermines her anger; there's a weakness about it. He peers up into the night and grasps her hand, and when he speaks again, his voice has weakened even more. "I don't think I could do it again, Kate."

"Tom." She closes her eyes. "You have to. Ben and Guy—you had to. You have to with me too. I have to with you. If you miss it, it's gone. And if we're taken, what will happen to Bea? How do you know I haven't just been taken?"

"Because you keep calling me Tom."

"Well, how do I know that *you* haven't been taken?"

"Because I know it's my name!" Evidently pleased with the functioning of his brain, he pulls her by the shoulder and she topples onto the ground.

"How do you know that we haven't both been taken and we're double-bluffing each other?" she says after a while.

He kisses her neck. "My name's Tom Hatfield. Our dog was called Rafa. I proposed to you with a ring pushed into an apple because they're your favorite fruit. Our daughter is Bea and we're going to find her, Kate. It's me. I'm not taken. And *all right*, I promise to watch you, so you better promise not to get taken.

Because now that I have you back, I'm never losing you again. Deal?"

She puts an arm around his shoulders. "Deal."

No people, little shelter, and hard days against a sudden rain that lances in from the west. It cools the air thoroughly and threatens to dash the leaves prematurely from the trees. No sign of the spiked van either, although they follow what they think are its tire tracks, and then they find horse manure, scant piles but fresh. It's like finding gold, and for a second they celebrate, before becoming steely, focused, following the tracks through the deluge.

"It's best to keep moving," Mark tells them, his voice raised against the drumming rain. "They won't be slowing down, I shouldn't think. We'll find somewhere warm for dinner."

"That's a long time yet," Tom mutters, and spits the rain off his lips.

"Not if we keep talking. Time flies."

When the rain gets even heavier, they are forced to shelter beneath the enveloping branches of a chestnut, its bark thick-notched, its roots rolling through the earth. They hug their arms to their saturated bodies in a vain attempt to keep warm. As they watch the slowly settling mist of rain, Kate glances at Mark. His lips are quivering, his eyes darting as he looks.

"Where are you going, Mark? What are you traveling for?"

He stares into the miasma, at the rain-ghosted trees as the drops prickle-smack around them. It seems he has ignored her and Kate turns away. But then, still staring at the rain, he says, "Because I've not found anywhere like home." She goes to probe, but he says the rain has lessened and makes them leave.

They walk and run at intervals, much faster than a laboring horse could travel. Tom reassures them regularly, driving them on, and points out the sporadic pats of manure, melting in the rain. They do find a warm place for dinner: an articulated truck, its front ripped and scattered away. Tom builds a fire in the mouth of the container and soon it's so hot that he and Mark take off their sweaters, roll up their trousers, and laugh as Mark pretends to tan.

Kate doesn't laugh and she keeps her trousers unrolled, wound hidden. There is no time to cause concern, no time for delay.

"It was late summer when it happened," Mark announces as the raindrops, slow and fat, fall in the mouth of the truck. "Do you remember?" Kate glances at him, at his bitten nails, and how his fingers shake, at odds with the keenness of his gaze. "Despite everything that was happening, at least we could say the weather was good! *Indian Summer.* And then the Feed collapsed and we were like cows. Our lives were so fragile and we didn't even know it. I didn't know what panic *meant* until then. But . . . listen . . . can you remember when you first *got* it?" His eyes gleam. "When you realized the power, as you first slid in, and the speed of the world it opened up? Who did you first share your thoughts with? It was the most intimate feeling, wasn't it? Nothing between you, no way to lie, just pure and perfect thinking. All of us, plaited together."

Kate watches Tom's back as he stares at the night. He can hear them, of course, but he's pretending not to. "I'd rather not think about it," she tells Mark. "It makes me upset."

"Yes." Mark sighs, sagging and rubbing his hands together. "Yes, I know."

Kate gives him a slip of a smile as she rests against the side of the container, actually sad to have curtailed his reminiscence for once. The spark in his eyes reminded her of the goodness of the Feed, the flow of it, the absorption. The precision of its knowledge. If they'd had it now, they'd already have found Bea. She could never have been taken if they'd had her enabled. Kate rests her hands on her leg and tries to hide the spasm of pain that makes her body jerk. Every day it's worse. Much worse. It's burning now. She is burning too. The fire crackles and she untucks her T-shirt, trying to get some cooling air onto her skin. Her eyes droop in the embalming silence.

"So here's a story," Mark purrs, jolting her out of her slumber. "There was a time when thoughts were in the air. They wrapped the world in color: busy blues, bloody-colored arguments, the peridot flash of joy. All plaited together, the web around the world." He leans back against the corrugated wall, the firelight scattering shadows over his face. "The patterns changed as thoughts did. In summer, vermilion swirls. Hard winter woven in darkness. The Water Wars created entirely new hues. Then the assassinations sparked violet in people's thoughts, and the shortages a deathly blue. Confusion coagulated and instability spread like some stain. And, you know, actual *thinking* stopped. We reacted to it like animals." Sparks fly into the darkness, drawn out on a plume of smoke. "When we discovered we were being invaded . . . that these assassinations were not accidental . . . well, the color of people's thoughts turned dark. The terminal velocity of a society, burning that web away. Paranoia. Unthinking fear. Inhuman things.

"So then: there was a man and a boy. The boy's

mother was gone, lost through frays that no one expected. But still, these two, the man and his son, were linked by thoughts of the liveliest living green. Every day the boy hid and the father hunted through the city's sudden ruins for food, but they were never apart, always linked at the speed of thought. Until the tapestry ripped. Like flesh tearing, everything was cleaved. The web of thoughts fragmented. People staggered, stopped, and crawled. The world on its knees when the Feed went down. When the man got home, it was empty. It may have taken him days or weeks, who knows? No boy. And the man can't remember the color of his son's eyes, let alone how he sounded anymore. It was all . . . too sweet . . . to store."

Mark has been talking quietly at his hands; now he surprises Kate by looking at her. "I'm better at telling stories about others. I hope you understand."

She gasps for air and comes quickly awake. Mark is squatting at her side, watching her, his hands out, close to her face, his fingers spread. "Kate?"

"Yes," she chokes out.

"Are you . . . sure? What's my name?"

"Mark," she says, sweat streaming down her back as she sits.

"And who's that sleeping there?"

She looks down at the sleeping body beside her, turned away, lying on his front. "That's Tom," she says. "Don't worry, Mark, it's me. It was just a dream."

"Some dream. What was it?"

She looks around, but not at what's there, fingering her clothes, pulling them away from her sweat-drenched skin to let some blessed coolness in. "I was in a tin. Burning hot. And . . . there were people there who I loved. My skin was scorching. Slowly it was dissolving away . . ."

Mark's eyes are soft with relief. He nudges her cheek with a knuckle before leaning back and making the wall of the container clang. "Welcome to the tin, Kate. Welcome to the tin."

She scrambles down from the truck. Leaning on its side and gulping from a bottle of collected rain, she tries to wash her dream away. She is very ill, she knows it. Her dream had merged with a fever dream she had before: she'd been weighted down and unable to move in a bed at the very top of the tower. The city was spread out below—she could glimpse it if she stretched—and Ben was there before her, although she knew he was dead. Tom's father crept around, but he was so, so sly she could never see him: whenever she turned, he wasn't there. She could feel his breath on her neck and the anticipation of his fingers, her swollen stomach lying prone. She could feel his soft, shuffling footsteps in her brain—

She rolls her trouser leg up. The veins around the wound are vividly colored and have now spread up to her knee. She can barely touch the flesh for the pain, and her hand is shaking wildly. A hard fever, taking hold. A gross infection. She wipes the sheen of sweat from her face, unscrews the cream lid with her teeth, and rubs the ointment thickly in, flinching as she does so.

She rubs it in continuously, discreetly, whenever she can as they walk the following day across a rain-stained overpass and down beside a reservoir, desperately trying to hide her limp. The surface of the water is weed-encrusted and swollen. Insects skit while crickets carve away. She holds the tube in her pocket, worrying at its half-empty form, worrying the horizon with her eyes, looking for the van, for tracks, for clues, for the van, they have to find the van before she . . .

"I was in advertising," Mark is telling Tom. Now that he has started talking about himself, he won't stop. "The Feed made anything possible. Quickcode adverts were a *dream*. But where are your consumers now?" he asks, gesturing at the world. "And that, ladies and gentlemen, is how most stories end: with silence. Folks just disappear. *Fin*. It's all horrifically unstructured."

At the end of the reservoir a signpost directs them toward a village, and while Tom pauses to peer inside a car, Kate and Mark walk on.

"Kate?" Mark asks, and there is something in his voice, in the way it lowers, and the way he glances over his shoulder. "I've woken a few times and Tom hasn't been watching us. Is he him?"

The starkness of the question brings her up short. Back to the world. The simplicity of how things can go very wrong. She looks back briefly. Tom passes a mossed-out coach, head down, and strides along the road toward them.

"Of course he is. I've asked our usual questions."

"Well, maybe ask him something deeper. I'm getting worried about him."

"So what can we ask *you* if we need to check?" she says tersely.

"Your names," Mark replies, "of course." Although he won't look at her, there's a softness now between them as he relents. "And my son's name was John. You know . . ." His voice is suddenly ragged with emotion. "I'll help you how I can, Kate. I'll help you find this spiky van. But I must say . . . You have to know how unlikely it is that . . . From my experience . . . people just . . ." He places his hands palm to palm, then he shakes his head and smiles at her. "I'll help you how I can."

They reach the village and walk through every street. Tom and Mark knock on doors while Kate scrutinizes the road debris for tracks, and in the end they shout, yelling at the silence, searching for anyone to ask. Their voices echo off rotten walls. The place is empty. Ghostly. There aren't even any bones. She falls behind. Pain courses so deeply into her thigh that it overwhelms her vision. She drops down to stop the nausea that consumes her and cries into her sleeve. With her eyes closed, the silence is such she could be anywhere—a farm, a valley, anywhere remote. But not a village. Not a place with houses and roads, where people should be, where—

"Kate."

She tries to stand but doesn't have the strength.

"Are you okay?"

Her head stays down but she raises a hand. She grits her teeth as Tom pulls her up, turns her face so he cannot see her cry. There's no time for her to slow them down. No time for weakness. Every minute, every second, something slips further away. She tries to hide her limp.

Some of the shops are shattered, others intact, their insides embalmed in darkness. Walking with her eyes closed, stumbling, some long-buried memory slips in: her final moments with the Feed. A bank of shops. A looter. A helicopter. Scintillating shards of glass. This little wormhole takes her back through another, knocked open by her fever dream, to when she'd first had it. She had woken and been convinced someone had been in her head. She'd *had* to know who. Tom had taken a lot of persuading but that morning she made him access the homeHub in his father's study. He'd riffled through her BackUps, her uploaded SaveYou states; he'd looked inside her mind. Recent, earlier versions of her, unfolding before his eyes. What she'd thought, how she'd felt, unfiltered; she was totally naked before him. It was the strangest and most wonderfully warming thing to see, knowing that he was inside her thoughts, sifting through her mind, and that she felt safe with him there. But when he came out, his eyes looked sunken.

"Yes," he had said. "He was in there. While you slept. My father came inside your Feed."

In the office at the tower's tip, they had been in the highest place in the city. Horror peopled the world below. Every day, more atrocities, paranoia; more people being taken or saying that their friend or parent, lover or child, had been and that was why they'd killed them. "*The demon eyes*," they said, "*I saw them.*" Their own eyes staring, twitching, looking around for the next threat, the next attack to resist. People they knew, people they didn't. People who may or may not have been taken. Who knew where truth ended and blended into fiction now? People killed. That was the only truth. They killed because they didn't want to die. But what Tom had just told her was more disturbing. His father had hacked inside her Feed? It was illegal and disgusting.

"But why?"

From his face, Tom evidently knew but was struggling to process the information. He had swallowed, then met her eyes. "He was analyzing the baby."

She takes Tom's hand tightly now as they pass a community hall with shuttered windows. Her other hand protects her stomach, the ghost of the shape it had been. The silence is so loud in this street, it's buzzing in her ears. A grotesque lurch hits her as Tom pushes open the hall's heavy door and a cloud of flies launches, battering off her face, borne on a stench that rolls thickly out. The buzzing is not the silence at all: it is from thousands of flies seething over countless human mounds. They crawl across the infection-smeared walls like moving paper. The stench invades her nose and blocks up her forehead. Her vision loosens and fades.

She comes to, minutes or hours or no time later, as Tom throws water in her face. She has been pulled away from the hall.

"You're all right. It's okay, Kate."

"Who's Sylene?"

Tom scowls. "Who?"

Kate buries her face in his chest, unsure with her head only half in the world whether the wetness is water or tears or sweat. "It's the fever dream," she gasps.

"Drink this."

"Tom, I'm worried."

"We'll find her."

"The cream's not working."

Leaning on the pavement, grasses growing up between the cracks around her, she rolls up the leg of her trousers and shows him the wound. Tom's face blanches.

"Kate. Why didn't you—"

"Margaret gave me this cream but it's not working. I feel very sick." Kate gives him the tube and puts a hand to her mouth, holding her breath. Tom grips it tightly, glancing blankly at the quickcode. Then he stares at her leg and the darkness spreading into her skin.

"Everything will be fine," he tells her, though his eyes say something else. "I promise, Kate. I promise."

"You're no use to Bea dead, Kate. You need to get to a Pharmacist!" Mark shouts at her again.

She is sweat-clammy. She has just been sick. Her trousers are rolled up in an attempt to dry her wound as they sit in the dewy morning just outside the village while Tom scavenges for food.

Mark stokes the fire vigorously. "That cream might buy you time but it won't stop the infection. Look at it, Kate, it's *horrific*! Why on earth didn't you *say* something? You *have* to find a Pharmacist!"

"They're a myth."

Mark shakes his head. "They're real."

"You would say that."

"I met one."

"You'd say that too," she mutters, and turns to look for Tom. "We can't delay finding Bea."

"I met him not too far from here." Mark makes a show of shivering. "But he has drugs and knowledge and you need his help. You don't want to delay finding Bea? Well, how would dying slow things down?"

"We have to find this van!"

Satisfied that the fire has taken, Mark settles on a log. "Kate. For fuck's sake, listen. The world is too big. Are we even on the right track? The nature of stories has changed: you can't willfully hope for a happy ending anymore. Look at me and John . . ." He pauses. Thinks. Decides something. "It's possible the Pharmacist would know about her. He's one of them, one of the taken. Or that's what he says, anyway."

They sit as the birds fly overhead and the clouds come in. Eventually a figure tops the hill.

"Here he is," Mark says, and Tom, in the distance, raises his hands. Mark rests a frying pan in the flames as Tom, his trouser legs wet with dew, drops mushrooms onto the ground.

"They're sneaky little buggers today. Must've heard me coming."

Mark looks up from the fire. "She needs a Pharmacist, Tom."

"It'll be fine. We don't have time to—"

"Be quiet a moment, Tom," Kate says. She stares into the fire. She imagines Bea. Maybe she's alive, maybe she's dead. The truth is she can't bear it either way. Because if Bea's alive, she's who-knows-where with awful things happening that Kate can see only too clearly. But if she's dead, then Kate is dead too, numbed to anything that matters. She inhabits these two possibilities constantly. She's living a double life. It drains her hope. She needs certainty. She needs relief. And if this Pharmacist might know . . .

"We're going to find the Pharmacist, Tom," she says through gritted teeth.

As the days pass, her leg hurts more deeply. The waves of pain warp what she sees. The veins darken and she cannot walk far. But she follows Mark, who seems to know the way. They doze during the day so they can walk in the coolness of night to manage her fever. Days, just days now, from this Pharmacist. One morning she wakes unwatched as sunshine touches her face and small drips of dew drop off the tarpaulin. Birds warble in the mulchy air, and she hears voices, and then they are gone. The voices again, indistinct but angry, are carried on the breeze and she limps between trees toward them. Through the trunks she glimpses Tom and Mark, their gestures fast. This fever has made time go strange, and sounds wash through her ears like water. Tom strides away and Mark follows, grabbing at his arm. "It's not the first time!"

"I was gone for a *moment!*"

Mark's voice lowers as he approaches Tom fiercely. "Why won't you watch us, Tom?"

"I don't like—"

"No one *likes* it!" he growls, pushing Tom back. "I've been watching *you* and I don't *like* what I see. So give me an excuse that makes sense!"

At that moment Mark sees her. He freezes as he mutters something to Tom, who turns.

"What's going on?" Her voice rings oddly in her own ears.

"Are you going to tell her?" Mark demands. After the silence, when Tom refuses to speak, Mark strides away. "I'd rather travel alone!"

Kate stands, breathing hard. She has so little strength. It's all she can do to continue.

"I only came to piss. I would've been gone for two minutes."

"What is wrong with you, Tom?"

"I was barely gone."

"Tom . . ."

"Fine." And he stalks deeper into the woods.

"Our daughter's called Bea, by the way, and my name is Kate," she says quietly, to his diminishing back, to the damp air, to no one.

By the time she returns, Tom and Mark have packed the camp away. They pick their way through the forest until they hit a road. Then they walk for miles in silence until, halfway through the day, Mark tells them he is leaving.

"I've no desire to see this Pharmacist again. Once was enough." He points up the road and tells her, "There's a camp twenty miles from here. You'll hit a city first. Don't go in, but skirt the orbital. Take the third road you cross and the camp has signs. Ask for Claire. She'll direct you to the Pharmacist." He will not look at Tom. Rather: "Watch him, because he doesn't watch you," he whispers as he hugs Kate, but he smiles warmly when he pulls away as if he hasn't spoken at all. "And if I find your daughter, I'll look after her. I'll try to find you, but . . ." He gestures at the world, the desolate road, the emptiness around them. "I promise I'll look after her."

Kate feels heat rising in her eyes. "And if we find John . . ."

"You won't," Mark says, nodding. "There are few happy endings these days. The world is too big and we're too small. We have to change our expectations."

"But there's still hope."

Although the wobble in Kate's voice betrays her, Mark pretends he didn't hear it. Instead, he salutes and jumps from the road, then simply strolls away across the expanse of grass. Tom turns immediately, and for a while, Kate follows. When she looks back, Mark is approaching a roadside shack where intertangled cars are rusted into a lump on the forecourt. He is clapping his hands and looking for movement, but she can no longer hear his sound.

———————

They walk through the night; they walk so they don't have to talk, and the following day it's the same. Even though her leg hurts chronically and her temperature soars, she keeps it all clamped in. The world is hallucinatory. The past and present mingle. She won't speak. Flashes of different futures. With Bea. Without. All she needs Tom for is to help her find Bea, and she's not sure she needs him for that. There is such a distance between them. Galaxies of space, where before there had been closeness. A distance inserted between them.

The next morning they crest a hill crowned with thick, thorny cords that they push back and stamp to the ground. In the bowl below them a city is revealed: a scuff of soot, a granulated smudge under a clouded sky. A motorway snakes down the hill and she follows its course with dried-out, burning eyes. Tiny cars are frozen there. More scatter the roads that split away in complex knots of elevated tracks. Between where they stand and the city, two giant skids score the plain. Crumpled knots of sky debris scatter the land.

"You know," Tom says, and then coughs. His voice is rough from disuse. "I know you didn't want to go to this Pharmacist, but if he is one of the taken, like Mark said, then maybe he does know things. Maybe he *will* know who took Bea. What do you think?"

Tom's hope again, starting to burn through. Give it time, that's all it takes. Even though he's merely repeating what she had said previously, it starts to work like a balm, salving something inside her more effectively than Margaret's cream. Hope sparks again. What else can she do? Within an hour this has become their refrain, his heartfelt belief and her hopeful pretense while she cries in silence inside: That the Pharmacist will know. That he will have information. That he will help them find their daughter.

They find the third road at dusk and track it across the countryside. They continue through the night until, with a deep gasping sound, the sky behind them is lit with fire as something in the city explodes. Nothing huge, not like the things they had seen before in the hellish chaos as they had journeyed to the farmhouse, but it's big enough to shrink them. A tanker? A fuel station? Does it matter anymore? They keep walking, Kate even slower than before. Stumbling, stumbling, she needs regular rest. She bleeds sweat. She slows.

The next day, Tom finds pignuts for her and then, when they come across a copse on a hill, they decide to rest. Kate bathes in a small pond at the foot of the hill while Tom sets traps for food. They secure the canvas beneath the trees and look out over the countryside as the sun lowers and the clouds steal its colors to glow above the earth. Sitting together, her shoulders shaking with the fever, she remembers a time long ago, sitting beside each other, jolted on a train. They were speeding past the darkened stations toward the tower. Tom's father had summoned them, so they were going. Her parents were missing; Southampton had gone down; maybe he had news. Tom had made her do anagrams, trying to calm her down, to anchor her to the real. But who didn't want to hide from *that*? Chaos was grasping the city. Of the children in Kate's class, only two had been on that morning. Even Jason-Stark27's Feed was not on anymore, and while there had been so many times she could have throttled him, she now desperately hoped the little shit was all right. She had held her stomach as the train moved on, had tried to send her baby—Bea, though she didn't know it yet—messages through the soothing motion of her palms. She had wished she could message her directly, but she didn't have an implant; they hadn't wanted her enabled *in ute*. So she had tried to breathe more slowly, to send her daughter the message that she could calm down too, she could stop her writhing around. Kate had been trawling every pool for news of her parents; that was why she'd been so buzzed. So maybe these anagrams were a good idea. Maybe it *was* better to be distracted . . .

"You'll like this one," Tom had said, his voice a veneer of calm. He'd stroked her face. "It's topical."

"Go on then."

"Dariancharles," he had said, and clapped his hands on his thighs.

Dariancharles. Or *dari ancharles.* Or *darian charles,* or *dari an' charles,* or something different because the vid had been so unclear. As President Taylor had died and Sergeant Vaughn, the assassin, had been wrestled to the ground, there had been something he'd shouted, or so it was being claimed in billions of pools, something he'd screamed before he was shot that sounded like *dariancharles.* Or *dari an' charles.* Or . . .

"The world is trying to work out what that means and you think it's an *anagram?*"

"I don't know." Tom had mimicked her voice. "But no one else knows either. It *must* be code. Some sort of message to his collaborators. He *knew* that vid would be seen by everyone."

He had pulled bits of paper and ancient pencils from his pocket and given her some. She had scribbled the letters *D-A-R-I-A-N-C-H-A-R-L-E-S* in a cloud to try to focus. She couldn't. Tom's pencil had raced across the page while her brain couldn't even move . . .

"Done!" he had exclaimed. "Five. You?"

She had lied. Said she'd gotten one. Told him to go

first, which he did: "Who killed the president? Well, how about this as a clue: *Iran Ash Cradle.*" He had looked at her meaningfully. "What we did to Iran—so they go *boom* in return. *Car Sandal Hire? Iran Crash Deal? Scar Heal Nadir!* That's four to me. And *here* it is: *Arid Ranch Sale!* These terrorists are from one of the dry zones. The AfricaBloc or AsiaSouth. Their land is useless now. These attacks are revenge for the Water Wars." He had snort-laughed before winking at her and tapping his head. Somehow his eyes were still vibrant despite how worn he looked. It had kindled something in her. "Well, at least we're keeping the wetware working. What have you got?"

She had shielded her empty paper. It had struck her suddenly that there must be conversations deciding geopolitics that sounded like her polls. *What region would you sacrifice . . . to protect your lifestyle? Africa, Asia, or Iran . . .* It had chilled her. Who would vote for *them?* Tom was waiting. She had gone on. A fraction of a second—3.5millisecs—and he hadn't noticed, and she had 21,593options, anagrams that made some kind of sense, and there was one she had known he'd like.

"China Lads Rear."

Tom had leaned back as the train sped on and mimed shooting at the sky. "That's good, Kate," he had said, and sighed as the train pulled into the station under the tower, nearly a mile directly beneath the homeHub, where Ben was waiting. "So you think it's the Chinese?"

She had gotten up painfully and told him she was going back on, that she had to find her parents. Tom had reassured her that Ben had promised he'd have news, had told her not to get too buzzed. Gently squeezed her hand. She'd be buzzed in an instant, she had known it, but in a disintegrating world it had been a comfort, even if it hadn't existed in the real, to feel the safety of the Feed.

"Do you miss the camp?" Tom asks her now, and she's pulled back, startled, into the sun-setting light with the birds around them, whipping about for insects, feeding in the evening sky. That dark underground afternoon echoes in her memory from years before.

"I . . . I miss Bea," she stutters, blinking the past away.

"Of course. I mean, when we find her, shall we keep doing this? Moving around. Finding places like this, like here. We don't need anyone else. Let's just be us. I'm sorry we didn't do it before, when you said we should. You were right. I was wrong. I'm sorry."

Kate puts an arm around him and leans into his body. They clasp hands.

"I'm so scared, Tom. I'm scared we'll never find her. I'm scared of what we'll find if we do."

Tom pulls her in close. They hold each other for a long time. It doesn't bring Bea back, it doesn't bring her any nearer, but it is comfort. When they are together, she feels less fear.

"It moves so quickly, when it's close to the earth," Tom says, nodding at the slightest clipping of sun over the hills.

"We're moving, not it. Come on, Tom, you know that," she corrects him, mumbling now, tired, and gently squeezes his waist. She smiles as something settles within her. Warmth fills her cheeks and the light gleams in her eyes as she watches the sun set behind the rough-treed horizon. She breathes in deeply. "But you are right. It would be a very good life. And I trust you, Tom. We'll find her."

The following morning she wakes scared and confused. Churning red dreams clog her mind, and a sense of freezing space. Absolute zero; icy cold. Blue canvas snaps and judders close to her face. The air here is clear. It cools and calms her skin. Her feet tingle pleasantly in the dewy grass but the ugly color seeping through the bandage on her leg is horrific.

"Looking good, Kate. It's okay, it's just me. I didn't leave you for long, I promise. Hungry?"

"Yes," she says, and finds some clothes bunched up in the rugs. "And exhausted."

"Let's see it."

She lets him examine her shin and apply some cream, and then she pulls on her trousers. She clumsily laces her boots as he rekindles the fire, then sits and watches him. He pours water into chipped tin mugs and she examines his face.

"Here you are." He strokes her hair. "You hang in there, right? We're nearly there."

She sits and waits, then drinks from the cup. It's warm, and pure, and good.

With more food and another day's rest, her body grows slightly stronger. They sit in the afternoon of the second day on the curve of the hill and talk.

"You're quiet," he says.

She nods. "I'm trying to fit things together."

"Like what?"

"Like exactly where we are."

"I don't exactly know," he says, mimicking her. "Pretty much bang in the middle of the country. From what Mark said, it's a couple more days to the Pharmacist. You'll make it. He'll fix you and he'll know. If he's one of the taken like Mark said, he'll know where Bea is for sure."

She thinks about that for a while and then says, "I can't remember what she sounds like. I'm not sure I can even picture her face."

He pulls her in to him and says nothing while they watch the pond below.

"Describe her to me?" she asks when he doesn't respond, and he rests his head on hers.

"Come on, Kate. Don't talk silly. Let's just get her back."

Later, while he's dozing in the sun, she descends carefully to the water. She has been watching the pond all day; it has virtually been calling her down. She tiptoes in until the water is high up her thighs and kneels. The hairs on her arms and legs stand, her breath speeds up, and her head rings as her pulse rate flies.

"I thought I'd lost you," he chastizes, stretching as she nears the top of the hill soon after.

"I had to feel the water. It's amazing."

He lies back on the rugs. "Well, you didn't miss much. I'm still me," he says. "Tom Hatfield. And you're my wife, Kate. Your sister was Martha. Who knows what happened to Rafa. And *those* are dangerously wet clothes. Why don't you take them off?"

She does and climbs in under the canvas. Her skin puckers as his hands run down her spine. They kiss. It has been a very long time. Tom moves and she moves too, tentatively at first, hidden beneath their canvas in their copse upon the hill.

After two more days' walking, as her body weakens again, she sees hand-painted signs on the road. She points them out to Tom.

IF YOU'RE GOOD TO US, WE'LL BE GOOD TO YOU. WE'RE HAPPY TO HELP, IF YOU ARE TOO. COME IN PEACE, OR LEAVE IN PIECES.

The entrance to the camp is set back from the verge, a gateway standing proud of a tall wooden wall. Daubs of paint around it nearly look like flowers. As they enter, she drags herself to a stop and asks Tom to take the lead: gesturing at her head and her exhausted eyes, she tells him to do the talking. The camp is centered below them around two train carriages, derailed and rolled down the hill. Tents and shacks circle them and huge vegetable patches radiate away. A woman in a colorful sarong leaves the plants she is tending nearby and sways up the hill toward them. Her skin is dark, her hair pulled back. After eyeing them cautiously, she waves at a wooden tower where a gun barrel flashes in the shadows and nods them on down the hill.

"This is damn impressive," Tom mutters as they pass furrowed rows bursting with vegetables. "They must have a real plow!"

She murmurs agreement but is distracted. People tending the plants examine the two as they pass. Two children careen around a row of beans, skid to a halt, and gawk. She waves tentatively and they do the same. The rhythmic sound of clanging metal rings out from a building whose roof leaks smoke. Behind the two train carriages are the skeletons of others. They have been cannibalized, their inner frameworks revealed, and an old lady covered with beads and ornaments sits on the grass before them. She has lost an ear and has a clipped lip. She shells peas, which she drops into a pot. "Sit down!" she calls out over the sound of metal, waving them forward with fat fingers. "My name's Claire. Give me a hand!" She steals a smile and tosses them a thick and uneven ceramic bowl, wafts a hand at the piles of pods. Her speech is slurred by her misshapen lip. "They're best out of the pod. Cook them, you lose the sugars."

"Thank you," she replies. "I'm Kate, this is Tom . . ." And then she becomes silent. She pops a pod open. It is lush, fresh, fibrous, green, and grown right here apparently. Seismic emotions heave within her. Exhaustion melts her body and mind. So much she wants to say, so much she needs to ask, but she knows she should leave the talking to Tom. She slips the pod into a pocket.

"So how long are you staying?" Claire asks over the sound of metal being hammered.

"We're not," Tom replies.

"Oh! Then thanks for preparing our dinner."

"We're looking for a Pharmacist," he continues. "I hear there's one nearby?"

Claire brushes the mound of empty pods from her skirt and looks sideways at him. "You know he's taken?"

Tom nods. "My wife's leg. It has an infection."

At Claire's gesture, she rolls the trouser leg up and shows her the bandaged wound. The smell is pungent and Claire recoils. "God knows you need it, but he may not help you. He's not a good person. Things"—she grimaces and twirls a finger at her head—"have gone wrong. Take something valuable to trade, that's the only advice I can give. How did you do it, Kate?"

She looks at Claire, frowns at Tom, and rubs her leg, muttering, "It really hurts."

"A dog," Tom explains.

"Well, go out the way you came in. Turn right at the road. Toward the end of tomorrow, you'll reach the edge of town. Be careful. There are people there who do bad things. Turn right at the fountain and keep walking. He lives in one of the more desirable addresses in the area!" Claire laughs. "Now, are you sure you won't stay for dinner?"

"We can't stop. We're looking for our daughter," Tom falters. "She was stolen. In a van with horses—"

"With spikes?"

"You saw them?" Tom gasps.

"They came past here last week. They know where all the camps are."

"Kate!" Tom grabs her hand, startling her; her thoughts are sloughing away, distracted, fuzzed out by exhaustion. "She's seen the van!"

"From a distance." Claire nods vehemently, her jaw set. "They've tried it on before, but I didn't know they were in the market for children."

"Do you know where they were going?"

"North," Claire states strongly, and then, her shoulders dropping and her face folding, her eyes lost in the expanse of her face, "I'm sorry. They're not good people either. The world these days. It's not unlikely that *they* were going to the Pharmacist, you know."

She feels Tom's grip tighten even more. He turns to her, and something has become steely in his eyes. "We'll get her back, Kate. We'll get Bea back."

"Good for you!" Claire has to raise her voice over the noise of hammering metal. She changes her tone abruptly. "Now, you get that leg fixed and get out of there! Find your child if you can. Come back either way. Have food with us, stay here awhile. Be happy!"

"What is that noise?" Tom yells.

"It's the smithy!" Claire shouts back. She nudges the side of the uneven bowl they've been dropping the peas into. "When they're not forging metal, we use it for pots." She points a chubby finger across the grass. A building of brick and flint has a squat structure of beaten metal panels clamped onto it. The furnace bows at the seams and the wall is smoldering black around it. A chimney at the top spits out filthy smoke. There is a man there, beating a hammer on an anvil: a lump of stone, covered with metal. "Tell Steve I said you could peek."

Leaving Claire behind them, they pass rows of cabbages and carrots, and tall and arching beans. Tom looks around them in wonder as they approach the furnace. The man, covered in dirt and sweat and veiled by the drifting smoke, hammers and hammers away.

"We could never have dreamed of this," Tom whispers. "We were living on a knife edge. Let's do it, Kate: let's find Bea and come back here!"

———————

Back on the road, she examines the veins of the pea pod she has taken. She can still feel the heat of Steve's furnace, where the moisture was sucked from her face. Dried-out skin. Dissolving. She rubs the leaf's wetness on her cheeks as she walks. Tom's face is still all scrunched. "Their knowledge was so far in advance of ours." He stops abruptly. "Do you think they were taken?"

She pauses in her stride and looks for a moment back over her shoulder.

"It's almost like . . . who cares if they were? They were doing so well," Tom continues, deflating and starting to walk again. "What's going to happen to us? This world?"

"Do you think we can change the future?"

Tom shakes his head. "I'm not talking about changing it. I'm just talking about *surviving* for it. Making a civilization that is going to last, and grow, and be good, and . . ."

He gesticulates passionately, but his voice trails away and he is lost in his thoughts. She pulls a stick from a bush and flexes it between her hands, thinking too and, like him, not sharing. Her hands are shaking with the fever now. She's burning up. Nearly done. She doesn't have long. After a while, she looks at him. "Tom, does the name Darian Charles mean anything to you?"

His face folds somewhat as he thinks, almost grasps something but doesn't. "Nearly. Maybe," he says. "Why?"

"I don't know." She sighs. "It's been in my mind recently. I'm sure it's nothing."

They sleep early, before they reach the town, and get up again before dawn. The earliest touch of sunlight hints at gold, but there is a haze to the air. They see the first person before the sun is up: a man partly hidden in the bushes, emaciated, his skin like a leather sheet shrink-wrapping his bones. He mutters and rants. They leave him. Later, when the sun has risen, they see two more people sitting by the road. "Stuff?" one of them spits, a woman as thin as wires. "Stuff? Stuff? Fuel?" She bares her rotten teeth. The man next to her chews something. Rags. He talks nonsense, mangled sounds. His spittle has dried into gray-flecked foam. He watches them. His eyes roll. They stagger on.

In the outskirts, they see the fountain, brown and dry. Soon the neighborhood Claire described becomes obvious: wider, tree-lined streets. Most houses were torched long ago and stand rotting, their ancient contents cascading out. Vines have overgrown the road like a knotted green blanket. The farther they go, the more people they pass. Vacant eyes. Tight skin, faces drawn. They moan. Reach out and shuffle. Some try to stand. They all seem to be going, slowly, the same way.

"What's wrong with them?"

"Keep moving," Tom tells her, eyes wide, as they are surrounded by the slowly shuffling horde for a while. In the distance, at the end of a particular house's railings that have been fortified with planks and razor wire, two men guard metal gates. "Any thoughts?" he asks her, taking her arm, glancing back at the brainless people behind them.

"To get drugs," she says simply, and limps on.

The guards recline in two torn armchairs with long guns across their laps, wearing black T-shirts, scuffed trousers, and sunglasses with thick colored rims. They do not stand.

"We want to see the Pharmacist," she tells them.

They move to look at her, these guards, like automatons, their eyes flicking like shadows behind their dark lenses.

"The Pharmacist," she reiterates. "We've come a long way."

One of the men, eventually, stands. He takes a heavy

key from his pocket and unlocks the gate. He heaves against what used to be an automatic mechanism and goes through. Shoots them a flashing grin. Locks the gate and walks leisurely up the drive.

A long time later, after the shadows of the trees have moved and the moisture in the air has turned chill, they are still waiting. The remaining guard hasn't stirred. His expression has not changed.

Tom points at the empty armchair. "Can my wife sit? She's hurt her leg."

When the guard taps the trigger, she lowers her rucksack and sprawls on the road. Takes the hat from her bag and a sweater. Tom sits on the tarmac too, beside her.

Sometime in the near-total darkness of the night, the guards swap. New ones sit and the retiring one walks up the drive.

"Any news?" Tom calls from the ground.

The new guards look at him blankly. One of them has a little box; inside it, a pill. He tips it out and holds it gently in his palm.

"Hey," she demands. "We want to see the Pharmacist!"

The guard's teeth glint in the darkness as he settles

into his chair. He palms the pill into his loose mouth and smiles dreamily upward. "That's nice, friend. Does he want to see you?"

It takes a day and a half. At night they shiver; during the day they move with the shade. Over time the group of spindle-thin people with opaque eyes edges down the road to lie moaning just a house away. The guards swap. Each new pair swallows their pills. And then, in the early hours of the morning, one of the guards kicks them awake and they stagger, unseeing, up the gravel drive. It scrunches as they stumble and the house looms before them. She watches its faintly glowing windows, like something strange is emanating, and as they draw nearer she becomes aware of fleeting shapes: slips of movement skimming past her legs. Some hiss and others mewl. Dim lanterns show that the raised wooden veranda writhes with cats. Fur shushes on wood and the prickle-clatter of claws makes her skin itch. A man with hock-sized fists, a monolithic face, and vacant eyes stands beside the door.

"The Pharmacist would like to see us," she tells him.

He jabs a blunt finger at their rucksacks. "Leave them. Shoes off."

Tom raises an eyebrow.

Another jab. "Socks too."

"Anything else?" Tom asks, but the man stays silent.

She passes barefoot into the house and finds the hallway, like the veranda, seething with fur. Beneath this living carpet the boards run bare up the stairs. But the guard stretches his arm toward a chipped door and, exhausted, finally she grasps its handle.

As soon as there is gap enough to escape, music slides out: a tenor saxophone thrilling above a band from the candlelit room within. The recording is crackly, dusty, like time itself has aged, and her eyes are black holes in the gold-tinged darkness. She makes out tables and chairs covered with the pooling innards of machines. At the far end of the room a long wooden counter fills the space, shadowed shelves behind it. The Pharmacist sits cross-legged on a sofa. His nose is angular and his mournful eyes hooded, his cheeks abnormally long, broad furrows in his raised brow. His greasy hair is brushed over his scalp. He wears trousers, a shirt, both scuffed and stained, and a frayed bow tie, tightly done. He does not move until he finishes reading and then looks slowly up at them. He claps his book softly closed and leans out of the shadows. His voice is like a desert breeze.

"What do you want?"

"We need drugs for my wife's leg. And information. Our daughter has been abducted."

"I see. And what would you choose if I were to grant you only one?"

Tom glances back at her, caught off guard. She looks at him, his fingers tense and clawed, and at the Pharmacist, relaxed, cross-legged, observing.

"Her leg," Tom explains. "She might lose it."

"And you have already lost the child. So that is your answer: keep the leg."

"No!"

Tom strides forward and the Pharmacist gasps with delight. His gaze, now sharp, shifts in the shadows of his face, flicking keenly between them. A smile lives at the corners of his lips as he waits and watches expectantly.

"What price?" she says, her voice scratchy as she breaks the silence, waiting no longer for Tom. She's leading this now. "For either."

"Ah." The Pharmacist releases the sound like a piston. "It depends."

"On?"

"What you have."

"So, we have a deal: we just have to find what we have that you want."

"If you have anything I want."

"What *do* you want?"

"What do you have?"

"Clothes!" Tom interjects desperately, and the Pharmacist falls silent, his smile tightening. "Beans?" Tom suggests, and the Pharmacist laughs: a sound like paper rubbing itself.

"Us," she says, staggering forward. "Ourselves! Me! What do you want from *us*?"

The Pharmacist's laugh dies out but his eyes do not change. The recording of the music continues, the band playing on from centuries before. Time rides the heartbeat of a rhythm that died long ago as the Pharmacist unfolds from the sofa until he is standing tall. He examines Tom without touching him: his eyes, his face, his ears. He gasps a laugh and shakes his head and then, a glint in his eye, a lilting walk, sashays to her side. He stares woozily into her eyes as though they share some joke before sidling in closer than he should. His hands brush her arms. He draws her hat off and drops it aside to finger her hair. He kneels, hovering his splayed fingers over her torso, her thighs. His face is waist-height and she can hear him sniffing. Then he prizes the hem of her trouser leg and pulls it up. She does not look at his balding head with its combed-over hair. She does not look to Tom. She feels the Pharmacist's touch on her, his fingernails on the painful dampness of her wound, and she feels her heart thump out of every inch of her skin.

The Pharmacist stretches upward until he looks directly, impassively, into her eyes. "This wound will kill you." And then, to Tom, but not removing his gaze from hers, "It will kill her."

The music plays, the saxophone hushed, the bass improvising, the brushes on drums.

"Can you cure it?" Her voice falters. Huge things well up inside her: the unfairness of it, of everything that has happened. She wants to scream at him.

"Yes, of course I can." He blinks smartly and his expression flattens. "But why should I?"

So many reasons cascade through her head, but: "Is it true what they say about you?" Tom asks before she can speak, and there's something odd about his voice.

A smile slits the Pharmacist's face. "That depends *entirely* on what they say . . ."

"That you're one of them. One of the taken."

The Pharmacist winks at her as he mimes weighing something. "People talk, people talk," he says, nearly sings. His movements carry him around the sofa to a sideboard, where he picks up a heavy glass tumbler, drops in some ice, and pours whisky on top of some leaves.

"Then that's why you have to help us," Tom implores. "Because we are taken too!"

The Pharmacist stoppers the decanter and turns

back around. He lifts a finger to his lips; then he lifts the glass and sips. Smiles. Satisfied. "Is that so? How long for?"

"At our camp, no one knew. We've been hiding. Secret. For years."

"Wonderful. How wonderful," the Pharmacist says breathily. "Then what is your name?"

"Tom Brown."

"Your real name."

"We've not stayed undiscovered by being indiscreet."

"But still, *Tom Brown*, given the circumstances . . ."

"What's yours?"

"Oh. No, I don't think so. You?" The Pharmacist raises his eyebrows at her.

"Her name is Kate."

"Her—real—name."

Tom shuts his mouth steadfastly.

"And what," the Pharmacist asks, "is your mission?" What little laughter there was in his voice is gone. "Can you tell me why we are here, then, if you're *one of us*?"

"We've told you our mission!" Tom cries. "To save our family!"

The Pharmacist laughs again, clapping.

"Is that really so funny?" she demands, unable to dam her words anymore, her hands shaking. Heat courses through her veins, flushing her skin. The heat of worlds burning. "That if we were *one of them* we'd want to save our family? Is that *funny*?"

"It's risible! Tom and Kate, you have to do better than this! You're so *unprepared*! How long did it take you to come here? Weeks? Months? So much time to *think*. And you know, you *know* that I'm, what did you say, 'one of them.' Yet this is the best you can do? Pathetic! Beans!" he cackles. "Clothes! What do I owe you? Nothing. Your world? *Absolutely* nothing! Your *family*?" He clenches his fist, blows onto it, into it, opens it out and throws it away. "I hate it and everything you stand for. So get out," he snaps. He leans heavily on the back of the sofa and rolls his shoulders. "Our mission is to kill you," he murmurs, circling his head around on his neck. "To kill you all. Tit—is that what you say?—for tat. We eat your flesh and harvest your bones."

He pushes himself from the sofa and approaches Tom, springing on his feet, his voice rising to a shout. "Now *you* are *lucky*. Because I'm not *like* the others. I don't love *violence*. But why should I waste my *time*?" He goes nose-close and they stand like that, the music still playing, until a tear leaves Tom's eyes. Another wells, swells, and rolls down his cheek.

"For kindness?" Tom whispers. "For good?"

The Pharmacist holds his breath before breaking away. "No." He sighs and collapses back on the sofa. "There are more important people than you." He picks up papers and slides some reading glasses on as the door opens and the guard trudges in. He pulls Tom by the arm and she follows them out into the hall, where the door, sharply shut behind them, cuts the still-playing music short.

Under the guard's stultified gaze they pull their boots back on and heft up their bags without speaking. They step from the veranda onto the gravel drive, and in the silence of the starry night the world feels vast and isolated as they make their way toward the gate. What else is there to do?

"Tom," she says, pausing by the hushing shadow of a bush and waiting for him to stop. "My hat."

When he looks blankly back at her, tears collecting in his stunned eyes, she takes his hand, squeezes it, and heads back up to the house. Pushes open the door. Back in the room, the Pharmacist raises an eyebrow. "You look familiar."

"I left my hat."

His gaze skitters around the shadows. It is on the

floor by the sofa, where he dropped it, and he nods for her to go. But she doesn't go; instead she opens her hands. "Why did you lie?"

"Which one?"

"'*We eat your flesh and harvest your bones,*'" she says. "Why did you say that?" She holds his gaze until it flickers. The Pharmacist removes his glasses and stands.

"Poetic license?" he replies.

She nods tightly. "Which Area were you from?"

A very slight smile curls the edges of his lips. "Well, hello, you. My name is Ethan Shore."

"Good," she replies. "I'm Sylene Charles."

Water gushes as steam heaves up in rolls from the porcelain tub. A muffled noise comes through the doorway as Sylene tests the water flowing from the tap and cups some carefully in her hands. She stares into it before letting it fall between her fingers and away. She wipes the steam back on the mirror and looks at herself, at this new face. Days now and, a rippled reflection in water aside, she hasn't known what she looks like. She examines the lines around the eyes, the shape of the lips, and the dips of the cheeks, every angle and curve. She probes the skin with her fingers, draws her blond hair through them, and then, sighing, places them to their reflection in the glass.

When she leaves the bathroom, smile in place, Tom is lying on the bed wearing just a towel, holding a book open above his face. He has shaved and his hair is still damp.

"What did you say, Tom?"

"I said, how do you think we can make him tell us about Bea?"

She stops smiling and drops her eyes. Clasps her hands and deflates. The effect is near instant.

"I'm sorry, Kate," Tom apologizes. "You just concentrate on getting better. I'll worry about the rest. Hey, this book," he says, flashing her the cover and lightening his tone, burying everything else under a veneer of ease, *keep hoping, keep hoping, you've got to keep up the hope.* "There's lots of words I don't get, but it's really good. I'm going to take this for Graham. Have you read it?"

She makes a face and shrugs.

"What did you say to him, though, Kate?" Tom whispers, glancing at the door and waving her to him. Sylene sits as directed. She feels his breath on her face and can see the candlelight reflecting in the orbs of his eyes as he reaches behind her and his fingers search her back.

"I said I'd sleep with him." She feels his grip tighten. Sees his throat constrict. She puts a hand to his cheek, thumbs his chin, lowers her face toward his. "Don't be silly," she soothes. "I don't know what changed his mind. Maybe what you said? Maybe he's kind," she prompts.

"I don't trust him."

She pats his chest, above his heart. "Then let's be on our guard."

As they go downstairs, music still sneaks out from the front room. Sylene leads the way, descending past paintings on the walls, limping as carefully as possible over the clumps of cats. She nearly knocks on the door but decides to simply push it open instead.

"Ah! Kate—and Tom Brown! Come in, come in, just a minute . . ."

The Pharmacist beckons them in before leaning back over the counter. With a magnifying lens scrunched over an eye, he eases something off a Petri dish with tweezers, lays it carefully down and then beams at them, rubbing his hands together. "Officially: Welcome! Are you rested and washed? Are you comfortable in your room? Tell me, would you like a drink?"

"Sure," says Tom, glancing at Sylene like he's humoring the man.

The Pharmacist strolls to the sideboard and pours the drinks high. His movements are now like a child's and less controlled. He is, Sylene guesses, excited. She is too. There is so much to ask, but for now all they have is fleeting glances when Tom looks elsewhere. As he wonders at the ice in his glass, the Pharmacist winks at her before heading back to the sideboard. He purses his mouth serenely as he passes under the gold-framed portraits on the wall. "My ancestors," he announces grandly, gesturing at the paintings and smiling indulgently at Sylene as he returns with her drink and a plate. Two colorful capsules roll on the china, knocking each other around the rim. "Shouldn't really have these with alcohol," the Pharmacist whispers, a hand up to his mouth, "but I think we're past that now—"

"Just a moment." Tom advances on the Pharmacist. "What are they?"

"Well, Tom, I'm glad you asked: it's an anti-infective, antiparasitic 23-dihydro-1-H-indolizinium chloride structure, and, I might ask *you*, what else would it be to treat such a chronic infection? I'm a very clever man; I made it myself. Crafted with my own loving hands for your wife. This will take a long time unless you trust me, but please, Tom, feel free, my equipment is at your disposal, so check it all you like. We have probably whole days until she dies." The Pharmacist invites Tom toward his shadowy worktop and the homemade scientific accoutrements with a slow sweep of his arm, but before Tom can move, Sylene knocks the pills back with a slug of her drink.

"Good girl," the Pharmacist says quietly, smiling at Tom all the while.

She watches Tom sleep like he asked her to. She still doesn't understand why. Candlelight dances on his face. The flickering glow of fire pricks tiny balls of sweat from his pores. She watches him until his hands relax their grip on the sheets and his breath catches in his throat. For a while he sleeps motionless, dead looking, and she thinks of her son before she buried him. She had gone to one of the deepest vaults that still had access to the earth, and she had dug it out with her hands. Her first son was buried there too, and her husband. She blinks the memories away and stands over Tom, her expression hardened. She pins points on his skull with her fingertips. He is now so deeply asleep he doesn't feel a thing.

"You took your time."

"I didn't know you were waiting."

"So why did you come downstairs?" The Pharmacist smiles at her and makes his spread-out fingers dance gleefully, like he's found her out.

Sylene points to the decanter on the sideboard. "For a drink."

The Pharmacist, sitting on the sofa, raises a tumbler where amber liquid already pools as she passes him. Lifting the lid of the ice bucket, Sylene thrills at the feeling as the stuff melts on her skin. Licking the water from her fingertips, she takes her time to carry her drink to a chair. The floorboards creak under her bare feet. She is wearing a gray tracksuit and white T-shirt she found in a wardrobe. Once sitting away from the Pharmacist, she sips her drink before raising her glass. They observe each other across the space. She won't speak first. He may be "one of them" too, but she doesn't know who he is.

"So." The Pharmacist sighs and dances his foot in the air.

"So," she agrees, and drinks again.

"To friends. Past, present, and future." The Pharmacist raises his tumbler at her grandly. "The continued good health of you, and yours, and the world. Which wave were you, Sylene?"

"Ninth. There was no one else left."

"I was the fourth. I've been here for years. Four. Five. It's difficult to tell. You?"

Fixing the smile on her face, Sylene observes the

darkness through the windows. Then she examines the leather-clad books on the shelves, the ancestral portraiture on the walls. She looks anywhere so he won't see the tears threatening her eyes: Kate's eyes but Sylene's tears.

"It gets easier with time," the Pharmacist calls softly. "What do you want to know?"

Sylene crosses to the bookshelves, her heart racing so her blood swells her cheeks. "I haven't found any targets yet," she says at last, and when her voice quivers uncontrollably, she flashes him a quick smile.

He assesses her and chuckles. "I think we're past that now, Sylene. Haven't you seen what's happened to the world?"

"But you do know who he is?"

The Pharmacist tilts his head, smirks, and gives it a slow shake.

"You don't recognize him?" she asks condescendingly. "Well, his name's not really Tom *Brown*." She turns to hover her fingers over the book spines and her tone changes abruptly. "The air is so different. Cooler, of course, but it feels thicker too, don't you think?"

The Pharmacist unfurls from the sofa. "You can touch them if you like."

The skin on Sylene's arms puckers as she takes the book he offers her. She opens it with trembling fingers, and as she does, the spine breaks and a page slides out under her thumb.

"I'm sorry," she gasps.

"They're old. And I can't read them anyway; they're not phonetic. Smell it."

"It's amazing. It's . . ."

". . . like history had a scent," he concludes. As he slides the book back smartly on the shelf, his arm brushes hers. She doesn't pull away even as, still close, he turns to her again. "Do we know each other, Sylene? I was from Area Nineteen. Scraper Forty-Two." This close together, his breath strokes her face, his teeth sneaking out from under his upper lip as he smiles hesitantly.

"No, I don't think so, Ethan."

"I do look different these days." The Pharmacist opens out his skinny arms as if revealing himself, and Sylene laughs. She lays a hand briefly on his chest before walking away.

"How's your leg feeling, Sylene?"

"Worse," she says over her shoulder. "What kind of a medic are you?"

The Pharmacist jogs to his counter, lifts a hinged section, and disappears behind the shelves. Soon there is a clinking and a rattle of pills. "A fake one," he calls cheerily, emerging smiling with his palm outstretched.

"But still better than anyone else on the planet. And me just a humble programmer, trying to learn new skills. We are resilient, you and I. Look at us. *Surviving.* Without friends, without family. So very nearly alone and yet so very strong in ourselves. Or, to be more precise"—he laughs, slapping his body and arms—"so very strong in others! It's pointless, by the way, to try to find people, Sylene. Are you searching for someone? Tell me, have you come here with high hopes to ask me to help you find your special person?"

Sylene regards him coolly before offering the slightest of shrugs. "His daughter. You heard him. Bea. We're looking for his daughter."

"No, no, no, no, *no,* Sylene." The Pharmacist shakes his head and edges closer. "Are *you* looking for anyone? Family, Sylene? Do you have any? It will hurt," he continues breathily, "until you realize you can simply stop the pain by *not looking for them anymore.* And I recommend you do. If your hand is burning, take it out of the fire." His voice has lowered. It carries too much weight for his whisper, cracking at the seams as a flickering darkness twitches deep in his eyes. "Trust me, Sylene, I've tried to find my family. But that way madness lies. The world is too large. Not enough of us made it. So many people died en route. You'll learn that you can simply choose to stop the pain. I'm telling you this as a friend to give you a little head start here, as I wish someone had helped me . . ."

Sylene knows the pain of loss, of course she does. She has seen her world collapse and her family burn. She has seen life sucked dry and everything consumed. She has been trapped and has risked all to escape. She has killed. No other choice. But while she has fought to keep her emotions hidden from Tom for days now, they have been burning her insides like the heat of a supernova all that time. The acidic despair of isolation. And the pain scalds her now with searing recentness even though it feels so far away, like it happened eons ago. Emotions break her from within. She's back there in her memory. The hiss and crackle of machines. The thrum of power; she'd felt it vibrate her feet through the tightly meshed grilles. The dried-out air in that stoppered-up room had been absolutely static. Sterile. A soundless density that came from being so far underground, contained in boxes. How much longer could they go on? The beeping of his life stats. She had been crying so much that the salt in her tears had scorched the skin of her face. But her son was so calm. Lying on the gurney, strapped up, plugged in, looking dead already, he had been so chillingly quiet.

"Don't," he whispered. His dark eyes had held her like gravity. "You know this is for the best. And you must do this too. We all must, until we've won." He slipped his dry hand into hers and his gaze continued to hold her frozen until her sobs melted and heaved again, from as deep within her as they were themselves sealed up underground, miles beneath the surface of the earth. He strained to nod at the men, who pressed a series of buttons. Pulled levers. Lights illuminated and a subtle alarm sounded as columns of colored light scaled up on a display. The metal room thrummed with power. As an alert chimed to indicate that something had hit an optimal level and as yet another alarm began to ring, the men depressed levers and, without any ceremony, the chemicals flowed through tubes into his arm.

She felt his muscles relax instantly.

"Don't!" she cried, and then gulped it back. "Don't forget: just say your name and I'll find you. I will follow you, I promise. Just do something big and say your name, and I'll find you!"

Whether he heard her she did not know. The displays flatlined and his muscles released as his body died. The columns of colored light flared briefly as the power in the room peaked and then dropped deeply to silence. Just the sound of her ragged breathing remained, the last breaths of the last of her family heaving out on the dry air. Tears had warped her sight. But nothing had changed; everything felt the same as always. Had he too just sacrificed himself for nothing? Given his life for an impossible cause? One of the men had spoken to her but she can't now make out the words. She listens harder, but his mouth is moving differently from the sounds that come swimming through her ears: "You can stay here with me, of course; you'll always know where I am, Sylene. But in the meantime, take these to stop the pain. The best I can do. And we'll work on the infection tomorrow . . ."

The Pharmacist coughs for her attention and Sylene snaps back. He shakes a cupped palm with pills pooled in the middle, his smile frozen, masklike. These pills are different from the ones before: chalky and white.

"What . . . what are they?"

"A basic form of physical painkiller."

"I don't need basic, I need effective," she grunts, swallowing the memories back down as she takes the pills in her hand. "Can I have more?"

"Not if you want to wear that body for long. There's much crudity in them. And it *is* a nice body, Sylene." The Pharmacist leans in close to her as she swallows the pills, and the sadness in his voice is gone. It is now, instead, so smooth, and his lips are close to her ear. "So, Sylene, who is he?"

"Tom Hatfield," Sylene says, the answer shocked out by his nearness.

"Hatfield?" The Pharmacist sucks in a breath and takes a walk around the room before turning sharply back. He beetles up close and takes her arm. "Does he suspect you?"

"No. All he's concerned about is finding his daughter. Someone told us you'd know where she is. But no, he doesn't suspect me at all."

The Pharmacist leans close, and instead of pulling away this time, she stares into his eyes.

"He looks at me *adoringly*, Ethan. He touches me and it makes my skin crawl. I let him—I let him because I'm so . . ."

The Pharmacist has come so near, he's now just not quite touching her.

"But it . . . it makes me sick when he . . ."

His hair brushes her neck. She doesn't pull away. She smells his greasy skin just before she feels his dry lips on her collarbone and hears him breathe her in. Then his hands are on her waist and she wraps her arms around his body and begins to sob. The contact is mindless and instinctive: feeling something real, some connection to her home, and grabbing it. When she realizes what she's doing, she withdraws from him straightaway. He stumbles and looks at her, surprised, before something closes down over the expression on his face.

"Are you all right, Ethan?"

The Pharmacist smiles fluidly. The mask is back but the mania dances still in the darkening pools of his eyes. "These are funny times, Sylene," he says, and shrugs. "Save yourself for Mr. Hatfield. We don't want him to stop the others from coming back. You might have to kill him yet."

The candle has burned low and Tom has turned over. A soft circle of skin pulses at the bottom of his throat. His face is so familiar to her. She had gulped so many old vids of him, and grabs, but this face is different from those images. It has not been maintained well; it is older, more worn than it should be at his age. Time has changed him; he is a different person now.

"Hey. Tom."

He lurches awake and slumps against her. He is naked and bed-warm, and as he burrows into her neck he fumbles to find her fingers, lifts them to his mouth and kisses their tips.

"Just give me a moment," he mumbles, and kisses them again.

Sylene stares ahead, unmoving, as he stretches and nuzzles her neck. She stares at the wallpaper as he makes a tired rumble in his throat, takes the hem of her top and pulls it over her head. His hands caress her bare torso, drawing down to the V of her hips, and he kisses the slight roundness of her belly. He hooks his thumbs into her tracksuit band, tugs it down, stands, and pulls her naked body to his. Sylene feels him swell. She slips a hand between them, runs it up his neck and kisses him quickly on the cheek. "Good night," she says, and slides into bed where the mattress is still warm.

Tom, head wilting with semi-sleep, settles himself onto an armchair, picks up his book and opens it carefully. "Don't worry." He smiles at her. "I'll be good watching till dawn. We'll get you well, and then we'll get the hell out of here. Find out where that van is and find Bea. All right?"

Birds wake her, or was it the sound of a door? Tom is naked in the chair, now asleep. She hears people moving on the gravel outside and a muttering hustle of voices. Bile rises in her—Kate's—gorge and she closes the bathroom door and vomits as quietly as she can.

Once Tom has woken, they go out onto the veranda. She walks slowly into the sunlight, her joints thick with exhaustion, still feeling deeply nauseated, and leans on the wooden rail. Cats patrol a precisely trimmed lawn, beyond which rows of flower beds stretch, regimented, down to large greenhouses and an encircling redbrick wall.

Tom gasps.

"He's been busy," Sylene agrees. She's never seen anything like it. The abundance is beyond her wildest dreams. What her sons would have done to see this. Look at the colorful surface of the earth: plants weave around trellises; their orange flowers droop and burst powder blue amid the leaves and tuberous stems. As Tom supports her across the lawn, she sees that smaller plants are segregated. The Pharmacist has tended them all. Some are soft like down, and everywhere the soil is mulchy, the air fragrant with dew. Not the dry and reddened earth she's used to. All this life nearly makes her cry. It's the most joyous thing she's ever seen. Beyond the beds, the Pharmacist emerges from a greenhouse wearing a wide-brimmed hat. He still has his bow tie on, even though he now sports gardening gloves as well. He makes a shooing motion back toward the house where, on the veranda, chairs and a small table await them.

"He walks like a bird, don't you think?" Tom says as he helps her back.

Sylene glances at the Pharmacist, now loping up the grass behind them. As she sits in the shade, she feels suddenly drowsy. Even this small amount of exertion has drained her. "Or a geklean," she concurs. She remembers seeing her first as a child as it crawled the plungehole, cleaning and resealing the glass, its padded feet spread, micro-claws finding the roughness in the strengthened polycarbide as it loped, neck long, past her gawking face.

"A what?" Tom crouches beside her. "Are you delirious?"

"No, it was something I read as a child . . ."

The Pharmacist scrapes earth from his shoes and steps onto the veranda. "Sleep well, all?"

"Ever heard of a geklean?" Tom asks him, still kneeling beside her.

The Pharmacist, hand paused on the balustrade, looks concerned. "A . . . ?"

"I think she's delirious. Are the drugs not working?"

The Pharmacist smiles with ease. "All will be well, Tom. Let's see what we have here . . ."

In his basket are various plants: one with light, flat sprouts, another with trifurcated leaves. He strips them, then Tom makes way as he kneels and flexes his fingers. Before the bandage is fully unraveled, the fabric starts to stain. The dirty mark widens as the lower layers are revealed. When fully removed, the pad is black with slime. Tom gasps in shock.

"No, no," the Pharmacist breathes from the floor, "this is good. We're drawing the toxins out. And this will now fight the infection." He flicks a viscous substance into a mortar before mixing it with the leaves. Sylene smells chemicals wafting off the cream and a light freshness easing up from the slowly crushed plants. The different smells compete but gradually the substances mix. As he works, the Pharmacist hums the jazz riff from the night before, and, clumsily, Sylene hums too, through her sleep haze, nearly following the tune. Tom listens. She closes her eyes. The air on her face, the coolness of the shade. The humming, her thoughts, melting . . .

"What is it?"

"Improvisation!" The Pharmacist laughs, and Sylene tries to blink her suddenly sun-glared double vision back together. "The cream is an antiseptic. Those," the Pharmacist explains to Tom, nodding up at a box on the table, "are antibiotics. And the plants . . . well, this place is limited and medicine hard to find, so I use what else I can."

"It's beautiful," Sylene slurs, raising her head weakly to survey the garden, its colors glowing mistily in the sunlight. "You've done so well. It's wonderful to see things grow."

"Where we are from," the Pharmacist tells Tom as he starts to spread the now-green cream onto Sylene's wound, "that's to say, where *I* am from, there was not the opportunity to grow. But all I have done here is to collect these plants and protect them. They've done the rest themselves. Isn't that amazing?"

Tom narrows his eyes. "Where *are* you from?"

Reaching for the bandage, the Pharmacist glances up at Sylene. He has a hidden smile in his eyes. She tries to speak first, but the effort is too much and the Pharmacist starts to hum the tune again as he takes a long time slowly rolling the bandage out.

"Where are you from?" Tom persists. "Why have you done this to the world?"

"Tom," Sylene warns, edging up onto her elbows. "Don't—"

"No, Kate, I'm happy to talk," the Pharmacist soothes her. He takes a stolen moment to frown her back into the chair and then smiles wanly at Tom. "You seem like understanding people. You seem like people who are *just*. There are at least two sides to this story, and we're not as bad as everyone thinks. Us 'taken' . . ." His fingers flex as they secure the bandage around Sylene's calf. Then he rests his palm on it, folding his hands around her shin, and leans back to look up at Tom. "We were abandoned. We were hurt too. We were left in pain for generations with no hope of salvation and no chance of escape, like you. Have you ever felt that, Tom? To see such pain in your loved ones that you would kill yourself for them? To feel such pain in yourself—not physical pain, but utter mental anguish, *that* sort of pain, you know?—have you ever felt so much pain like that that all you desire is to escape your own head? Because otherwise you will lose your mind? Tell me, have you felt that, Tom?"

Sylene stares up at Tom as he shifts slightly in the face of the Pharmacist's unwavering gaze. Are those tears in his eyes, as he blinks and nods, or just an illusion caused by her own?

"We were damned, Tom, actively," the Pharmacist says curtly. "There were always other choices, to avoid what happened, but they were never taken. What happened was inevitable. Ignorance is no defense. Everyone knew what was coming to pass. We were not considered important, it's as simple as that. We were not cared for like people who matter. We were set up to be destroyed. And this is revenge for that."

"Destroyed by whom?" Tom asks. "Can you slow down a bit here?"

The Pharmacist glances at Sylene from the corner of his eye and then back. His voice is devoid of emotion, his eyes are hard, but, she notices, his hands tremble. "By you."

Sylene's heart rate rises as Tom's face screws into a frown.

"So you're . . . what, you're from Iran? You're . . .

Chinese? What on earth did we do that you wanted this revenge?"

Myriad emotions flicker across the Pharmacist's face before he snorts and shakes his head. "You don't deserve to know."

A hollow lump of laughter resonates in Tom's throat. "We don't deserve to know? You destroy our lives but we don't deserve to know why?"

"You destroyed ours first"—the Pharmacist shrugs—"and never told *us* why."

"Our daughter has been abducted! By people turned into *animals* because of the state you've made of the world! And we don't even get to know *why*?"

"If only you knew," the Pharmacist says, smiling with hollow eyes, "how many children you condemned to death. If only you *knew*—"

"You people killed my brother!" Tom cries.

The Pharmacist stands so suddenly that Tom jumps. Sylene hauls herself to her feet too, dizzily, behind them, reaching out for the Pharmacist's arm, but he pushes her back, snarling at her. "Brothers, sisters, children, hope—you took everything before we even *had* it. You didn't give us a chance! You consumed our world and left us to die. You *annihilated* us. Look at you—you're so self-obsessed you don't even know who we are! So conceited! You *disgust* me. And you thought there could be no retaliation, because we had no way to get back at you! Well, surprise! A desperate creature is capable of anything, Tom; you, with your technology, with your *Feeds,* did you never stop to think that someone might surpass you? That someone might find a way to use it all against you? We had no choice! You made us lose our minds! What other hope did we have? We escaped the hell *you* made, leaving our bodies to burn behind us, and we sent our thoughts out wildly for sanctuary, looking for somewhere safe to tether ourselves, and some of us found you, with your surprisingly open minds." The Pharmacist's expression has frozen in contempt, but now it slowly warps in realization of something and he turns to Sylene. "You are *animals.* Stupid, unaware, incompetent animals. You're not even worthy of the destruction you've caused."

"But wait," Tom says. "The people you take? Jane. Guy. My brother. What happens to them?"

"Gone."

"Their memories?"

"There's not enough room for two."

Tom's eyes dart wildly. "And do you choose who you . . . inhabit?"

"No." The Pharmacist laughs, looking down at his body apologetically. "We can't."

"And . . ." Tom slumps and then regains himself.

"How does it feel? To be free from that turmoil, to escape the mental anguish? How does that feel?"

The Pharmacist looks suddenly surprised. He runs a hand through his greasy hair. His eyes flick to the dressing on Sylene's leg, which he bends to tuck in tightly before grinning at her. They hold each other's gaze. There is something mournful in his eyes. Sylene's heart pummels her chest. She stood. She stood there in the heat of the sun and knew that it would kill her. She had wanted to die. Like her husband, like her sons. It was their destiny to burn.

"Like a *relief*," the Pharmacist replies.

The next morning she is sick again and, sweaty, sits on the veranda in the dew. Something is changing with the days: the temperature is dropping and clouds firm up around the horizon. Tom sits beside her. He is always beside her; he will not leave her alone. He asks her who she thinks "they" are and where exactly "they" are from. He reminds her of an anagram, years ago, about China—something about *China Lads*—and whether she thinks it was them. She takes her pills. A wooziness smothers her mind. An inner swell of sickness. She can no longer string thoughts together; they detach and splash apart. She takes more pills.

The pain in her leg subsides, but that night the rest

of her body worsens. A heavy fever takes her and she
is violently sick. Tom bathes her and the Pharmacist
re-dresses her wound. She hears them talking, discussing her, their mutual hatred roiling beneath the surface
of their words. They can't leave here now. Tom will
not leave her alone. The Pharmacist strokes her skin.
In the morning, Tom feeds her soup the Pharmacist
has made. She hears him swimmingly through her
dreams—dreams of her sole surviving son, of being
buried and burning in the sun. She hears him ask the
Pharmacist about Bea, about the van; how Claire *told*
them it had come here. She can hear the hatred in his
voice. The Pharmacist must hear it too. He tells Tom,
"Let's get that leg healed first." Then he feeds her
more pills, and makes her drink, and scrapes out and
recleans her wound.

Fever dreams swirl for days until they curl away as she
cools. Her body relaxes and at some time her thoughts
take grip again and loop together as she comes back
from the shadows, where flickering ghosts of things
that were and things that might have been had ap-
peared equally real.

They are sitting, Sylene and Tom, in silence on the veranda, as they have been doing for days: she in a chair

with a bucket at her side and he, as always, beside her. His chin is thick with stubble and his eyes will no longer settle. Every day he asks if she's well enough to leave, when can they leave to search for Bea? They watch the Pharmacist tend the garden and talk politely when he returns. She wants to ask the Pharmacist things, they swell like a deluge inside her stomach, but Tom is always there, he is there right now between them.

Then, as the birds take to the air in the early-evening breeze, a guard rounds the hedge by the lawn. "A rabble!" he shouts, waving, raising his gun toward the gates.

"Ah!" The Pharmacist curls out of his chair and tilts his hat. "What have they got?"

The guard shrugs and calls, "Fuel and stuff. They said that's what you wanted."

"Well, tell them next time we want *meat*!" He spins to Tom and Sylene and lowers his voice. "You do like meat?"

"Sure," says Tom.

The Pharmacist nods. "It tastes good if you ignore what it is. And it's full of natural protein," he adds, and strolls into the house. The guard waits, watching them.

"What's going on?" Tom murmurs. When Sylene says nothing, he nudges the empty bucket with his foot. "You're doing well, aren't you? Maybe we'll be able to leave soon. What do you think, Kate? Can we go? It's ripping me apart being here." His eyes are pleading as he searches hers. Sylene feels her face twitch as she tries to hold his gaze. "What's the matter?" he asks.

"Nothing, Tom. I'm just exhausted."

"But we're losing so much time! *Kate.* You're well again! We have to go or we'll never find her. And I can't go without you—we have to stay together."

"Tom . . ." And his expression, firmed up with anger and confusion, breaks, and she sees deep in his eyes a vulnerability, a fear of ceasing to hope that they will somehow find the girl. She recognizes it in herself: her own hope, her own hurt, and what she feels for her son—

The Pharmacist sighs, stepping back out onto the veranda. He tosses a rattling bottle between his hands. "Be a pal, Tom. Take this down the drive, would you?"

"What is it?"

"Payment," the Pharmacist remarks. He rattles the bottle again and then morphs the movement into a syncopated swing down by his hips and speaks in time with the rhythm. "A mildish opiate, I think is what it is. Just two pills each, now, Tom. And make sure that they give the stuff to you first." He stops dancing, strides over, and pats Tom's shoulder, a gesture that turns into a grip and then an encouraging lift before he pushes him down the stairs. Tom turns to protest but the Pharmacist lowers the bottle into his hands like a chalice, then puts his finger to his lips and points firmly down the driveway. Tom turns and the Pharmacist exhales, watching him go. "He really never leaves you alone, does he?"

"He'll make us leave soon for the girl."

"Do you want to stay here? You can, you know."

"I should stay with him. We don't want him closing the breach. So what do I need to know?"

"It's difficult, Sylene. Knowledge is in very limited supply. We got President Taylor. We hit China soon after, but things fell apart so quickly it's hard to know who else we got. Some power stations. I think that's what did it for the Feed. Energen was pulled out of the Arctic by its CEO. An announcement from nowhere, apparently. He had them creating cold-fusion plants, started promoting utterly unheard-of technology, so we definitely got to him. But I don't know any more. The Feed hasn't transmitted for years. It all broke, Sylene."

Sylene rubs her face. "So we've done it? It worked?"

"I don't know. It seems so."

"And can we use the Feed to find each other?"

"Not yet. There's no power, so the Hubs are all down. SaveYou still runs, of course, though. Don't let Hatfield work that out or he may try to close it down.

I don't know . . ." The Pharmacist glances at her from the corner of his eye. "Have patience, Sylene, we'll make the Feed work again. And the world. There are quite a few of us, you know. And still some more may come."

"Really?"

"We're all dotted around," he says, and nods. "There must be thousands of us at least. Maybe more. Who knows? There are a couple close by, for example. They head up some little camp. You know, she actually seems to *care* about these people."

Sylene frowns, remembering the pea pods, the furnace that they'd made. "Claire's one of us?"

"Is that what she's calling herself now? Gosh, she really has gone native. The body she got is fat," the Pharmacist describes with relish, and blows out his cheeks. "Missing ear. Lower lip incised."

"So . . ." Sylene stops talking as things come together. Like that: they click. The lost child. Tom's daughter. This Bea. And that SaveYou still works, of course. So there's an obvious way to find her. And with that she realizes how she can find her son—if, that is, he survived. But she won't know unless she looks, and using Bea like this is the best she's come up with yet. Her voice comes quickly on the hammering of her heart: "How did you look for your family, Ethan?"

"Who are you searching for, Sylene?" The Pharmacist's words are too fluid. She sees the dart of his tongue around his lips before he snaps, "Forget them!" And then, warmly again, "Who is it? Who have you lost? Are you all sad?" He examines her, leaning to stare into her eyes, and his voice stops crooning and spits, "Well, they're dead! Whoever they are. Stop torturing yourself."

"What happened to you, Ethan?"

"Hurt breeds hurt. I can't describe the *hatred* I feel. I thought it would stop, but no, it grows. I *hate* them, Sylene, I—"

"I hate them too, but—"

"Enough." The Pharmacist nods down the lawn to where Tom is marching back toward them, straining with gasoline tanks and a bag across his back. "The Hatfield himself," he sighs. "And be careful, Sylene. Slips like the geklean are unforgivable. A-*ha*! Splendid!" he cries as Tom drops the tanks on the ground.

Tom's voice shakes. "What you're running here is wrong."

The Pharmacist scrutinizes him. "But you enjoy the light and the warmth and the food and water?" He knocks his hat back from his brow. "All things that wouldn't be possible without a little suffering passed off down the line. Isn't that life?"

"Those people are destroyed. They're animals!" Tom cries, pointing back at the gates.

"You have a choice." The Pharmacist's fingers mark time in the air. "And so do they. So do I, Tom. I choose to play."

Tom's voice is seething. "You remember those people we saw, Kate, when we were coming here? Well, they're all outside, addicted to . . . what is it?" He throws the plastic bottle up the stairs.

"As I said, I don't know," the Pharmacist apologizes, snatching the bottle up off the floor, opening it, counting the remaining pills. "But they seem to like it, and I have a whole lot more inside."

"And there you are. Fuel and stuff." Tom kicks one of the bags. "There's a chicken too."

"Ah, excellent!" the Pharmacist exclaims. "Meat for supper tonight!"

Tom stomps up the steps and sits between them. He scowls out at the garden, his fingers twisting over themselves. Sylene glances at the Pharmacist behind Tom's head and nods him to go inside. "Well . . . let's get these stored, then," the Pharmacist says mock tactfully, and stoops to lift a tank. Wheezing exaggeratedly, he stumbles into the house—but as soon as he disappears, his footsteps become unlabored and they echo easily away.

Tom deflates. "All those people. He has them addicted. One woman, she gave me that chicken—a *chicken*—for a pill."

Sylene takes Tom's hands. She examines his skin like a map. "It's not a fair world, Tom. But you've got to harden up. If we're going to find Bea, we will have to fight. Never give up hope. We'll find her. You'll see."

Tom stacks their packed rucksacks by the door that night. Sylene's strength has returned. She spends the next morning in the gardens, walking between the plants. She lies on the lawn and feels the wet depth of the earth beneath her. She smells the flowers deeply. She is better now, apart from one thing: while the fever has disappeared, the swelling waves of sickness remain.

"So . . ." says the Pharmacist, rubbing his palms as she sits on the counter before him. He unpeels the bandage and smiles up at her with hooded eyes. "Well, haven't I done well? You are free to leave whenever you like. *If* you like. You can always amuse yourself with me here. Wouldn't that be nicer than heading off with *him*?"

She ignores his suggestive glance and bends to examine her shin. It's still bloody but the colors have gone from the veins. As the Pharmacist spreads more cream on her leg, he holds the muscle of her calf firmly, kneading her skin, and his hands slowly move up her thigh.

"Thank you, Ethan."

"My pleasure. *Hmm*." The Pharmacist purses his lips. He trails a finger up her leg before raising it into the air. "You're still getting sick, though?" He feels her glands. Puts his hands on her waist and presses her stomach with his thumbs. When he looks up, his expression is excited. "You know, Sylene, this is quite a thing! All I can think is that you are—"

"Don't. The infection's gone?"

"Yes, but I—"

"Then you're a clever man. Well done. We should go now to find his daughter."

"I can give you something to solve it, if you like?"

Sylene frowns, but his steady gaze is immutable. There are many worlds in her head: one where she finds her child; one where she doesn't; one where she goes with Tom; one where she stays with the Pharmacist instead, with someone who would understand what she's been through, which is companionship of sorts. But with someone who seems so casually inhumane? So set to destroy people and their lives? To say that he could *solve* it?

"What's happened to you, Ethan?" she whispers. "Why would you suggest that?"

The Pharmacist smiles and shrugs. "Don't you find it so lonely being alone?"

"But we're not alone anymore. That's the point. Why are you so determined to destroy things? I don't understand it. Those people outside. This—"

"Oh, look at *you* playing happy family with Mr. Hatfield . . ." Contempt drips around the sides of his words. "Look how *good* you are, Sylene!"

"I'm not . . ." Anger burns her cheeks. "I'm not playing anything, I'm trying to—"

"Listen," he says, and he puts his hand on her leg again. "We could build a life here, you and me. It could be *lovely*. We would be everything for each other. Don't leave me alone." He lays his hand on her belly and lets it linger there. Blinking shyly, he leans toward her until she pulls away.

"Thank you, Ethan, for curing me. I can't thank you enough—"

"Oh, I'm sure you can. You offered it. And I have *totally* cured your leg. Listen, I'd rather you didn't go, I'd much prefer you stay with me, but if you *are* leaving, well, that was the deal you proposed. You *offered* me yourself. So if this is good-bye, let's go!"

"Ethan . . ."

"I just want a bit of what *they* get, Sylene." His tone has changed again. It has thinned, become pleading, but with the whiplash potential of a tightly compressed spring. He smiles and strokes her cheek. Licks his lips. Smiles again, his long face stretching. "I'm human, after all!"

Sylene shrugs his hands off her and slides away from the counter, shaking her head. In her mind she is already out of the house, planning their journey and the next moves she must make, when his voice stops her, halfway to the door.

"If I told Tom Hatfield who you really are, do you think he'd want you then?"

Sylene closes her eyes. Bites her lip. "Why would you do that, Ethan?"

She hears him crossing the room behind her, and his voice when he speaks, though quiet, is sinuously close to her ear as his fingers curl around her hips.

"What are you planning, Sylene? I know you're up to something. It's in the things you never quite say . . ."

"Like you said, I have to stay with him, we can't let him close the breach!"

"Well, I might just let him know that his wife's no longer herself. That's the charitable thing to do. Because it's cruel, isn't it, really, that the poor man doesn't know what he's lost—"

"Don't!"

"Then what will you offer in return? What's in this

for *me*? I make myself vulnerable to you and you treat me with contempt. I make you well and he takes you off. I'm left alone again. You're not even giving me some fun with a body that isn't even yours!"

"Tom!" Sylene calls loudly, and then, turning, whispers rapidly, "I'll come back to you, I promise, but let me find his daughter first. Think about it, Ethan, he may be useful to us. *She* may be useful, because if we have the girl, we can make him do—what—we—want." She has a hand on his face and strokes underneath his jaw. She kisses him quickly and he, briefly, closes his eyes and sighs. "And when I come back, then we'll see what the future might bring—for us."

Things flicker across the Pharmacist's face. A sudden loosening and expansion of his pupils in hope; faint quivers of doubt. Then the door opens and Tom enters. He glares at the Pharmacist from the threshold.

"Kate? Did you call for me?"

"I'm cured," Sylene says, and hurries toward him. "He's done it, Tom, my leg! Let's leave here now, let's find Bea!"

"You're definitely leaving then? Is that what you've decided . . . Mrs. Hatfield?" The Pharmacist, swaying slightly, watches Sylene, his eyes on fire.

Tom blanches and turns on her. "You told him who we are?"

"He forced me to!" she hisses. "That's why I called for you. Come on, let's go!"

"Oh!" the Pharmacist croons across the room, laughing. "I tell you what, Tom, listen to this. I'll give you a choice, all right?"

Tom hesitates as Sylene tries to pull him out.

"*Kate* here hasn't really left me any choice at all, so the choice *you* have to make is between your *wife* and your *daughter.* Like we started, all that time ago. What do you say, hey?"

"What do you mean?"

"Let me have your wife," the Pharmacist explains, ambling daintily across the carpet, "and I'll tell you where your girl is. What do you think about *that*?"

Tom squeezes Sylene's hand. Indecision cracks his voice. "Kate?"

"I saw her not too long ago, you see," the Pharmacist muses. "She is a pretty little thing and will be fertile, I'm sure, like her mother."

There is a potent pause before Tom leaps forward. "Where is she?" he cries. "Why didn't you tell us before?"

"Will you let me have your wife?" the Pharmacist spits at him. "Tit for tat, come on!"

"Please!" Sylene appeals, struggling between the two of them. "Why are you doing this?"

"Because," the Pharmacist says tartly, "who wants to be alone? I'll tell you where your daughter is, *Kate*, and you can stay with me while he gets her! Then, when they return, how happy we can be!"

They stand like that, the three of them unmoving, shaking, until, like a wire under tension snapping, Sylene relents. She grabs the Pharmacist's hand and leads him across the creaking floor, Tom staring after her, flushing, as she leans the Pharmacist against the counter, strokes his chest and runs a hand up his arm. He relaxes, closes his eyes, smiling; hums as she caresses his neck and leans down toward his lips. Then both her hands are there, one behind his head and the other squeezing his throat, and the Pharmacist's eyes jerk open, along with his gaping mouth.

"*Tell us where our daughter is!*" she snarls, but the Pharmacist, bent back, holds his breath and grins determinedly at her. He forces out a wink. "What happened to you?" she whispers. "This isn't how we should be!"

"We owe these people *nothing*," the Pharmacist chokes out. His stale breath caresses her face; they're so close together, speaking so fiercely quietly. "Don't leave me! Look after your own. That's what this is all about, Sylene—"

"Don't—"

The Pharmacist strains to raise his croaking voice as

she squeezes harder. "Mr. Hatfield, I have to tell you that your wife—"

She cracks his head against the countertop. His legs bow and then his feet scrabble for purchase on the floor. From the corner of her eye, Sylene sees Tom tense, but he stays where he is, too far away to hear. "It's my son!" she whispers desperately in the Pharmacist's ear. "All right? It's my boy. That's who I'm trying to find, Ethan! And if I can find him, I'll come back here, and if I can't find him, I'll come back too. I won't leave you alone, I promise, but *please* let me have a chance! If you tell him who I am, I'll leave you alone forever, I swear it. Keep the secret and tell us where his girl is, and there's a chance, isn't there, that I'll come back for you. It's the only one you have."

The Pharmacist starts to shake as Sylene squeezes his throat harder. It's as though an electric current courses through him as he tries to keep his lips clamped together while his face turns redder and redder, until—

"They came here for supplies!" he croaks, bursting, gasping in some air.

"What supplies?"

"Sedatives," the Pharmacist wheezes. "That's what they always want."

"And where did they *go*?" Sylene demands, releasing her grasp slightly.

"I don't know!" The Pharmacist heaves in a breath. "Truly I don't—at least not exactly. But they went north. They're holed up in some valley. I heard they've taken a village."

Sylene glances at Tom, whose slowly nodding face is deathly pale. She releases the Pharmacist and, wiping her hands on her top, staggers back toward Tom. Takes him by the elbow. They walk unsteadily toward the door.

"Oh, Mrs. Hatfield?"

Behind them, the Pharmacist sprawls by the counter, his hair disheveled, his clothes awry. There are tears on his face, but he's smiling. He closes his eyes and savors the air as if smelling spring flowers on a breeze. His fingertips linger along his throat. His other hand scuffs his groin.

"That was lovely," he whispers. "Thank you."

At the bottom of the drive the guards roll the gates back, and it's almost like no time has passed, except now she can walk without pain. Ivy clogs the canopy. Birds roost and coo. It's not long before they pass a group of racked and starving people. Most lie on the road, staring up at the sky. One, a woman, pale-eyed and spattered with muck, cranes to stare at them. She reaches toward Tom, her face stretched in a pleading grimace.

"That was her," he says quietly. "With the chicken."

They soon leave the suburbs behind them and they walk northward for days toward the hills. They eat very little and stop only briefly to sleep. They reach a track that coils into a valley, past farms and rusting threshers. Searching for this village. But no one lives here now. Time has passed and a new world opens up before them. The landscape changes and a wind whips down from the dark and vicious rocks that rise to higher ground.

At every high point, Tom searches the land. His gaze is keen and at the same time forlorn. Sylene watches him as he looks for the spiked van. She does too, but not really. She can't let them find it; she must do everything she can to stop that from coming to pass. Tom not finding Bea, she has realized, is how she'll find her son.

For days the rains fall. They run through them and shelter beneath the trees until her skin is a puckered, floating layer. She's never known anything like it. Her limbs hurt from shaking and her fingers become blunt with cold. They find a cottage in a wood at the foot of a gully that glints dully in the rain. The door is off its hinges but the windows are still intact.

"Shall we see if the rain gets lighter?" Tom asks, his

teeth chattering as the icy water flows down his chin. "We're no use to Bea dead."

She nods, of course she does; she has no intention of letting them find the girl and every delay will help. And she's freezing; her nod is just a slightly deeper dip in the constant juddering of her drenched and shaking head. She has never been this cold in her life and it scares her. Inside, she is indescribably terrified. So they approach the derelict place and force the rusty door open. Stale air eases out. Aside from a slow-creeping leak of mold, the hall is undisturbed. The staircase and the rooms upstairs are the same. It's like people were here and they only just left, or they are hiding around a corner in the soupy, unmoving air.

In the kitchen the surfaces are clean, hardly even dusty. It looks like a museum piece. A plastic-wrapped casserole by the oven has mushroomed up with mold. Only one more room to check, and Sylene is aware of the smell as she jerks the door. What had once been a dining room has been ransacked: the furniture is up-ended, photoscreens on their sides. Old-style LCD pictures and wallpaper have been ripped to shreds and fur lies scattered everywhere. There has been a fight here between animals. The glass garden door is pivoted open and the carpet and walls are drenched and stained. On the table and on two of the chairs are the faintest re-

mains of people: an imprint of their arms on the tabletop and of what had happened to their bodies on the
floor. A crisp layer of dark blood coats the lacquer,
tongue-laps smeared across it. And two knives, stuck to
the surface of the wood. She finds a blood-flecked let-
ter, taped closed, and gives it to Tom.

Darling Paul and Jenny,
If you make it back, come join us. We're happy, but
we miss you. Cut deep.

> *We love you,*
> *Mum and Dad*

They rearrange the room as best they can, heave
the garden door closed and barricade it with the table.
Then they find tins in the kitchen and eat from them
raw. Limbs aching and eyelids heavy as the sky gets
dark outside, they climb the stairs and into the freezing
bed. It is damp and moldy. Rain hammers against the
windows. After a while, Sylene sits.

"I'll watch first," she says, touching his arm. "I'll
watch you, Tom; you sleep."

"Fine," Tom says. "As you like."

She used to joke with her husband that their son Darian was their mistake. But then so was their firstborn,

Gabe. Because who would bring children into their world? All the advice was against it, as was common sense. So what counteracted rationality? Animal instinct? Hope? Their boys were the youngest people in the Scraper, probably in all the Areas around. They had grown up angry as a result; they were too young to have known anything else, any other way of life. Never setting foot outside in their lives, they were hell-bent on fixing what had happened and on doing more besides, she began to realize as she overheard them talk. They never said the word *revenge* but it was always there.

She watched them train. Thousands of them had signed up when the operation was conceived, and there were thousands more in reserve. That was in their Scraper alone. That it was patently a suicide mission spoke chapters, she thought; she could only imagine how their hatred sounded when it was discussed openly behind closed doors. It was their fuel, their drive: you hurt us and so now we will hurt you. We *hate* you. And for good reason too. She was deeply proud of them. They had undertaken a terrifying ordeal. But she was absolutely scared of them as well. Their zeal. She didn't understand it; their language didn't sit right in her brain. She no longer recognized her world.

Their training reverberated through the metal halls,

the low-level light in the corridors creating a world of shadowed struts and grilles. Metal, metal everywhere. The atmosphere control had been unpowered for years. They were forced to deeper levels to avoid the building heat. So they planned their reckless escape. All odds were against it and she was powerless to protect her children from the world or from themselves, yet she was utterly desperate to try; it ripped her apart at the seams. They trained. Their time was running out. The heat was rising. Their father had died already. There was no more energy, no more fuel. This was it, where it had been going all along: the burning, futile end of things. Tens of thousands of them had gone. In other Areas, many more. She had to be strong as first Gabe, then Darian, had left, sacrificing themselves for the cause. She had watched her sons die for it; she had held their hands as their bodies died, clutched them as she clung on to the hope, the unproven chance, that their minds had somehow survived.

The rains still pour the following day. Wet trees cover the cottage. The sky is crowded with clouds. The roof drips. In the garden, two tanks have water swelling their brims.

"Would you like a bath?" Tom asks, turning back from the view.

"Sure," she says, still in bed. "Yes please."

She watches through the window as Tom builds a fire in the garage, smoke rolling along the ceiling and out the open door. They heat saucepans of water and run with them across the wet grass and upstairs, filling the bath until it's deep and warm. Steam condenses on the mirror, revealing like invisible ink ancient hand-sweeps across the glass.

"In you go," Tom says, and goes to close the door, but she doesn't let him. He wavers.

"Would you like to get in too?"

"You enjoy it."

She stands in the bathroom until her limbs begin to tremble with the cold. Just with the cold? Tom is behaving differently. Her survival is tenuous at best: an elastic energy, the surface tension of water, at any moment ready to snap. She undresses and wipes the condensation from the windowpane. Rubs her neck with her freezing palms. Presses her cold fingers to her forehead and then her stomach. She probes her stomach until, shaking too much, she slips into the water.

By the time she comes downstairs, trailing her fingers along the dusty wallpaper in the stairwell, there is a rich and heady smell rising to greet her.

"What's this?" she asks quietly from the kitchen door.

"What's this?" Tom remarks. "What's *that?*"

Sylene fingers the edge of a white cotton bathrobe, the trim with stripes of pink. "Do you think she'd mind?"

Tom smiles faintly and then turns away to finish laying cutlery and plates on the table. He places a platter in its center before pulling back a chair for her to sit.

"Dinner," he announces. "At lunchtime."

As she eases past him into the chair, he moves only slightly away. His voice is incredibly quiet. "Kate. *Kate.* Look," he says, "I'm sorry. I've been in an awful mood."

"Tom . . ."

"No, I . . . I didn't like being there. I felt so powerless. I don't blame you—but—and he was . . ." He kneels, and they observe each other as his words fall apart. "I didn't help you," he utters in the end. "I didn't save you. You did it all."

Sylene puts her fingers through his hair as he bows his head to her chest. She doesn't know what to say. They stay like that until Tom, quietly sniffing back his tears, fetches a tin of anemic vegetables and puts them on the table. Then he goes on his knees again, takes her head at the back of the neck, and kisses her. His grip is strong. She refuses to respond but she doesn't pull away. He lays his hand on her thigh, where the robe has fallen open, until, finally, she turns and nods at the food. "This looks amazing," she whispers. "Thank you."

"I love you, Kate."

"I know." Sylene picks up her cutlery.

Clearly smarting, clearly choking something back, Tom lifts the platter to reveal a colorful block of metal, its label scuffed and torn. "It's tin-baked salted beef à la firewood." And suddenly he's crying. "Kate, I'm so sorry—"

"You don't need to apologize!"

"But I don't know how to find her. How long can we hope? I'm so tired! How can we *find* her, Kate?"

The food steams as the rain pours down the windowpanes, its shadows running like graying floes on the floral-patterned tiles. She puts her arms on his shoulders and sighs. Carefully, now. "Maybe we've lost her, Tom. Maybe we won't find her by wandering. Can you think of another way that we can work out where she's been?"

"I'm not like Mark," he says, something hardening in his voice, and he pulls away suddenly, some strength flaring up beneath his tears.

"Mark?"

"I won't give up like him!" he says, searching Sylene's eyes. Something changes there; something resolves. "We're going north, like the Pharmacist said. We'll get up high and look for the van. Look for the smoke of their camp. Let's look for their fires at night. We will *find* her, Kate, I *promise*. Come on! We mustn't give up hope!"

"I know," she says, backtracking before the glare in his eyes. "I agree, but . . ." But she can't tell him about SaveYou without revealing herself. Because Kate wouldn't know. So she must help him work it out. She has to get them to the tower; she must gain access to their homeHub. ". . . but surely, Tom, *think*," she pleads, and runs her fingers through his hair. Down his neck, where she rubs it at the base. She imagines the implant there, woven gracefully into his brain, into his very being. She kisses him softly and smiles. "There must be a clever way to find her."

By the time they leave the cottage, the trees are saturated and their bark is dark. The gully looms rottenly above them, its rocks jagged to the sky. The air is ionized and the ground sodden, leaking up into their boots.

"That smell," Sylene says. "It's amazing."

"It's autumn. It's turned. I hope they've harvested at home."

They walk through the wood on mulching leaves, a wood that has stretched over fields and tracks without care. Sunlight slides through the branches, lighting up the moss. Birds skitter and stop, bowing at the moist ground, pecking for worms and grubs. They camp in the most sheltered spots they can find—in hollows and caves with fires built at their entrances to kill off the increasing cold—but still they shake through the nights. That smell she loved becomes the herald of shiver-aching joints, fingers numb with cold. They scramble up into the jagged hills and survey the land. It is tough and very steep. Rain makes the moss-covered slate slippery and sharp. Tom stops often to check that she's all right. She nods every time. Of course she is. She's climbed worse than this.

She remembers climbing the Scraper after Darian had died. *That* had been a climb. She had signed up to be in the next wave, what looked to be the final one because there was hardly anyone left. She had enough provisions for the two days she thought it would take her to reach the surface and return, scaling the hundreds and hundreds of levels of the Scraper by stairs. The tubes had been down for decades. All the screens in the emergency stairwells were blank—down for decades too. She could remember in years gone by all the beautiful vistas screened on them when energy supplies were too low to run individual Feeds anymore, the rivers and grasslands and lakes replaced now by the bland grayness of the obsolete screens. The daily domestic aspects of the Scrapers had been powered by people's harvested footsteps as they went about their lives; but with too few now there just weren't enough steps. Energy had become sacred. The cold-fusion generators couldn't keep up with the demand for the long journeys back. There was no way to manufacture parts for the solar arrays above, being pummeled by the heat, and anyway it was too dangerous to go onto the surface to fix them. Rather, they had to preserve energy. The Feed was largely shut down. Entire Areas had been closed, thousands of Scrapers sealed. Their vast central plungeholes provided limited natural light, their arrays of mirrors twinkling in the void making the habitats places of diamond-flecked darkness. The energy needed for the atmosphere control had simply been too much for years, so the air was stale and the temperature out of control. The temperature. Always mounting, even though she still had four hundred levels to climb. Already the air here was baked, the handrails too hot to hold. Deep breath . . .

"There!" Tom hisses, and grabs her arm.

She sees nothing; and then movement on the road

far below, twisting below the cliffs where they stand. Tom's grip tightens.

"There," he growls. "Do you see it?"

She isn't prepared for this. She doesn't expect the terrible thing that she sees. There is no denying its spiked shape. It is small with distance, but definitely round, and prickled with spines all over. This far away she can't see what's pulling it, but it's moving slowly for sure. Tom's grip is viselike. His hand trembles intensely. His face is ashen, stunned. And then he breaks out in a cheer.

They stay up high to keep the vehicle in sight. It's Tom's idea and it works. Sylene is impressed; she wouldn't have thought of something so obvious, though she is disappointed, of course, that he has. If they find Bea now, she doesn't know what she'll do; she can't allow it to happen. But how can she prevent it? she wonders, as they keep running along the ridge, parallel to the valley floor. Their route up high is more direct than the road's, a curling ribbon of mossy green. They close distance that afternoon and Tom stays awake all night, watching the tiny fire in the valley. When it is extinguished, he paces around until dawn, when he wakes her and tells her they're moving. They run, and approach, and start to descend the ridge, and she still hasn't worked out how to thwart this. She needs Tom not to find Bea but she still needs him to trust her. So she needs to alert these people whom they track throughout the day, closing in, stalking carefully.

Dusk falls as they reach the valley floor. Tom has hurried them on and they have dropped down beside the road, ahead of where the van will come. They rest outside a thicket through which the vehicle must pass, hiding behind huge ferns whose buttery smell clogs her head. They wait until the night is pitch. No movement but the whispering wraiths of trees, the gasping hustle of the grass. And then, finally, she hears creaking. It draws effortfully up the road: the roll of rusted wheels crunching over moss and soft wood, the squeaking of the vehicle as it trundles ponderously past.

"Can you see them?" Tom whispers, and she shakes her head. It's too dark. The vehicle is obscured by the trees. There could be many people flanking it. Or no one. And they may all have gone past or not. Sylene snaps around: maybe they're being flanked; maybe the vehicle is a trap, a lure for *them*. The ferns bristle silver in the moonlight. The cliffs rise above them, their jagged edges defined by the scattering of stars. Wind. Silence.

"Okay, what do we do?"

She makes a face at Tom; she really doesn't know.

She says they should wait until dawn—it's all she can think, to buy time—but he won't wait any longer. The hopeful plan is formed that she will follow the van along the road while Tom runs to overtake it. They'll follow it until it stops. She is there to watch, that's all, to see if an opportunity arises; Tom, meanwhile, will get close, right up and inside the van if possible. If he can sneak up and steal the kids away tonight, then why wait until morning?

"Listen," he says, and takes her hands. "If anything happens, to me or either of us, the other must save Bea. All right?" He raises his eyes and seems like a ghost in the moonlight. "I love you, Kate," he says, and she can hear the tears in his voice. "Let's get her back. We'll go back to Claire's. And we'll never be apart again." He kisses her and peers through the darkness. "Kate?"

She lets his hands go and takes his cheek. "I love you too, Tom," she tells him.

She watches him disappear between the ferns and then pushes through the trees to the road: a more open darkness, though smothered with slippery moss. Sodden branches collapse softly beneath her feet as she skids onward. The world is sketched out in gray. The trees' branches wave above her. The silver, mossy road. Black tracks of wheels are churned up where the van passed just before. A crashed car crumpled into a tree across the undergrowth. And Tom somewhere ahead, running through the dark, risking his life for the child. She can't let it happen; she needs him alive; she needs him desperate for his daughter.

Birds screech somewhere ahead. She wades through the deep grass off the road back to the crashed car. Its hood is burst open, its doors flung out wide. She fumbles around for a large, firm stick and then, lifting it high, smashes the rear windscreen as hard as she can. The glass fractures into cubes and scatters like a sneeze, near silent. Some birds beat into the canopy but the night is barely disturbed. "Fuck!" she spits, and her face is contorted as she raises the stick again and brings it down onto the roof. The flat thump echoes, drumming into the trees. *Boom.* She does it again, again, and again, smashing more glass and rattling the stick around the frames, booming the roof, sending a tumult into the night.

She finally stops, panting, and the sounds echo away.

The road is empty behind her. No one in the woods that she can see.

She climbs back up to the road and runs until she sees the van ahead. Abandoned. Alone in the moonlight, taking up half the way with its smooth-domed spiky bulk. It has stopped below a slight clearing in the trees, and as she watches, Tom sneaks from the bushes beyond. Moonlit, keeping low, he looks around quickly and runs to the vehicle. As he nears it, he slows and reaches out to touch it, and something clangs into its side. Something else does too, and Sylene sees a small rock smack into Tom's arm before hearing a shouting cry coming from the trees. A figure runs out and shoulders Tom to the ground. They roll in the earth as Sylene runs out to help him, but Tom has already won with ease: he has his hands around the throat of a small and flailing man.

"Don't hurt us!" the man cries, and tries to bite Tom's wrists.

"Who's *us*?" she demands, and lowers the stick to the side of the man's head. She glares at the trees around them, her heart pounding. "Who's there?" she shouts. "Or I'll kill him!"

After some silence, another figure emerges. Small, bundled, and shaking, a woman approaches, her hands raised in the air. "Please don't hurt him," her weak voice calls.

Tom lets the man go to scoop him up again and push him between two of the thickset spikes on the van. Sylene has never seen him like this, snarling in the night. His frenzied eyes are deadened, like an animal's.

"Who are you? Where are the children?"

"W-what children?" the man stammers.

"Please don't hurt him! Take anything you want!" the woman cries.

Tom, still fiercely holding the man, falters. He glances back at Sylene. "Open it," she orders, gesturing at the van with her stick. This close up, the spikes look less forbidding. She touches the flaking paint on one of them. The spike is made of wood.

The weeping man pushes his wife aside and opens the doors of the van. It's then that the woman starts screaming: *"Please don't take him, please leave us the boy!"*

Inside, the van is nearly bare. There are empty wooden shelves and some boxes, but nothing else besides a pallet on which a body is strapped. The corpse of a child, all bundled in rugs, more bone than anything else.

Tom gags from the smell. "What the hell is this?"

"Our son!" the woman cries. "Please don't make us let him go!"

Once the sun has risen, she takes another look. The oval shell is metal, but the wooden spikes are moldering. Decoration, the man tells them; this is the first time they've not deterred an attack. Tom is sitting, distant, down the road. He hasn't slept all night. Sylene opens the back of the van again. There is nothing of any use. Some shards of tech and lumps of wood.

Hardly even any food. Some leaves. Are those potatoes? A box of near-rotting apples. And the child. The bones. These pitiful people's son. Dead for over a year, by the look of him.

"Be careful," she tells them. They still won't meet her eye. "You shouldn't light fires at night."

And they, skittering around her, pick up the bridles and start rolling the van away themselves. Sylene watches them go. Then she turns to Tom. He looks up at her from where he is sitting on a disintegrating mossy log. His expression is entirely eroded.

"It makes no difference now," he says. His voice is husky. Bone dry. "But what was that noise? Before we got them? They knew we were coming."

"I don't know. It must have been them. Were they trying to scare us off?"

She reaches her hand down. Tom looks at it, dangling in front of his face, and then, taking it, with effort stands.

They spend two days going more slowly, but pick up pace as they near a town. Tom's fire has collapsed, hope barely kindling anymore. They have approached along a stream and they reach a crumbling bridge: a redbrick hump with low-arched sides. "I know where we are," he says suddenly. He has been so quiet these last two days, and withdrawn, but now something brings light to his face. "Do you recognize it, Kate?"

"Are there any Hubs around here?"

"Hubs?" He frowns. "No. We're in the middle of nowhere. Don't you recognize it?"

"Remind me."

A fence bursts outward from a paddock, the earth all churned. There's a church amid the trees with scorch marks on its walls. The stained glass is warped. This place is like nowhere she's ever seen. Of course she doesn't recognize it, and the slight enthusiasm in Tom's eyes is dimming as he waits. Cottages line the road. One rosebush has taken over three front lawns. There is movement in an upstairs window, a flash behind curtains, and then nothing more.

In the end she just smiles at him and nods.

"We need to get up high." Tom turns away from her. "So we can see around. Look for their camp, for smoke. We have to be *tactical.*" His eyes are exhausted; there is so little light left, but still he scans above the houses, points at a ridge of rock that stands tall. "That will give us a good view. Let's see if there are any supplies here. You'll soon recognize where we are."

They follow the road as it curves past a village hall. Notices for rummage sales and fetes and posters for films are still up behind cracked and milky glass.

"Up here, I think," Tom says as they hit the main road, and points. "Yes, look!"

The shop's doors are still locked but its windows have been broken. At Tom's insistence, Sylene goes in under the hanging shards. Bodies of mannequins surround them, tangled in ropes, harnesses, and clothes. She skids on the dusty floor.

"Remember it?" Tom asks again. "It's where we bought this old thing."

He lifts the hem of his jacket. Sylene smiles and laughs and looks around the shop.

"A while ago," she agrees, and walks away. She finds a large rucksack and transfers the contents from her own, turning this whole thing over in her mind. Food, a pan, some mugs, her hat; she puts aside the small T-shirt with the airplane on it . . . and repacks it all as Tom furls a rope. She watches from the corner of her eye as he takes some ancient vacuum-packed biscuits from a dust-laden shelf, spots some map packs and waves one at her.

"France," he says. "Do you remember those trips we went on?" And then, when she says nothing and just goes back to her packing, "Do you miss teaching the kids French?"

"Of course I do. So what else shall we get?"

"Some waterproofs and some wax. Let's get a tent.

In fact, let's get two. When we find Bea, we'll need the space. Have you seen any knives? And test those flashlights. I'm sure the batteries will be gone, but who knows . . ."

They camp at the foot of the ridge. Rain clouds have built but come to nothing, and as the sun sets, they lift, their undersides reflecting red and gold back onto the earth. They eat a weasel that Tom has caught, tangled in a contraption of wire and lured by some moldy biscuit. Birds fill the sky, sweeping the air for bugs.

"I tell you one thing I liked about his place," Tom says.

"Whose?"

"The Pharmacist's. And that was the music. That Wynton Marsalis when we first went in."

Sylene eats from her bowl with her fingers. "That wasn't Wynton. It was Sonny Rollins. I'd know that old stuff anywhere."

"Well," Tom says levelly, "it was nice to hear music, anyway. It's something I miss. When was the last time we heard any? Can you even remember?"

"I like the birds," Sylene says. "They're enough for me. Just hearing them now, with the light, and the air . . . it's like being free."

"What do you mean?"

"It's good, that's all." She frowns. "All this nature is good. Are you all right, Tom? You seem a bit . . . you know."

Sylene continues to eat but Tom has stopped. He stares off into space. Sylene takes the stick from the fire and slides off more meat while Tom surveys the rocky ridge and the ribs of cloud hazing out.

"I wonder how Margaret and Nigel are," he says.

"This really is delicious."

"They made a nice couple, didn't they?"

She licks her fingers. "Can we have it again tomorrow?"

"Don't you think?"

"Yes, Tom," she sighs, "they did."

"And Jane, I wonder how she is. She'd love this sunset. Do you think she's still painting?"

"I hope so, Tom."

"Yeah," he says, and puts his plate on the ground. "That would be nice."

He stands and walks toward the woods.

"Going far?" she calls, but he is gone.

Sylene takes the remains of the weasel off the fire and kicks the ashes down. She finds some leaves and wipes the plates, and lays out their rugs beneath the canvas. She watches the sky and the birds. She breathes deeply on the air. She smiles to herself, lost in thought, and something melancholy hazes her eyes. The last sky she had seen before she left was blazing. It had taken her over a day to climb the Scraper, and at the top, barely able to breathe, she'd unsealed the airlock, fighting the crippling heat. The metal had seared her palms as she had gripped the handle and twisted. She cried out, gripped it and twisted again and again and again until it finally released. Some ancient alarm sounded as she opened the outer hatch, and that was when the heat really hit her. Smacked her down. It was like her face had been flayed in an instant. She could feel her throat blistering with every breath as she climbed the final rungs and hauled herself outside.

The sky was bleached. The earth stretched away, red-soiled, dried out and jagged. Dry wind roared in her ears. She stumbled a few steps, already feeling her skin burn away and peel. Parts of her clothing were melting. Before her, the vast circumference of the plungehole dropped down, the curved walls of its windows obsidian black, wormholing toward the depths of the earth, so many miles deep. She was taking the journey. She had decided to follow Darian and she had signed up to go. But she had to be sure she'd do it. It terrified her too much. It was suicide to go, she was sure of that, and how could she make herself die? It was against nature. Self-preservation: that most powerful of instincts.

So here, on this utterly barren plain, she threw her arms back and opened her chest to the sky, embraced the heat and all the other things that, never mind the actual light, had for the last minute been ravaging her body. Ten seconds was enough to kill someone, but she wanted to be sure. It had seen to her husband in thirty. So she stood for a minute, and for a minute more, until her dark hair curled and she couldn't see for the dryness of her eyes. She felt things run underneath her clothes but didn't know if it was fabric or skin. The gurney was waiting for her. To send her back. To do her duty. To stop this from ever coming to pass. And if it had worked for him, she was determined to find her son.

It is dark by the time she hears Tom return. The night has become chill and Sylene is under the rug. She sees he has bulges in his pockets as he stands above her, looking down.

"Do you mind if I sleep first?" Sylene asks, already nearly there.

"Sure."

"I'm exhausted."

"That's fine," Tom says, and removes the rocks. Two large and heavy things. "For the dogs," he says. "I don't think we're safe here."

When he slides in beside her, Sylene rolls onto her

side. She looks out along the earth and listens as he fidgets, as he takes off his clothes behind her. She hears the rocks clink as he drops them next to her head.

"Good night, Kate."

"Good night."

In the morning they climb the wide-toothed rocky hills. She is sick again as they go—she had told him she'd catch up—and she retches behind a bush. She looks out at his back, trudging slowly up ahead of her. Did he hear it? Did he not? She doesn't know anymore, has no idea what he's thinking. He keeps on ahead and now, near the top, the wind turns her hair to little whips, which flick her face. He is away and small in the distance.

Tom has stopped on a wide, flat rock where two valleys converge below. She sees he is waiting for her, but she is exhausted by the climb and goes slowly, her hands on her thighs as she hauls herself up the last of the slope. The slate clinks under her surely splitting boots as the ground gradually flattens out. As she approaches Tom, she can see into the other valley behind this spine of hills and there are lakes, long ones, the low sun reflecting off them through the early-morning haze. It makes the colors glow. The water is striated. Woods checker the landscape with the rolling fields and roads. It is perhaps the most beautiful view she has seen.

"A beautiful enough view?" Tom's voice, quiet for so long, knocks the silence apart.

Sylene nods, hands on hips, as high as the sky, looking down on all below. "Exactly what I was thinking. I can't see any smoke, though, or camps," she says. "There are some houses over there, and there—look—that's the village we've come up from, isn't it?"

Tom nods as she continues to scan the land.

"But I don't see any life. How long will we watch? Tom, this could take forever. We need to find another way. Is there anything about the Feed that could help us?" She turns and he is standing surprisingly close. With the sun in her eyes she can't make out his face; she raises a hand to shield them.

"Let's sit, Kate. I have something for you." Tom reaches behind his back.

Sylene is tired. Her limbs are weak. The taste of vomit stings her throat. She sits. Tom kneels in front of her and pulls from one pocket an apple and from his other pocket another.

"Thanks, I'm starving."

He watches her eat, his own apple held tightly in his hand.

"Where did you get these?"

"The van. In a box. I took them."

"You should have gotten more."

Tom rests his hands on his thighs and looks out at the view. There is so much air around them and so, so much light. It is clear for miles around. "You have no idea what this is, do you?"

Sylene stops eating. Tom is speaking very quietly.

"You don't know," he says, almost musingly. "It's not that you can't remember."

"What," Sylene asks, slowly wiping her lips, "don't I know?"

"Over there." Tom nods. "It was on the other side of this valley. We walked up for sunrise, set out before it was light. We sat there looking down and you said it was the most beautiful view you'd ever seen. That was where we stayed, that lovely B and B. Can you see it?" He points into the valley at a tiny building by a river, half hidden by distance and trees. "And you've always checked your apples since."

Sylene looks down at the fruit, half eaten, the juicy flesh exposed. When she looks back at him, he lifts his hand and flicks his wedding band with his thumb. She glances at her own hand, at the two rings there, one glinting with diamonds.

"Can you remember what you said?" he asks. "Apart from yes."

She can't hold his gaze. She looks down at the rock they're on and lets the wind whip her hair about her face. So this is how it happens . . .

"When's your birthday?" he asks.

Sylene stays silent.

"What was your sister called? How about our dog?"

Her hands are shaking and she feels tightened to her core.

"What was Bea's first word? What's your favorite book? Who the fuck are you? What was our wedding song? Who are you? Kate? You made that racket by the van, didn't you? You tried to stop me from finding Bea!"

Sylene looks down, at the stones worn to sand between the fissures in the rocks. Worn and worn, worn down by time, the unbearable weight of its crushing.

Tom's hands are clenched, different bits of his face stretched and compressed at once. "Please," he groans. His head drops and he starts to cry. "Give me *something*, Kate, *please*."

"I was a language teacher. I taught kids French."

Tom lunges at her and pins her to the ground, knocking her skull onto the stone. "No, you didn't! You taught English! You just heard me say that in the shop!"

She tries to push him off. She heaves at his chest but he forces her back. She kicks his shin, her knee connecting with his thigh. He tumbles and she manages to roll away, but is only halfway to her knees when he grabs her legs and pulls. Her arms collapse, her face smashing into the stone. Her chin and palms scrape along the ground until he flips her. Pinning her wrists above her head, he forces her legs out and lies, crushingly, across her, his face down close to hers.

"Who are you?" he snarls.

Stones bite into her back as he shakes her, lifts and drops his weight, winding her, again and again and again. "Stop," she gasps, but there is no air in her lungs and no room for her to breathe.

"Who are you? Where's my wife?"

Sylene tries to speak, tries to push him back, but Tom kneels on her stomach. His hands are around her throat. His fingers tighten and she can't draw breath. He chokes her. He throttles her. She can feel the cartilage stretch in his grasp and can't gasp any air. She claws his face, rakes her thumbs across his eyes. Tom screams and throws himself away. Then he comes at her once more but she is on her knees by now with a hand to her stomach and another out to stop him.

"The baby," she gasps. "You'll kill the baby."

Tom stops, his hands shaking, inches from her throat. The wind ripples his trousers. Whips at his jacket. Blood runs down his face. He staggers.

"The baby," she pants. "Don't hurt us."

And the look in Tom's eyes and the space in his mouth as he collapses to his knees. His shoulders drop as something drains from his face. Sylene staggers aside. The wind pulls her, flips her hair. She works her palms flat around her stomach and continues to back away.

TOM
Animals in the Ruins

He stands in the river, waiting, his feet made ageless by the eddies of water and the layering light. They are cold, cold enough for him to feel the pebbles only when he flexes his toes. He moves his fingers, also icy stiff. The water rushes past his ankles, pulling at his shins. It flows before his eyes, passing away, until it could be him that's moving and the river's standing still and time has been inverted or lost. Then there's a flash of something: a glinting writhe amid the roiling water. He lunges. His fingers connect with something firm that bounces away. Before his heart has beaten again he sees another flash of scales and stabs a numb hand down and grabs. He hefts the fish out and pushes it to the ground. He tries to lift its head, to snap its spine, but it won't break, so he leaves it to flap in the mud, gills gasping.

He pulls wood into a mound. Takes the damp matchbox, wastes three matches whose like will never be made again and whose heads crumble without a spark. He lowers the fourth, sputteringly lit, to the kindling. Smoke curls, lazing heavily into the air. He feeds it until it's glowing hot, until the wood is translucent, its edges charring to white. He holds a pan above the heat and slowly sears the fish, first on one side, then the other. Simple. The sound of its sizzling seeps into the other night sounds of the birds and the breeze and the sparks from the fire. Behind him rise the tooth-shaped ridges of rock, silhouetted against the star-pricked sky, a day's chase away to the west.

Tom eats with his fingers and watches the stars. He sees a hundred of them and then, dizzyingly, a thousand more. The world around him is simultaneously hit by their light and blindingly dark. The fish is delicious, but something about the caustic taste of seared scales teases at the loose memories in his mind. The scrape of cutlery on a plate, and anger. The fire pops and the trees rustle. His tent is pitched behind him. He takes the pan from the fire with half the fish's white flesh and charred scales still there and waits for his eyes to grow accustomed to the light. Once he can see, he trudges up the verge and onto the track: a country lane that has become covered with soil, blown on the wind and carried on the hooves of animals. The grasses down the center stretch have grown thigh-high. His boots fall heavily and his breathing fills the silence of the night. His eyes search the darkness, and in the end—there: he sees an unnatural shape, too angular. He scuds the frying pan along the road.

"There's some food," he calls. "If you want it."

Food, and the fish, and fear, and the sound of water running. The pool beside his tent. They spark off memories, facets of his past, as sleep resolutely will not come. He forces his eyes closed, a T-shirt wrapped around his face. His heart pumps and a dark memory emerges like oil.

It had taken them years to negotiate contact. There would be no talk of the business, nothing about their past, and they'd learned to avoid their parents. Those things had been too confused, Tom's and Ben's different interpretations of history coiled like electricity wires: they were too sensitive and, pressed, the conversations would spark into senseless anger and defensiveness. Neither had been entirely clear on the cause of the difficulties in their relationship, what precisely had brought this all to pass, but there it was. All they had to work with were the consequences.

"So have you read any good books?" Tom had asked. In the silence, troubled only by the ornate water feature beside them, Ben had given him a look and he'd known that even this had touched on something. "I didn't—"

"It's not our fault. Fuck, Tom."

Tom opened his hands up. "I didn't even mean it like that!"

Just two weeks previously, the final printers had closed. Books had been obsolete for years, but the event had been symbolic. "If there's no market for something," Ben had persisted. "Their business sense was . . ." He shot himself in the head.

Tom had nodded and taken a drink of water. He was trying to go slow on the wine. "I didn't mean it like that, Ben, I was just making conversation. Been watching any good ents?"

"The old stuff mainly. *Other Kinds of Furies*. And they've remade *A Mirror for Monsters*."

So they had reminisced about old ents and they had the conversation stabilized by the time the food arrived. It was an international cuisine: a fusion of everything, from everywhere, which was the way the world had gone. Tom's main course, a dissection and repositioning of scale-seared fish with tiny vegetables and an artistic splatter of jus, had prompted him to ask, "It's not a fusion if it's just the norm, right?" and then they had talked superficially about the Water Wars and the instabilities of the European Bloc. How the Feed had finally been allowed into China and how its government was now suspected of eavesdropping on people's very thoughts. All they discussed had been surface, easy padding to keep the conversation flowing, until Ben had mentioned as he'd inspected his food that he'd been on Kate's pool.

"What would you sacrifice . . . to make the shortages stop? It's a difficult balance, progress," he had said, and something in his tone had made Tom reach for the wine. Ben finished his glass of water, obviously gauging his brother, flicked a finger at the waiter and twirled it downward for more. "And Dad doesn't mind that the Feed was one of the options to sacrifice, but he hopes she's noticed that every time she puts it in one of her little polls, it doesn't get voted for once. Customers love it. So the question is, why does she keep putting it there?"

Tom had thumbed the wine list. This was definitely out of the agreed parameters, and he had felt himself flush. He and Kate were getting married in a month and it was still unclear whether his family would come.

It was more unclear whether he actually wanted them to, though Kate was outraged on his behalf. For him; she was angry *for* him, unable to understand how his family worked, and he was hardly better placed to enlighten her. If Tom had been on now he would have glanded some melatonin, but that had been another of their rules: they'd go slow when they were together. It helped them keep control.

The water feature tinkled away. Tom could taste his fish again, acrid now. Ben eventually stopped staring at him, but Tom's flush wouldn't subside. Ben's words agitated his mind. He was trying to remember them precisely (difficult without the Feed) to report them fairly to Kate. He stopped. Maybe *that* was why Ben had agreed they go slow—or in fact had he first suggested it? No record of what was said. No proof. His heartbeat had quickened and there had been nothing he could do.

"Tell me about SaveYou then, Ben," he had said, his heavy-pounding chest barely allowing his words more weight than breath.

"You know we don't talk about the business, Tom. You chose to opt out of that."

"Let's talk about ethics then, because from what I understand, you're now in the business of supplanting God."

"Tom—"

Too late. Tom's pulse had already created a rhythm of its own. "I'm speaking as a *customer*, Ben, and this SaveYou service—which, by the way, I notice I've been upgraded to automatically—"

"You have the Premium Service, free of charge. People would—"

"Oh, thanks, Ben, but you've digitized heaven here, haven't you? Let's take the good or the bad out of the equation for now, because I don't think we'll see straight on that; let's even ignore the morality of what it *means* for people to have their brain states *stored* because *ditto*. What's ethically dubious, *Ben,* is that you're not giving people a choice. Their minds are uploaded, *saved,* as you put it, and whether that's wonderful or not, they've got no choice about it. This technology is changing us as a race, but we, humanity, are not in any position to decide."

"People choose to buy the Feed. It's democracy on its feet."

"But what gives you the *right*?"

Ben had stared at him like he'd gone insane. Then: "You don't even know the half of it." He'd smiled and Tom had recognized it. He'd known that smile since he'd been a child. Whatever it was that had bound Ben to his father more closely than him, this smile had always shown it. They had the same smile, and Ben had known it. It was his trump sign that Tom would stay the outsider.

"SaveYou is merely a by-product, Tom. And one," Ben stated, pointing, "that consumers have *asked* us for. But it's not the main goal. We're investigating travel. I won't tax you with the unethical details, but by downloading someone's mind state and uploading it somewhere else, travel becomes near instantaneous. Even interstellar distances: we'll be able to travel them on the fastest-moving wave. All you need is a host to catch you."

"A . . . ?"

"A synth. You should see them, Tom." It had been clear that Ben was goading him and probably equally clear that it was working. They had left the confines of their agreed space and were circling each other in the wilds. *Come on then. Strike first.* Maneuvering for the moral high ground. "A synthetic being. They look really nearly human. Quite sexy, some of them."

"Enough," Tom said.

"Would Kate like one done of her?"

"Fuck you, Ben."

"It wasn't me who started this, Tom."

Tom had been seething. There was so much that was out of his control, but that he felt he was responsible to influence. Even though he'd run away. Was training to be a psychotherapist. How could he and his brother have the same genes but be so far apart, have such differing opinions that combusted when put together? Like matter and antimatter, only a galaxy's distance could keep them from exploding.

"I don't think we should do this anymore."

Sleep does not come; his body won't allow it. Every time he falls, a bubble of the past bursts in his mind and his brain boosts on to solve things. Ben. The Collapse. Kate and Bea flicker through his thoughts with a rapidity that feels familiar. It almost feels like the comforting sensation of the Feed. But he has no control over these images, these bursts of memory; they simply come and go. And what can even be solved here? He has lost everything, and all his brain's kick-start panic does is cost him energy and sleep. The tinned beef, the bath, screaming on the cliff. At the Pharmacist's, where suspicious fear had infected him. Her silences hadn't been the same. Holding her naked there. Claire's camp, the trails of sky debris on the plain; when had he actually *known*?

He listens to the water flowing in its tiny brook outside the tent, the high, sparkly tinkle of the ripples clinking pebbles. He remembers the sensations of Kate's pool: "What Would You Sacrifice?" Anything, he realizes suddenly, if it would work. If he could go back in time to change what had happened, he would sacrifice *anything* now. Killing Sylene when she had first arrived, yes, of course, *but when had that been?* And Kate would have been dead then anyway. So . . . leaving the camp sooner, as Kate had wanted to. But would that have stopped Sylene? The Pharmacist had said they had no choice who they inhabited, that it was purely random chance. Bea would be safe if they'd left the camp sooner, that is undeniably true. But Kate? Maybe. Or not. It's impossible to know.

Possible histories, impossible to predict. But what would he have had to do to stop this from coming to pass? When the assassinations first began—could he have helped his father? No, of course not. He'd been uninvolved in the business too long. He hadn't ever been *actively* involved; he had never been given that choice. Even with his birth, his involvement had been requisitioned: he had been the first person to be enabled *in ute* purely because of who he was. "The Experiment," as his father's friends had called him. The deeper wound was that his mother had allowed it. She must have condoned the bone-deep tests he'd undergone as a child. "*Testing for what?*" he'd asked, but in a world replete with communication, his father's greatest trick was silence. Secrecy. Revealing the fait accompli.

So maybe that's what he would change: he and Ben wouldn't have been so abandoned. Maybe they would even have liked each other if they hadn't been competitors; maybe they'd have been a team. And from there—how would the future have been different? If he had run the Feed? He would have put a pace on technology. He would not have let it evolve faster than their morals could keep up. And in the tent, Tom's heart thumps him back to reality as stark loss seeps through his thoughts again. He can fantasize about changing the past all he likes, but it won't change the future and what has come to pass; it can't bring Kate back.

By the time he has washed and trekked up the lane again, the other tent has gone. All that remains are a dew-free square of flattened grass where it had been and his pan with the uneaten fish.

Tom has two ways to run—the way they came or the way they were going—and he chooses the latter, the lane gnarly with plants. Fallen branches have crumbled to a layer of mulch that makes him skid and slide. When he hasn't found her soon, he searches wildly, glimpsing snatches of the bushes as he trips, searching for any place she could hide. His chest is burning and his eyes streaming when he eventually sees her, a distant figure on the road. He can barely shout for breathing.

"Stay where you are!" Sylene yells as soon as she hears him. He approaches, nonetheless, and then stops. There is nothing between them but silence and sunlight, clear on the crisp morning air. His breath courses out in clouds and the sweat on his body chills instantly. Sylene has her rucksack on, the straps clasped around her stomach.

"Where are you going?" Tom calls.

She shrugs, an exaggerated gesture to be seen this far away.

"Can I come closer?"

When no answer comes, he starts to walk. Sylene stays silent, her lips pursed and her pale cheeks flushed until: "That's enough!" she shouts.

"Listen. I'm not going to hurt you."

"You tried to kill me."

"I was in shock," he says. "I didn't . . . That was before I . . . You're carrying my baby!"

Sylene turns, her hands on her shoulder straps, and starts marching on.

"Please, wait!"

"Don't follow me!" Sylene shouts without turning back. But he keeps a constant distance between them, walking faster than is comfortable to keep up with her quick pace.

"Can we talk about this? Will you please stop? Sylene!"

She stops. Even from this distance, Tom sees her shoulders heave. He slows and waits. After a while, she part-turns, one arm out in a shrug. "I didn't ask for this, Tom. I didn't choose this. I don't know what to do."

"Well . . . thanks for stopping. That's a start."

A flock of birds disperses from a bush and skims to sit in a tree, their heads cocking, their tails bobbing. They chirrup. One skits back to the bush, and then the others follow, a flock again.

"Is that it?" Sylene asks impatiently.

"I . . ." he starts. "What are we going to do? Sylene? Is that what you said you're called?"

"I'm going to find people who aren't going to kill me."

"I'm not going to kill you."

"Actions speak louder than words."

"I can't let you go. You're carrying my child."

"Well, we've got a problem then, because I don't trust you."

She stands in the light falling between the trees, one leg bent. Her jacket is open, her stomach revealed.

"Are you sure you're pregnant? Have you, you know . . . ?"

"I know how it feels, Tom. Are you going to propose something? I'm getting cold."

"Wait," Tom urges. He balls a fist and pats it into his palm; watches her; clocks the gesture; stops it. "Will you wait for me if I get the things, then? And then we'll continue together?"

"Not for long."

"Promise?"

"Yes."

"Because," he says, moving on his feet, "I don't know how well you know how to survive, or what you can and cannot eat. All I know is that if we separate, we'll never find each other again. Okay, Sylene? A little time, a little patience . . ."

Sylene shakes her head. "Tom, you tried to kill me."

"I was scared! I'm not going to— How can I now? Please, listen, don't . . . Let's just talk. All right? I don't know why you're here, I don't know what you want, but I'll help you. Whatever it is, whyever you've come and invaded people's brains, I'll help you. Just, *please* . . ."

Sylene watches him steadily. Then something seems to thaw and she nods.

"Okay. Great! Twenty minutes and I'll be back. I'll

run!" He heads back down the road, stops, turns back, and shouts: "You'll stay?"

"Yes," she calls, weary-sounding again.

Tom nods, turns, and runs again, glancing back occasionally to see her, smaller and smaller each time. Soon the curve of the track and the trees hide her, and he jumps into the undergrowth and runs back, parallel to the path, as fast as the foliage will allow. He peers between the trunks. She is still there, in the road where he left her, looking at the sky, her hands on her lower back. After a while, she sits on her rucksack. Tom watches her as she kicks the roots growing over the road. Her hand strokes her stomach and Tom can see it now, the tautness of the thing. The growth.

The sweat on his skin has cooled and crystallized. Sylene looks back up and sighs with the waiting; she won't stay for long. He emerges from the foliage and coughs. She looks up, startled, and then her face hardens.

"Happy?" she says. "Twenty minutes. From now."

By the time he reaches his tent, his shirt is sodden and his heart's every thump makes him dizzy. He throws the tent down, rolls it, forces it into his pack. Thrusting his stuff into his rucksack, something solidifies around his stomach and the bile rises in his throat, but he breathes it down and starts running again, back down the path.

"**So we've** got to solve this," Tom tells her as he walks. Sylene in Kate's body. Close enough to touch yet infinitely far away. He can never be close to Kate again. She's no longer there. They've gone in silence for hours. "We mustn't get this wrong."

"And how are we going to do that?"

"Sylene, this will be fine. We'll work it out. Listen, just give me time—"

"To let me go to sleep so you can kill me?"

"No! To get used to this, to—"

"Tom, this isn't going to work. I wanted to help you find Bea, I really did, but now, I—don't—trust—you."

Tom grabs her arms to plead with her, but Sylene mistakes the gesture, wrestles him and tries to pull away. She kicks his knee and he falls, cracking his elbow as he lands, and the weight of his rucksack pushes his face into the earth, stunning him, jarring his teeth. "I'm not . . . I didn't!" he cries, spitting soil from his mouth.

"Don't come near me . . ." Sylene's voice quivers as she backs away.

"I wasn't going to hurt you. Sylene. Please!" He kneels, his hands stretched out. "Bea's gone. Everything's gone. Kate, my wife, my child. It's impossible to find her!" His cheeks are slicked with wetness, his saliva tear-thickened. "Everything's lost! I don't know what to do! What you have is all I've got. Don't take this away from me. Please don't leave me! I know you're not Kate. I know you're . . . Sylene. And if you're pregnant, you're pregnant, but please don't leave me alone!"

Tom cries for a long time. He cries until he cannot see and he is deaf to everything but the noise; crying is what he becomes. When, with time, he calms and his face feels clear, he remembers where he is and sees that Sylene is still there too. "Eat this," she says, giving him a biscuit. She's been waiting. "And here's some water." She passes him a bottle and he drinks from it, deeply, the tears still fizzing his nose. She didn't leave him. "Eat." He does, his shaking hands guiding the biscuit with difficulty to his mouth. "Now come on," Sylene says, hauling him to his unsteady feet, "let's find a place to stop."

Tom lies still, not sleeping, but looking at the clouds and listening to the water churn and roll. They are camped in the middle of a wide pasture with a gauze of waterways. They have set the two tents up on opposite sides of a stream; it's impossible to cross it silently. It used to be that he'd stream a vista like this to give him peace. *Savers*, they'd called them, so the brain didn't get locked, something to give you pause now and then and some virtual space to breathe. They were the official solution to early, concerning signs of potential addiction to the Feed. People personalized them: down-time views based on their favorite cities or ents. They often slept with them on. His had been of nature. Old-time "photos" and vids of the real world, from before the Water Wars, when he imagined things had been simpler. And here he is inside one now: a real-life vista, the world back to simple once more. But so incredibly complicated.

He hears a light splash and a crunch of rock on rock, then another splash, and another, and more. He rolls his head and sees Sylene, arms out for balance as the water rolls around her shins. Sylene in Kate's body. Kate crossing the stream toward him—

"Can I come over?"

The water gushes around her legs. He doesn't have the energy to reply. He just stares at her and feels the cold depth of the earth on the side of his face. The huge mass of the planet, and his tiny head beside it.

Sylene wades across and stands, not too close, but nearer to him than distant. "I'm sorry," she says quietly. "I don't know what to say."

Tom looks at the tent behind her on the other side, at the mountains around them, at the trees, nearly bare. Their bark is darkened by the moisture in the air. The vista is huge. It's cold. A large crow works at a nearby branch. This place, so quiet, so desolate; it all feels so alone.

"I can't imagine how you feel," Sylene says. "What would you like to know?"

"How long has it been?"

"Weeks. Since before the Pharmacist. Just before Claire's camp. When did you know?"

His eyes barely flicker. "I suspected," he whispers, "at the Pharmacist's. I didn't want to know. Kate always said I was blinded by hope. I called it my strength." He snorts a humorless laugh. "Was it you at the facility?"

Sylene makes a face and shakes her head. "We were on a hill, in a wood, with a bit of water below. You made me a hot drink. I'd never tasted anything like it. I'd never seen grass. I'd never felt water before like that pond. Not synthetic. You talked about your father and about us finding Bea. You said I have a sister called Martha. Where is she? What happened to her?"

Tom feels sick.

"I didn't know what to do," Sylene admits, and sits on the ground, still not quite next to him. For a long time the only sounds are the water and the crow, cracking at the bark and cawing.

Tom's hands shake with whatever courses through his veins. "So who are you?"

"My name is Sylene Charles."

"That's not what I meant. What happened to Kate when you . . . ?"

"Honestly?"

Just the tone of her voice makes his eyes hot, makes him want to pause time, rewind it, undo everything. But he can't. He sees her shrug through his tear smears and turns to look away.

"We had no way of knowing what would happen to the host. I don't think we really believed it could work. But there's . . ." A hand lifts to the side of her head and points. "I can't feel her here. There's not enough room."

Tom picks at the grass. His arms are quivering, his whole torso shaking uncontrollably. From the cold? From the shock? His jaw judders. "Why are you doing this?" he pleads.

Sylene looks down and sighs. When she raises her face, her eyes catch the light of the gray autumnal air. "When you're alone and desperate, you'll do anything. It's not our fault, Tom." She appraises him. He can tell she is doing it; he can almost sense that she is deciding whether to stay silent or to lie, whether she should tell him the truth. There is a clarity to her eyes and clearly doubt, but also a frown of something else. A commonality in pain, perhaps, that she recognizes in him? Some form of connection? Who knows what's happening in her head?

"We're from here, Tom. Earth. This is our world too." She sighs again. "We destroy it. You do. *Did*— from my point of view." She studies the sky, the mountains far away and the clouds that coalesce above them. She holds her hands out, hovering her palms above the earth. She almost smiles. "It took some time from now. I don't think you'd believe the destruction you cause." She points to the distance. "Dry earth. Everywhere. All the life sucked away. All the metals, the chemicals, the oil, everything you could plunder: gone. Devoured. You consume it all. You leave us with nothing, without even hope. You killed your own children with your lack of balance." Her hands are shaking, but not from cold. "We were alone. We had to save ourselves, to find a way to escape. But, Tom, do you realize how huge the universe is and how small we are? There is nowhere to escape *to*. The world got so hot the ground was burned from beneath our feet and we had nowhere to jump. How stupid is that? A billion people died in two weeks of starvation. The next two billion were killed in under a week. Then the big weapons were mobilized and the world fought for water again. Still consuming, of course, even during the final Resource War, still pretending that life could go on as normal. I think everyone thought that someone else would save us, that this couldn't *happen* in a civilization like ours. But it did. Everyone was deluded. Everyone was culpable. Oh, we collected all the information, we weighed the evidence, and yes, we judged you. And you're guilty. All of you."

Sylene looks at Tom, at the views around them. She inhales very deeply.

"Sometimes I think this is a dream. That I didn't make it back. That I died, and my body is there on that slab in the future I grew up in, and with these last few seconds of consciousness I've found a heaven that I never had the option to live. We had screens, you know? They showed images of how the earth used to be, and it was so beautiful. But then the screens stopped. The Feed stopped. We didn't have enough power because not enough people survived. The sun cooked us. Killed us. Every living thing on the planet. You made the world a furnace, Tom, your generation and the next."

Tom's heart expands into the cold air, thumping harder the longer her silence runs. When she starts again, she talks quietly. "Thousands came back at first, charged with changing the past to stop the destruction of the planet. Our intentions were so good. If we stopped things back here when we could, if we changed the course of history, then perhaps we'd have a chance to survive in the future. But we didn't hear from those who had returned and everything stayed the same where we were, so we assumed they must have died. Still more went back. All of us. Hundreds of thousands in the end, fired randomly back through time, knowing that only a fraction of us might make it. It was assured death to take the journey by the time my turn had come, or so I thought. We had no choice. It was that or burn."

"But how does this work? How are you doing it?"

Tom sees something glaze in Sylene's eyes: a look that freezes, a pursing of the lips. She assesses him and goes to speak, but then she shakes her head. "That's enough for now."

"No, it's not. Tell me."

Sylene rocks back and looks the other way. Her face folds into a scowl and she shakes her head again. Tom staggers to stand. He can hear his voice change without his meaning it to, its sore roughness tightening as something builds in his chest like floodwater. He could break something huge with his hands right now.

"Tell me, Sylene!"

She looks at him straight. "It was you." There is no

emotion in her tone; she is giving him information. Plain fact. "You helped get us back here, Tom. You showed us how to do it."

Her words roll in his head like clouds—clouds made from wood and iron and flint and ancient hazed-out glass. He can't hear anything. His vision is obscured, as though a gauze is there between him and the world, but the sound of the stream crashes like it's gushing into a ravine and his breath is slight and high as his heart shakes itself to bits.

He kneels in the stream and douses his head. Cold water to clear it. Freezing water to solidify his thoughts so he can slow this down and process things and think.

Tom's hands shake, barely able to grasp the mug Sylene holds out for him. The water level rollicks as she lets it go. His eyes spasm so much, his whole head is twitching. Kate. Ben. Danny. Bea. His parents. Anyone. Please. No one to help him. Alone.

"Would you like some food?"

He rubs his wet hair back from his brow. Pulls his legs up and holds them tightly. "N-no. Tell me, Sylene, wh-what happened," he demands through tightly clenched teeth. His face is twitching. Feed reflexes, or because he's freezing? What difference does it make?

he thinks, as he squeezes his eyes shut and tenses his face until everything shakes and then he gasps it all away.

"When I grew up, we lived in earthscrapers, massive cans drilled miles and miles deep, with walls so hot we couldn't touch them and air recycled a hundred thousand times. We still had the Feed, for a while at least. It was everything, Tom. It made us whole. It unified humanity because everything we had was shared." She strokes her face, brushing over her eyes, her fingers delicately tracing the shape of her eyelids, and she smiles. "Everything was common knowledge. Including history. The birth of humanity, democracy, religion, the microchip. Communism, consumerism, we knew it all, the evolution of society. How our world had come to be. What would have become the future for you is ancient history for me. I absorbed it all as a child. Vids of your father at the launches of the Feed. Grabs of you as a boy, as an adult when you ran the company yourself. It was all old history for me. Big stories, becoming myths, but the Feed froze the facts and truth in time. Like when you became a whistle-blower on your father."

She puts her hands together and thinks. She chooses her words precisely. "Look, we've changed things. By coming back in time, we have evidently disrupted the world's progress, as we originally intended to. This is not what the history pools told us happened. But it didn't change *our* future. Where we were. We didn't see any changes *there*. So we've created something parallel here, we must have. A different universe? Just a different bubble of reality around our own? I have no idea. Does it really matter? But now, this," she says, looking around. "This isn't how history went for us. There was no—what did you call it?—Collapse. In my world, in *our* history, that didn't happen. None of what is going on for you *now* happened for us *then*. For us, in a few years' time, society was still intact. The large corporations continued to cannibalize the earth. Animals were killed. Buildings were built. The temperature soared. The world warmed and yet still there was no restraint. You never strived for balance. Just growth. The Feed expanded too. The next big thing was travel. It granted everyone in the world who could afford it near-instantaneous travel, throwing your thoughts from place to place. You created synthetic hosts, and they didn't come cheap. And the *energy* you needed to power it . . . Everything you did, consumed. Oh, the energy even to store your mundles and your thoughtlessly taken millions of grabs! The Feed wasn't the worst company in the world, but it was just another one that damaged things. And you became a whistle-blower on it. You shattered consumer confidence in the company because you revealed to the public that their Feeds could be hacked."

Tom watches her, examines her face for traces of lies or indications of truth. This face he knows so well. Kate's face. Her eyes. It sounds just like her: her tone as she describes these corporations and their negative effects on the world. They'd had this discussion about consumerism and morality; they'd had it so many times. At home, in restaurants—he has flash-burst memories of Kate's ire and her righteous determination to save the world as she shouted him down with hot tears of frustration and concern, as she sprayed another poll on "What Would You Sacrifice?"—her small attempt to change the world. And she was right, it seems—she was right.

He jolts as Sylene puts a hand on his arm. He throws it off and scuffles backward along the earth. Sylene stays where she is, waiting until he settles. "You revealed in a post on Kate's pool that people's Feeds could be hacked. Through SaveYou, Tom. It was still a young program then, sending out people's memory states as BackUps. But the door opened both ways. You could go *in* through the program too, into people's Feeds and effectively into their brains. Potentially, as you revealed to everyone, it was the perfect identity theft. Within weeks the breach had been fixed and no one had been hacked. Everyone still had the Feed, the product was safe; in fact it was better than ever. You were still famous, though, Tom, in my time. There was a vote of no confidence in your father. He had tried to hide it; you came clean. People trusted you. You saved the world. All the enabled, you protected them before anyone could abuse this breach, you fought the company on their behalf and won. You exposed your father as careless at best and negligent at worst. Who was better placed then to run it?"

"But . . ." Tom's head is swimming. He squeezes his eyes shut to keep track of his thoughts. "You've hacked us now, before the breach was closed?"

Sylene looks at the ground. "Yes. With the benefit of hindsight, we had history on our side. We knew the Feed was vulnerable at this time and that we could, in theory, colonize your minds through SaveYou. But we didn't know until we tried. Our world was on fire. We were about to become extinct. You'd try anything in that situation, believe me."

"But going backward in time's not possible."

"Not with people, no. Or with mass of any kind. But with thoughts, which are stored on matter but aren't actually matter themselves . . . Your father inspired the technology: if there's a transmitter and a receiver, a beacon to draw us in, and hosts like yourselves to tether to. The hosts don't have to be synthetic . . ."

Tom laughs, like a vibration, like his body just needs something to do and this is all it has.

Sylene is crying now, though, and his laughter makes it worse. "We broadcast our thoughts out blindly. We had no control, no way to aim for any particular person, no assurance that it would even work. We must have lost a quarter of a million people before it worked. But some made it back. I know that now. Some people made it back, because *look:* we've changed the world. We *have* saved the future. The planet is going to be fine. So SaveYou *must* have helped us be received."

His laughter gone, Tom muses silently for a while. "So you're not Chinese? Or from Iran?"

Sylene closes her eyes. "No, Tom, we're not Chinese or from Iran."

"And you did this to survive?"

"We did it to change the future. We did it to save the world. We couldn't choose who we inhabited, but we had hopes for who we might hit by chance. Whose actions we could change. Politicians and key people, heads of corporations, who history showed had harmed the planet. If we couldn't inhabit them and literally change their minds, the idea was we would kill them; get close, if we had inhabited someone they trusted, and take them out of play. President Taylor was killed, right?"

"Yes," Tom says, remembering suddenly where he had been: the restaurant, that kid with the tattoos, the shockingly bare billboards, and how they'd sprinted home, PresidentTaylor1's assassination clogging every stream. The curfew that started that night became a state of emergency without end. That moment had started all this. Kate pregnant with Bea—and suddenly Tom's memories open up like a portal through time. He is exactly back there briefly, he inhabits it, it exists again, and then with a gulping whoosh he's in the here and now and crying, his whole being defined by a sense of absolute loss.

"Well, he had a chance to stop it!" Sylene's voice is hard with hatred. She spits the words from her mouth like dirt. "Five global summits and none of them delivered on their promises. Pledges made in public and deals done behind closed doors. History is transparent, Tom. He promised to fetter the oil companies and didn't. He swore to make the Feed and all the other tech companies hit energy consumption targets on their storage towers. Every vid, every grab, cost the earth. The very real footprint of information stored. It's all archived. And who was responsible. We could read it all. He damned the world to die because it was expedient at the time. But not just him. We targeted everyone like him to try to save the world. The greedy. The selfish. The charming charlatans. History made them plain to see, and what's one misguided, thoughtless life to save a billion, or a trillion, or more? This"—she gestures around at the world, at the here and now—"this wasn't supposed to happen! We wanted to slow things down, to make key, simple changes to stop you from destroying the planet. At worst we wanted to evacuate the few of us survivors back, now, so humanity would survive. But we didn't want to destroy it all. This wasn't the plan at all."

Tom is laughing near silently again, his mouth a rictus grin. "Well, congratulations anyway; you've made humanity destroy the world twice, then!"

He kneels by the stream in the gloaming. Midges fuzz the air. The sound of the water seems sharper for its coldness: a precise and high-pitched ripple. He cascades the icy stuff over his head and rubs it into his chest. Sylene is in her tent already, lit up by the murky light of her flashlight. The grasses are dark. The running water is silver stippled black. The earth feels so cold and the water so true, so perfectly real, that what Sylene told him feels impossible but somehow inevitably true. Kate had always been saying it. With her pools where people sprayed about saving the world. Other people, with influence, had lobbied for it too, but the future was a far-flung place. Was this threat real? Who honestly cared what happened there? Devastated people *there* didn't count. And besides, technology would solve it. That was what he always thought, though he would never have admitted it to Kate: history showed that people came up with solutions only once the problem was really dire. That was when self-preservation kicked in, when business and survival meshed. It was just a question of *when* that solution would be found; everybody knew that, right?

That night, he watches the world. He is exhausted but cannot sleep. His thoughts turn with the stars. He watches the shadows on the inside of Sylene's tent until she turns off the flashlight. He walks. He washes again. And then, just before dawn, he lies down.

He is in a dreamscape world in his father's office, hanging in the air. He can hear the skin-creeping rustling of leaves, but it's only the city he can see, stretching to the horizon, gray and granulated, a constant veneer of buildings being consumed by fire as the Collapse takes final hold. The Feed holds on by a thread—just one last power station's collapse away. On a bank of machines behind him, under a static-laden screen, Bea drums her feet on the memory banks of the homeHub, where all the family are stored. She's not been abducted; she's been saved somehow, and she's singing a song whose words he can't quite hear with a mouth that looks like her mother's, with a face like Kate's, while her girlish song-voice sings—

He's awake, looking at the smudge of skylight below the upside-down curve of his tent, the mountains where the sky should be. His face is freezing. His limbs are dewy, solid with cold. He's on his feet and running across the stream. "Sylene! *Sylene!*" By the time he gets to her tent, she has halfway emerged. Tom grabs her shoulders and she screams. They tumble as she hits his leg and he has to hold her tight to stop her blows. "Stop, stop, stop! Sylene, listen!"

Her hands are up, her eyes wide with fear, her skin made paler by the early light of day.

"SaveYou!" he pants. "If that's what you're using to come back through time, then it's still working! Whatever's happened to the rest of the Feed, SaveYou is still on! We can find out where she is, Sylene. *We can find out where she is!*"

There is frost on the grass when they leave. The stars are still visible, just, and the mountains like bite marks in the sky. They make hurriedly for the road.

"But isn't it more dangerous?"

"Yes."

"Is there another route we can take? One more sheltered?"

"No."

"You're no use to Bea dead, Tom."

His breath steams, his fingers flex against the air. He looks around them, spinning, for another way. "We *have* to take the road," he appeals in the end. "It's the fastest route. We have to get to the tower; we must get to the Hub."

"Tom. You are no use to Bea dead."

He steels himself. "So we must be on our guard."

Sylene holds his gaze. Something pulls at the sides of her mouth, something in her eyes nearly smiles, but then she nods, sternly, and with that they both turn for the road. They scramble up onto the tarmac and set off. Tom is silent, determined. It's all Sylene can do to keep up.

They walk half the morning at full pelt, and their pace has only slightly slowed when he stops dead. He stares at the horizon, unmoving. Sylene stops too and follows his gaze. They are at a place where the road hugs a hill, curling around a valley. A flock of birds circles like a black cloud in the pass. Closer around them, animals have fought over something. Clumps of fur, bloody chunks clinging to their roots, are scattered around the burst tires of a car . . .

"What is it, Tom? What have you seen?"

Some birds on a fallen pylon. Old girders, rusted and wilting like flowers . . .

Tom goes to the ground, breathing loudly, and cradles his head in his hands.

"Tom? What is it?"

"I was wrong," he moans. "I'm . . . an *idiot*. She doesn't *have* it." He punches the ground.

"Have what?"

"She doesn't have the Feed."

"But everybody has the Feed. Come on. Let's get to the Hub now."

Tom swipes her away and shouts while she stumbles back. "Maybe where you come from, but don't tell me about my own daughter! She wasn't enabled, Sylene!"

Sylene stands some distance away, her hair falling loose from her hat. She stretches her hands out to slow him down or keep him away; he doesn't care what she's doing as he paces up and down. He kicks the car. Kicks it and kicks it again and again until the rusted metal ruptures. Birds launch up all around them.

"Tom. Listen to me. Please. You'll hurt yourself. Listen. Did you have it removed?"

"She was born after the Collapse, Sylene. *She—never—had—one!*"

"But, Tom, the Feed's genetic."

Wind rolls, blowing leaves off the edge of the road toward the valley floor. They stand apart, facing each other. Tom searches her eyes. "Maybe when you're from, in the future, but not here. Not now. It's not."

But Sylene is nodding before he's finished. "Yes, Tom, it is. You're *in ute,* aren't you?"

"Yes."

"Right. You were the first. I saw the vids of when your father launched the product. It was revolutionary, implanted while you were still in the womb. And the implant was genetic. It bonded with the human machine."

Tom's face creases. He looks past her, over the barriers at the side of the road and across to the scree and the hills and the space over the valley. He remembers the tests, the bone-deep samples taken from his body. The scientists, some of whom he knew better than his family by the end. His blood, thick and dark as it was drawn into syringes throughout his early years. Tissue samples being tested—"*For what?*" he'd asked. Ben's face, and his father's face, when they found out Kate was pregnant. Expressionless. Thinking very hard. The fait accompli.

All he can say is: *"What?"*

"It all came out when you were running the Feed, that the implant in utero was genetic. Some people said it was your idea, but you maintained it was your father's. You said you were 'the Experiment'; you told the world, full disclosure, and people, by and large, believed you. They trusted you even more. Whatever the truth, the Feed blended with us, became indistinct, the first true wetware, passed from parent to child, a living part of our brain."

He points at her stomach. "And that one?"

She nods. "Yes, of course, it'll have the Feed."

Tom is hushed. "It's immoral."

Sylene shakes her head. "The Feed became free for all: you bought it once and you bought it for all the generations to come. Knowledge became a human right. Everyone knew *everything*! It closed geography, it closed class. It leveled society in a decade. Eons of evolution—biological and social—in a life span. It took us past human versus machine; it was human *with* machine, a pure entity, a bio-algorithm, and you made it free."

"I would never allow something like this!"

Sylene moves uncomfortably. "Tom, all I know is what I learned in the future, from the Feed, about you, your father, and your son. You were running the company when the Feed's coverage went global, when it was in us all, in everyone in the world. You completed it, Tom."

Tom puts a hand out. "My *son*?"

"Yes."

"I have a son?"

"In my version of your future, you had a son. Daniel Hatfield."

"But no daughter? Not Bea?"

"Different things happened, Tom, different paths," Sylene explains tersely. "We have changed things by coming back in time. We're in some sort of parallel event, I guess from the first moment one of us got successfully back, so any time from when SaveYou was first installed, my world and this one parted ways. Cleaved away from each other. Changing, probably very subtly at first, before things got so extreme. In my future there was no Collapse. Society continued. The Feed evolved for centuries. Everyone was corrected. Knowledge and communication became basic human rights. You made travel instantaneous, Tom, flipping a mind state around the world. You stopped brain death, because everybody was backed up, everyone was saved. You made us immortal in effect, until the world was destroyed."

"What about Kate?"

"What about her?"

"Was she . . . ?"

"Yes. You were married. I'm wearing a dead celebrity's face." Sylene stops herself, and although her expression drops, she does not break his gaze. She reaches out for his hand. "I'm sorry. That was unthinking of me."

Tom walks away to the barrier by the ravine. Sylene stands watching him, from the body of his wife; he can feel it. He can ignore it, forget it even maybe, and then it thumps him in the guts. He closes his eyes. The fizz of tears takes him back to the tower, after Ben and his father had found out she was pregnant. Kate had woken one morning adamant that someone had trespassed in her mind. He had taken a lot of persuading, because what she wanted him to do was immoral; but that afternoon they had gone to his father's office and accessed the homeHub. With her permission—but still—he had entered Kate's BackUps and tunneled into her dreams. And there he had found, like footprints between her thoughts, places his father had been. He had been analyzing their baby, the data around their child. At the time, Tom had felt horror. Disgust. An animal instinct to escape, to protect his wife and child. But now it makes sense: his father was looking for early traces of the Feed, when Bea was still inside. The experiment hadn't just been with Tom. He had only been the start.

Eventually he wipes his face dry. "We have a lot to discuss." He turns to Sylene. He is surprised by how calm his voice sounds. "But for now: Bea has the Feed."

"As far as I know."

"And SaveYou has been backing her up, it will have been storing her memory states."

"If—"

"If there's enough latent power in the implant to act as a beacon for you, to attract *you people* through time to use us as hosts, then there's enough power to send out the BackUps! Am I right, Sylene? We are its battery. So even though there's no power in the Hubs to transmit *at* us, we have enough power to send signals *out*. And if *that's* right, *we can see her latest BackUps!* Is that right, Sylene? We can see exactly where she is?"

"I don't know, Tom. It looks like it."

"Well, that's good enough for me."

The seasons change in the weeks that follow, but Tom's determination doesn't. The slight clouds high in the cooling sky lower and thicken like wicking until they are scaled and lumpen. The sun moves on a different plane. The rains break. Thrown on harsher winds,

they blot the sun for days. The birds withdraw. Cobwebs thicken, heavy with dew. And Tom and Sylene
continue, heading for the tower.

One evening, after countless weeks, the clouds dis-
solve around the setting sun. The light is different now.
It carries none of its previous warmth, but things are
dry tonight. Tom finds the least wet wood he can. He
uses five big firelighters and, after rolls of heavy smoke,
flames suck at even the damper logs.

He glances at Sylene, sitting with her legs out of the
tent as he makes supports on one side of the fire. He's
sure he saw people doing this in the ents he streamed
with Ben. People marooned, cooking things on a spit.
Or . . .

"If madam would like any clothes to be dried . . ."

Soon socks, trousers, and T-shirts steam over the
flames. Sylene burrows back into her tent for more,
and as the door flaps close, Tom can half see, half
imagine, as the tent shakes, her sliding her trousers off.
As she stretches to remove her T-shirt, her foot pushes
the flap open again and he sees the curve of her stomach: the way her tummy now protrudes. By the time
she has pulled on a sweater and new socks, he finds his
hands are shaking. He remembers the first time, when
Kate had told him she was pregnant; he'd shaken uncontrollably then too. Shaken with excitement and joy,

and he'd promised her that he'd protect them, that he'd never abandon them—absolutely no matter what.

They make a stew of what soft-looking roots they can find. They make enough to eat and more to store, banking on more rain to come, which it does, for days. They walk through the sideways-slicing sheets sometimes, and other days they rest. Sometimes they lie in their tents with their door flaps apart and the rain cascading between them as they talk. Other days they zip themselves away and grow sticky with their tent-contained sweat. He asks Sylene about the future, he asks about her family, but she shrugs and won't reply.

Warm days return for a while, and the land looks lush and green. Grass snakes bask on the road. Somewhere the landscape changes. They walk. The muscular folds of foothills slide into gentler rolls. The woodland becomes thicker, the trees more round, the horizon lower down. They avoid the villages nestled in the nooks between hills, eyeing them warily as they approach and then checking over their shoulders for days. The landscape will have to change again before they reach the tower, many times more. The villages must merge into long expanses of town, of suburb, and then city, with buildings lumped and crushed together and high roads looping between.

Weeks later, they are halfway up a rise, looking back over the land they have traversed. Dark clouds clog the east and the earth is unnaturally black. The sky is a mix of citrus, and a river running toward them looks like it has leaked wetly from the horizon.

"Shall we stop here?" Sylene asks. "Make some food. Enjoy the view."

Tom looks around. The air is fresh, the vista expansive. "Why not?"

Sylene starts to lay out her tent as Tom pulls the air deep into his lungs. "Back in a while," he says, and leaves toward the trees. Soon he can see far back behind them, the way they have come, and yet the silence is complete. He stops kicking the leaves, under whose sludgy matter he finds only disintegrating lumps of wood, and pulls thin branches off the trunks. The hilltop is small and he is soon on the other side. Walking has become their way of life. Planning routes, gauging distances, setting the best direction. He looks out at the way ahead, and close enough to shock him is a sodden hulk he recognizes: the angular concrete blocks of the old storage facility. The same one near the camp.

Threading through his mind from now to his memories of those months past.

The fire that night does not take. Tom scratches a stick on the ground. They drink rainwater and sit in the doorways of their tents eating soggy biscuits and nuts.

"Do you have enough?"

Sylene rubs her hands on her trousers. "It was one of those things," she says, nodding, "getting used to food. Mostly ours was synthesized. The air in the Scrapers had bumps: vitamins and things for our health. So the volume of food you eat here is . . . I've never felt this full."

Tom purses his mouth. "I've never eaten this little."

"Are you hungry?"

"Constantly. But I'm more worried about you. Are you getting enough of all the things that you need? I don't know. Before, Kate took all sorts of pills. She was always monitoring stuff. Levels of . . . I don't know what you . . ." Tom gestures at her swollen waistline. The quiet here is far removed from the vortex of swirling stats and numbers that Kate had streamed him from the moment she was pregnant, showing him the progress of the baby, sending him gulps of information, dolloping it directly into his brain.

Sylene places both hands on her stomach. "Well, it's getting bigger, so I think we're fine."

Her expression makes him laugh, and Sylene laughs too.

"You can come over here if you want," she says. "I could use you to heat my tent."

Tom throws the stick away as she shuffles over to make room for him in the doorway. Night is falling, darkness draining into the sky.

"If you snore, though," she says, "you're out."

The following day, Tom glimpses the facility again fleetingly between the hills. They must be near the camp. They cross a road whose sides have collapsed and whose tarmac is powdered and sodden. It leads directly to the facility. The dirtied glass curve above the main entrance is dwarfed by the building's size. Graham comes to his mind, a recent memory that he'd already nearly forgotten, and Danny after him with the cart. Concrete fragments as they're shot at and running as fast as they can. Such a recent long time ago.

He jumps down the other side and continues into the field, away from the facility.

"Can I have a hand?"

Sylene skids down the bank, holding her hair out of

her face. He hurries back to her, takes her hand, and helps her reach the ground.

"Where was Kate from?" she asks as they set out across the grass.

Tom opens his mouth, but says nothing and closes it again.

"I'm sorry, I shouldn't have asked."

"No. It's not that—"

"No, I'm sorry, it's not my business. It was a stupid thing to ask."

"Listen. At our camp, we were trying out rules of how the world might work again. We . . . I thought it was healthy not to dwell. So we weren't allowed to talk about the past."

"At all?"

"We had to live in the present and look to the future. So, of course, if we could remember knowledge that could help, we would. One of the camp members, Graham, he was writing it down. He used to be a journalist and old habits die hard. But emotions stopped us from being present. They paralyzed people. They made Feed reflexes kick in to try to solve what was wrong. People had fits trying to connect to the Feed. Seriously. It killed most people, the shock. For us, the survivors, the question was how to deal with that grief. How to process it. Our brains were fried, the emotional stuff was raw. The Feed had done *everything* for us before: stored information; told us what to eat, when to exercise, how much to sleep. It communicated for us more efficiently than we ever could on our own; it recorded our memories. It's only recently that mine have started to come back."

"How big was the camp?"

"Oh, small. It's actually quite near here." Tom glances toward the facility, now hidden behind some trees, and works out directions in his head. "It was the best. The house had been Kate's aunt's, but the others had already found it. It was a real community. We built a dam in a stream so we had a washing area, and we'd just worked out how to filter the water through soil so we were no longer getting sick. The farming was really coming on. It was great, Sylene, you would have loved it." He can't stop talking. He wants her to like it, he realizes. He wants to defend its memory. "Nothing huge, like Claire's camp—now *that* was something else. But ours was something to be proud of too."

"It sounds lovely."

"It was precarious. We didn't know how a harvest would go. All the machines were breaking. We had no idea how to fix them. But we were working out new ways of surviving all the time. Sean had nearly perfected cheese before the animals died."

Sylene smiles. "I know what it is, but I've never had it. No . . ." She doesn't have the word. She hunches her back and plods her arms along, puffs out her cheeks and, with her fingers above her head, heaves out a *moo*.

"Cows!" he croaks when he finally stops laughing. He gives it a go too: an impression of her imitation of a cow, romping along the earth. It makes him laugh even more. "Well . . . we'll find you some cheese someday. When we've found Bea, let's make that our next mission."

"And where did you and Kate meet?"

"At my brother's wedding. It was very over-the-top. You were . . . Kate was there to swell the numbers. She'd only known Ben briefly, at college, but there were so many people invited by my father, businesspeople from around the world. Ben wanted to fill it out."

"Describe it to me."

"Really?" He exhales fully. "Well, my father wanted it to happen at the tower, to close the mall and hold the event there. He wanted to have augmented content through the Feed depending on what your perception of a perfect wedding was. And to be honest, my brother wanted something no less extravagant, no less over-the-top: he just wanted it to be *real*. A ridiculous house with grounds and a lake and all sorts of lights in the trees. Fireworks and a banquet and helicopters and musicians and massive screens. The company made the largest flexiscreen ever for the day. They floated it on the lake. After the dinner, during the fireworks, they streamed all these vids so it looked like someone pulled a plug and the water had drained away. Then it looked like someone filled the lake up with champagne, and then there were all these lights and effects, and grabs of Ben and Miyu zooming around, and lasers."

"It sounds amazing."

"It was pure distraction, the way we lived."

"But where you met Kate, so not all bad."

"We met over dinner. Sorry, the *banquet*. I'd gone for a drink, and by the time I got back I was stuck at the back of the room. I could barely see the head table, where my father was giving a speech. And next to me was you. Kate. You know what I mean. You looked up at me and, brazen as you like, rolled your eyes. Then you mouthed along to what my father was saying, like you were imitating him. And then—and this was the moment, I think—you did this . . ." Tom draws his hand in front of his neck and mouths, *Go off, go off the Feed.* "And I did. I went off. My father's voice disappeared. The room was suddenly silent. Kate revealed it all for what it was: nothing. There was nothing there. It wasn't real. It really didn't count for *anything*. And I felt . . . liberated. We talked for real, slow, at the back of the room, while everyone else was buzzed. It was the most amazingly private thing I'd ever done. My father would have been furious." He spreads his hands as he walks. "Of course, when she realized who my dad was, it was embarrassing for a moment, but I didn't care, she didn't care, we both felt like we were somewhere we didn't belong, so off we went."

"Just like that? You knew?"

He flushes slightly and loses the confidence of his speech. "Well, no, that's not quite what I meant. I mean we went upstairs. We kept our Feeds switched off and left everyone else to it. You remember the lake I told you about? The lake with the screen?"

"Of course."

"Well, we saw that from upstairs. While everyone else was outside. We were upstairs in one of the bedrooms."

That night as they lie in the tent, Sylene's breathing slows and it sounds like she's asleep. Tom is also dipping into dreams. They'd stopped watching each other long ago. It had happened in a moment's understanding between them, a pause in a look: How could either of them kill the other? And why would they? Knowing what he knows now, Tom can easily see a way to forgive the killings, or understand them at least, and such understanding encourages acceptance. If he were to be taken . . . at least his death would not be in vain. There would be a continuation of sorts, he thinks as he nearly sleeps. Words meld and mean different things. The world changes in his mind. He is aware of the cold earth under the tent but feels like he's flying above a desert at the same time. Fragments of buildings point up, collecting sand. Office blocks, clock towers, churches. Sand collects in drifts against their sides but the scale of things is impossible: How large are those future ruins beneath him?

"Tell me another story," she says, and Kate's voice sucks him back. She rolls to face him. She doesn't touch him, but he can feel how close she is. "About the past, Tom. Where did we live?"

Her voice is sleep-smothered and he's not quite sure he heard her right.

"We . . . we lived in a house . . . it was in the old part of the city, not one of the new domiciles. You hated all those new-builds . . ."

He listens to her breathing. He can remember their home without trying. Their kitchen in the basement, their bedroom upstairs. They'd prepared the baby's room with new LCD wallpaper and carpet; every time he went in, he set the colors to blue, and whenever he returned she'd changed them to yellow again. All the other things in boxes that they'd bought: the clothes, the toys. Essentials, they told each other, all. All that potential there, a different future, boxed and gathering dust in their house. Their home. If it's still even there, in the ruins of the city, where they are going back to. He'd fled it before to save Bea; now he's returning there for her.

Sylene prods him in the eye.

"Okay, I'll tell you a story . . . This was a few years ago. We were at the camp, in the study in the farm-house, watching Bea. We had the fire burning, but apart from that it was nearly silent: just the sound of her piling blocks on the rug. She never got the tower very high; two blocks, maybe three, and then it would fall, and she would start again. She always had this *smile*, like she was the most patient person in the world. I was aware that things had gone quiet, that her little grunts of concentration had stopped. I opened my eyes, and just as I did so, I saw her reach up to place the sixth or seventh block on the tower, and she caught my eye and the thing collapsed. She stopped and *looked* at the blocks, and she said, 'Fuggit.' That was her first word. *Fuggit.* And the expression on your face as you looked at her and looked at me, and we both said at the same time: 'Well, I didn't teach her that!'"

Sylene sighs and seems to sink lower.

"Is that enough?" Tom whispers. "Are you asleep?"

"Thank you. It's almost like I can remember it."

They come at the camp from a different angle from when he had returned with Graham and Danny, their desperate journey back from the facility. They approach down a narrow lane with balding hedgerows lining its sides and birds warbling from the branches. Their boots clump past wrecked vehicles on the soil-covered track. And the air, something about the trees, smells familiar.

"We're nearly there," he says.

"We're going to your camp?"

He nods curtly. "It's on the way. And you asked about home, so . . ."

They walk on, arms swinging, boots banging, birds singing.

"Also," Tom says, having thought some more, "we can stock up on supplies. We can take some food with us."

Sylene glances at him.

"What?" he asks.

"If the camp was attacked once, it may have been attacked again."

Tom frowns. He hadn't thought of that. A bird speeds into a bush and hops from stick to stick. The sky is already losing its light. Their breath steams.

"I'm sure it'll be fine."

"I'm just saying, Tom," Sylene maintains, "that we should be careful."

They carry on walking.

"But when we get there," Tom says, "you know you'll have to pretend." He scans the horizon, looks up into the trees. "Do you know what I mean?"

"Yes."

They leave the lane and enter a field; the gate is crumpled and the hedgerows haven't yet quite over-grown the gap. Nearby rabbits scatter. He sees at least fifty more, farther away, unconcerned.

"Well, at least we don't have to go far for dinner."

"Tom." Sylene has stopped. She has her hands clasped and her face is furrowed.

"Are you all right?"

"Yes," she says, "I'm fine, I . . ."

"What?"

"It's the baby."

He nearly reaches for her but doesn't. "Are you okay?"

"You do know it's still Kate's? That just because I'm . . . just because of me, it's not . . . The baby is still genetically Kate's and yours."

The sun has sunk and the light catches the sides of their faces. The hedgerows cast thin-fingered shadows and the group of rabbits is dissolving, scampering swiftly away.

"Yes," he says. "I know."

They leave the field and drop into another lane. They are close to the camp, he knows it, but he can't find the track. The evening is already sketched out in darkening gray, and this stretch of road, with its over-turned cars and jackknifed trucks, looks familiar, but he curses. He's lost. He's sure the turnoff was *here*. He glances at her. Strands of hair fall from under her hat, whose woolen rim halos her head. Her cheeks are pink and her nose bright white. She catches him looking and smiles.

"We should just camp, Tom, if we can't find it soon."

He looks away. When he turns back, he sees, just for a moment, melancholy on her face. She, seeing his glance, smiles at him again. He takes her hand and pats it. Her fingers squeeze his—did they?—before she lets him go.

Tom watches her from the corner of his eye. Her near-familiar gait, the way her arms swing like they always have, the fullness of her belly between the cur-tains of her coat. It's just like it used to be, the first time they came looking for this place, having battled from the city, having clung to life, surpassed their stunted thoughts, communicating somehow with malformed words, a degenerate language of grunts. And at last, with the sun's last light dropped below the earth and bouncing only dimly off the clouds, he finally finds the track.

"It's been hidden," he murmurs as he climbs into the pile of wet branches.

She starts to climb too. Bits of bush and strands of ivy have been curled around and interspersed to hide what it is. What it is is a barricade. She nears its top and rolls over.

"Careful!"

She looks back from the other side and smiles. "Precious cargo," she says, patting her stomach. "I know."

Tom looks back along the road. Nothing. Still. Apart from the wrecked van and the motorbike, it's empty. He was here with Danny and Graham not too long ago. How times change the world. He peers back into the murk of the forest and scales the barricade. At its top is gloom: dark earth and black trees beyond. A dizzying lack of light.

"Kate?" he calls, and checks himself. "Sylene?"

The rustle of trees in the darkness; these trees; the sound that returns in his troubled dreams, and with it the fear rises within him. He can't see anyone. Running through the woods again, searching and desperate. To stay with Kate or search for Bea—what choice was that? He scrabbles and falls down the other side.

"*Sylene?*"

A hand grips his arm, and—"*Roagh!*"—she collapses into him, laughing at his face, shaking his shoulders and roaring at him, getting high on his quaking fear. Tom raises a shaking finger. "Don't . . ." he starts, and the quiver in his voice makes her face fall. "Don't do that."

"I'm sorry."

"Not here." He smiles without meaning it, puts a hand on Sylene's shoulder and moves her down the track. The gentle incline feels so familiar to him and also from another world. The wizened trees reach over them, spindle-thin, and click like insects in the breeze. "This is where she was taken. I must have been so close."

"Oh," Sylene murmurs. "I'm sorry."

He examines the bushes as they pass. They are nearly leafless; it would be impossible to hide here now. But then they had been full. And smoke had burned the air. And his heart had jolted with panic; he'd had no idea what to do. Then. Not now. He's looped back around to find her now. He'll save her. She'll be fine.

By the time the track levels out, Tom notices that he

and Sylene are holding hands. They break out of the trees and the air is instantly cooler. He doesn't let her go. There is nothing between them and the stars. The long grasses whisper. He squints, looking for shapes, looking for lights. Looking for anything at all.

"Should we wait until morning, so we can see things more clearly?" Sylene's voice is quietly earnest. She shivers. He sees that she is scared.

"No. Let's get a bit closer." He squeezes her hand.

"But maybe they've left." She withdraws it.

Tom points into the night. "Look, there it is." He directs her sight at a darker patch and they take high steps over the grass.

With his gaze locked on the house, the first hut, Danny's, surprises him, out of the gloom. Its windows black, its wood wet-dark and glinting, it has a heavy presence in the night. It is burned, chunks of it charred away like a cindered skull carved out.

"I'm beginning to think," Tom whispers deeply, "that we shouldn't have come back."

"We can still leave."

Yet he sets his jaw and continues. The house gradually appears, a stroke of gray in the darkness. The skeletons of trellises have collapsed. A smear of soot is shadowed around the kitchen door and Tom walks to the window, where jagged glass is still in the frame, a board now fixed in behind it.

"It's deserted."

"Then why are you still whispering?"

Tom coughs. "There's no one here. They must have abandoned the camp after we left." His voice echoes in the darkness.

"So. Shall we go?"

"Let's go in."

"I don't like it here!" She pulls him back, digging her feet into the ground.

"There's no one here!" he explains, and is surprised by the harshness in his voice. Something more than impatience, more than hope snuffed out. "Come *on*, Sylene."

He drags her forward with him. The scorched kitchen door is rough like hide as he wraps his fingers around the handle. His thumb sits snugly on the latch as if he'd never left, as if they're creeping back to bed from a midnight walk. The door sticks in the frame. He heaves once, twice, and with the third, harder shove it falls open and he lurches into the kitchen as a clatter of cascading metal beats the silence apart. It resounds throughout the valley around them. Sylene pushes her way into the doorway as Tom looks back out, into the darkness, gaping at the shadows of the huts, looking for movement, looking for light, for—

"*Who's there?*"

Tom freezes. He shrinks into the doorway and forces Sylene back into the cold kitchen behind him.

"I have a gun!" the voice shouts again, and a sharp crack echoes around the hills.

The silence draws out.

"Who are you?" comes the voice once more—a man's voice, tremulous with age.

"Graham?" Tom calls quietly. "Is that you?"

The windows are boarded and an armchair has been moved next to the sofa, but apart from that, the study is the same: the desk, the cupboard, the pictures on the walls, even the worn-out rug. A fire burns in the grate.

"I only use the back door now," Graham chatters, "and this room and the kitchen. I don't want anyone noticing me. I really don't need that much space. It's quiet sometimes but I'm quite, quite comfortable."

"You sleep in your hut?"

Graham nods.

"Wouldn't you be safer here?"

"It was all theory until tonight, Tom. You're the first people to have disturbed my peace." He gets slowly to his feet and takes the pot from the flames. The skin under his eyes has a translucency to it that it hadn't had before, and his hands shake as he pours. Somehow he looks less substantial. "More, Kate?"

"Thank you, Graham," says Sylene.

He hoops the pot back over the fire and settles onto the sofa. His movements are effortful. For a while before he speaks he looks around the room, as if admiring people who aren't actually there. Then he turns to them abruptly, as if no time had passed. "I thought people would be drawn to the house and not come looking in the huts. *I* thought: *The prominent door of the house, that's where they'll go, so I can keep the back one for me!*" He tilts his cup at them. Smiles over the rim with glee. "Cheers, Kate. Cheers, Tom. Welcome home!" He drinks. And then, "So . . . tell me . . . did you find any—"

"We'll help you tidy up in the morning."

"Oh." Graham swallows. "Well. It's just pots and pans tied across the door. I'd completely forgotten I'd set it. You scared the life out of me."

"You scared the life out of us!" Tom laughs, keeping the conversation moving, away from questions about Bea. "Didn't he, Kate?"

"With this?" Graham's eyes scintillate as he pats the stick leaning against the sofa. It resembles something like a gun, in silhouette at least. "I clapped two big books together!" he chortles, and stretches his feet toward the fire. When he stops laughing, after some calming silence in which he watches them, he asks carefully, "Did you go far, then?"

"North," Tom says. "Where's Sean?"

Graham spreads his hands in a way that says it all.

"And you didn't go with him?"

He stares into the fire. "Sean went to find Jack. You'd gone to . . . find Bea. And I'd be going to look for . . . what? I'm old. I'd just get in the way. No one needs to have me around. I'm just . . . My mind has . . ."

Tom glances at Sylene sadly as the old man drifts off. Even though Graham is smiling, something in him has gone. Or maybe *because* he's smiling, at the fire, into nothing, for no reason at all.

"Is the generator okay?" Tom asks after the pause has trailed on for long enough that he is sure there are no more words coming, that the previous thought has become lost somewhere as Graham stares into the flames. "Graham? How's your Chronicle?"

The old man starts and then turns away, his face darkening. "What about this is worth recording?"

"Well," Tom says, clapping his palms gently together. "Is the generator working?"

"The last time I used it, yes." Graham's voice has a sudden veneer of enthusiasm. "It's so much bother to get going, though, and I . . . well, I find I don't really need it. The thing, the—what is it? You have to dry the sparky bit out each time. And I'm fine without hot water, Tom. I don't really like electric light. I've missed your cooking, though, Kate." He leans forward and clasps Sylene's hand.

"It's good to be back, Graham," Sylene says. "Bea's first words were in this room, you know?"

"Ah, yes," Graham says. He steeples his fingers, raises his eyebrows, and smiles. "Yes, yes, I remember well. Jane really loves that girl. Have you said hello to her yet?"

Tom chokes, halfway to speaking. Graham's expression stops him. He's smiling, hopefully, determinedly, yet he's crying silently while he nods and nods away.

They leave the study when the fire dies down and go through to the darkness of the hallway. Graham stoops at the back door and shuts it firmly behind him as he heads out into the night. Tom meanwhile lifts the candle and lights the way upstairs. It throws a tentative light along the corridor as Sylene stops at the top. Tom waits for her to go to their bedroom, but she doesn't.

"Sorry," he says with a start. "It's the first door on the right."

At the threshold to the room he stands close enough

to smell her hair as the candle reveals their unmade bed and the chair beside it and the cupboard and the drawers. Everything as it was, but freezing and dark. He draws the curtains, surveys the bundled comforter and lifts it, throws it out and plumps it up. The last time he had slept here the camp had been attacked. Panic was the last thing that had happened in this bed. Nothing has been the same since. Bea had been in the children's hut, being watched by Danny, while Kate had been watching Tom sleep.

Sylene is already unlacing her boots, her sweater off. She lets her trousers fall. The curve of her belly is pronounced.

"You take the bed," Tom says. "I'll go in the chair. Or I can go back downstairs if you want. Graham's in his hut. He won't know."

Now she pulls the comforter up, kicking her legs to warm it. "Don't be silly." Her voice is already getting lost in the pillow. "You can get in here."

Tom heel-toes his shoes off and the floorboards creak just, once they've done it, as he remembers. The candle shines in the cut-glass mirror as it always did. He watches her, the rise and the fall of Kate's body as she breathes, the vulnerable curve of her throat. She is sleeping on his side of the bed.

Tom wakes to sounds he hasn't heard for a long time: rain smacking against glass and clattering onto the roof; wind working its way into the house through its ancient chinks and cracks. He pulls the curtains back. Through the cracked windowpane, the sky is balled up, the ground looks sodden, and the air between them thick with rain. Sylene spreads out. She forces an eyelid open.

"Don't make me go outside."

Laughing, he says, "I won't. Sleep. Rest."

He dresses and goes downstairs. The grandfather clock, he notices, is silent, and all the rotas have been pulled from the board. He collects the pans and pots from the kitchen floor and piles them by the sink, then opens the door to let in the wet gray light. The larder smells like it used to. Kate's secret stash of whitened chocolate is where it always was. He takes things down: tins of what is, hopefully, fruit and sealed containers of greening flour. With everything laid out on the table, he runs into the rain. It is cold and very damp in the shed, where he pulls out and dries the spark plug and pulls the starter cord five, six, seven times until a jet of sooty air coughs out around his ankles. Who cares about conserving fuel now?

Back in the kitchen, he makes a mixture for biscuits as the oven growls beside him. He tries to remember how Kate did it. He is spooning far-too-viscous stuff onto a tray when Graham enters, his legs sodden.

"You've brought the weather, Tom." He sighs, then chuckles, and then frowns as he sits, looking around as if for something lost. Tom watches the old man scratch the tabletop absently. So many meals, so many camp meetings here, and now just the two of them.

After a very long silence, he asks, "What's wrong, Graham?"

The old man looks at him as if he had forgotten he was there. For a split second he seems confused, and then he spreads his hands across the table and a wan smile across his face. "In sooth I know not why I am so sad."

"Are you missing Jane?"

Graham shrugs.

"And everyone left the camp, so . . ."

Graham, his voice barely a grumble, mumbles, "*Everyone* didn't. I'm still here. Life is what it is. And if you've got that straight, no one can ever touch you."

"Graham," Tom says softly, "I'm just saying that you have lots of reasons to be sad."

"It's the awful pain of hope, Tom." Graham sighs again. His posture is strong, his chin held high but clearly straining. His eyes are moist. "If life has taught me anything, it's that none of it is permanent. Property, happiness, *things*. I've been alone for months now, and do you know what? It's been *pure*. No one could touch me because I had nothing to lose anymore. So it's lovely to see you, Tom, but at the same time . . ."

Tom nods slowly. "Would you like a biscuit?"

"When they're cooked. They'll still be raw. Where's Kate?"

"Resting."

"She's pregnant again."

"Yes." Tom grins. "We're very excited."

Graham nods, his eyes on the floor. "And Bea? I know you didn't want me to ask yesterday, but I *have* to know, Tom. Did you find her?"

Tom wipes his hands on a cloth. How to tell the old man that he is right: that they will be going again soon; that, indeed, he has nothing much more to live for?

"We've come back for supplies, Graham. We think . . . we may know how to find her." He chews his lip and bobs his head deeply, wanting to speak, wanting to fuel the hope glinting in Graham's eyes, but afraid in the end to explain it to this ages-old Resister. "SaveYou. Your memories were saved in case you had an accident, so your thoughts could be rebooted if you suffered trauma or an attack. It helped police solve murders, because the evidence was there—very clear what happened, before the moment of death. It was part of the Premium Service. Were you aware of it?"

Graham brushes Tom's question away, his eyes darkening. "Of course."

"Then what's the matter?"

Graham fixes him with a look of disgust. "We're not computers."

"I'm not saying you have to like it, Graham, but this"—Tom starts to talk more quickly—"if you think about it, is how we find Bea. She wasn't at the facility and we can't find her. We've tried. But we *can* find out where she *is* because her thoughts will have been stored. We can see what happened to her, where she was taken, where she is now, via the Feed."

"But, *Tom* . . ." Graham blinks, confused again, before continuing, sure of himself once more. "The Feed went down."

"But SaveYou, the program that sends out the Back-Ups, is still active," Tom continues rapidly. "Listen, Graham, the Feed implant is biotech, right? No batteries needed because the battery is us." He hits his chest while Graham sits back in his chair, shaking his head.

"Playing at God," the old man mutters, and stretches out an arm as he declaims, "Technology outstripping our moral capacity. Ripping this world apart! For money, for greed, for—"

"Graham, please!" Tom wants the man to understand. He needs him to believe. "I agree with you, we've discussed this all before, but put your Resister dogma to the side. *Please.*"

"Let it go, Tom." Graham leans forward, his eyes icy. "Leave it. Because all I'm hearing from you is thoughtless hope. If you hope blindly, you can't protect yourself from *what really is.* I can see the pain it's giving you! It's obvious: it's right there on your face! So *stop* it. Live in the real world. Bea's gone. Like Danny, like Jane, you've lost her, she's dead—"

"I met one, Graham." Tom's words threaten to break his speech apart. "I met one of the taken and they told me the truth. SaveYou is still transmitting. That's how they tether to our minds—"

Graham recoils. "Who do?"

"You're right, Graham, our morals were spent: they're from the future and they had to escape the world because we had devoured the planet in their past. They sent people back to try to change history, to stop us from destroying the earth."

Graham stands. "I'm not listening to this anymore."

"It's the truth," Tom retorts.

Graham's fists are clenched as he shakes with rage. "I want you to find Bea, of course I do—the poor girl! But, Tom, this is lunacy! She doesn't even have a Feed!"

"No, you're *wrong,* because . . ." Tom shakes his head vehemently, even though his voice has lost its drive. "Because the Feed became *genetic,* Graham! It didn't *need* to be implanted anymore!"

Deep sorrow sags in Graham's eyes. "Tom, this all sounds so willful. The Feed became genetic? We're being invaded from the future? Who on earth told you all this? You say they invade us through the Feed?"

"Yes," Tom replies. "Yes, that's correct."

Graham's expression is exhausted; there is no victory there. "But Jane didn't *have* the Feed, Tom. So how did they take her? Have you really been told the truth?"

When the rain stops, they put on boots and hats. Tom finds a scarf for Sylene. Outside, the sun is already low enough to shine slantways across the land, rounding the bellies of the clouds with molten gold. It refracts in the amber beads of rain clinging to the grasses as they climb the hill. At the top, a lone piece of planking links the earth and the clouds. The grave has been tended and words carved inelegantly into the wood. Jane's name. Her dates, and a cross.

"What do you remember about her?" Graham's voice is thin. "Because for all the years, I can't remember much. Her smile sometimes. But I can't hear her voice anymore. I wonder sometimes if I . . ." He turns to Sylene apologetically. "What do you remember about her, Kate?"

"Oh, Graham—"

"She was a happy soul, Graham," Tom interrupts. "She had the wisdom of the earth."

That alone is enough to make Graham weep, and as time stretches out, Tom glances awkwardly at Sylene. He is surprised to see that her eyes are also wet. Her hands are clasped so tightly that her knuckles strain. Her lips are moving, whispering something to herself or someone who isn't there. Whether she senses being watched or not, she angles her face to the ground. He turns from her too and gulps something back as the wind wraps around them. A very light rain passes like a shadow, like a sketch from a curling wisp of cloud. By the time Graham has collected himself and leads Sylene over the rise, the clouds have stretched to scuffs of pink. Lagging behind them as he leaves Jane's grave, Tom's own tears fall suddenly free. Although he tries to stifle the sounds, Sylene waits for him and wipes his cheek with her thumb, and in that moment he sees something in her eyes—does he?—a sorrow, perhaps, before she leads him on, linking her arm through his. And he realizes then that he trusts her. What other choice does he have?

Graham waits for them by the forest. Under a layer of softening leaves, another grave lies.

"You did everything you could, Kate, but the stitches didn't hold. It was too large a wound to cauterize. We tried to pack it shut with wax."

Sylene gasps. "Didn't you use medical aids?"

"What do you mean?" Graham peers at her.

"I mean . . . I'm sorry I wasn't here to help."

"Sean thought the camp unsafe. He left. And it's all because I killed that man."

Graham's face contorts into a disgusted scowl. He turns away and stares into the woods steadfastly, shrunken somehow in his coat. He looks haggard, depleted in his skin. Sylene glances at Tom, who shakes his head for her to stay quiet before his gaze is pulled back to Danny's grave.

"I don't deserve to live anymore!" Graham wails suddenly. It's a strangled voice, not one that should be heard. "The children gone, Danny dead, in revenge for *what I did*! I think I'm . . ." He wheels back around to them and gestures at his head. "Sometimes I think my mind is going, my memory, like my mother's, and . . .

It would give me peace, *to forget would give me peace,*
but I'm *terrified,* I'm—"

"It's not true, Graham," Tom interrupts. He scrambles over Danny's grave and stumbles into the old man.
"We went to the facility and it wasn't them. They didn't
take her. It wasn't your fault." He shakes his head as a
fresh patter of rain scatters over the leaf bed. He holds
Graham's thin hands and stares into his animal eyes.
"And I'm sure you're not losing your memory. With
your mother—"

"It's genetic," Graham says pointedly, and his expression stiffens suddenly as the trees shush and wheeze.
Leaves roll heavily across the ground. Then he walks
away; he just turns and heads back to the camp.

Tom and Sylene follow. Graham is suddenly and
resolutely taciturn, musing hard on something as they
trudge their way over the oozing ground. When they
reach the porch of his hut, Sylene breaks the silence:
"Graham, would you like to sleep with us tonight? We
could sleep in a rota. For safety."

"To be honest, Kate, I think if they take me, they
take me, so what," Graham mumbles, slapping his
chest. "Someone else could probably make better use of
this old thing than me, whoever the hell they are. And
it's not like there's anyone here anymore who would

need to be protected from me, is there? Some nights I hope they do take me!" Then he raises his arms and waves at them cheerily before closing the door hard.

They stand in the darkness.

The wind in the distant trees sounds familiar, which is either Tom's imagination or because he is home.

"Home?" he asks her, and as they walk, he puts an arm around her. "That was kind of you."

"He looks lonely."

"I'm sure he is. But you know he can't be taken? He doesn't have the Feed. His wife . . ." He shakes his head. "Poor Jane. She was enabled when she was young. Then she met Graham, who was a fundamental Resister, and she didn't ever admit it. She hid it from him their whole life, and she never came to peace. I always thought her incredibly heroic: she protected him from knowledge that would have hurt him. She took that hit, and he was happy. Originally, she wanted to have it uninstalled, but who had that done? The operation was too expensive. This was all first-generation tech. Once you were in, you were in. Which all makes it doubly unfair."

"What?"

"That she was taken. One of your lot came through and Graham had to kill her. She was sleeping in their bed, in their hut there. That poor old ancient man.

That's the world you made, Sylene. When even people like Graham . . ."

Tom stops and looks up at the sky. He puts his hands in his pockets. Then he veers away around the farmhouse. The gazebo is dark at the back. The power cables and light wires look like fractures across the sky. Not so long ago, they were lit up. He and Kate danced here. Bea heard her first music beneath these lights. They all danced around the fire to celebrate her birthday . . .

"It's cold, Tom. Shall we go inside?"

"I just wanted to say: I'll care for you, for you and the baby. You know that, don't you?"

"Tom . . ."

"You're a good person, Sylene. Do you recognize it here?"

"No, I—"

"You remember that music in the Pharmacist's house?"

"The Rollins? Yes."

"Well, Kate hated jazz. I always loved it." He takes her shoulders and kisses her. At first she doesn't move, but as he presses closer, she pulls back and turns out of his grasp.

"Kate, I just—"

"I'm Sylene!"

"I'm sorry. It was an accident! Your name, calling

you that, was an accident—not the . . . You're a good person, Sylene." Tom can't see her in the darkness, can't make out her expression as she looks up at the stars, breathing heavily. The echo of his own voice reverberates in his ears: its hoarseness, its pleading tone. There is a roaring sound in his head, and his chest heaves as if a valve in his neck has been drawn tightly shut.

"I had a husband, Tom."

He feels suddenly how cold the ground is, feels it soaking into his feet. And he feels how small he is compared with the depth of the earth, and the height of the sky, and the very age of the world.

"Of course," he mumbles. "I'm sorry."

"Don't be." She takes his hand and squeezes it. "Let's get back inside."

They fumble through the empty house. In bed they have a strange half-hug and then they turn from each other. After some time he feels her relax and hears her breathing deepen. He turns, silently, and raises himself on an arm. He waits for his eyes to get used to the dark and then, when he still can't see, he slides to the edge of the bed and pulls open the curtains. He can soon make out the outline of her body as she sleeps, her mouth relaxed, her hands by her face as if praying. Her eyes twitch beneath her lids in deep sleep. He watches her.

Wonders what she dreams. Whether she too could now be taken. Not that he could bring himself to kill her. Nor would she him, of course.

She rolls onto her back, sighs and shifts. Then she turns on her side again, facing away from Tom, and, reaching back, pulls his arm around her. She places his palm on her stomach. There is nothing for a while, just the sense of something full, and then the surface warps, and what was soft is suddenly firm, and relaxes, and then is firm again, as the baby moves beneath.

When he can, he pulls his hand away and turns back to the window. He stares out through the cracked and dirty pane. The lawn is a silvered rug rolling up the hill. The forest is dark there on the other side, over where Danny's grave is.

"Hey, pal," he whispers. "I wish you were still here. I don't know what to do."

Up early, he makes more supplies: biscuits and a simple mulchy stew. There are some old Tupperwares whose plastic has become opaque, and even some scraps of foil. Graham enters midmorning, sees what he's doing, and says he's going for a walk. He won't be drawn into conversation, and Tom watches him from the doorway as he ambles across the grass and turns to his hut, then walks the other way before pausing, trembling visibly even at this distance, and turns back. He plods past his hut and away up the hill.

Sylene comes down, wearing the robe—Kate's robe—that had been hanging behind the door. He puts some biscuits on a plate for her and they share a quick smile. Then she warms her hands on the cup of tea Tom gives her and looks at it deeply as she drinks.

"It's not poisoned," he remarks to break her solid silence.

Sylene sips again and frowns. "My brain knows I don't like it, but my body says I do. I can't describe it."

Tom goes to speak before he thinks better of it and turns back to the sideboard. Sylene watches him as he wraps up more supplies.

"Will Graham be okay without us?" she asks.

"I'm sure he'll do just fine."

"How much longer will it take to get to the tower?"

Tom glances out the window, at the hills and the sky and the distant horizon. "A few weeks. Maybe a month."

"And . . . did Kate like tea?"

"Yes," Tom says, trying to sound casual. "Very much."

Graham waves them off cheerily as they leave that afternoon, but when Tom turns back, he has gone. The

air is chill as they ascend the track beneath the few remaining leaves. Water drops shiver on their browning
edges and fall occasionally to the ground.

"He was a nice man," Sylene says.

"Yes," Tom replies, "he was."

Sylene breathes in deeply. "It smells different. The
air." She glances at him, her breath steaming out. "You
shouldn't feel bad, Tom. The world's not fair. Survival
has a different code."

"Things change," Tom says. "It's the only given constant." And they do: the days harden. They stay bright
but the air becomes unkind. Then the clouds roll in
and stay for good, sitting above them like a frozen layer
of sky. They sleep in their warmest clothes under the
rug they took from their bedroom, and sometimes they
talk, and sometimes they sleep, but time seems to stop
watching as they inch their slow way south.

After many days they pass a town, a small one, with
decaying buildings in its distant core. Streams of vehicles knot around its domes. The rains have been strong
and the earth off the tarmac is bog-like, so they walk
the road again: it affords them some stability, even if
they are now more exposed. Huge billboards ahead
have broken and drooped. Tom looks behind them at
the looming clouds, heavy with another load of water.

"I don't like the look of them."

Sylene glances up, and when she turns back, she is smiling.

"What is it?"

"Nothing. It's just funny."

They pass a row of rusted cars crushed into one another. From how they're positioned it seems some slewed to avoid the collision, while others took the force full on. A long time ago now. All have been raided and the insides are torn, the bodies gone.

"What's funny?"

Sylene sighs. "That was the point of no return, when you killed the clouds. You made the world hot enough that they could no longer form, and after that the heat became exponential. The clouds"—she points up and then gestures, with both hands flat, one above the other—"protected the planet from the sun's rays. So once they were gone . . ." She hitches her rucksack up. "Clouds were myths by the time I was born. One of those things that became extinct. So these," she says, pointing up again, "are lovely. Even if *you* don't like the look of them."

"I meant I think they're going to rain on us."

"Yes, I know."

"But I'm sorry we killed the clouds."

The billboards here have collapsed across the road, massive things, their white expanses covered with mold, the vast quickcodes barely visible beneath.

"What are those things?"

"Quickcodes? Very clever. Didn't you have them? Mark loved them." He frowns. "You didn't know Mark. He was . . . Anyway, they were scanned directly by the Feed and only relevant ads were shown. A huge source of revenue, and for the consumer—such convenience. The Feed knew what you thought, what you bought, even when you needed to drink or what your body should eat. So food packaging was personalized. A million ads, personalized for each and every product. For me, for you, for children—different for everyone, depending on your needs."

They climb down into the jagged foundations from where the concrete pylons supporting the structures were ripped. Cables protrude from pits of water like exotic grasses. The metal legs curve over them and twist like clay.

"What was Bea like?"

They scramble up the other side of the crater. Tom reaches the top first and waits for her to clamber out behind him, examining the road, the clouds above them and the waterlogged country spreading to the side.

"She's lovely," he says in the end. "She's blond, like you, and has your eyes and nose, though the rest of her face is like mine unfortunately."

"I meant what's she like as a person?"

Tom inclines his head and nods down the road. "Shall we?"

They climb onto the tarmac, grabbing the creaking fender of a truck to pull themselves up.

"Spirited," he continues. "Like you. Clever too. She saw things—*sees* things that I can't. You know what I mean?"

"That's kids for you."

"She sees things that are obvious, but that somehow we just don't see—"

"Or have the time to notice."

"That's right," he says, returning her smile.

"I had children," she says. "My boys."

"Really?" he says. And, after a while, "Did they . . . ?"

"I buried them."

Sylene has her thumbs tucked into the straps of her rucksack, up by her chest. Her head is down, looking at the road, watching her footing among the debris. She has to lean forward slightly now to see her feet over her stomach. "My parents died first, a long time ago. Then my husband. He had been trying to fix the solar array. And then my eldest son, Gabe; he was one of the first wave to try to come back, but we knew it had gone wrong straightaway. The second, Darian, he came back later. We thought it was working by then. I wanted him to come back before me so I could bury his body. Even if the transfer worked, our bodies still had to die."

"So maybe Darian's here now? Maybe he made it back?"

"Maybe. But how can I find him?" Sylene looks at him levelly.

"I'm sorry. No one should have to—"

"No," she says, and catches her breath. "No one should have to, but here I am. They saved the old for last. I hoped I wouldn't make it."

It starts like the sound of a rattle, or guns in the distance. Tom doesn't know what it is until it gets louder, and he turns and sees that it's nearly upon them: a striated wall of rushing gray, drilling into the car roofs, rattling them like cans. "Cover!" he shouts, but the raindrops thrill over them, piercing and hard. His hands are icy in an instant and his fingers ungainly as he fumbles a car door open. He throws himself inside and reaches over to grab Sylene's rucksack as she forces it in and squeezes into the passenger seat. The car has the cold smell of empty years and their breath instantly condenses on the glass. The air outside takes on an early darkness and water coats the windows.

Sylene says something that he doesn't hear over the cascading rattle.

"What?"

"It's loud!"

After his ears get used to the stunning noise, Tom reaches around his seat for his bag. He emerges with two hard biscuits. They eat in companionable silence as the raindrops pummel the car and he looks at the patterns in their flow.

"So your boys, they were adults?"

Sylene nods, swallowing her dry biscuit down.

"Children of their own?"

"No. It wasn't a world you'd wish on anyone. My husband and I . . . went against the advice we were given. We thought we only had enough energy for a decade's more air when we had Gabe, but we found ways to make it last longer. We knew the heat would kill us first."

He nods, thinking. "So . . ." He turns to her. She turns to him. "How *old* are you, Sylene?"

"You shouldn't ask a lady that. And anyway, age was different where I come from. We lasted a lot longer. By that reckoning, I'm not even middle-aged. I'm comparatively younger than you."

"Are you ancient?"

"None of your business."

"But you are a woman at least, aren't you? I mean, you're not a man in there?"

"This conversation," Sylene says, flicking the end of his nose, "stops right now."

"I just wanted to check."

"Well, you're being offensive!"

"Why are you smiling then?"

"I'm not. This horrible biscuit you made." She sucks her mouth. "It's all stuck in my teeth. Fill this up, would you?" She turns and rummages in her bag, and he stares at the stretched skin of her waist as her sweater and jacket ride up. She puts a tin cup in his hand; when he doesn't move, she nods at his window and points. "Come on then, boy."

He grins, opens his door, and holds the cup outside. The rain whips in, drenching his leg, but when he presents her with the cup, it's full to the brim.

He watches her drink. "Liquid cloud, right?"

"Tastes so good."

The road is slick in the morning and the autumnal colors of the cars have been brought out by the rain. Their doors creak open painfully. Hers shuts, spraying water into the air, but the hinges of his lock, halfway closed, and the door will move no more. They walk for an hour, and when an elevated junction appears in the distance, fenced off with billboards that could be hiding anyone, he takes them off the road. They cut a course across the fields until they reach another. They cross it, descend the other side, and continue across the sodden earth.

By the time they camp, nights later, they are eager for the warmth of the tent. "It's beginning to feel like home," Sylene jokes as she throws the tarpaulin out and begins to peg it in.

Tom smiles at her over his shoulder, bending down to lay a fire. "Better than your tin cans?"

Sylene narrows her eyes. "Those cans were progress, boy. State of the art in their time. I'd like to see this thing stand up to some serious solar rays. I bet it doesn't even have beta-particle protection." She fingers the fabric, challenging him with her smirk.

"I have no idea what you're talking about. I'm just a primitive, an ape." He taps his head. "All I know is all I got. What are beta particles?"

The expression of Sylene's eyes sinks somewhere else. "Nothing. They're not important yet. They killed my husband, though, after we destroyed the clouds."

Tom continues to pile the logs up as Sylene carries on with the tent. "Are they a type of radiation or something?" he asks after some time.

Sylene inserts the structural poles and the tent is up. She climbs inside and connects the inner tent to its shell. She takes far longer to do the job than she normally does, and after a while Tom returns to laying the fire. He cooks in the peace. Surveys the land around them. Sylene comes out when the food is nearly ready, her eyes, perhaps, slightly red, and Tom watches from a rock as she pours stew from the pot. She looks more tired than she used to, but generally happier with it too. More relaxed somehow. Her stomach pushes her jacket aside like someone peeking through.

"Here we are."

Tom takes the tin bowl she hands him and first of all warms his hands, lowering his head to feel the steam. "It's perfect."

"You haven't eaten it yet."

"It is the most lovely smelling radiator in the world."

She settles next to him, breath escaping as she lowers herself down.

"I'm sorry about your husband; that must have been awful. But are you happier now?"

When the silence stays unbroken, he rolls his head to look at her, not wanting to take it away from the warmth. She is watching him quizzically. "Yes," she replies. "Doing all right."

———

Once dark, the temperature drops and the night sky is clear, the stars precise and bright. They sit outside wearing two sweaters each under their jackets, gloves, and hats. Their breath steams: the only clouds in the sky.

"Did you know," Tom says—they are leaning back into each other, their shoulder blades connecting—"that over seven years all the cells in your body will have replaced themselves? You will literally, physically, be a different person."

"Says who?"

"Says . . . someone I know. I think it's true."

"We had nanobots that replaced our cells weekly. A constant clean, renewing them before they had a chance to deform."

Tom looks up at the stars, his lower lip out. "It means I'm a different person from who I was before the Collapse."

He feels her nod, the roll of her skull through their hats, and he can see her steam clouds rising upward as she speaks behind him: "There's no point fighting it. It's what makes the world go round."

Tom watches the stars some more.

"It was Danny," he says. "Danny said that. I wish you could have met him. It sounds silly, but he's the best friend I can remember having. We weren't similar, but I understood him. I liked him. He was kind. He really loved Bea. And I don't want to ever forget him."

The landscape ripples up to little folds of hills. Sometimes when the wind courses over them from the east they smell a briny sea. They cross roads, but they're only small in this part of the country. Expanses of emptiness stay silent in the salt-licked air.

Late one afternoon they crest a hill. There is a river below them, an area that has widened into the bowl of an estuary where the slopes are thickly covered with trees.

Sylene gasps. "It's so beautiful!"

Tom looks at the view again. Before, he had been thinking only about how to traverse it, only seeing the half-sunk boats in the water, the length of a pontoon snapped and scattered like floating matchsticks, all the signs of destruction. But now he sees the trees, the stillness of the water, the silhouettes of the distant hills sketched out in the miasma of the afternoon's late light. It *is* beautiful, he realizes. And to the south, in the distance, maybe—is he seeing this right?—he makes out the faintly notched shapes of the city, one of which, he knows, is the tower.

These are flat days now in the terrain they cover and the way time seems to stretch. They walk constantly, talk occasionally, sleep rarely, and eat not enough. But the city grows upon the horizon. The smell takes Tom by surprise, even though he had been expecting it. Sylene mentions it as they pack up the tent one morning. It seems to slick the air itself, turning it fetid and cloying.

"It'll get worse," he says. "If it's coming from the city, it'll get worse for sure."

And suddenly something becomes real. All this time they've been walking, the hundreds of thousands, maybe millions of steps they've taken; with each one, somehow, the memory of Bea has softened. Her image has become more and more opaque, the essence of her in his head less real. An imaginary child, not a true one. Their mission had, somewhere, at some point, become the mere act of it, but now, with this smell, he realizes: this is it. They may find her here. And if they don't, she's gone. Like so many others, snuffed out, deleted from the world, from life. This smell, he understands, is death.

They meet a motorway and flank it. Keeping their distance, they look for people, animals, anything that might be a threat as the vehicles go from sparsely scattered wrecks to a frozen floe of rusted metal and filthy glass. The city becomes clearly visible: a spread of something covering the earth; the low-slung sub-city domiciles; the huger edifices farther in. He points at one, at the horizon, and tells her that's where they're going. That's the tower. His father's place. Where their homeHub stores their BackUps and Bea's—as Sylene has told him it will.

Then, soon, the cars are packed so tightly together they act like a scab across the road: a rusted layer of metal, bleeding onto the tarmac. They walk along its top. Slowly. Stepping from bumper to roof to bumper, going from car to car. Gaping rusted holes reveal rotten innards of stained fabric and shredded seats. Ten lanes on the motorway, all packed with crushed-up cars, all of them stopped as they tried to escape, and going nowhere for years.

The crunch and boom as they climb echoes into the evening. They pass under vast rain-darkened billboards. At dusk they drop down underneath the crust and they eat, and sleep, and hold each other for warmth as their breath condenses on the windows. Skeletons watch them from some of the wrecks. Most of them are empty.

The next morning they pass rancid sewage plains and warehouses that dwarf them. A sign welcoming them to the city suggests they drive carefully, except the *R* and the *V* have been blown away by bullets, changing the hospitality of the message.

Soon they are in the suburbs, and the smell of rotting reaches a peak as the road is swallowed between the vaulted malls. Domiciles curve around them like so many giant suds. The road rises up on massive legs and beneath it, between the stanchions, are the remains of older buildings. The previous centuries' places. A lot of the newer domes are smoke-blackened from the inside. Others house a darkened fuzz of moss. Many, most, are cracked like eggshells. Creepers grow out, birds fly in, and there, way down on the ground, a pack of huge dogs waits in line. One by one they prowl through a car-sized smash in a wall. And out flows that smell, like the thick and rancid odor from a putrefying wound. It sits heavily like a layer of fat on everything, greasing their faces, seemingly making even the road surface slippery.

They continue as the super-road rises and the stench gets lighter with height. Before them the city spreads: conglomerations of smooth-sided buildings, glinting like glassy hills. In the far distance, toward the river, the famous buildings of the older city emerge from the water. Shards of glass. Cross-anointed cupolas that, in centuries past, had been the must-see sights. Sylene clings on to the barricaded edge of the road, the wind catching her hair. Unearthly silence surrounds them.

"So here it is," she says. "This was one of the vistas we had up on our screens."

They camp on top of the next super-road, where the pegs won't penetrate, the tarmac being clear of soil up this high. They position the tent between cars to shelter themselves from the wind. The sun is setting, melting into the city's distant reaches. It makes the buildings to the east look like they're on fire. That was where their house was, Tom thinks, but he can't quite remember enough to pin it down, its location lost with his habits and GPSmaps of the past. Then the stars come out and the city, empty, is peaceful below them. In the darkness the destruction is veiled. It is the quiet of winter country nights, but here surrounded by glass and concrete and air. There are noises, carried on the breeze. Dogs, birds, and at one point something cascading: a colossal sound as a building settles at last, giving up the ghost. Tom wakes halfway through the night and sees a fire in the distance, on another super-road, floating.

"Is this how you imagined it?"

They curve around an off-ramp, walking past spindly streetlights, a putrid and gaping underpass descending to their right.

"Are you joking? None of it is how I imagined it. The city. The world. The people we've seen."

"What's different about the people?"

They join another super-road, the translucent barriers melding together at the junction in midair. Blank posters line the sides, lines of nothing but regular quickcodes.

"You're all different colors."

Tom snorts back a laugh. "You can't say that!"

"By the time it gets to us, we're all a golden-browny mix."

"Sylene . . ."

Tom takes her arm, cutting her laughter off. Ahead, coming around a car, is the stocky form of an animal. With a low, square jaw and muscled ridges on its shoulders, this dog ducks as soon as it sees them, stretching its legs into the ground. It reveals its teeth. Its eyes flare darkly. Saliva strands between its lips as it unleashes a massive gulping bark.

"Get behind me, Sylene!"

Tom pushes her back as the dog approaches. Snarling, legs quivering, when it growls the sound vibrates in Tom's guts. It finds purchase and lunges, and he, dodging, manages a kick on the side of its head. It barks and lunges again, teeth rancid and sharp, and smashes against him with its snout. Its eyes are crazed, pure black, nothing emotional there. He swipes with an arm, kicks out again, and lands a lucky blow on its mouth. It yelps, surprised, and recoils, then skulks away down the road, snarling, growling, padding sideways, never taking its gaze away.

Tom carries a pipe now, the exhaust of a car. The road drops, narrowing from three clogged thorough-fares to one as it enters an older zone. The stream of solidified cars is continuous: wedged two abreast in the single lanes, mounted on the pavements. At ground level, they enter streets where disorder rules: the dev-astation is random, it seems. Sometimes single houses are gutted while their neighbors appear pristine. Walls have crumbled into the road and entire blocks have been razed. Scraps of building point up like black-ened broken teeth. One mound of rubble is mixed with twisted metal. A plane? A satellite? Something hurled down from the sky. Everywhere the trees are unruly, their branches grown too low, too wide, freed and con-trolled no more. Grass sprays up between the paving slabs. Down here on the ground, away from the super-roads, everywhere Tom looks lie bones. Some still snag tendrils of fabric, or maybe it's matter, but most are sun-stripped clean. Sometimes there are recognizable configurations: two attaching at a knee; a rib cage like a spider; vertebrae with the jawbone attached. Pieces of people discarded like toys.

He realizes he is walking alone.

Sylene stands between rows of cars whose tires have sagged and split. To one side of the road is a line of old houses. The doors are all unhinged. The gutters have burst. One house has been blackened by an explosion, the windows of the cars blown out. On the other side are the rusted railings of a park. A tree has crushed the seesaw. Its roots are still embedded and its branches grab the slide. Only birds now sit on the rusty-chained swings. Tom goes back to her. Tears flow freely down her face, and her hands, raised to her mouth, are shaking.

"We didn't mean to do this," she sobs, the tears stranding between her lips. "This isn't what we meant at all."

Tom takes her in his arms and she buries her face.

"Well . . . I don't think we meant to destroy the world either," he tells her, and her shaking sobs stop for a second before they start again, louder and unrestrained.

It's like they walk through the rings in a tree, the city around them aging. A super-road stretches far above them, but the residential area they reach is one of the oldest of the city. Instead of curving glass or the concrete behemoths they have seen before, these houses are centuries old. Tom climbs some steps at random, the asphalt cracked and frozen-flowing down. The ornamentations and window frames are streaked brown, the windows fuzzy with dust.

"We're nearly at the tower," he says, "but let's stay here for tonight." He tuts and points at a panel by the door. "A BioLock. We'll leave this one for the archaeologists." He steps over the small wall dividing this set of steps from the next house and examines the front door, running his hands along the frame. "Looks good . . . Wait here. I'll do a quick scout."

He descends the stairs and turns down a few more at the side of a small front garden. At the bottom is another door. He smashes one of its panes with a brick, reaches through, and twists the latch. Pushes through the silken cobwebs. A short, dark corridor leads into a kitchen, where the air is damp, like a tomb, but the room is shockingly peaceful. All the chairs are upright. It's like life. His old world. If he could forget everything that's happened in between. The memory of Bea clutches him, terrified, desperate not to be let go. And he feels nauseated. Should they stay here for the night or push on toward the tower? Its summit, his family's homeHub, where Bea's memories, he prays, are waiting.

Shaking, he glances into the next room: a dining room with glass doors looks onto an overwhelmed garden. Again, everything intact. Leaning on the walls as he climbs, on the next floor he finds a living room with a gray three-piece suite. The floors are carpeted with burlap. He pushes his knuckles into the firm weave. They'd had carpets exactly like it in their house. He goes to a wall that looks bare, but yes, he can feel the stretch of a thinscreen just where they'd had theirs. Atoms thin and translucent; no archaeologist will be finding this piece of tech. There are two bedrooms upstairs where theirs had been. Had they all really lived the same way? Hadn't it seemed strange at the time?

Tom stands at a window as the last of the day's light catches the side of the frame. Sylene, arms across her stomach, woolly-hatted, looks up and down the road. A quiet late-autumn evening. If only none of this had happened. He goes back downstairs, his boots clumping on the floor, and puts his head outside.

"It's nice," he says. "With some modest refurbishment, it could be our dream home."

In the cupboards, there is very little that hasn't rotted or rusted through. Some brown sauce and a tin of fava beans, colorless but seemingly edible. Tom opens their last sealed Tupperware and they shovel the beans with biscuits and splash them with the sauce. Framed posters line the walls. At the end of the table is a high chair, its plastic seat covered with mold that spreads along the straps. Tom notices that Sylene's gaze keeps returning to it.

"Is this how you lived?" she asks.

He turns to the window. Not far off, and not too far away, though he can't quite get his bearings. They had a kitchen in the same place, and exposed brickwork too. Kate had refused any quickcoded artworks, so they'd had real posters on the walls. To buy them would have cost a fortune, but these were heirlooms, she'd said, from when her parents were young. Plays and films they'd seen. Concerts they'd gone to. Antiquated public events they described in detail to their children. They were dubious about Tom having them, but they were delighted their daughter liked them.

"Not exactly the same, but similar."

"It's like a museum." Sylene laughs and shakes her head in wonder. "I like it!"

They lick their plates clean. Tom takes them to the sink and twists the tap, from which nothing comes, of course. He did it, he justifies to himself, to feel some routine, some familiarity with what was once before; not because he forgot. Sylene clears her throat behind him.

"It's a girl, I think, Tom."

He puts the plates down and turns. Leans back against the sink. "How do you know?"

Sylene looks at the high chair, her hands on her stomach. "It doesn't feel like a boy."

"What will we call her?"

Sylene doesn't respond, so he sits and reaches his hands toward her.

"Sylene?"

She gives a very brief shrug. She doesn't take her eyes off the high chair. "It depends on who she looks like."

He wakes just after dawn. He has barely slept. All night he heard noises: scratching, movements. Ghosts in the house, he had thought while he was still murkily asleep. How many ghosts must there be around them? Protecting their homes, haunting the streets. When he had managed to sleep more, the dreams had been confused. Nothing had been stable. A house, his and Kate's, with flooded foundations; having to hide some things there—books, he thought, grabbing the dream before it evaporated, as posters floated past on the tide; he was suddenly in a very tall building he no longer knew, but he knew he was being watched. Gas building up, wherever he was, waiting for the spark to ignite it.

He goes downstairs, leaving Sylene asleep, and puts the smeared dishes back in their cupboard. Sparse light comes through the plant-clotted doors in the dining room. He picks up a paper photograph in an old-fashioned frame, leaving a crevice in the dust on the shelf. Parents, children, grandparents, sitting on a bench. A dog lying on the grass. A cat half leaving the frame. The youngest child pointing after it. There's a small, colorful slide on the lawn.

Black leaves and strange tendrils suction onto the garden doors, and he turns the handle, pushes the door open an inch, then harder, tearing the ivy away. Years of untending have left the garden wild. The top of a plastic slide emerges from recently grown bushes. A fence running along the side of the garden is smothered with roses. He wades into the undergrowth and, yes, finds it: a mossy bench, soft, cracked, and buried deep in the grass. How long ago was that family here? The dog is more likely to be alive than them. And today he will find Bea.

A knocking brings Tom up. He looks up at the house for Sylene, but its windows are cobwebbed and empty. The tapping again. He looks to the house next door and sees a figure in a window, no cobwebs, the glass wiped clean. Its hair is long, matted, and gray. Its cheeks sag. As the figure leans forward, even from this distance he sees its eyes are pale, like the irises have been bleached, before its breath fogs the glass. It ducks to see him again. A smile twitches its lips and it waves at him tentatively. Tom lifts a hand and waves back, and it smiles fully now, this creature, revealing black and broken teeth, and a clip in its lower lip that shows brown gums. It points at him, and smiles, and then lowers a hand to its stomach. A dirty tongue protrudes from its mouth and draws slowly around its blackened lips. Then it jabs a finger at him, eyes flaring wide, and disappears from the window.

Tom stands for heart-lurching seconds, and then he is jumping the grasses back to the house in an instant. As he races toward the doors, he notices that the next-door garden is tamer than this one. There is netting there, hung between two trees, with a slowly flapping bird caught in it. Back inside, he scrabbles to lock the doors—watching the fence to see if anything scales over it—and then he heaves the table toward them, slides chairs across the floor wildly as he runs into the corridor. He hears one of them—or something—smash the glass behind him.

"Sylene!" Tom crashes into walls running up the stairs. "Sylene! Get up, we have to get out of here!" He grabs the bags and forces their stuff in as she hurries out of bed, pulling on her clothes, collecting her things. Then there is a noise.

Tom holds up his hand.

It sounds like something is being dragged across the floor in the house next door. Then there is a scratching, scrabbling sound that spreads rapidly out across the wall.

Tom doesn't know what to do. There's nothing he knows, no experience he's had, that can help him deal with this. This house. That thing. A human animal. They've worked so hard to get here, and now his hope burns away as fear scalds through his body. He points at Sylene's boots, at the bags, at the door, and gestures downstairs, shaking. As they creep from the room, something heavy is hurled against the wall. The entire floor shakes, and they jump. Then a cascade of footsteps tramples the staircase next door. He doesn't think. He grabs Sylene's arm and they run, his legs jarring on the stairs, his arms smacking the walls as he wrestles his rucksack on.

It's dark downstairs, and cold. Is there a breeze coming in? As Tom goes past the dining room, he hears, he thinks, the open doors banging. They dash into the kitchen. Empty. The table undisturbed. Back down the little corridor, and a thin chill draft slides through the pane he'd smashed for entry. Quickly, quietly, his heart choking his throat, he ducks outside and peers around at the main steps above them. Nothing. He scans the windows of the house next door. Nothing there either but dust, cobwebs, and shadows. He waves at Sylene, who climbs up behind him, her hands on her stomach, effortful, pale-faced, very scared. Tom maneuvers her through the gate and takes her hand, and they run as quickly as Sylene can manage past the empty-looking houses and seemingly abandoned cars.

Gardens have claimed the streets. Weeds push the paving stones awry. As they approach a corner, Tom slows, pushes Sylene ahead again, and squints back along the pavement. Small puffs of cloud hang high in the sky. It's a bright day. No one follows them down the street. He breathes out in relief, but as he turns, he sees from the corner of his eye Sylene's head jerk sideways, and in a moment's realization that comes as she stumbles and collapses, he knows he saw a flash of something smack into her head. He ducks, adrenaline rising like bile before he is even conscious that the next rock is spinning at him. It smashes into a car. Another hurtles past his ear, and then there is one for his face.

Sound is sharper than ever, and the colors pop. All this precision and yet everything wavers moltenly as he sees a figure leap upon Sylene. She stirs, woozy, and then struggles as the creature, this tendon-thin, rapacious thing, squats stilly on her thighs. This person, this human animal.

Tom knows he should be moving, but his thoughts and his body detach. His sight swims and he feels strangely calm. He watches as the creature claws at her face, her arms, her belly, and tries to tear her clothes, and through the flashing of limbs he sees Sylene's face, which is Kate's, twisted in terror and screaming, and with that hat and her skin cold, face flushed, she looks like Bea, he sees Bea's face, and her cries reverberate, shocking his mind.

The thing pulls a blade and Tom lurches up as the knife swipes down. There's a collision and a fall and his face cracks into the ground. Stunned again, he feels the thing's head beneath him and he punches it hard, hard, again. Something scalds through his arm and he twists and pummels wildly. The thing beneath him scrabbles, its movements too quick, and they roll across the pavement, Tom clinging to the figure in a brutal, shaking hug. The blade rushes again and Tom blocks it with his arm. He kneels on the creature, wrestles with its arms, grabbing for its clawlike hands. It's panting rancid breath straight into his face, its eyes widened in excitement.

The blade stabs Tom's shoulder, hot and clean, and he hits it away with his fist. His skin is sliced to the knuckle, but he grabs the creature's hand and punches its stomach, punches its chest, thumps the hard hip bones with his elbow. He smacks its spine and the ridged ripples of its ribs. He tries to twist around so he can thump its face, its grimacing face with its cloven lip, but this person—bloodshot, ravaged, hard to think it was ever a human—this thing bites his arm with broken teeth and the blade is back in his face. It scores his chest, nearing his eyes, catching his brow with a swipe, but he blocks it again with his palm—he catches it and holds the blade, despite the pain as it sinks into his flesh and hot blood runs down his wrist. His arm shakes as he screams. He punches the creature's forearm, smashes and smacks the bone, waiting for a *crack* that doesn't come, so he *bites* until a saggy lump of flesh comes loose and his mouth floods full of warm and salty blood and the knife falls finally free. He snatches it and embeds it in the flesh. He swipes it out and through its throat, and stabs its chest, clipping a rib. Its stomach splits open as the metal tears right through, and he's stabbing down to the ground. The figure flaps beneath him.

Tom drops the knife. His hands are sticky with blood, viscous and dripping slowly from his wounds.

He spits and gags. He turns to where Sylene was, but she's not there anymore; now she's standing, holding a bleeding arm to her bruising face, and Tom realizes that the sound in his ears, over the snarling and gnashing and his own grunting cries, the awful sound he has been hearing is her screaming.

They break into another house many streets away. The wounds on Tom's hands and face burn with each contorted pulse. There is something rancid downstairs but they raid the drawers and cupboards on the upper floors. Looking for bandages. Looking for ointment and water with which to wash their wounds. Sylene comes into the bedroom, where he is tearing T-shirts into strips. Her hands are full of tubes, all of them marked with quickcodes.

"Any of these?"

"No idea," he says, grabbing them, squeezing, smelling the curls of gel. "I think this is lip balm. I've no idea about this. Here—does this smell right?" He holds a tube under her nose, palming some of the cream.

"I've no idea. Medicine's very different for me. The nanobots . . ."

He nods briskly. "Well, this is going to have to do. Did you find any water?"

Sylene shakes her head.

"Come on."

They go to the bathroom: once-white enamel is now stained and crusted; a shower curtain hangs furry with mold. The toilet evaporated dry years ago. Tom licks and sucks his hands. He hawks thick blood into the sink. He spits into his palms and rubs his fingers into the wounds on his face, wincing, gasping with the pain, smearing the surprisingly hot blood into whorls.

Sylene stands close. Her voice is quiet, her face bloodlessly pale. "Tom. Are you all right?"

He stops. Looks in the mirror. What looks back is covered in layers of dirt and blood, mixed like a painter's palette. It is a different man. He is gaunt, his cheekbones prominent, with deep dark bags beneath his eyes. They stare, wide and angry. There's something animal in them. He's never noticed it before. His hands are shaking. And his face now starts to judder. He blows out his cheeks as he lowers himself slowly to the edge of the bath. A whimper comes out, unintended. Sylene puts a hand on his head and runs her fingers through his blood-soaked hair. He takes her arm and turns it gently to look at the wound.

"Does it hurt?"

"I was lucky."

He brings her arm to his face. The wound tastes sharp, the blood warm. He sucks and spits. He flicks his tongue along the cut and spits again, and then he wipes his lips. She lowers her arm, and spits on both her thumbs, and sets about cleaning his face.

They leave the house with bloodstained ribbons of fabric wrapped about their limbs. They walk like each step costs them, but they are walking hand in hand. The city is silent. Golden sunlight slices down from a powder-blue sky through crisp and frosty air.

"We're not far now. We'll hit a super-road soon."

"Have you killed people before?"

They kick through piles of dry and scattered leaves. Dogs bark somewhere, their gnashing yelps echoing the ruins. Once quiet, Tom and Sylene proceed.

"Twice. You?" he asks, and she shakes her head. He nods. "Then it's my job, so you never have to."

They reach the super-road and trudge up the ramp, the city warping in the wraps of thickened glass at its sides.

"What did it want?"

Tom glances at her, at her life: the warmth in her cheeks, the fear darkening her eyes. He remembers its gaunt face. The expression in its eyes, dilated, excited, desperate.

"Food? Does it really matter?"

She nods. And thinks. "And what was with its lip?"

"It must have been a Resister. An extreme one." Tom gestures at his own face and ears. "People had augmentations: microphones and speakers implanted in their skin. But then there were stories about people being bugged. Government and corporate surveillance. It was expensive to have them removed, so it became a mark of honor, among some groups, to do that to your face."

They are on the top of the super-road now and leaving the older area behind. Houses spread. Maybe not all of them are empty. Maybe humanity, in some form, survives. The road arcs over a band of newer-builds, each upturned bowl containing blocks of buildings and overgrown parks, the domes like drained and broken globes, the dwellings like models within. Ahead, in the distance, the river spreads like quicksilver. Standing tall before the swollen water, the tower pierces the sky.

They reach the sloping sides of the super-mall, its contours, once crystal, opaque. It rises above them massively like a sunken, landed cloud.

"I don't think we want to go in there," Tom says, pointing into the dark tunnel where the road carries on into the side of the thing. "But up there . . ." he continues, raising his arm toward the tower, the glassy canine that erupts from the center of the mall and makes him feel so very cold, "that's where we'll find Bea."

As he lifts Sylene up the wall beside the road, his wounds split and his bandaged hands darken with fresh blood. He scales the wall himself, trying not to use his left hand at all and only the fingers on his right. As they traverse the narrow sloping walkway, the road drops down into the bowels of the building below them; to their left lies the patchwork spread of broken roofs, the Sunday-morning feel of empty streets in a crisp fresh breeze. He hasn't known for years what day it is. What does the world care about that?

They hug the curved building until they emerge onto a wide plaza, tiny amid the brown-boned arc lights and the huge translucent curve framing the entrance to the mall. They walk slowly across the expanse and up to the rolling side of the thing. "Careful," Tom says as he bends tiredly through a jagged hole in a twisted-framed door. But it is his own rucksack that catches on the shards, and he panics, stumbles, landing on his hands on the glass-showered floor. Sylene drops beside him as he sits there, stunned.

"You've lost a lot of blood. You should eat."

"I'm fine," he says, struggling to stand. He can't stop now: he *can't*. Bea flashes in his mind, crying, imploring him on and on. But if she isn't here . . . if her BackUps haven't actually been saved . . . "I'm just tired, Sylene. Come on—"

"No. We should eat." Sylene takes the rucksack off him and pushes him back to the ground. "We don't know what's here, what we have to be prepared for." She peers over his shoulder. Escalators ascend from this white-walled atrium. At the top is a high-domed space of struts and light, but more than that they can't see.

They sit in silence, with food, and Tom stares at the ground—for all his stillness, his thoughts are awhirl. Each step they take now brings them closer to the Hub, to Bea, to see if Sylene told him the truth.

Once they have eaten, she helps him stand and pull his bag back on. She tightens the straps and holds his shoulders firmly. "Listen," she says, and takes his hands. "Whatever we find, Tom, whatever has happened to Bea, I'm here. I lost my family too. I know how you feel. I can still be here for you."

Tom knows there are tears in his eyes, and he expects that she can feel his heart beating in his hands, it's thumping so hard. After a while he puts an arm around her shoulders and pulls her to his chest. In the absence of words, it's all he can do. But soon she pushes him away.

"I can't breathe!" she gasps.

On the escalators, the sensation of the metal and the sound it makes under Tom's boots is disorientatingly familiar to him. At the top, though, the mall opens out into an expanse of refuse and glass that knocks back his memories of this place. Shop windows are hillocks of cascaded crystal. Bags and packaging clog the way. The tables, chairs, and umbrellas outside cafés are overturned. The plants in the raised beds have died.

Air escapes him.

"This was a good place," he whispers. "I broke in with Ben to play here when they were building it. And then at night, when it was finished, when everyone had gone, I'd come down here alone."

"You lived here?"

Tom gestures with his head. "In the tower, above the Hub. All the offices and our apartments."

Over them, the white struts are laced with dirty webs. Filthy cocoons dangle down. The curved glass of the complex is mottled, but he can still just see through it and glimpse the tower that rises above, the top few floors his childhood home.

"So that's where your homeHub is too, up there?"

Tom nods and they move on. Most shops have been ransacked and all the corridors are layered with dust. Wide paw marks trail through it, and the circular sweeps of tails. Cobwebs block entire corridors with gossamer layers, stretched tight and lumpen in places with trussed-up things. They cross dark patches on the marble, deep stains of blood, but there are no bodies to be seen. Two domes of the mall meet above them in an atrium, beneath which an oval light-well drops. Tom leans over the balcony and looks at the darkened floors below. Grayish piles in the food hall move ceaselessly; rippling things writhe. An ammonia stench is so pungent it gives the air a heat-like haze.

"It's the smell." He breathes heavily as tears come to his eyes. "I never wanted to see this."

"Well, let's find Bea and get out."

"I'm scared they're alive, Sylene."

"Who?"

"My parents."

"Well . . ." She puts a hand on his shoulder; looks at him, thinks, and then clearly chooses to say something else. "Well, we can leave. We can find Bea another way. We'll work something out. However hard things get, Tom, there is always a choice."

The gentle clatter of scattering glass echoes around the space.

Along the oval balcony, at their level, from the mouth of another wide corridor, a dog emerges from the shadows. Its thick neck and heavy shoulders catch the daylight as it sniffs and turns things over with its nose. Its pelt is filthy, its jaw hard-set. Canines protrude from its lips. Another beast follows, and another behind that. They circle the balcony toward them.

"Sylene—" Tom whispers, but she already has a finger to her lips.

The animals have come halfway. One has found some cloth to chew and grunts as it tears it apart. Tom points back the way they have come and they move, treading lightly, the smallest crack of glass making them freeze in fear. Two of the dogs disappear down another corridor, their silhouetted hulks lurching in the reflected light, but the last one stares through the glass of the balustrade at them. No—it's panting, openmouthed, peering down at the food hall below. Its breath steams the glass, its eyes fixed on something. Then it shrugs itself after the others.

Sylene takes Tom's hand and pulls him quickly along the corridor. They stop halfway down and Tom takes them to a set of double doors that open into an enclosed concrete stairwell. What little light there was is lost as the doors close, and he feels back for her hands in the darkness.

"We're going seven floors up," he says. "Hold on to me."

He shuffles forward. Reaching out blindly, he connects with the banister and starts to climb. There are things on the stairs, lumps that he works his way around. Sometimes things scratch his legs, sharp like bone. He pretends he's a child again. Eyes closed. He used to know this place backward and forward, with Ben, at night, when only the faint red security lights were on. He stands on something that slides across the step and flies into the stairwell, clanging its way down, bouncing off the banisters, until it lands. A screaming barrage erupts from the darkness below, setting off similar screams above and around and the sound of scrabbling claws and writhing fur, until it slowly succumbs to silence.

Seven floors up, they struggle to find the door, banging their hands against the perfectly smooth wall until a chink of light expands. They heave against a weight that keeps the door wedged closed, but they force it slowly open and squeeze out into the corridor. The ceilings are lower up here and the floor is covered with more debris: piles of things that had been bodies. No flesh now, but cloth-wrapped bones. Dissolved matter is stained into the marble. The mass weighing the door closed is a skeleton, contorted and confused, disjointed.

Sylene groans through the hand that's at her mouth again.

"You didn't mean this, Sylene," Tom tells her, though his voice is dead. "Remember, it wasn't your fault."

He has to remind himself of this too, as they climb over the bodies toward the oval light-well. Struts crisscross the space this high. The foyer of a cinema. Quick-code poster boards flaying. Popcorn shriveled in its bins. Something has ransacked the sweets. Tom stops by a patch of empty wall.

"This is the way in?" Sylene sounds dubious.

"This is how I came down at night. Look . . ."

On the wall, below his knee, part hidden by scuffs and time, but still there, is etched a *T*.

"The tower is nano-proof and sterilized. Or at least it used to be."

"So how do we get in?"

"Magic," Tom announces, and sweeps his hand out wide.

When the wall remains shut, his face falls. He runs his palms over the surface until his fingers find a protrusion whose tiny perforations are clogged with dust. He blows on the BioLock, hard, and the wall jolts back and disappears to one side. Tom turns, beaming through the crusted blood and filth on his face, and gestures for Sylene to enter. Hands on her back, he hurries her into the darkness and the door seals tightly behind them. They ascend stairs, plunging deeper into the shadows. It's just like it was, running through the place, the night-timed lights subdued. Ben and him as kids, slightly older than Bea was—than Bea would be. *Is.*

Nearly there. There is a strange spring in his step as he overtakes Sylene and rushes on, pulling her along curved corridors until they mount a walkway that takes them up and devastation emerges around them.

Sylene gasps and stumbles over the debris as the space expands above.

"Well," Tom sighs, "I'm not surprised. Nothing's impregnable." He is light-headed and his hands are numb. He spins around, arms out, gazing up into the space. *Then* and *now* collide: as a child, he stood here, awed by it all, by the people busy around him, searching the crowd for his father, too busy; now he stumbles on a mound of wires. "They must have gone *insane.* Being here, in the Hub of the Feed, but unable to make it work." The Hub is battered and smashed. Circuits ripped out, the metal gantries surrounding it dangling from the walls. "Is it how you imagined it?"

They are standing in the innards of the Hub, knee-deep and unsteady. Sylene's forehead creases, her arms across her stomach. The room is very, very high. The Hub towers for stories up to a distant roof of glass. Machine parts have been hurled down and lie in piles, cortices of wires tangled across the floor.

"Tom, I'm so sorry."

"Oh, I never thought it would be intact." Tom grins.

His thoughts are racing as he spreads his arms out and, his voice echoing, cries up into the cavernous space. "And even if it was, the power's down! The emergency generators would conserve their power for the locks and lifts and doors."

"Tom . . . So . . ." Sylene's face is crumpled and flushed. "What are we going to do?"

"We're going upstairs."

His voice hardens. He yanks Sylene over the twisted debris. Even when she stumbles and falls, he pulls her, dragging her from the Hub, ignoring her pleas to slow down. No time. It's now. To see if she was lying to him. To see if he's lost Bea. Faint light stretches around the curves of the corridors, strange silhouettes dancing on the walls until they reach a portal in the rain-dirtied wall, a dense reflective door.

"Go on." Tom pushes her forward hard, and she stumbles.

"What do you mean?"

"The BioLock. Your turn." And when she doesn't move, he continues as if explaining to a child. "This is the private lift to the apartments. So go closer," he urges. "Wave your hand. Breathe out. It'll know Kate's here."

"But—"

"Do it!"

Sylene shakes her hands toward the portal. It turns opaque, slides back to reveal a booth.

"See. It doesn't know that you're not you. You're family, Sylene!"

"Tom, you're scaring me."

But he is past her and inside. "Come on, Sylene, come *on*."

"You're scaring me, Tom."

"Get in the fucking lift!"

The door slides shut as soon as she enters, and the acceleration is immediately smooth. They score up the building in the light of the cityscape and the widening horizon beyond. "That's where we came from, look!" He waits for her to turn, then continues as if without a pause. "And there—you see all that water? The barriers have burst. That's the river. Why are you crying?"

"Tom, you're manic." She pulls away from him as he dances from foot to foot. His hands are pumping. Eyes wild. "What are you going to do if there's bad news?"

With perfect deceleration the lift stops. The door illuminates, turns translucent, and opens.

"Welcome home!" he announces.

Mezzanine levels rise above them. The air hasn't moved for years. The curved glass wall sweeps up for stories, holding out an immensity of view. Huge floorboards, painted white, and glass tables and arcing lights. A wormy woolen rug stretches away to the sofas. Screen plinths by the walls, atom-thin and dull. Vases where the flowers have died and become dirty impressions of themselves. Tom remembers when they arrived to live here, without knowing that was why they'd been summoned. Ben had welcomed them in. Right here. Told them the theory: That people were being invaded. That someone was taking over their brains. Sitting there on the settees. When his parents were still here. When Ben was alive. When Bea was—when Kate was still—

"What shall we do?"

His chest won't move, his lungs stuck.

"Tom? Shall we look for your parents?"

Nothing here has changed.

"No," he gasps. "We're not here for them!" He crosses the expanse, strides through the kitchen, and mounts the stairs carved into the ebony wall at the heart of the apartment.

"Tom!"

He turns. Sylene is standing below him, framed by the dark wooden walls of the staircase. Her face is flushed and she is panting, out of breath. And the look in her eyes is . . . fear. For him. Concern.

"Do you want me with you or would you rather be alone?"

He looks down at her, at Kate there, pregnant again, back in this place he thought they'd escaped for her good. For the good of the baby. He has been alone, he knows, for a long, long time, but not, he realizes, recently. With a gasp his tears finally burst and he collapses on the stairs. Something gives. His frenzy snaps. "Of course I want you with me!" a voice he barely recognizes wails, but he knows it must be his own. "You *know* I need you now . . ."

Sylene runs up the stairs and holds his shoulders and kisses the top of his head. They both cry, with hope, with fear, because it's the only thing they can do as she helps him stand and stagger up the stairs and onto an open walkway. Many wooden doors open onto other rooms; they hurry past . . . but Tom returns to one. His face is bloodless. He pushes open the door. A room with a deep-pile carpet is revealed. Huge windows show a vista of devastation that sweeps forever away. The flooding is clear from here, the swollen waters shining, swallowing the city, the lower tower tops breaking the surface like reeds. The utter devastation.

"This is their room."

"No one's been here for years, Tom. You can stop worrying. Where do you think they went?"

"My father was in his office when the Feed went down. That's the last I knew. But he would have had something planned, I'm sure of it. Some way to survive. He always looked to the future. That was his life."

And he's back, in this room, over two decades before. There was a bandage on his leg. Whatever it was ached deeply, it was so very sore. That was why he was here, in the night, terrified because his parents were asleep but he was desperate for their help. It hurt too much. The loneliness and the pain. He heard his father breathe. He reached out toward him, in the dark. He'd had a test that afternoon, a deep one. Some bone marrow, his father had told him. And now, Tom knows, it was to make sure the implant had taken, that it had become latched on to his DNA. He was an experiment. A test to see that it would pass the Feed down through generations to come, and it's like something flows between Tom now and his younger self then: an echoing dark loss, a loneliness and pain that is somehow companionable when it joins him together over time. A loneliness and pain that was solved, by Kate, by Bea, and now—

"And your mother?"

Tom looks around at the shelves and drawers and the sculptures—so familiar, so distant, so dead; at the bedside tables and machines; at the wardrobes, thrown open . . . but empty.

"I don't know. She wouldn't let me share her Feed."

"Why?"

"Because I killed my brother." He folds his fingers together and bounces his hands on his thighs. He nods over Sylene's shoulder, remembering as he tells her. "We were in the room next door. President Taylor had been killed, the Chinese premier too. They had worked out we were being inhabited. We didn't know why. They had one of you imprisoned, Ben told me, but he never talked, even though I'm sure he was tortured. There must have been many of you, waiting, and then inspired by Taylor's death to action. It was carnage. People killed in the streets. Who knew how many sleeper cells there were? So fathers killed children, children killed mothers. Everyone was watched while they slept. How many innocents were killed? Who was going to be taken next? The fear was devastating, Sylene. It was everywhere. It poisoned us all in our heads. This is what you made. This is what you did. People hallucinating with fear. Lack of sleep. *Terror.* People killed without proof. But I saw those signs, I *know* I did, while Ben was next door, one night, asleep. He was taken on my watch."

"And your mother wouldn't forgive you."

Tom raises a finger, scolding. "Oh, no. She didn't *believe* me. She had always said I was jealous. It's funny

what success does. She came from a very modest family, but isn't it interesting how having *more* makes you
less secure sometimes? She thought I couldn't actually,
honestly be happy with a comfortable life, an unambi-
tious life, she called it. She had always assumed I hated
Ben. Which, I suppose, I did. But not the way she
thought. Because *they* liked him. They were kinder to
him than to me! And I wish he wasn't dead!" He weeps
suddenly, fiercely, looking at the empty bed through
burning-hot tears and remembering those who had
slept there. In the end he turns back to Sylene. He has
no barriers anymore; he's too tired to hold anything
back. "I killed him," he says quietly, emptied. "And
I killed Guy. But I could *never* do it to you. I didn't
watch you, I didn't want to see it happen. I loved you
too much; I wouldn't have been able to bear it."

"I'm *sorry!*" Sylene cries. "We didn't have a choice!
We didn't know it would be like *this!*"

They fall into each other's arms and cry until Tom
strokes her flushed face and smiles. "Oh, we're past
blame now, Sylene. We're not here for that anymore."
Then he grips her wrists and pulls her from the
room, back along the mezzanine and up more flights
of stairs. The stories narrow the farther up they go,
tightening and turning until they break out at the

top, where sky and slanting sunlight surround them. Dizzy, dizzyingly high. Sylene gasps behind him as Tom strides onto the platform, the city spread below.

"I remember being up here before they finished the building," he murmurs. "Before the glass was put in. I don't know what came first, his God complex or this."

Sylene puts her arms out for balance. The view to the hills and the gleaming estuary is larger than can be absorbed. Clumps of clouds collect at their level and darken in wisps around them. There is glass, she sees, but it is almost invisible. And there, sitting opposite each other in low dark chairs, are two skeletons. Grinning at each other. They are clothed: one suited, the other in a dress with a handbag on its lap. Their skin has embalmed to the bone.

Sylene takes Tom's hand as they approach them. The silence of the place is deathly.

"So they are dead, then. After all. I beat them."

"Tom . . ."

"They hurt me so badly, Sylene."

"Come now," she says, trying to turn him away. "Forget them. What about the homeHub? That's why we're here, Tom, not for them. Let's find our children!"

Tom pauses, frowns, and turns to look at her.

"Bea . . . I mean, let's find Bea."

He squints, and thoughts furrow his brow. Then his

face relaxes. He nods at her before saying, *"Hub?"*—and something thickens the air. A high-pitched whine. A signal tuning back into life. It expands and, deepening, resonates in his bones.

"Did you feel that?" Sylene gasps. "Did you *feel* it?"

A molten lance weaves through Tom's brain and connects to the implant there. His forehead rises as he senses something acute. Then his eyes twitch minutely. Incessantly they rove and dart. They jerk and snap around. His arms grab out at her as his legs go, and Sylene tries to catch him. She guides him, staggering, to a chair and he slumps back, his eyes widening, and flickering, and widening again, and his legs jerking as his head rolls. He spasms and kicks.

"I'm *glowing*, Sylene, I'm flying!" he gasps. *"Look at me now!"*

His back arches and his hands crush hers. His eyes stare flickeringly ahead, unseeing, as he sweats. So much information. So quick, so clean, so pure. His heart is going to burst. He pants, "You were right, Sylene, she's stored. It *has* become genetic. All Bea's BackUps are here. And mine. And Mother's, and Father's, and Ben's." Clenching himself, he turns to Sylene. Strange noises come from his throat, non-words, until, "They escaped."

"Who did?"

"My parents. Sylene, they . . ." Tom palpitates. "He sent their mind states somewhere else. He sent them far away. They didn't die at all! He—"

"Forget them, Tom!" Sylene pleads, grabbing his face, clutching his arms, his hands, his cheeks. "What about Bea? Can you see what happened to Bea?"

"I will," he says. "But first there's you. Kate. She's here too. Her BackUps are saved here. Right up to the very last." His lips contort. Sweat pours down his face. The tendons in his neck are stretching. Every word is a pain, but something victorious slides in. "You can find out who you are, Sylene. Look. Look, here, you can do it. Here, she's still here. Oh, Kate . . ."

Sylene pulls back, but Tom's eyes are hard on her. He grabs her wrist. Will not let go.

"Reinstall her, Sylene," he growls. "Bring Kate back and erase yourself."

"Tom, I thought we—"

"*Listen* to me, Sylene. Your children are gone. Your husband too. They died and you buried them. But *her* family is still alive." He stretches a hand toward her stomach, his mouth still moving, gulping out breath without words. Even he doesn't believe his argument, but what else can he say but appeal to some kindness, some form of human care? "Make *something* right, Sylene. That was why you came back. To make the world a better place. So give Bea back her family. Reinstall Kate now."

"Tom . . . find her. Find out where Bea is. I can still help you find her!"

His eyes do not blink as he engages a different place. They flicker as he accesses SaveYou, scans what has been saved, looks for what happened to Bea. Something locks. His expression catches. A noise sticks in his throat. He shakes. Deeply. Spasms to the core of his soul. No one should see what he's seeing. Water swells the rims of his eyes. He chokes. He tries to breathe but can't. He tries to shout. For Bea. For help. Nothing. His body shudders. Nothing can be done. He can't turn away from what he is seeing, what he is experiencing secondhand, the emotions of the girl, the final memories of the child, his eyeline tethered inwardly as his face screws into a scream, a silent, shaking scream as—

He collapses.

Sylene pushes his head back but he doesn't move. She wraps her arms around him and tries to pull him up. Limp. His head lolls. She lifts it. As she tries to force his eyes open, his breath surges and he punches her in the face. He tries to defend himself, tries to fight her away. He finds himself. Finds her before him and cries: "She's gone, Sylene, she's gone!"

"What did you see? What happened?"

Tom pulls her toward his bloodshot eyes, and Sylene clings to him as he howls.

"You'll get through this, Tom!" she yells, trying to hear herself above his cries. Animal sounds shake his body without form, with senseless, guttural pain. "We'll get through this! It feels insurmountable now, I know, but I promise you, I *promise*—I will get you through this, Tom!"

"Sylene!" he gasps, then withdraws, abruptly quiet, and fixes her with a stare. He takes her arms in the sudden silence and searches her eyes. A sense of control now changes his tone. His voice drops. For all the pain in it before, it's empty and burned out now. What he says to her is simple: "You can put something right at least. You can access the homeHub. Go into Kate's Feed. Her BackUp states are saved. Bring Kate back, Sylene."

"Stop, Tom!" Sylene says, yanking him forward.

"No. I'm going back to when we escaped the city. Kate and me. The Collapse, when she was pregnant with Bea. I'm resetting myself, Sylene. I'm resetting my memories to then."

Sylene shakes him. Grips his wrists. Grabs his face, trying to look into his eyes. "You can't do that. Listen to me!"

"I can!"

"But you'll forget—"

"Everything! I'll forget *everything* that's happened since then. Exactly! And there won't be this grief anymore. There's nothing I want to remember. It'll be like we'd never left the city. There will be only hope. It'll be like the Feed's only just gone down. We can start again, and I'll never know. I'll never know about you, I'll never know that Kate died. I'll never know that Bea . . ." He reaches out and strokes her stomach with his blood-soaked bandaged hand. "You can tell me whatever you want, Sylene. You can tell me this is Bea. Whether you reset yourself or not, whether you bring Kate back, whatever you tell me, I'll believe it," he whispers fiercely, before his eyes roll and defocus. He gasps again and shudders. Sylene grabs him. She tries to physically force the jolts to stop as his head slumps and his body quivers. As she collapses into his shaking arms, he goes totally limp beneath her.

Sunlight streams through the glass, through the clouds.

The skeletons in the chairs smile at each other still, their minds, their inhabitants, far away.

She goes—

—plunging myface into a freezing pool and I am here, here, I'm *on,* and mynerves cascadingly *scintillate* because I haven't felt this in solong! This sensation. It's like home. I'm purethought, alive and unbound! I haven't felt this rush, this purity, for such a longtime as I'm connected to theFeed but—but—but—wait, no, there is nothing else here there is nothing

nothing at all

there is void, cold darkness like an ancient buried tomb. I am buried again, I am blind, I see nothing out there—nothing in the world at all—so I look inward, toward this homeHub that lets me in because I have KateHatfield1's BioPrint, KateHatfield1's Access, KateHatfield1's DNA, & here like leafskeins are the BackUps of them all. All their SaveYou states. They're saved. Bea. Here's Tom. Here's his father, his mother & Ben. & Kate. I riffle through them & they spring to life, their thoughts, their emotions, their memories through the years, sparking bursts of— *fireworks,* of color in this forsakenworld, & I see that yes, his parents have fled, they sent themselves away, they uploaded their mindstates to somewhere else & then their Feeds go blank, their BackUps empty after that. I abandon their memories & curl deeper into me, into KateHatfield1, past the pain that ended it all on the hill above the pond & the fear & the upturnedtruck, the fire & deliriousdreams. (& I feel a pulse of myself in these. It's like looking into a mirror & *being* a mirror at the sametime & feeling the decades cascade between us.) & then I see a man who is Mark, whom I never met though I know him now because Kate does & because I am one with her, & Tom, who KateHatfield1 didn't trust anymore; she used to love him so deeply but she doesn't trust him now, doesn't trust him as much as I—SyleneCharles29471—do, I realize. I realize not only that I trust him but that I can protect him, I can help him, & I realize that I *want* to keep him safe.

Back in the mundles, & going deeper through them, is like getting to the core of things. The blond-haired dog. Another one ravaging myleg. The camp. It thrums with people & Graham & life & Bea—Bea—*Bea*—in thereal I choke, I know, I gasp, & tears come with the memory-surge of *whatIfeelforBea*. *WhatIfeelformychild*. It's the deepestfeeling, the fullestconnection I've ever, ever known, & I *know* it. I love it. *Love* is not enough of a word. It makes chemicals release in mybody & I follow them, the emotions, I follow the emotional addiction through the mundles as Bea grows younger, as the plants shrink & the huts deconstruct & I feel the slick weight of her as a baby. In the farmhouse bedroom. Darkened. Graham, younger. Tom, younger. That must be Jane. How Bea, the baby, looks. How she *feels*. The firstimpression she makes in the world. On my skin. Then earlier, Tom & I crawl across the country, Bea, a baby, unborn, back inside me, safe within my skin, never more protected than deep inside me now. The feeling of complete-ness, of being whole with someone else, is inde-scribable, it floods me, but the chemicals I must analyze to understand it, jetting through my veins, they say it all as eloquently as can be: the formula of love, burninghot, it's the truest thing that matters.

Our heads were destroyed as we escaped the smolderingruins of the city & Kate's/my memo-ries scramble out & distort, for weeks they blank away in the shock of theCollapse, & suddenly the world is *alive* with people & planes & cars all moving, all living, restored, so detailed, so real, all these memories & smells & sounds, & mymundles of theFeed explode into life. Every-thing is saved. I'm surfing like I did through my/her mundles of theFeed & in thereal I stretch in the sun over Tom's inertbody & I know I've nearly made it! Darian, my boy, I'm here! In the ruins of thereal I can't help but smile as I trawl Kate's BackUps, as I search Kate'smundles of theFeed for just two words. For Darian, my son, my boy, for Darian, please. Let me find you. If you're alive. If you made it back at all. I told you

I would. I've worked so hard! I've fought so hard. To find you *here*. & after everything I've endured, you're now just a simple search away, & neither of us will be alone again!

& with the search through KateHatfield1's memories for [*dariancharles*] comes *Arid Ranch Sale, China Lads Rear, Car Sandal Hire, Iran Ash Cradle* while she/I sit with Tom in a train, & I search for the first occurrence of his name & I'm in a restaurant with a tattooedwaiter & she/I have been pooling all day about Energen (she/I *reallycared* about theworld, I didn't know peoplethen actually cared thismuch about the planet, & I love her pool, [*WhatWouldYouSacrifice?*], which I dip into for a millisec, and I think I might have *liked* her if we'd ever actually met, I think we would have liked each other for sure, but I don't care now *because I need to find my son*), & there it is, there, I see, is [*dariancharles*], & with a stomachplummet I see hisname a thousandbillion times—why so many?—fractalling across theFeed & the first time Kate/I heard it was—

[*dariancharles*] the news is that PresidentTaylor1 has been killed. Everything goes quiet. All Feed-

IDs are stilled. *President Taylor1 has been killed.* It fractals across theFeed, then mutates to say *assassinated.* Already there's chaos in the U.S., contagious panic, the economy has flatlined & weapons have been mobilized toward the east. My cortisol levels are up 18.2%, my heart-rate beating 2.93times too fast, & there are now 100,000s of thisvid & as fast as 1pool is dammed, 2,000others appear, & I'm looking up what's the difference between *murder* & *assassination* & Mum is still shouting but she's drowned out by the roar & it's something to do with the word *hash,* which is an archaic term for $C_{21}H_{30}O_2$, & I access one of the newspools & what's there, the thing that everyone's absorbing, that's at the center of all these newspools coming repeatedly and unstoppably into existence, is a vid tagged [*Richard-Drake62SeniorSecurityAnalystWH. USA.StaffFID#22886284912*] and time-stamped 7.23secs ago. I go into his memory bundle. I have no idea where this room is because the GPSloc is blocked, but it looks like every special-ops room from any ent I've ever gulped. A lacquered table reflects cold-buzzing neons. Thinscreens & decks adorn the soundproofed walls. Then PresidentTaylor1 walks in with a creamsweater (the new line from [*Muitton*], an ident links me) slung across his shoulders, a big mug of dark and fragrant coffee (the [*arabeanica*] blend from [*Nesspro*], an ident links me) in one hand, & this is the WhiteHouseUSA, this *was* the WhiteHouseUSA 7.34secs ago, & this mundle getting out is an insane security breach, no wonder pools are being dammed, &—

—Good morning all, PresidentTaylor1 says in thereal with that warm-gruff tone, and sits. I understand, he says, given Energen's surprising news, that the race is now on for the Arctic South. We will not let it fall into the wrong hands. Folks, we have war in a cold climate. But before the president's smile can fully form, RichardDrake62's view is obscured as a silhouetted figure—PatrickVaughn59, it's tagged—stands & raises a gun. The president's head becomes a cloud of red. The room upturns as RichardDrake62 dives for cover & RichardDrake62's mundle crashes to black & there's the sounds of upheaval & someone screams something that sounds like "Dariancharles!" & right away [*dariancharles*] is spurting off into thousands of pools saying [*whoisdariancharles?*] & then the vid repeats—repeats—repeats.

I search again for a laterlink because that mundle is cutshort & there it is: Kate/I resprayed it the followingday. After the silhouette stands & PresidentTaylor1 is shot there is a turmoil, a chaos
in the room. The gunman is thrown to the ground &—here, now—he shouts, *Darian Charles!* I hear him. I hear him shout his name. It's him, it's my son, I've found him! He shouts again, his voice breaking, *Darian Char*—&

a gunshot silences him. 2, 3, 4 shots & no one speaks until people shout. For medics, for help, but not for Darian, my boy—they're running to help the president. To help PresidentTaylor1. Him. Who helped humanity ravage the planet & leave it burned & dead. & us. & me. & my children, damned to never have children of their own. These people! These animals! These stupid, careless *animals*! They abandon Darian, leave him on the ground, & run for the president as—

I stop the mundle, I pull out of KateHatfield1, &—

Sylene kneels above him, in silence, for hours. It is a place of stillness, a place of total loss. As it gets dark outside, Tom stirs.

Sylene dips back briefly into the Feed. She riffles through Kate's BackUp states. She has time, now, to do this. She searches her SaveYou files. She travels through their lives. She unpicks things and savors them. When they met, where they lived, their secrets and their fears. Their arguments. She feels it all. Both of them. She understands them. She sees that Tom told her no lies. She looks at everything. She experiences it all. The sort of life she was never allowed. The joy. The fullness of it, of everything they had. Of all they took for granted.

With a very simple impulse, she could reset.

She could allow Kate to live again.

It's there, in her brain, like an itch.

But Darian. Killed on the other side of the world just six short years ago—six tiny, tiny years, a pathetic fraction of the time they had both traveled back through the absolute cold of the void, as thoughts without form, the hell of it all, the torturous hell of that!

She has found him, as she'd promised him she would, if only he said his name.

She told him to do something noticeable, and he definitely managed that.

She feels pride among a mixture of things. The overwhelming urge to protect. Fierce familial love, Kate's memories of Bea burning still, acid-hot, through her veins. This baby she has been carrying, growing, and the fiery heat of self-preservation kicking in. Fear as the Feed went down. Hatred and despair. President Taylor. That disgusting man. If only he'd stopped this when he could have. He could easily have prevented it all. No one needed to die. But Taylor's death had set off so much. The devastation of the world. And she'd told her son to do it.

Tom groans.

She turns her connection to the homeHub off and feels the Feed echo away. Her mind is quiet again.

Tom breathes heavily beneath her. His face, this still, looks peaceful. Wounded. She would fight to protect him in this wonderful, wonderful world. But Kate would too, she knows.

She turns her Feed back on.

The option to reset, to forget everything she's lost and to feel blissful nothing. Or the option to have it all. The knowledge and the loss.

"Kate?" Tom whispers beneath her.

Six Years Later

KATE
Forgive and Forget

The memories of those early days are packed away like hazardous waste, as if my mind doesn't want me to touch them. I certainly don't want to talk of them, of what we had to do—to Tom, to anyone at all. The first days were the hardest, let's just say that, but the rest were incredibly hard as well. It toughens you up, this life. I broke into a house and we stayed there. Tom was addled and confused. I wasn't much better. The grief. His speech was stunted, his thought processes pained. He spent days in a wallowing daze. The weeks. The time it took us to travel. I knew where we were going, but I was so unclear how to get there. But we found the camp in time. I gave birth. A girl, and she looked just as I'd imagined. I suggested we call her Beatrice. His mind was still sporadic, but from that scrambled state he learned. We both did. We learned new lives. I told him everything he needed to know. Nearly two years later, I became pregnant again. A boy. Daniel seemed to fit; I thought really hard about that name. We made a family. We made our lives. We made a world that works and is fine. From when we got down from the tower to six years later, all that work, all that time, to now.

We go walking, Danny and me, in the hour we have before dinner. That lovely slow time of day. We brush the pig feed from our hands and run through the camp, pretending to be birds.

Once past the forge, past the buildings, with their oiled-paper windows and freshly limed walls, we race up one of the furrows and look for worms in the field. Danny loves worms. He's fascinated by how they move. I took them for granted until he showed me one, and now I could watch them writhe for days. Kids point out the taken-for-granted in things. That's what they're here to do, and we have a duty to listen.

Outside the camp's gates, we take the little track through the woods, and Danny trots by my heels as he chatters. I've promised him a honey lick if he can catch a pigeon, and he falls for it every time, trying every approach he knows: the casual stalk, the stealth attack, the all-out run, arms flailing. He's never caught one yet, but it tires him out before bed.

The heat is coming off the day. Early-summer plants sway and insects curve around them. As we reach the slope, Danny becomes tired. He's only four, and though his body hints at an athletic build, he doesn't want to climb. He arches up at me and raises his arms.

"Mummy-y-y-y-y?" He droops and whines.

His whole hands fit inside my palms as I twist him onto my shoulders. They are dirty, rough, and smelly from feeding the animals, I realize, as they grasp my face. We should have washed them clean. Dirt is dangerous in a world like this. But then so are many things, and we can't be protected from them all—we need some hardness to survive. Halfway through the woods the railway line still cuts a path, and Danny asks to be let down. He lies lengthways on the thickly crusted tracks, hugging them, his mouth lolling in glee. He loves the way they smell. He loves the way they stay warm. He loves the way they're buried in plants, secret, deep, and hidden.

"Why are they so hot, Mummy?"

"Because they're made of metal."

"Why is metal hot?"

I admire my son, hugging the track. How does he know to ask these things?

"D'you think we'll see a train, Mummy? One that's still alive?" The boy's head cranes to look along the tracks.

"They're all extinct," I tell him. "There are no more left at all."

Danny stands up. He sighs and kicks the track with a tiny foot. "Stupid thing."

I reach out my hand and he takes it.

"Do we have to go up the hill?"

"Yes, we do."

"Why?"

"Because your daddy has something to show you."

"Is it a witch?"

"No."

"A troll?"

"Come on, Danny. It's not far now."

The boy's face contorts as his shoulders hunch and droop, and in that moment he looks like Tom. Tom when he's tired. Tom when he's required to do something he doesn't want to do. Tom as I led him from the tower, from the city, six years ago, ever-increasingly pregnant. Bury those memories away.

I lift Danny up again; laughing at him would make it worse. "Keep your legs tight, then. And give me your hands."

I trudge up the rolls that ripple toward the summit, and near the top, we turn. Danny stretches his arms out as we spin around in the breeze. He sees the camp below and kicks and shouts and waves.

"Woo-hoo! Clai-aire! Ste-eee-eve! I'm up hee-re! Look at me! I'm flying!"

But they don't hear him, Claire and Steve. The height and the breeze take Danny's words away, so we turn and head for the top, where Danny sees the others. He gasps and claps and pulls my hair with excitement. "Daddy and Beaty-Bea!" He scrabbles to get down, runs to them, and jumps up into Tom's arms. Then he leaps down and wrestles with his sister.

Tom disentangles the children and smiles as I approach. His hair is graying now, and his skin is leathered from working outdoors. But mine is too, I know, my brow as furrowed as the fields. My own hair is going gray, this body getting old. Even that climb was exhausting.

But at the same time, while of course we're getting older, I love how slowly time goes.

"Hello, you." I take his hand and lean on him to get my breath. "Does it work?"

"I don't know, I was waiting for you."

He grins like a child. A wide scar scores his forehead. His hands and arms are covered in them too, from when we left the city. I told him all he needed to know, like Jane did for Graham, because I saw how he fought for me, what he did to keep me safe; he wears his scars only on the outside now, I've made sure of that.

"Let's see. Hey, you two," he yells at the wrestling-again children. "Come here *now!*"

He slings the knapsack off his back as Danny and Bea dash over. Bea is nearly six now. Her birthday is in a week. She stands there patiently, looking up at Tom, interest glowing in her eyes. It's like a living thing. She's a thoughtful girl and more considerate than her brother, who pushes her aside to grab for the thing that Tom pulls out.

"What is *that?*" Danny asks, his eyes goggling.

"Be—very—careful," Tom says.

"What is it?" Danny whispers, which makes his sister laugh, a light and glorious sound, which in turn makes Danny scowl.

Action: reaction—it's how the world works.

"We can't remember what they were called in the past," Tom interrupts to distract their bickering. "But do you know what it's made of?" He points at the tightly stitched hide and, in response to their vacant expressions, explains, "It's *leather.*"

"Can I hold it now, Daddy?"

"*Wait*, Danny. Be patient. What's this, Bea?"

Tom flips the thing around and points at the clear globes held tightly at each end. The leather has been stitched, like a collar, around them. Bea's fingers tap them, stroke them. Her skin judders across their surface and she raises her hands to her mouth in thought. "Stone!"

"No."

"Metal?"

"Nope."

"This game is *silly*," Danny interrupts.

"They're glass, kids. Come on, try it."

The children attempt the word—"*G-lass*"—but Danny's interest is waning.

"Look!" Tom puts the thing quickly to his eye and then gives it to Danny, who stands on my foot while leaning against my legs and raises the tube to his face.

"I don't get it . . ."

"Close this eye," I tell him, smiling at Tom and leaning down to touch Danny's face. "No, this one. *This* one, Danny. That's right. And look through here. *Here.* Now, what do you see?"

The boy is silent. Then: "Eh?" he says, and "Wow!" He wriggles, looking around at things. If I wasn't supporting him, he'd fall over. "Is it magic?"

"No, it's not magic. It's science your dad made."

"Is that looking into the future?"

"No." I laugh at the thought. "It's what's here now, just farther away. Can I?"

Tom nods. He's pleased with it.

I ignore Danny's huff and raise the thing to my eye. It's defective. Most of the view is warped and unclear. But a small part at the center is perfect. The world whips past as I pull the thing around, swollen in the orb—the green of the leaves, the furrowed fields, the tall wooden walls circling the camp. Those ridiculous painted flowers. The skeletons of the train cars that had been at its center when we first came here have now virtually disappeared: over the years, all of their metal has been used, stripped and flayed away. The forge pumps smoke into the sky. Claire and Steve have been vital in making this work.

"Well done, you," I say, and Tom beams at my words.

Again, action: reaction. The world is shaped like this.

His voice is excited. "I think if we make it smaller we can get the glass more precise."

"And maybe something other than leather?" I suggest. "It feels like it's bending."

"Steve doesn't think we can make a metal tube small enough, but time will tell on that!"

"It's good," I reassure him. "I'm very proud."

I rest a hand on his chest and pat it. The children have run away and are playing in the grass. Rather, Danny is trying to wrestle with his sister while Bea persistently explains something to him. Something about the land, something about the earth and the way things work, it seems from the way she's pointing. But Danny is restless and bored. It's nearly time for food.

I admire the view over their heads. There is a deep silence to the world. A weight, a strength, a peace. Birds are flying in the distance. I am here, and that is it, the wind blowing through my hair. It seems we humans are in balance once more. Our power is simply our own. Without buttons to press, or weapons to unleash, each person's effect is just that. We have refound our humility. This view is huge. I can't affect it at all. And it's a tiny proportion of the planet. All I can hope to control is my little area. Here. The vastness of the world disconnects everything but a few strong relationships. We mustn't overreach ourselves. So we make the thinnest veneer of security through all the work we do. We hope it will hold back the dangers. The space we create, that we forge with our lives—that's what we

have to protect. We work hard for such an inconse-
quential space, but it is absolutely everything to us.

Bea and Danny are still arguing. Tom's looking
around at me. They all want to start the walk home.
What little we have here thrums alive with the greatest
possible value.

"We were lucky to find this place." Tom takes my
hand. "We were so, so lucky to find it."

I smile. We *were* lucky. But I knew it was here. It
wasn't chance. In an uncaring world you must make
things work for yourself. It's all about advantage, this
fight for preservation. If you don't take it when you can,
who will? It will be taken. I squeeze his hand. "Claire
wants a camp meeting after dinner, so we better not be
late. And Steve says the forge needs some repair work
done."

"Doesn't it feel like we're nearly there?" Tom says,
and puts his arm around me. "That somehow we've
nearly made it?"

"It does. This is close enough to perfect."

"We've got to protect it, Kate," he says, and strokes
the back of my neck.

"Yes," I agree. "We do."

In the distance, the dull blur of an old city lies halfway across the plain. Below us is all that matters: small
buildings and fields, and the smoke from the forge,

and, closer, our son and daughter. The future of this world. Playing in the grass. Beatrice Sylene and Daniel Darian. Our children. Our future. Our all.

I take Tom's hand and we start down the hill toward camp. Tom thought their middle names were strange when I gave them. But it's how we'll be remembered.

Acknowledgments

Many people have influenced this novel. Writers, musicians, filmmakers, family, friends, and others—you might notice these bits, you might not. You might not ever even read *The Feed* or know you influenced it. In any case, I'm very grateful.

Over the years, *The Feed* has passed through many drafts, sharpened by feedback from the people who read it, some numerous times. Thank you—this book would not exist without you. Over the years, I've gone through a few drafts too, shaped by feedback often from those same people. I wouldn't exist without you, either.

Thank you Tara W., Julia C., Will W., and Jessie B. for advice.

Thank you Miles C. and Mary W. for the numerous

reads and support. Thank you James W. for not pulling the punches. I'm sorry I hurt your brain. (And thank you, Kate W., for getting us relaxed again.) Thanks, Tom E., for the reads and the many conversations about many stories, not just *The Feed*. Looking forward to more.

Many thanks to Joanna B. and all at the Faber Academy, where pen was first put to paper, especially Soph T.T., Hugh C., and Ali MacD. Thank you Helen D. for the advice generally, but especially for your guidance when things were getting exciting. You are sorely missed. And thank you Chris McQ. for your kind phone advice, too.

Matt, Sean, and Fred, I think you would have enjoyed this book and I wish you were here to read it. Ditto my grandparents (with many thanks for influencing me and this novel in many ways).

Thank you Jen D., Kitty S., Emily G. (it was all too brief!), and everyone at Headline. Thank you David P., Priyanka K., and the William Morrow team. Sue H., Sara M., and Channing P.—who knows what the future will bring . . . and I'm looking forward to the adventure!

Juliet—it's been a blast and boy am I looking forward to more. What a dream come true. Agent, editor, guard dog, friend, and precision-guided missile with notes. And there I was thinking I couldn't do any more drafts! *Thank you.*

Steve and Mashton. Thanks for helping me get here. Let's get the lunches back on.

Thank you to Mum and Dad for encouraging me to read in the first place. From that, everything comes. Mum, thank you for your experienced red pen on the many drafts of many novels you've read since. You've always been there for me, unquestioningly. Katie— thank you for all the support over all the years. Isla and Perry—I stole some dialogue from you. It was too good not to.

And Eleanor . . . how can words do it justice? Thank you. Not just for encouraging me to write again (but that belief was like lifeblood). Not just for reading this story many times. Thank you—so much—for everything. If there *are* parallel worlds, there will be somewhere we never managed to meet, and none of them are as good as this one.

—NCW, London (July 2017)

About the Author

Nick Clark Windo was a student in the Faber Academy "Writing a Novel" course. He studied English Literature at Cambridge and acting at the Royal Academy of Dramatic Art, and he now works as a film producer and communications coach. Inspired by his realization that people are becoming increasingly disconnected from one another, as well as by philosophical questions about identity and memory, he wrote *The Feed*, his first thriller. He lives in London with his wife.

HARPER LUXE

THE NEW LUXURY IN READING

We hope you enjoyed reading
our new, comfortable print size and found it
an experience you would like to repeat.

Well – you're in luck!

HarperLuxe offers the finest in fiction and
nonfiction books in this same larger print size and
paperback format. Light and easy to read, HarperLuxe
paperbacks are for book lovers who want to see
what they are reading without the strain.

For a full listing of titles and
new releases to come, please visit our website:

www.HarperLuxe.com